The Sinners' Club

D.W. Plato

Cover art by Dustin Peterson at Apex Digital Media

Edited by Eliot Chavez at Publishing Assist

Musical Lyrics Credits:

Lennon, John. McCartney, Paul. Beatles, All You Need is Love, Parlophone Capitol (July 1967) London, England

Keagy, Kelly. Night Ranger, Midnight Madness, Sister Christian, MCA Records (June 1984) USA

Stump, Patrick. Wentz, Pete. Trohman, Joe. Hurley, Andy. Walker, Butch. Hill, John. Fall Out Boy, Save Rock n' Roll, My Songs Know What You Did in the Dark (Light Em Up), Island Records (February, 2013) USA

Germanotta, Stephani. Khayat, Nadir. Lady Gaga, Pokerface, Streamline (September, 2008) Hollywood, USA

Pearson, Carol Lynn. de Azevedo, Lex. My Turn On Earth, Carlton Pearson (1977) USA

To Tishelle and Jen.

Thanks for the inspiration.

Prologue

It couldn't be, no, no, no. The directions said the additional line could take two to three minutes to show up. The extra blue line showed immediately, before she even set the testing stick on the bathroom counter. It was probably a faulty test. An error. Her heart pounded so hard it was causing a headache. With shaking hands, she fumbled with the box as her anxiety escalated to panic. She dialed the 800 number the packaging provided and pleaded with the call representative to tell her the test was mistaken.

The agent explained, "The only time they've ever been wrong is on occasion the test will say negative and it's really a positive, but if it says positive, they're accurate every time."

As she hung up the cordless handset her body retched as if adding confirmation of the test results. This was not the way her perfect summer was to end. Damn. A part of her longed for her mother. Would it be easier or harder to have her parents here for this crisis? Would they be thrilled to be grandparents or upset she had gotten pregnant with someone she barely knew?

Was she in love? Puppy love, summer love, call it whatever you want, but it was a love that had made a baby. She was almost twenty years old and virtually on her own. After applying for a government internship and not getting it, she took a temporary job for the United States Park Service. There were up sides and down sides to every job, but this one had more up sides. The biggest plus was they provided housing wherever she ended up, the bad side was she never knew where she was going to end up. The most recent assignment had been in a remote and relatively unknown national park in central Utah.

It was beautiful there, picture perfect, like living inside a postcard. The terrain was somewhere between mountain and desert. The cedar trees and wild sage gave a pleasant aroma to the dry air and the colors of the earth were different than she had ever seen. Red, verging on purple in places. The weather was extreme and she loved that too. It had become her favorite national park. Some days truly felt magical, especially after meeting the tall, dark and handsome local boy. They had fallen fast. In love? Lust? In bed.

Although they didn't know each other that well she knew he was going to want to get married. He would want to 'do the right thing' and walk her down the aisle. They would buy a house in the little town he was raised in; they would probably live a few doors down from his overbearing parents. Holiday get-togethers, PTO meetings, soccer games, chickenpox, playdates, strollers, car seats and all the other countless responsibilities she would have to face became foreboding in her thoughts. None of it sounded appealing. Besides, she had only known the baby daddy a short time, not long enough for a lifetime commitment. Gagging, she dry-heaved into the sink.

Her heart ached for her mom. Regardless of how her mother would have felt about her current predicament, she would have offered comfort and assured her she was loved, optimistic and positive no matter what. Sadly, her parents were dead, killed by a drunk driver just a year and a half before. Who knew that only a few months after she moved out, they would both be gone? This baby situation was something she was going to have to figure out herself. Maybe settling down in the middle of nowhere Utah was just what she needed to do for the unborn child she was now responsible for.

Needing to get out of the claustrophobic cabin she currently called home, she bolted out into the sunlight and headed into the little town to find her baby's dad. He was working so she left him a note to meet her at 'their spot' when he was done with his shift at the local Frosty Freeze. Deliberately the note was vague, she was sure he would have shown up even if she had left a detailed essay.

'Their spot' was the farthest campsite at the top of National Park's campground. It was used for overflow and wasn't often occupied. The most appealing part was the privacy. The hidden site was where they had made love the first time and where they had spent the majority of their time together throughout the summer. To assure no one else would be there, he had booked it over the fourth of July holiday so when she could steal away from her job duties, he would be there waiting for her. They had a candlelight dinner that night and he told her he was falling in love. That memory brought tears to her eyes. The wind whipped her hair as she gazed into the cloud dappled sky. They seemed to be smiling down at her, as if to lighten her mood

The idea of becoming a parent was overwhelming and the thought of an abortion was crushing. She sat on the picnic table and waited. He showed up on time, all smiles. Damn, he really was striking with his irresistible boy-next-door sweetness. He looked like a modern-day Prince Charming with his angular jawline and adorable chin dimple. And those eyes, so dark blue the irises were lost. Without warning he wrapped her in his arms and started to kiss her neck. While he nuzzled her, she blurted out the truth in the simplest two-word sentence.

"I'm pregnant."

Pulling away from her she could see his eyes dancing, no apprehension, and no worries. Holding her hand, he immediately went down onto one knee. It had been expected. She shrugged, not saying yes or no.

"I love you, Sue," he said still holding her hand, she remained silent. He continued as the idea of parenthood settled into his face. "Heck, yea. A baby. *Our* baby! Dang! My folks are going to be..." He hesitated, a look of dread flashed on his face before he continued with a forced smile. "Let's not tell them about-" his eyes dropped to her stomach, "Um, in fact, let me deal with them. We'll just tell them we're getting married, okay? I'm supposed to go on a mission, but instead we're going to have to set up the missionary lessons and get *you* baptized," he smiled with reassurance. "When will you start to show? Oh honey, I'm stoked. Eventually we can be sealed in the temple, but that'll be down the road. Dad's gonna be royally bummed, but we'll figure it out..." She noticed a troubled look that had taken over his handsome face. It had knotted into nervousness, he was rambling. *What have I gotten myself into?* She thought.

Chapter One

As he stood in the Memorial Garden it felt as if he was in a dream. His black hair hung over his face as he looked at the small marker to honor his mother. 'In loving memory.' She had written her own obituary, picked the memorial placard, prepaid the cremation. Basically, she had planned her own funeral down to the last detail. Her face materialized in his mind, her crooked smile and friendly eyes. He recalled the conversations they had regarding her final wishes. She had explained to him she didn't want to be buried: no cemeteries, no coffins. But still there should be a place to come together for friends and family when the time came. She was always thinking of others. More importantly, she had told him that when he wanted to talk to her there needed to be a place he could visit. Not just any place, but a peaceful place, not creepy like cemeteries so often are. A place full of nature where the sky looked big and wasn't obstructed by buildings or cityscapes. In the memorial garden by the cement bench, under the pine tree.

Tiny water droplets rolled off his nose and hair, fitting since it had rained all day. It was over. The funeral made it final. It was as if he was on auto-pilot, just going through the motions. The people around him were calling the get together a celebration of life. Everyone was reminiscing about her, recalling their favorite times with her, toasting their drinks to the air. "To you, Sue."

In his mind, it was indeed a funeral, an ending of the life he had known for so many years, and a final farewell to his favorite person on the planet. He let Toni steer him back to her car, and they drove through the rain out of the memorial park and back to his neighborhood. Walking through the front door of the small house, it was as if it wasn't really his home anymore, as if the essence of it was gone, as if her death had stolen the breath of the structure itself.

Gaius took a paper plate of food from someone he remembered meeting when he was a child but couldn't place her name, he put a forkful of casserole into his mouth. The food tasted bland, his stomach was in knots; he felt like crying. He tried to engage in conversations with her friends, their neighbors, and the blur of unknown sympathizers; but he could not recall who he talked to, nor what he had said.

Now the guests had meandered out, the old house was quiet and he was alone. He started to go through the envelopes people had been handing him all day. Many had money in them, and the accumulated total was enough to pay the mortgage and utilities for a month. Sighing, he read the signatures and comments in the cards, the one large card from work had dozens of signatures. She had touched so many people's lives.

'Such a neat lady. Work won't be the same without your smiling face.'

'Going to miss you Sue! You were truly one of a kind.'

'You were an inspiration. Beautiful inside and out, I'll miss you.'

'Our thoughts are with you during this difficult time.'

'So sorry for your loss. Please call if there is anything we can do.'

'You'll be in our hearts forever, Sue.'

Soundlessly, the tears started to flow. It wasn't like he didn't know this day was coming. Sue had been dying since he was a kid, or so it seemed, on and off for seven years. Not once, but twice the doctors had diagnosed her terminal; they told them both she wouldn't see another birthday, yet she marched on and on until she couldn't anymore. Now her precious life was over. Gaius had only her memories now and the life lessons she had taught him. He heard her voice in his head clearly.

'Remember son, there are only two things in life that are for sure...'

That thought made him giggle, the laughter turning to something else as his eyes refilled with water. His silent tears turned into a torrent, then full blown sobs. Everywhere he looked he saw her, younger, healthy, happy. Standing at the stove cooking chocolate chip pancakes, the Mr. Coffee she had for a decade even though the carafe had to be replaced four times, the curtains she had made with sheets she had bought from a yard sale, the few small throw pillows for the worn out couch she had made with the matching pillow cases, the coffee mug collection, the 60's style Formica table, the worn out swivel chair and ottoman with the tall antique lamp that was her grandfather's. Flashes of her over the years bounced in his mind. He could picture her sitting in her chair doing crossword puzzles, needlepoint, reading paperback books, watching TV, crocheting him a throw for his bed and eventually a throw for the chair. Picturing her talking on the phone, a landline with the cord stretched from the kitchen, he remembered her drinking coffee, drinking wine, laughing, sleeping, and crying, all from the chair. He couldn't remember the living room without it.

There was also the house itself, full of a lifetime of stuff, stuff memories are made of, stuff that some say defines the person. Gaius knew those things didn't make his mother. Those things didn't *define* her. He knew what made his mother so special was her soul, her attitude, and her kindness. She was a terminal optimist. There was always a bright side to everything and everyone. Sue saw past the flaws of most people. As Gaius matured, he wasn't sure this was a positive trait. He had once heard that a person's greatest strengths and their greatest weaknesses were the opposite sides of the same coin. He never fully understood that until he grew to be a young adult and witnessed his mother's forgiveness of stupid people over and over again.

Sue loved people, genuinely. It was her greatest strength. She would offer someone the shirt right off her back as the old saying goes. Sue loved people, genuinely. It was her greatest weakness. She was forever drawing the wrong types of people into their lives. Damaged men, emotionally unavailable women, or vice versa. Part of the problem was people also loved Sue. They were drawn to her goodness. They hung around due to her generous manner and good humor.

Sue's best friend, whom Gaius had known as 'Aunt Toni', had been known to chastise Sue for being 'a goddamned saint'. She was definitely the more cynical of the two. Crass and blunt, she was one to never sugarcoated anything. Toni's voice had the unmistakable roughness of someone who smoked their whole life, and although she was the same age as Sue, she looked at least twenty years older.

"What?!" He recalled Toni's voice sharp and irritated; he was reminiscing about a heated conversation years ago after an ex-lover of his mother's had stolen her bank card and all the cash in the account. "Of course you're going to press charges! You think you can save the world, Sue? What are you a fucking saint or something? Feeding the masses with two loaves of bread you bought with your EBT card? For fuck's sake kiddo, save yourself first!" Toni had finish her lecture with a long toke from a Camel cigarette, or maybe it was a joint, he couldn't recall.

There had never been religion in their house, so sometimes Gaius didn't understand Toni's references and ribbing. Sue had said she lived and practiced her own religion. Often she had joked she could become tax exempt if she just turned their living room into a place of worship. In her everyday life there were basic what goes around comes around rules with Pagan roots, plus a lot of spirituality as she called it. Sue had referred to God as a 'her' or 'she' and stated that organized religion missed the whole point. She taught Gaius pre-Christian Pagan rituals like decorating trees for the Winter's solstice and decorating eggs in the spring. His mother had taught him about the sun, moon, stars and ancient practices before organized religion 'messed everything up'. Gaius enjoyed the science aspects of it.

"Pagan," Sue explained one day, "means 'Country dweller that isn't baptized into a specific religion,' so technically, we're Pagans," she declared this fact with a full smile on her face, eyes dancing. Her stance on life in general was to leave the world a better place than one found it, that included people, places and things. Gaius K. Stuart had adopted many of her philosophies, although not necessarily her beliefs.

At an age when most young men were starting school or a family, he had committed to her when she had gotten sick. The cancer seemed to never fully flow out of her, and each time it returned it seemed more ravenous than the time before. The doctors and nurses had told him on several occasions, her prolonged life was partially due to his abilities to care for the sick. He had learned to cook for her and made her vegetable smoothies and her favorite Caesar Salads with home baked croutons and tomato soup. There was nothing he wouldn't have done to give her the simple comforts and basic needs she provided to him over the years. She had taught him it was what you did for your family.

One of Sue's favorite songs was the Beatles', "All you need is love," he believed her when she told him that's all they needed. They didn't have much, but they had plenty of love. It was just them, no dad. Before he knew about the birds and the bees, his mother had told him she had followed a rainbow to the end, and instead of a pot of gold or leprechauns, she had found him. Jokingly, she said she almost left him there, he was lucky she was such a sucker for a cute baby. As he got older and wiser to the world, he had pressed her for the truth.

The story was always the same. His father was killed in Iraq before he ever had a memory of him. In his mind's eye, he had always pictured them all together, the perfect family, until duty called and the war hero didn't return in the name of someone else's ideals. By the time he was old enough to really understand why he didn't have a traditional nuclear family, America had moved on to 'protecting' a different country for a different cause.

Over the years, he had fantasied about the family he could have had, the father that he never knew, a stereotypical all American hero. In his daydreams, his dad had played football, married his high school sweetheart and had a son before bravely marching off to serve the country he loved. Gaius pictured him looking handsome in his Army uniform, his loyal and beautiful wife swearing her allegiance in a tearful goodbye. This was the vague story from his mother every time he asked about his dad. His imagination had filled in the blanks. When pressed for more details, Sue would say he had been incredibly good looking, smart and funny, and had wanted to be a teacher after college. She also suggested Gaius looked like his father, same dark wavy hair, same thin but strong build and the same piercing blue eyes that, in the right light, were so dark blue they appeared purple. It had to be true, he didn't look like his blonde-haired, green-eyed beauty his mother had been.

On her deathbed, Sue painted a slightly different picture, as if to unload her secret burden of single-motherhood. One afternoon, while she ran a low-grade fever and the disease continued to move through her body like food coloring placed in warm water, she told him that she had gotten pregnant by his father out of wedlock during a summer she worked for the National Park Service in Utah.

"Puppy love," she called it with a fondness. She told him ideally she pictured them getting married and living happily ever after, but things didn't always work out like a person pictured. "Ah, the delusion of the youth." Sue smiled with the memory. As she continued, the smile faded. "His parents refused to allow us to be together," she said bitterly.

"Why?".

"Due to religious differences."

Religious differences? Clearly he didn't hear her right. He was born in the early-nineteen nineties. Religious differences? Sue continued and used words he thought he knew, but she used them in an unfamiliar context like 'the ward', 'sealed forever', and 'the relief society ladies'. As she continued, she got agitated, stating his father's parents insisted on him cutting all ties with her and shuffled him off to join the military, specifying he needed to get his 'head on straight' and become 'temple worthy'. They encouraged her to give the baby up for adoption, stating there were many families that would be thrilled to have her child. They never said 'their child'. According to his father's family, it was her baby, her problem. They emphasized how young she was and told her not to throw her life away and give up her youth only to struggle to raise a child alone. Sue was young indeed, she was almost twenty, barely more than a child herself. There were suggestions of abortion, but no one could come out and say the word. It was insinuated by saying things like, 'It's not too late to take care of that condition'. Regardless of the young lovers' feelings, his parents insisted the two would never be together.

After hours of crying and negotiating with his parents, Sue agreed she alone would take care of 'the problem'. Feeling defeated, she told them not to worry about her, she would be fine. It was what they thought was best for *him*. There was never mention of what was best for *them*. He joined the army. She moved to Colorado Springs. He was deployed over-seas. She got a job at a call center. She never heard from him again.

"I tried to reach them when you were born, but..." her voice faded off.

Gaius' stomach was in knots as he became aware of the first phase of his life, Sue had no family, no friends and had to take the city bus to and from the hospital when he was born. She worked hard and made her son's life as comfortable as she could.

Sue had always given a positive impression when speaking of his dad, usually with a blissful far-away look in her eyes, but she had never gone into any type of details. She had never even told Gaius his name, and he had never asked. Since they both knew the end for Sue Stewart was near, he ventured the question.

"Kimball," she replied. "Kimball Smith."

"Kimball?" he repeated.

"It's a Mormon thing," she replied matter-of-factly.

"Smith? As if Stewart isn't a common enough last name, but, Smith?" he chuckled and shook his head. "Is that my real last name?"

"Oh no, I gave you my last name. It's Stewart," she said firmly, "If his parents are still alive, my guess is they don't know you exist. They have no idea I decided against the adoption, or abortion or whatever. And there was no reason to keep in touch with them. Like I said, I tried right after you were born, then that was it. They didn't want us. They told me I wasn't good enough for their little boy, that I didn't fit their mold of the ideal daughter-in-law. We weren't the forever family they were hoping for."

"Well, dying overseas probably wasn't either, Ma. You know what they say about Karma."

"Oh Gaius! No one deserves that! Goodness!" Her words were sharp and he noticed a little shadow pass across her eyes and mouth. She sighed and continued, her voice soft, resolute. "Honestly though, I'm the one that lived happily ever after. I won the grand prize. I told them I would take care of the pregnancy and I did! I never specified *how*. You know me, I'm proud to say I'm a feminist and you know I'm pro-choice. You have to know, son, it was my *choice* to have you. I wanted you! It was time for me to settle down and it was the universe's way of making me. Wouldn't have changed a thing," she smiled warmly at him.

"Mom, you were nineteen! C'mon, time to settle down, really?" he rolled his eyes thinking how far away he was to settling down. They cuddled on the couch, he put his arms around her frail and thin body. She laid her head on his chest and listened to his heartbeat.

"Your heart beating is my favorite sound in the world," she paused and listened a few more seconds then continued. "I remember the first time I heard your heart beat at the doctor's office. It was so fast, like a bird," she closed her eyes and smiled at the memory.

"Is Kimball what the K in my middle name stands for?" he asked absentmindedly. When Gaius was young, he had always wondered. Only once he had asked and she had replied, 'It's just Kay, baby, like Homer Simpson's is just Jay. Remember that episode?' But even then there had to be more to it.

"No, Kimball is a nice enough name and all…" She sighed deeply. "But I did not name you after your father. Your middle name is Kinza."

"Kinza?" he was grateful they weren't facing each other and did his best to hide the smirk on his face, but his mouth itched terribly as it demanded to laugh.

"Yes, Kinza," she replied brightly, "C'mon, it's a cool name, Gaius! It's Arabic for 'hidden treasure', which is what you were, what you became. You've been my hidden treasure your whole life, *my* treasure, my world, my son, my shining sun. My life! Always know you were wanted. I mean that." The talk was wearing her out and her speech started to slur slightly. "I wouldn't have changed a thing."

He could tell she was fading, worn out from the conversation. "Get some rest you wild and crazy woman," he laid her down as you would a child and pulled the light blanket to her chin and tucked her into it. "I love you, *mamacita*. I love you to the moon and back," he spoke softly as she began to nod off.

"Love you too," she slept quietly for several hours as he started to make dinner. Mac and Cheese or Campbell's soup? He opted for the Mac and Cheese and ate his little meal spiced up with a generous smattering of Tabasco sauce and washed it down with a can of Coke.

A death bed confession, Gaius thought. It would be the only conversation they would have about the subject. Mind whirling, he wondered how much truth there was to the story, was his mother's relationship with Kimball Smith a one-night stand? Puppy love she said. Was the narrative of his sperm donor just the ramblings of a dying woman or did he really have blood relations out there that didn't know he was alive? 'Family' would be pushing it. Blood doesn't make a family.

Another thought crossed his mind. If he *did* have blood relations out there, would he want to find them? Would they want him or would it be one big disappointment? Would they even remember his mom? He knew his dad never remarried. He died, right? Or did he? Could that have also been a lie Sue had told him all his life to protect his feelings? Was she painting a picture she knew he'd buy into, and what about his grandparents? Sue's parents were both killed in a car accident a while before he was born. What about Kimball's parents? Did they have other children? Didn't the Mormon Church people have a reputation for having big families? Multiple wives? That *was* the right religion, wasn't it? His mind reeled as the conversation spun in his head, illusions, and handful of 'what if's'. The uncomfortable thoughts were a welcome relief. He needed something just to take his mind off the situation, off his reality. Sue Stewart was withering away to nothing. She was going to die.

That conversation may have been when the truth of his world started to sink in. Gaius had been caring for his mom for so long, that he knew this cancer was different. Her energy, the pallor of her skin, the whiteness of her eyes, it wasn't right and he had known she wasn't going to make it this time. She must of too.

Now she was gone. The funeral was over. He was alone. There were decisions to be made. Big grown-up type decisions. Gaius was barely twenty-two years old. It was a lot to process. For the last two and half years he had been working part time for a local locksmith. Donovan Gray of Gray's Keys had been good to him and had been flexible working his schedule around his mom's sickness, but it was a part-time job, not a career. Sell the house or keep it? Taking over the mortgage would mean more hours, steady hours. He would be literally locking himself into this... this house, this town, this lonely life without his mom.

Chapter Two

Elizabeth Ord Anderson, or 'Sister Anderson' as she was now known, loved Jesus Christ. She loved sharing her testimony of the Church of Latter Day Saints. Living the religion was all she had ever known. Three-hour church meetings every Sunday was a way of life. Each week it was the same; Sacrament meeting, Sunday school and then one more class where young women were taught how to be good wives, neighbors and daughters. Eventually, she would participate in the Relief Society, the church's group for women. Her brothers would go to the Priesthood meetings to learn how to be good men, husbands and patriarchs.

Elizabeth was definitely the second mom in the house, always helping with the other kids and housework. In her life, there was never a question of whether or not she would be baptized at age eight. Instead, it was another event she looked forward to, her first rite of passage. Looking back, one of her favorite Primary Hymns was 'I hope they call me on a mission.' She remembered belting out the tune off key with the rest of the Sunbeams in her class. The lyrics went like this:

> "I hope they call me on a mission,
> when I have grown a foot or two,
> I hope by then I will be ready
> to teach and preach and work
> like missionaries do."

It was her theme song as a child. It was a year and half she couldn't wait for, dreaming of the exotic lands she would travel to, and the people she would meet. *Interesting how perfectly kids picture the real world,* she thought to herself, thinking back to her previous comfortable life. Serving her mission had been different than she had expected or imagined. Not necessarily good or bad different, just different.

At home, her family was like every other family in their ward. It was their way of life. Attending church, taking the sacrament, getting baptized, baring your testimony, having bi-annual meetings with the bishop, and going to the mutual dances and camps in the canyon. Once young adults, kids were expected to serve their missions. Since she and Paul were so close in age, it made sense they got their callings at approximately the same time. Because the Elders' missions were two years, and the Sisters' only eighteen months, she would leave later and be back earlier than her younger brother. Paul was called to Stockholm, Sweden. In her mind, it didn't get more glamorous than that.

Although close in age, they had never been close. There always seemed to be a competition between them. She never understood it, but felt it with their grades, sports and the approval from their parents and older brother. It was as if Paul was bitter at her for already being there when he was born. Was it because she was a girl? He didn't seem to feel the same about their older brother, Zeb. They had gotten along famously. Paul had just been miserable all his life. Most blamed his ill behavior on 'middle child syndrome.'

Their mom would have two of her five children serving at the same time. Elizabeth's older brother, Zeb, had served his mission in Madrid, Spain and was still fluent in Spanish. Shortly after returning, he was sealed in the Manti Temple for all time and eternity to a high school alumnus, Tiffany Johnston. They hadn't gotten pregnant yet, but they were still hoping to have a little one anytime.

With Zeb being married off and both Elizabeth and Paul gone, there would only be two kids in the house for at least a year. The two youngest, Giselle and Jozette, were born just fourteen months apart and couldn't have been closer if they had been twins.

How long had it been since there were only two kids in the house? Elizabeth wondered. She didn't remember because her first memories were with both her older and younger brothers. In her young, child mind, her mom was pregnant like an elephant, for two whole years with the girls. The diapers and laundry seemed to last a lifetime. Sometimes Elizabeth felt as if she was the nanny to them all and not really related to any of them. She was the one periodically put in charge, when their parents had been out for the evening, to make dinner and make sure everyone did their part in clean up, homework, and scripture reading before prayers and a nine sharp lights-out bedtime. Zeb often had after school activities with sports and boy scouts. Their parent's outings were usually based on their weekly trip to Provo to do the temple work they were devout to, or to volunteer at the Missionary Training Center, more commonly called the MTC.

Now, all the kids were grown. Zeb was twenty-four, Elizabeth was past the half way point of her twenty-first year, her younger brother was already nineteen, Giselle was sixteen and Jozette fifteen. Five kids in less than ten years.

Elizabeth's best friend since junior high was Tish. She was also from a large Mormon family, number six of nine. Born Patricia, it had switched to Tish when one of her older brothers couldn't pronounce his P's as a toddler and just called her Baby Tisha. The 'a' on Tisha had been dropped about the same time the 'baby' part had, but Tish had stuck. The boys in their family were all named with the letter J. All the girl's in their family had names beginning with P: Phoebe, Pamela, Patricia and Prudence. Tish was proud of being the oddball and using the T for her first initial.

When she was little, a teacher wanted to call her Patty, she recalled bawling to her mother about it. "My name is Tish," she had whined. Her mother had made a phone call and requested the teacher and other student's address her as Tish, unless it was official documentation. Tish had always been a little disappointed her diploma had her legal name.

Once, Elizabeth and Tish had been reading a popular teen magazine with an article about names and what the initials meant. The T was for Tiger, proud, a leader not needing a pack or herd, just one mate to have her back. Tish had solidly declared the magazine article truth, explaining that it answered the question of why Tish was her name instead of Patricia. She was no porcupine, she was a Tiger through and through. The porcupine, the animal for the P, was a timid creature, often being misunderstood because of its outer quills, wanting sociability but struggling with it. Tish had pointed out her other sisters were definitely more like that. Elizabeth had thought of her younger brother, Paul. Misunderstood was unquestionably his most prominent personality trait. Her letter, the E, was the baby harp seal. She had thought it was the dumbest one on the list. The baby harp seal was tolerant, kind, and patient, but on the downside, it could fall into the trap of victimhood. As much as she wasn't crazy about being a seal, she had to admit, the definition did sort of fit. One of her struggles as a kid, and even as an adult, was losing sight of her gratitude while mumbling, "why me?" her last name was A, the dolphin who was intelligent, social and chatty. That definitely fit her mom, who had two A's for initials. She read several of the other ones, thinking of her older brother and little sisters.

Now she was ready for her mission, the next rite of passage. Tish had not applied for a mission calling, stating she wasn't sure she could be that committed while being on her own, but promised she would write. She laughed as she confessed to Elizabeth that she would skip church all together if it wouldn't let her parent's down so much. Not Elizabeth, she loved her Lord, loved the church, loved the services every Sunday, loved the scriptures and couldn't wait for her mission.

When the calling finally came she learned she was going to Kentucky, she couldn't have been more disappointed. She wanted somewhere foreign, mysterious and exotic. Not wanting to play the victim baby harp seal, she painted on a smile and pretended to be happy about it.

"Everything happens for a reason," Tish had assured her, putting an arm around her friend. She could read Elizabeth's feelings so well, nothing needed to be said.

Elizabeth fought back the tears in her eyes as she heard her mom on the phone gushing. "Well I prayed and prayed she would stay state-side. God always listens to the prayers of mothers."

Tish's giggle was infectious, "Well, you lucky girl. Your mom has a direct line to God." Elizabeth felt a smile tug at the corners of her mouth. "Sister Anderson, my friend, it is what it is," she put her arm around Elizabeth and continued. "You're gonna be great, have a little faith that there is a reason you are supposed to go to Kentucky. Maybe you'll met a guy and he'll come back here and be your husband and you can have a dozen or so kids, get a mini-van and-"

"Stop, Tish, please," Elizabeth was laughing and feeling better. She reminded herself she had never been to that part of the country so it was foreign to her. Tish was right, everything happens for a reason.

Chapter Three

Thank goodness for his Aunt Toni. She was heaven sent to be sure. A week or so after the services, she showed up with cleaning gloves, a stack of empty boxes, trash bags, a large coffee, a box of fresh Dunkin' Donuts and her graying hair tied up in a bandana. Without even discussing anything with him, she went into Sue's room and started the process of packing her things. Gaius grabbed a chocolate cake donut with chocolate frosting and stuffed it in his mouth, picked up a second one with sprinkles, wandered into his mom's room and flopped down onto the bed. It smelled different now. It had gone from smelling like her deodorant, incense, make-up, and hair spray to smelling like a hospital, and now, it had gone back to the more familiar smell and feel of his house, but emptier.

There were two framed pictures on her nightstand. One was a 5x7 snapshot of them together when he was a baby, the background was somewhere outside. In the woods, the mountains...camping maybe? It was something they had done together often during his childhood. Tucked into the frame was a photo cut to a wallet sized picture of them on his graduation day. It was frayed at the edges as he knew she had always carried it in her wallet. Both pictures were all smiles, all love. The other picture was an 8x10 of just him when he was an infant, his opened-mouth smile showing no teeth. It was taken at a mall photography studio. Sears maybe? JCPennys? He was so cute, all cheeky and soft. She had told him over the years it was her favorite picture of him. He could see his resemblance to her in that specific shot, even though the coloring was different. She was so much lighter skinned, her hair blonde and straight in contrast to his dark, curly locks. He picked up the photo and placed the picture against his chest as the tears welled in his eyes.

"You doing ok, buddy?" Toni asked from the closet where she was pulling down boxes from the top shelves.

"Well enough," he said, as a single tear fell across his temple and ran into his hairline.

"Thought I'd pack up her things for you, perhaps you should consider this room for you. It is bigger and nicer than yours, and it has a bathroom."

"My room is fine," he replied. "My bathroom in the hall is fine. Everything's fine... just freaking dandy."

"Did I detect a little sarcasm in your tone, G? Or just normal I-just-lost-my-mom sadness?" She had started calling him G when he was in elementary school. Sue had insisted everyone call her son Gaius, she had even been known to correct people when they called him Guy. "Had I wanted his name to be Guy, that's what I would have named him," she had said to anyone who slipped up. Toni said he needed a one syllable nick name. "Like a dog," she had explained, so G it had been for years. He had called her Aunt Toni when he was little. It was shortened to Auntie as a teenager, and just T as a young adult.

"I don't know," he sighed, replacing the picture to the nightstand and sitting up. "I just don't know." The tears kept coming. "I feel horrible. I cry every day."

"Yea," she replied sympathetically, "I don't blame you, I don't know what to tell you. I have no answers."

He noticed the boxes she had taken from the closet and opened the first one. It was full of papers: past year's taxes, receipts for appliance purchases, manuals for said appliances and manila folders marked on the outside with titles like 'Gaius' school stuff,' 'bank statements,' and 'phone bills.' "I think this one is probably trash."

"Don't throw it away just yet," she answered. "There are a lot of things we can toss, but let's go through it all to be sure, okay? I cleared my incredibly busy schedule and freed up my weekend so we can figure it out together. I'm here for you, G, lean on me."

"Busy schedule, T? Really? Now it's my turn to detect some sarcasm?"

They both smiled. "Figured out what you want to do with the rest of your life?" Toni asked, turning back to her task at hand.

"Nope." Gaius replied and opened the next box that Toni had set on the floor. "Don't have a lot of resources, so I suppose I'll stay right where I am and do exactly what I've been doing for the last couple years. Stick with the comfort zone, you know?" In the box there were little parcels wrapped in faded pink tissue paper, and he unwrapped the first one. It was a little white and green ceramic bird. He unwrapped the second and it was a like bird, but in a different pose. They were obviously supposed to sit together.

"With one minor exception, sweetie." Toni interrupted his concentration on the figurines. "You don't have a mother to take care of anymore. Let's face it kiddo, that was a full-time job the last few years. As harsh as it sounds, as hard as it is to say this, maybe you should look into selling the house, look into getting out of this nowhere's-ville. Maybe go to college, be a normal kid, enjoy your youth. You did a fine job of caring for Sue these years. God knows it bought you a pass to heaven, but honey... it's a big wide world out there and you're not getting any younger. In no time you'll turn around and be old, like me!" She was trying to be cheerful, but he could tell she was hurting too. They had been friends since Sue had moved to Colorado Springs. They had been in the same training group at work and had their shifts and days off as close as they could to spend time together when they were off.

"Did she ever mention my dad to you?" he ventured cautiously, deliberately not meeting her eye as he changed the direction of the conversation. He was looking at the last tissue wrapped package and could feel it was bigger than the birds, and not bird shaped at all.

"Not really," Toni remarked absently, "nothing other than he was from some po'dunk town called Pleasant, Utah. I only remember because...really? Pleasant? Not Pleasant Hills, or Pleasant View or Pleasant Grove, just plain Pleasant. Sounds like a made up place, right? And my guess is, it ain't very pleasant," she chuckled at her own bit of humor.

Gaius unwrapped the last item in the box and discovered it was a ceramic nest. Inside of the nest was a stack of twenty-dollar bills folded in half with a rubber band around them. "Holy Shit!" He said as he scrambled off the bed towards Toni. "How much do you think is here?"

Toni turned to see what he was holding and her eyes widened. "Oh, my gawd! I don't know, count them, where did you find this? In the boxes? Holy shit is right! Pennies from Heaven, well twenties from Heaven. Much better, right?" she gushed and giggled.

Gaius had already taken the rubber band off and was counting to himself. As he reached the end he counted out loud. "Forty-eight, forty-nine, fifty. And yea, found it in the box with the birds."

"Fifty? That's a thousand dollars! Holy crap. I wonder if there's more," she said, glancing at the other six boxes she had just extracted from the closet.

Gaius arranged the little birds into the nest. They nestled perfectly together, and he noticed they were painted slightly different. One was male, one female, the male sitting a little higher than the female in an almost protective posture. There were no markings on them to identify how old they were or where they came from. He turned to see Toni unwrapping similar tissue off a large vase. It was blue, yellow and orange with an amazing glaze on it, the colors running together but not blending.

She looked inside and smiled. "Bingo kiddo, another one," she turned the vase over and an identical looking wad of money, bound with a single rubber band, slid out. She placed the vase next to the birds. The money she handed to him, and he set both stacks on the nightstand with the framed pictures. "Next?" she motioned with her hands to the remaining four boxes. "What's behind door number three?"

The next one was obviously a nativity set after they unwrapped two of the dozen or so pieces. Feeling the items, they didn't need to unwrap each one. They only took out two pieces that were big enough and the right size to possibly be hiding another stack of cash. Toni unwrapped the manger with the baby Jesus. "Nothing here, what you got?"

He slid the paper off to reveal a ceramic camel and tucked between its four legs and the bottom of the stand was another fifty twenties bound in a rubber band. "So my mom," he smiled at Toni. "The camel, of course. Not the infant savior, but let's hide the money in the legs of a camel," he softly laughed and shook his head thinking of his Arabic middle name as Toni opened the next box. Wrapped like the others, it was a similar vase to the first, but squatter and with a lid. It was two toned gray, and there was another bundle of money hidden inside.

"Four, four thousand dollars, ah, ha, ha," Gaius said in a mock accent of The Count from Sesame Street. The next two boxes produced other treasures with hidden money like the first four. One stack was stashed in a music box that played 'When the Saints go Marching in.' Also in that box was a small hand crafted vase with the initials KS and the year 1991 carved into the bottom. It also contained a thousand dollars. Additional items included crocheted doilies and a stack of old greetings cards with 'Sue' written on the outside of each envelope. It was obvious it had been years since these items had seen the light of day.

The last box. Another pack of money was in a sealed envelope with the word 'Kinza' printed in Sue's neat script. This one had ten one hundred dollar bills. The rest of the box was filled with photo albums and 45disc records. Buddy Holly, The Supremes, and The Jackson Five were just a few.

"Kinza?" Toni said with her eyebrows arched and turned the envelope for him to see.

"Apparently my middle name. It means 'hidden treasure' in Arabic," Gaius answered, opening the first photo album. Tears welled in his eyes as he saw the picture of him and his mom just days after he was born. She looked so young, so beautiful, so naïve, but the smile was the same, a bit cocked to the right, no teeth showing, her left eyebrow slightly raised. He looked like all newborns, dazed, confused and a bit like a potato. Page after page 3x5 snapshots and 5x7 school pictures were displaying Gaius growing up and his mother growing old.

"Hidden treasure, huh?" Toni said, putting her arm around his shoulders. "You were her treasure that was for sure!"

After going through a couple of the albums, crying a bit, reminiscing and eating a light breakfast of hard boiled eggs and toast, they went back into Sue's bedroom with the plan to separate everything into three piles: the keep pile, the donate pile and the garbage pile.

Knowing he did not ever want to sleep in the bed she withered and died in, they drug it to the pick-up truck. They had decided the dump run would be first and loaded the bed of the truck with two sacks of garbage, a broken chair, and other miscellaneous items that was definitely trash. They tied the bed and box springs to the top and Gaius drove off to the local land fill to discard a chunk of his mom's life, the Beatles on the radio filled his heart with the acute feeling of loss.

When he got back, Toni had emptied Sue's dresser and closet and had piled the clothes on the floor, placed the shoes in one bag and the purses and miscellaneous bags in another.

Together, they took the dresser to the truck to start the donate truckload, and went back to go through the clothes.

"Most of this stuff is so outdated no one will want it, even at the thrift store. Too old to resell, but not old enough to be considered classic. Let's donate it anyway, we'll let them sort it out." Toni continued to fold the clothes, stacking them in a large box. Eventually, she came across a dark brown leather jacket. "Always loved Sue in this, she wore it for years."

"Try it on," Gaius encouraged. He also had good memories of his mom wearing the coat.

Toni grinned slightly and shrugged into it. Surprisingly, it fit pretty well. She put her hands in the pockets to strike a super model type pose, when she suddenly stopped and withdrew another rubber banded stack of cash. "Oh my god!" she shrieked.

"I think that one is for you," Gaius said. "The money and the jacket. Dang girl, you are rocking that thing!"

Laughing out loud, she reluctantly agreed and stated she was going to put it in her car. "G, grab that box and put it in my car too," she indicated the very first box that was taken from the closet shelf, the one filled with paperwork. "I'll go through it before we throw it all away."

The truck filled with donations for the Goodwill. Sue's dresser, nightstands, clothes, shoes, hair dryer and curling iron as well as a stack of paperback books. There was a small shelf with some hardback books, and Gaius started to pack them in a box when he picked up a leather bound copy of *The Complete Works of Shakespeare* and thumbed through the pages. The book opened to a pressed purple flower, the play was Romeo and Juliet. There was a line highlighted in pink marker that said:

'For never was a story of more woe, than this of Juliet and her Romeo.' Another line was marked with the same pen, it read, 'Don't waste your love on somebody, who doesn't value it.' "I think I'll keep this one," he said and placed the book on his bed with the nested birds. Gaius had decided he wanted to keep them too. There was something about them that appealed to him, something unique. He was pretty sure they had been hand painted and glazed, although the glazes didn't exactly match. It was weird there were no markings on them indicating where they were from or who the artist was. It didn't matter, he liked them.

They discussed the other furniture in the house and for now, he opted to only get rid of his mother's personal belongings. Although, technically, everything was his mom's. When and if he decided to move, he could decide what else to keep or donate.

After a run to the local Salvation Army to drop off the donated items, Gaius grabbed a pepperoni and pineapple pizza, his favorite, and a side of extra crispy hot wings to take back to the house. The sun was going down. It had taken all day. Sue's room was empty and clean.

"Mission complete," Toni announced when he walked in.

"Let's eat!" He plopped the pizza and wings on the table and went to the fridge to grab a beer. "Brew-ha Tia?" he asked.

"No thanks, hon," she said, opening the wings and dipping one into Bleu Cheese dressing before asking, "What's your schedule this week?"

"I haven't gone back to work yet, but I've been thinking about it," he replied. "Donavan's been great, he said my job is there when I'm ready to come back. He told me to take all the time I need. With our greenback treasure we found today, it looks like I've got a little more time to make a decision."

"True that," Toni said, grabbing a fourth wing from the box. "I'll come back in a day or two. Let you have some down time, and give me some time to go through all that paperwork. Call me if you need anything," she grabbed a paper plate and two big slices of the pizza. "Gotta run for now though, taking this to go. Anything else you need, sweetie?"

"Naw, you've been a god-send today though. Thank you!"

"No problem, you'd do the same for me," she winked at him.

"Would I?" His eyebrows shot up as he mocked surprise. "You don't know me very well," he added in a low dastardly tone.

She laughed. "Oh, I know you buddy boy, I know you *really* well. And *yes*, you would be helping me if I needed it! I'd bet my last dollar on it," she winked again and headed for the door calling over her shoulder, "Love ya, buddy!"

"You too T, love you too."

Chapter Four

The next day, he surprised himself by sleeping fifteen hours. When he first had gotten up, he thought maybe the power had gone out, and that the clock was wrong. He checked his cell phone, and sure enough, he had slept the morning away. There were two missed calls from Toni, and one voice mail.

"Hey Gaius, its T, call me. I've got good news, better news and fantastic news!"

The calls and message were left at about noon. He hit the callback button and listened to the Night Rangers' 'Sister Christian' ring tone. *Such eighties girls* he thought, her and his mom. His mind automatically slipped to his mom.

Toni answered cheerfully. "Good morning or shall I say afternoon? Did you get some good sleep?"

"Yea," he answered, a little groggier than he felt. "What's up?"

"Well that box was full of good stuff, and of course, some junk too. First of all, there was an envelope that said Gaius on the outside, and inside is your original birth certificate with your father's name on it!"

"Kimball Smith," he said flatly.

"Yea, you knew that? Kimball Kay Smith."

"Didn't know his middle initial was K, but yea, she told me a few weeks before she died."

"You didn't tell me that, honey," she said, sounding a little disappointed he already knew. "Well, you have your birth certificate now and there is also a passport, but it's almost expired."

Such a good mom, he thought, *gone too soon.* A wave of sadness washed over him. He shook his head and turned his attention back to what Toni was saying.

"...it looks like the policy is two hundred and fifty thousand dollars, so not enough to become independently wealthy, but enough to move you just about anywhere you wanted to go. I mean, a quarter million dollars is a-"

"What? Policy?"

She could hear his confusion. "The Mutual Life Insurance policy I found in that box. Its dated way back to nineteen ninety-five, so you would have been about three or four when she bought it. I don't know if it's valid or not, but I'm going to do a bit more research. Did you get an official death certificate? I'm sure we'll need that too."

"Wow, yea, cool. What else did you find?" he yawned.

"Well, I'll tell you what I didn't find. Those two vases we found, I have no idea where she got them. I've never seen them in my life and can't find anything online that remotely looks like them. One says MRS 85 on the bottom in tiny letters, but I couldn't find anything with that. The vases themselves are well crafted, most likely thrown by hand."

"No shit," he said amazed as he started making a pot of coffee. One in the afternoon or not, he just woke up and wanted a cup.

"Couldn't find anything on the birds, but I'll keep looking. There are no markings on them, nothing to really go by, you know." Gaius watched the coffee drip into the carafe and heard Toni draw and exhale a cigarette, or maybe a joint, he was never quite sure. "Dude… a couple hundred grand would be a wonderful aid to start a new life. You could look into selling the house, or not…"

For the first time, he actually started to consider a move. But where? Pleasant, Utah was the first town that popped in his head. Gaius rubbed his forehead and took a gulp of coffee and sighed. "What else?"

"Well…" The way she drew out the word made him unsure if what was coming next would be good or bad news. "In the envelope with your birth certificate is an old fashion polaroid picture of your mom with a handsome young fella. He only looks familiar because he looks like you. I'm ninety-nine percent sure it's your dad, but it's kinda blurry. There's a younger version of your mom's handwriting on the bottom that says KS and Me,1992."

He suddenly thought of the clay pot they had taken to the Goodwill the day before, on the bottom was etched KS 1991. He should have kept the thing, maybe he would go to the Goodwill and buy it back, surely it would still be there. Seriously, who would buy it? It was obviously handmade and although it was pretty, it was unremarkable.

"Anything else?"

"No, nothing else too exciting. Appliance manuals, a few of your report cards, your high school diploma, *her* high school diploma and a couple pieces of your childhood art work she must of fancied. I'll bring the good stuff by tonight and drop it off. I tossed the junk."

"Sounds good." They said their goodbyes. After his second cup of coffee, he went to log on to the old laptop computer. It wanted to update, shut down and update again. Then, it needed a new passcode. *Good grief*, he thought, running his hands through his hair, *when did she get this thing, five years ago maybe?*

The seven thousand dollars in his dresser came into his mind. *Yea*, he thought to himself, *it's time for an upgrade.* He showered, brushed his teeth and put on clean clothes. As he did this, it dawned on him, he hadn't showered since the funeral. He had brushed his teeth, hadn't he? What day was it? He walked into the bathroom and looked into the mirror, but only his mother's shifting reflection looked back. A wave of sadness came over him as he realized a whole week had gone by without his mother, his *mamacita* as he called her. He thought of the Polaroid Toni was going to bring by later. Like it or not, he could feel the pull in his heart to know his missing parent.

Looking now at his reflection, he thought again of her eyes and her smile. When she looked at him, there was always love brimming in her face. Those warm memories were replaced with images of her withering body and the scars where the surgeons had gone in and cut away parts of her body, the fast forward aging process she had endured. Sometimes it seemed she aged a decade in only twenty-four hours.

He remembered her last day. Her sunken cheeks, opened mouth and the pooled blood in the bottom of her legs, arms and back before the morticians came to get her body for the cremation. The funeral home had asked him if there was something specific he wanted them to dress her in beforehand. It didn't matter to him at all. What a weird question. The funeral home folks took her in her flannel pajamas, so he assumed that was what she was wearing when her body was turned to ash. He hadn't gone down to the funeral home that day. It had been an option, but he didn't want to see her again like that. Lifeless. The urn sat in the living room still, in the same place he left it after the service. Tears stung his eyes. *This is going to take some time*, he thought. Another strange thought crossed his mind. He was an orphan. A twenty-two-year old orphan, just like his mom.

He finished dressing and grabbed one of the packs of money. It felt nice in his front jean pocket. Death is one of those occasions when money can't buy happiness, but never the less, it was the most money he had ever carried on him. The eight thousand dollars he and Toni had found was the most money he had ever seen. He knew his mother would approve of this purchase. He walked to the living room and placed his hand on her urn. They had picked a silver one with a black stripe around the middle. It wasn't the most expensive or the cheapest. It was important to him her remains be in something nice. No clearance.

On impulse, he ran back to his bedroom and grabbed another wad of cash and headed to the mall where he knew there was a Sprint store. The sales clerk was a young lady about his age with long, straight blonde hair, an eyebrow ring and a bit too much make-up. He must be feeling better if he was thinking of the opposite sex. He briefly told her what he was looking for, a tablet with mobile service for road trips.

"Top of the line with all the extras," he said. She delivered. A black iPad with a hotspot, Google Maps, Siri, 128 gigs of storage for music and unlimited internet. With the two year contract he signed, it was less than a thousand dollars, much less, so he pre-paid a year's worth of service. Impressed, the cute blonde sales lady gave him a quick lesson on how to access his apps, sold him a cool looking case, then slipped him a folded piece of paper he deposited in his wallet without looking at it.

When he got home, he took the paper out. The name Brittney was written out, big and bold. The name and phone number were going slightly uphill. Gaius knew that meant she was an optimistic person. He had gotten that from a handwriting book his mom had. He had read it five or so years ago, when she was going through the first round of chemo...or was it the second? The dot over the *i* was called a tittle, he remembered. A word like tittle was not easily forgotten. Brittney's tittle was a heart; that had something to do with her ego, but couldn't recall what.

It was amazing how tired he had become. Losing his mom was harder on him than he had expected. Looking at the slip of paper, he thought of the girl at the mall. Brittney with a heart over the *i*. Her name fit her. In his mind, he saw the way she smiled at him when he took her number. Too cute. Too seductive. Not real. She was pretentious through and through and was probably more impressed with the wads of cash in his pocket than with him. *Not many women in the world like my mom*, he thought. *Real, genuine and sweet*. Oh, how he missed her!

He thought he would nap until Toni got there. She worked until four-thirty, so she wouldn't be there much earlier than five-thirty. Yea, a nap was in order. He laid down and thought of the mall. When he walked out of the Sprint store and to the west side exit, he remembered seeing a tee-pee sign with Free Adoption written on it. *Maybe I'll adopt a pet to keep me company,* he thought as he closed his eye and drifted to sleep.

Chapter Five

Toni showed up at a quarter after six with dinner in Tupperware. It was leftovers from her house. Gaius was still asleep when she knocked once and opened the door.

"Hey hon, dinnertime, get up, get up!" she sang while going into the kitchen. "Brittney? Who's Brittney?" she asked from the other room.

Gaius was waking up, feeling a little groggy and surprisingly hungry. He remembered the scrap of paper he left on the table. "Just a girl at the mall, T. I got an iPad today with a hotspot. Brittney was the girl at the Sprint store that signed me up," he answered nonchalantly, grabbing the plate of food he was offered.

"Is she cute? Does she give all of her favorite customers her private number?" Toni asked with a gleam in her eye. "Gonna call her?"

"Yes, she's cute, yes, she probably gives out her number on a regular basis and nope, not gonna call her," Gaius responded while still chewing his food, not even looking up.

"Well why not?" Toni sounded indignant, like Brittney was a personal relative and she was offended by his quick response.

"I don't know," he swallowed, "she's not my type, I guess."

"Oh and how would you know what your type is?" her tone was almost scolding. "Just how many girls have you been with, lover boy? Tell me, when was your last date?"

"Toni, seriously. A woman in my life is the last thing I fuckin' need right now!" His tone matched hers. Their eyes locked. She looked away first, he went back to his food.

"I'm sorry hon, I just thought a cute girl may help lift your mood, that's all. I don't want you mad at me, I just love you and want what's best."

"I'm sorry too, T. I just haven't been myself this week. I feel sad all the time. I sleep too much. I eat too much. I *drink* too much," he sighed audibly, and she noticed his eyes were moist with tears.

"That's called depression, honey," her tone had changed again. It was caring, soft and loving this time. "Does it help to know that's all normal?"

Tears fell over the brim of his eyes. "No, not really. I just want her back. I sound like a little kid saying it, but I want my mommy! Even sick, even in the state she was..." His words trailed off as he put his head down on his folded arms and cried.

Toni walked over to him and put her arms around his shoulders. "It's okay honey. It's barely been a week. Cry it out," she rubbed his back and repeated herself. "Cry it out, honey. It's going to take some time. You really should consider doing something fun. I'm not tellin' you what do, G, I'm just making suggestions. Get out of the house. Enjoy the sunshine. Go to the mall and visit the cute girl that's not your type. Take her to a funny movie, order popcorn and pretend you have someone else's life for a night," he sat up and wiped his nose on the sleeve of his shirt, nodding slightly. "Until then," she continued, "eat, drink, sleep. You're doing just fine, and you'll *be* just fine. I know it hurts, you miss her, but you're tough and she would want you to be happy and healthy."

He nodded again. "Thanks for dinner."

"Sure, hon, anytime. I'll stop by again tomorrow after work."

"You don't have to do that."

"I know I don't," she replied, "but I *want* to! You're important to me, I love you."

"I love you too."

Toni gathered her plastic containers and left. Even with the nap, Gaius felt exhausted and headed back to bed though it was only 7:30p.m. He slept another fourteen hours. Maybe he was depressed.

As he made himself some instant oatmeal, he thought about his conversation with T the night before. What would it hurt to ask Brittney out for a movie and maybe a bite to eat? He had some cash, and he could afford it. It wasn't about the money, and if he remembered right, there was an Adam Sandler movie that just came out.

Brittney was lovely to look at. It was just that she wore too much makeup for his taste, her blouse was a bit too revealing, and he thought he had noticed a tattoo peeking out from beneath her sleeve. It wasn't like he was a prude or anything, and tattoos were great on other people. It just wasn't his thing. Gaius was simply more attracted to girls who were more natural, earthy. He was attracted to girls he knew his mom would like, and ones that would like his mom. He supposed that didn't matter now. Yea. Perhaps he should go down there, talk to Brittney and ask her to the movies.

Gaius always parked in the same spot at the mall, or at least the same area, in the west side parking lot. That way he never had to really *remember* where he parked. Another little trick he learned from his mom to make his life a bit easier. There was a crowd just inside the doors. *What was going on*, he saw the sign he vaguely remembered from the day before. 'Free adoptions, this weekend, vaccinations included, half price spay/neuter'. Moving away from the people and animals, he made his way towards the Sprint store. His paced slowed as he approached. Not wanting to appear too excited or needy, he took mental inventory of his facial muscles and body language. When he looked up, prepared to ask her out, he noticed she was leaning over the counter giving the male customer a full view of her exposed cleavage with that same pretentious smile on her face, batting her fake eyelashes under way too much make-up. *I can't do this,* he thought, but she had seen him and started waving. Gaius turned and started back towards the exit. What was he thinking? This was not a good idea. He heard a woman's voice. "Guy, Guy!" He kept walking, it really bothered him when people called him Guy. Brittney caught up with him and touched his arm, he slowed and turned towards her. "Hi!" She beamed.

"Hi," he answered, not nearly as enthusiastic.

"What'cha doin'?" The fake niceness was too much. The coy smile, the yellow Sprint shirt that was probably two sizes too small, the doe eyes, the batting fake lashes, the sticky sweet syrup tone in her voice...it was all too much. Did he just notice gauges in her ears?

"Oh nothing," His voice was flat. "Just coming down to support the animal rescue, you know. Been considering a new pet," he glanced around at the people and commotion. "I understand there are free adoptions this weekend, so I'm just supporting my community. That's all. Community support."

"You're so sweet," Brittney said, pouting out her lips while using a sing-song voice, as if she was talking to a baby, "You didn't lose my number, did you?" She flashed a full-toothed smile and he thought of an alligator, just briefly.

"I still have it," Gaius assured her, then turned and walked into the shelter shop trying to put space between them, watching her over his shoulder. She continued out the glass exit doors and opened her purse, lighting a cigarette and holding it between her lips. *What a turn off!* Gaius thought. If she had been attractive before, she wasn't now. Brittney took out her cell phone and started texting. The smoke circling around her face made her grimace in the most unattractive way. Looking around at his unintentional surroundings, he noticed a young boy with his parents. The boy was about ten years old and holding a grey and white American Staffordshire Terrier puppy, grinning from ear to ear while his parents finished filling out the adoption paperwork for the newest addition to their little family. He overheard the shelter worker talking to the family.

"Congratulations, that's the last pup. That little guy came from a litter of twelve! Now we just need to find a good home for their mom. She's a sweet dog, was a good mom to all those babies. The pups all have good temperaments. It's that way when the mom's a bit older." The new adoptee's said something, more to their child than to the worker. "Okay, looks like that's it. Have a great day, and congratulations again, Billy, Mr. and Mrs. Jameson. Great meeting you. Take good care of that pup and you'll have a friend for life," she smiled as they exited.

Gaius looked up and saw the too tight yellow Sprint shirt coming back towards the shelter. Brittney was texting and walking at the same time. Cuter from a distance, he assured himself. He certainly didn't want to take a chance of running into her a second time, so he slid onto the chair the little boy had just occupied. "Hi," he said to the rescue lady, "I'm interested in getting a new pet. A dog maybe? What about the mom of the little puppy that just left? I heard you talking about her."

"Oh she's a sweet mama dog. A little older, we estimate her to be four, maybe five. Maybe older. This was definitely not her first litter. Do you have other pets?" Gaius shook his head. "Do you rent or own?"

"I live at my mom's house, she owns," he gave her a wan smile. *Is that the proper tense if she is deceased?* he wondered to himself. Owned? Owns? Either way, there was no landlord to have to contend with. Either way, his mom was still dead.

"Okay!" the animal humane employee said eagerly. "Come this way. I'll introduce you." Gaius followed and noticed

Brittney had gone back to work. His intention was to leave when he knew the coast was clear, but as they approached the kennel where the mama dog was, he thought the nameplate had Sue Stewart written on it. Like a cartoon character, he shook his head a little and looked again. Focusing specifically on the letters, he could see it said Sassy Sami. How in the world did he get Sue Stewart out of that? The initials S.S. were the only correlation. Gaius thought briefly about how the brain worked. Science was always one of his favorite subjects. He remembered reading that there are findings which provide convincing evidence that the brain can sometimes use memories to fill in what it doesn't know. The brain was very tricky. Nevertheless, his mom was now on his mind.

His eyes dropped to the dog as she heartily jumped up to greet them, her tail wagging so hard it appeared she could lift off like a helicopter at any moment. Sassy Sami was a grey and white American Pitbull, just like that one that just left, but she was thin from nursing twelve pups, and even though her tail wagged, he could see she was sad. She had an almost pleading look in her eye as she met Gaius, tail still wagging. The lady was talking to the dog as she opened the door to the kennel. "Hi sweet thing, your babies are all gone now, all have good homes..." she trailed off and started rubbing the dog on both sides of her face. Gaius swore he saw the dog smile as he turned his attention to the shelter employee. "I have some paperwork to file and some administrative stuff to get done from that last adoption," she spoke while putting a leash on the dog. "Why don't you take her out to do her business, there's a patch of lawn we use on the other side of the parking lot. You'll see it, there's a bench and no other grass, so it's pretty obvious. Then, let's talk and see if this sweetheart is for you. If not, we most likely have something else that fits your pet loving needs."

Before he knew it, he was walking out the auto-slide glass doors with Sassy Sami leading the way. Thinking about Toni, and what he would tell her about his botched attempt to ask out Brittney, he just allowed the dog to lead him without really paying any attention to her. She suddenly stopped and sat down on the asphalt of the parking lot. "What's up doggie dog?" he said out loud to her. He looked up and realized she had stopped at *his* black Toyota truck. He glanced at the truck and back to her. Again, he got the impression she was smiling.

She winked at him. "C'mon," he murmured. "Seriously? Did you just walk up to *my* truck then smile and wink at me? Is this for real? Why are you messin' with me like that, dog?"

He looked around all of a sudden self-conscious. Maybe he was on some weird hidden camera reality show. How could they have gotten the dog in on it? *Paranoia for real*, he thought. Looking back at the grey Pit, he realized her expression had changed. This time she wasn't smiling. She wouldn't even look directly at him. Instead, she laid down at his feet, exposing her belly to him with her eyes closed. Her tail started to thump rhythmically on the hard ground. Gaius glanced around again, waiting for someone to jump out and announce he was being videoed on a hidden camera. When that didn't happen, he tugged the leash slightly and started walking towards the patch of grass. Sassy Sami followed and just sat on the lawn, not appearing to have to go. Gaius shrugged and headed back.

Once back inside the mall, he noticed the lady that had been helping him before was beaming as they approached. "She's a doll, isn't she?"

He noticed her name tag read Kathy. "Yea, she's a good girl," he answered, thinking of the doggy magic trick the Staffordshire terrier had just executed. Knowing what vehicle was his was absurd. It was a coincidence, right? The double S initials...was that another sign he was supposed to adopt this dog? His mom had always taught him to pay attention to reoccurring thoughts and feelings, numbers and happenstances. He could hear his mother's voice in his head. *The universe always seems to know what a person needs, and delivers.* "Free adoptions this weekend, huh?" he said out loud.

"Yes," Kathy replied matter-of-factly, "Sassy's current on her shots, but we'll insist you make an appointment to get her fixed. Had she not been nursing when she was brought in, she would already be spayed. We just hope she's not one of those puppy mill dogs that they just kept pregnant her whole life. She's got such a good temperament, don't you, girl?" She rubbed the dog affectionately on the head.

"Where'd her name come from?" Gaius inquired.

"Oh, we have an auto generating computer app. People adopt cute names, not numbers, so we've got to name those that aren't an owner surrender. Those folks are the worst! You know? Those jerks that dump off their pet cuz of any excuse they can come up with, usually a move, but whatever. So you know, a dog is a minimum of a ten-year commitment," she gave him a sharp look. "Anyway, you asked about her name, the app goes alphabetically and produces a male and female name. With her, the names were Sassy and Sam, but both names suited her. Some of the workers started calling her Sami, some called her Sassy. She does this talky thing that sounds like she's having a conversation with you. She's vocal, but doesn't bark much, so we kept both names and she's our Sassy Sami, aren't you, girl?" Kathy again rubbed behind the dog's ears.

"I don't know," Gaius hadn't had a pet since he was thirteen, and it was a cat. Louie was a Siamese mix, and they had him for seven years, until one day, he just disappeared. At that time, his mom took care of everything like feeding, cleaning the litter box and going on vet visits. There was a saying that Gaius once read which said, 'Dogs have owners. Cats have servants.' Louie was that kind of cat and Sue had doted on him. In his mind's eye, he could see her sitting on the old chair with the cat splayed over her lap. Was he ready to have that kind of responsibility? Kathy was talking to him and he concentrated on her words.

"...just take her home with you now for the weekend. The first day we can get her in for the sterilization surgery would be Wednesday. If things don't work out, you can just leave her when you bring her back. The surgery will be half price if you sign the papers this weekend. You can pick which veterinary clinic works best for you, you know, location wise..."

She kept talking, but Gaius had stopped listening as he began hearing voices in his head. Gaius heard Toni in his head first. *Pppssshhhh... afraid of responsibility? C'mon G, you've been taking care of your mom for years, a dog will be a cakewalk.* He heard his mom's voice in his head next. *Everything happens for a reason, son.* He heard Kathy's voice, her advice for little Billy. *Take care of that pup and you'll have a friend for life.* He was lost in thought when he realized Kathy had stopped speaking and was looking at him expectantly. "Okay, let's do it," he sounded more committed than he felt.

Gaius smiled. Kathy smiled. Sassy Sami smiled.

Chapter Six

Service. Mondays were what was referred to as P-day. The missionaries were able to wear regular clothes instead of the church clothes that were worn the other six days. On P-day, they didn't schedule lessons to convert those that weren't of their faith, but instead served the community. Often they helped members of the church with small tasks like yard or housework. It hadn't taken long for members and non-members alike to take advantage of these young people on their missions. Rules had to be established worldwide about the number of hours that the missionaries could donate to one particular family or project.

Sister Paula Cooke from Idaho, Elizabeth's current companion, called Sister Jolley early one P-day morning inquiring when they should come over for their community service project. The Jolley's had six kids. A big family regardless of what religion you were. Sister Jolley had said to wear 'grubbies'. She wanted the sister missionaries to help her paint their toddlers' bedroom. Their two youngest were ages four and two, both boys. Their room had seen all of the other four children at one time or another and desperately needed a good cleaning and sure, why not, a coat of paint.

So this was Baptist country. One thing that was blaringly obvious to Elizabeth was there were as many Baptist Churches in this part of the country as there were Latter Day Saint churches in her little corner of the world.

Sister Jolley asked them to go with her to the local Walmart to get some basic painting supplies. As they walked in, Elizabeth couldn't help but notice the way the locals were dressed. Just about everyone was wearing camouflage pants and tee shirts with pro-gun slogans. Elizabeth couldn't help but think of the *Thou shall not kill* commandment. Others wore tee-shirts that advertised their faith with sappy church slogans like: 'Act your praise, not your shoe size', or 'A cold church is like cold butter, it doesn't spread well', or the one that made her wince, 'Fifty Shades of Grace'.

The jewelry cases were loaded with crosses of every size and color imaginable. Big crosses and little crosses. Everyone wore crosses on their necklaces or earrings, or on the back pockets of their jeans. There were crosses on the bumpers of their cars and on their tombstones. The Mormon church did not ever use the cross symbol. When asked why, Sister Anderson often referred to a quote from President Hinckley, the fifteenth president of the church:

> "Because our Savior lives, we do not use the symbol of his death as the symbol of our faith. But what shall we use? No sign, no work of art, no representation of form is adequate to express the glory and the wonder of the Living Christ. He told us what that symbol should be when he said, 'If ye love me, keep my commandments' (John 14:15)".

She could have referred to a comedy act she watched years before. The comedian had compared wearing a rifle pendant in Jackie Kennedy's presence to wearing cross jewelry in Jesus' presence. *Just thinking of you, John.* It wasn't the *method* of Jesus' death that was to be remembered, but the *why*. President Hinckley was right, the commandments were the true symbol.

At the Walmart, listening to the locals talk, she wondered if some of the conversations were even in English. Maybe Kentucky was more 'foreign' than she had given it credit. Shirts with the confederate flag were on the shelves. Prejudice and intolerance was alive and well here. Between the crosses, guns and rebel flags, Elizabeth could feel herself becoming judgmental, one of her own personal pet peeves. She reminded herself why she was there, as the familiar tune of her favorite childhood hymn started to play in her head.

> 'I hope that I can share the gospel
> with those who want to know the truth;
> I hope they call me on a mission
> while I am in my youth.'

As they checked out and loaded the painting supplies into the cart and headed to the car, the three women were approached by a fifty-something year old black woman with cropped short hair and a missing tooth in the front-bottom of her mouth. "Ma'am, 'cuse me, sorry to bother you, but Imma needin' some help, missus any change you could-"

"Get away from me, you filthy animal!" Sister Jolley screeched. "You sure as shit do need help, but you ain't gettin' none from me. Now go on home before someone comes along and beats your black ass!" *Did that really just come out of*

Sister Jolley's mouth? Elizabeth wondered, glancing at her companion. Sister Paula had a look of pure shock on her face. They loaded their purchases into the trunk of the car and climbed in as Sister Jolley started the engine. "Fucking niggers," she said. "Sorry ladies, I just hate using the eff word, but for real! I don't know why they don't just stay down on their side of town. Why they gotta be up here, slinking around, beggin' for change?"

The eff word was the least offensive of the two words, Elizabeth thought, but said nothing. "Right?!" Sister Paula agreed. "Do they have no shame?" *What was happening? Why were they talking like this?* Elizabeth thought. Okay, so she hadn't actually met a black person before her mission, nor anyone that had a bad thing to say about blacks, but she had met several African Americans since coming here and had found them all to be rather pleasant, and some of them were downright funny. Not to mention, the black children were some of the cutest kids she had ever seen. Elizabeth listened intently to the two women to see if she had missed something. Both of them were acting as normal as could be, Sister Jolley driving through traffic and Sister Paula staring out the window. They were having a pleasant conversation about the weather.

Once they got back to the Jolley's, the day went back to normal, and Sisters Anderson and Cooke got to work cleaning the room. They threw away broken, worn out toys and bagged up trash. After several hours, the room was ready to be painted. *Now that it's clean, it doesn't look so bad*, Elizabeth thought. Paula made a motion pointing at her wrist, and Elizabeth understood it meant they needed to figure out how to leave before the painting got underway, or they would be there another four to five hours.

"Sister Jolley," Paula said gently, "Sister Anderson and I have a few other appointments this afternoon and need to get on our way, could we say a prayer before we go?"

"Of course, dear, I'll do it," Sister Jolley said, climbing off a step ladder before bowing her head. "Our dear Heavenly Father. Thank you for these sisters, these young, dear missionaries doing your work. Thank you O' Lord for their service. We ask thee to bless and protect them as they travel back to their home, and we pray that they are not accosted by any darkies or other unholy beings. We ask unto thee that they return safe so they are able to continue to spread the gospel of the one true church. Again, we thank you for this beautiful world in which we live. We thank you for everything you sacrificed so we may have a life full of free agency. We are proud to be your humble servants, Lord. We say these things in the name of Jesus Christ, amen."

Amen? Elizabeth couldn't shake the feeling that she was surrounded by long standing hatred between white and black people. She had lived here over a year and was just now noticing things that she simply had not before the service-day at the Jolley's. At the ward she attended, there were very few blacks. In fact, she could only think of one black family, and she didn't always see them at Sunday service. There were black people she had met along the way during her mission, but they were all from trekking and knocking on doors in very particular parts of the town. In fact, now she really *thought* about it, there were no white people in *those* neighborhoods, with a few exceptions. Poverty stricken families, that some referred to as white trash, were dotted throughout the area the locals called the ghetto. She couldn't believe there were parts of her country that still had racial intolerance. Many times she had heard or read of racial separation, but didn't really think it existed. This was the United States of America for crying out loud.

A few days later, the mission president had suggested doing splits, a system where each missionary is paired up with another individual in a short-lived capacity. Successfully meeting people, teaching their lessons and introducing the idea of baptism to a family is strictly a numbers game. The more people missionaries came in contact with, the more real chances there were for follow up visits and potential conversion. So on occasion, they split the missionaries with other LDS members to canvas more territory.

Sister Cooke was paired up with Sister Jolley's oldest daughter, who was twenty and still entertaining the idea of applying for a mission but hadn't committed. Elizabeth was paired with a woman she had only met in church a couple time, Rebecca Armstrong. She would have guessed Rebecca was in her early to mid-twenties, exotic looking with dark hair, hazel eyes and a body any Victoria's Secret model would envy. Rebecca sported a simple gold wedding band and a matching necklace with a sideways figure eight suspended by the ends of the delicate gold chain. On her right hand she wore a gold version of the CTR ring Elizabeth was wearing on her right hand.

CTR stood for Choose the Right, and is a lesson drilled into children's minds from the youngest of ages. When a Latter Day saint child reaches the age of eight, they are baptized on a Saturday and confirmed on the following Sunday to become an official member of the church. All of their sin is washed away and they are cleansed. It is a very exciting time for a Mormon child, an important rite of passage. There is usually a celebration of sorts, and they are recognized by the bishop on that Sunday's service where they receive their CTR ring as a reminder to always Choose the Right.

The mission president was happy about the pairing of these four women and suggested if it worked out, perhaps it could become a regular arrangement, "No more than a couple times a week," he said, smiling a little too broadly, looking directly at Rebecca. He continued. "For safety reasons, I need to know your routes today."

Sister Cooke was quick to say they would stay local in the ward and hit up the elderly couple that were not members just a few blocks away. She and Sister Anderson had already made an initial contact with the couple and they were responsive and positive about continued lessons. The mission president beamed, and nodded, turning to Elizabeth and Rebecca.

"We'll tract down to south valley," Rebecca said flatly, meeting the mission president's eyes.

"If you're comfortable with that, Sister Armstrong, I see no reason why you shouldn't. Sister Anderson, are you okay with that part of town?" The mission president looked expectantly at Elizabeth, as if she were a child getting ready for an adventure.

"Yea, sure," Elizabeth replied, "why not?"

"Why not!" Rebecca repeated a little too heartily. The mission president and Sister Jolley gave each other a doubtful look as the girls, scriptures in hand, headed out, two going north, two going south. As they walked, Elizabeth attempted conversation with Rebecca about her life. If she had lived in this area long, what about her husband, did they have kids? Sister Armstrong answered in monotone, one syllable replies. They fell into silence as they kept walking. Elizabeth's mind wandered, she loved the scenery here, thinking it looked as if they had stepped into a Hollywood movie set, it was that picturesque.

After about ten minutes of neither of them talking, Rebecca finally spoke, "Sister Anderson, I've got to confess something to you, I don't want you to think I'm something I'm not. First, I'm a convert. I was born in New Jersey, baptized Catholic at birth. My real last name is Schmitty," she said. Elizabeth kept walking without replying, but glanced at her temporary companion just so she knew she was listening. "I'm not married. I wear this ring to keep the weirdos at bay. I was a drug addict, homeless and living in the gutters of New York City. Then I met Elder Nelson from White Fish, Montana." Rebecca smiled at the memory. "White Fish, great name for a town, huh?"

"Not as pleasant as Pleasant, but yea..." Elizabeth smiled back.

"What?"

"Nothing, never mind."

Rebecca smiled warmly back. "Funny? Is it pleasant where you're from?"

"Pleasant enough," she laughed, "I'm kidding... the name of the town is Pleasant. We have fun with the play on words. Continue your story, I'm sorry, didn't mean to interrupt. You were homeless in New York?" Elizabeth returned her face to a more serious expression.

"Yep. Homeless and strung out on heroin. So glad I didn't O.D! *That* would have sucked!" She shook her head at the memory and her face turned solemn. "Then outta the blue there's Elder Nelson from White Fish. Him and his companion had gotten turned around and ventured down the alleyway where I had been camped out about a week. I was nasty at the time, living in the streets, no shower or toothbrush, I stunk, my hair was a mess. I had even turned a couple tricks just to survive. Well, no, that's not exactly truthful, I blew a fella a couple times for a bit more smack."

"Smack?" Elizabeth was confused, she wasn't entirely sure what a trick was and was completely lost on the word smack used as a noun and not a verb.

"Heroin," Rebecca's eyebrows raised "do tell, Sister Christian, where is that pleasant little town you speak of? The moon?"

"It's Anderson, I'm Sister Anderson. And it's in Utah."

"Well, that explains a lot," she chuckled to herself. "And I called you Sister Christian as a joke, I didn't mean to offend you. I know your name. You're one of *those* Mormons." A sly smile played at the corners of her mouth.

"What do you mean? I'm so confused. Mormons are Mormons. You're playin' with me."

"Oh not exactly little mama."

"Little mama?" Elizabeth was feeling like she was still on that Hollywood set but didn't know the script or what was being said or what she was supposed to say back.

Rebecca's giggle was turning to a full blown laugh now. "You're so cute and innocent it makes me want to barf!" Elizabeth didn't know what to say so she didn't say anything. Rebecca continued. "As I was saying, I was homeless, a drug addict; one step away from becoming a total derelict when I was converted by Elder Nelson and his buddy. You know, I wanted him to be my knight in shining armor and come to my emotional rescue like good old Mick Jagger says...coming to my emotional rescue on a fine Arab charger?"

"Who? What?"

"Oh my H. E. Double toothpicks! You don't know who Mick Jagger is? Seriously, you've never heard of the Rolling Stones?"

Elizabeth noticed Rebecca's dumbfounded expression. "Yea, of course, I know the Rolling Stones... sure. 'I can't get no satisfaction,' those guys, right?" Elizabeth was hoping she was referring to the right band. She really didn't know any of their music. *They were old dudes, right? Been around a long time, right?* She thought this and didn't speak it aloud as to not appear anymore ignorant than she felt.

"Okay little missy, you're off the hook... where was I?"

"Elder Nelson. Heroin. Streets of New York."

"Okay, yea, yea..." Rebecca got back into her story mode as they turned down third street into a neighborhood Elizabeth had never been to. She was just assuming Rebecca knew where they were going. "So, Elder Nelson and his companion were a little lost and happened down my alley. I saw them coming in their clean white shirts, all young and innocent looking, just like *you* Sister Christian! They were so clueless. My intention was to rob them."

"What?!?" Elizabeth turned in shocked horror and looked at Rebecca. For the first time, Elizabeth really looked hard at her companion and suspected this girl was closer to thirty than twenty.

"Yup, yup, yup." Rebecca's memories made her golden hazel eyes look distant, yet they sparkled at the same time. "I jumped out holding a seven-inch butcher knife in front of me and demanded their money and wallets!"

"Oh my, gosh!" Elizabeth was enthralled now, yet a little horrified.

"Right?" Rebecca continued. "The look on those boy's faces. Priceless! They both threw up their hands, their scriptures falling to the ground. Elder Nelson explained they were missionaries from the Church of Latter Day Saints, and they didn't have any money, and asked if they could please be on their way," she paused for a minute. Again, Elizabeth didn't know what to say, so she stayed silent. "Fine', I told them, 'skedaddle then, this is *my* alley,' and turned back to my makeshift shack. Elder Nelson's companion was scrambling to get his stuff and go, but Elder Nelson asked if he could bless me, and asked me if I would pray with him."

"What'd you say?"

"I told them it was a free fucking country and they could do whatever they wanted, just get out of my alley." Elizabeth had never heard anyone use the eff-word so casually, especially a woman. Rebecca went on. "But Elder Nelson had a revelation, so he sat with me on a cardboard box bed I had made and asked me my name. His companion was still unsure, looking like a scared rabbit ready to bolt at any given minute." Rebecca continued talking as they made another turn onto a street called Hayward. *We're walking like we have a destination*, Elizabeth thought. "So good old brother Nelson takes my hand and starts to pray, asking the Lord to help me see the light and enjoy the gifts He has given all of us. He prayed that I might find my way without the use of drugs and without compromising my body. It was weird, but when he said that it was like he knew I had done things I wasn't proud of, knew I was hooked on some really bad shit, like he saw through me, into my soul. I mean really, how did he know I was shooting up and giving BJ's for dope? I just met him two and a half minutes earlier."

They had been walking about an hour at this point and Elizabeth realized she had never been in this part of town and had no idea how to get back if she had to. The houses looked shabbier, the yards smaller and not as kempt.

"So they got done praying and Elder Nelson asks me, is there anything they could do for me, and I say, 'yea mother fuckers, I'm hungry.'" *The language from this woman,* Elizabeth thought, *serious potty mouth.* "So Elder Nelson takes my hand and we walk to the end of the alley like a couple of lovers with his third wheel bringing up the rear, and we come out on Broadway near Champ's Deli. He opens the door for me to go in, and all of a sudden I'm aware of myself, my clothes, my smell, the fact I couldn't remember the last time I brushed my teeth or combed my hair, and I just stopped dead in my tracks. 'It's okay,' Elder Nelson assured me, and his companion caught up with us and went in as I just stood there, feeling conspicuous and exposed. 'You okay?' Elder Nelson asks me. 'Sure,' I said, 'but I'll just wait here for you.' 'Promise?' he asked. I mean really, where else was I going to go but back to my cardboard bunk, so I promised. They went in and came out with four big bags of food, and we all crossed the street to a little area where there were tables set up. Elder Nelson's companion blessed the food and started taking out big containers of coleslaw, potato salad, a *huge* baked potato wrapped in tin foil, and three sandwiches, handing one to me. I said to them, 'thought you boys were broke,' and Elder Nelson said..."

Elizabeth interrupted and finished her sentence for her. "The church pays for it on these pre-paid debit cards."

"Right you are!" Rebecca confirmed. "And he handed me the card, told me there was only about twenty dollars left on it, but they would be fine until they got another one, and he wanted me to have it. By that time, I had torn into the sandwich and was stuffing my face with ferocity as Elder Nelson would later recall it. They sent me home with the leftover salads and the baked potato. And that, my little Missy, was the beginning of the end for me," she turned onto a sidewalk that lead to a small brick house with a big front porch, as she knocked and yelled, "Hattie, you here? Hat, open up, it's me, Beck."

The door was flung open by a thin twenty-something, shirtless young black man with a shaved head and a thin mustache outlining his full lips perfectly. He had many tattoos on his chest and arms. Without staring, Elizabeth stole a couple glances and realized many of them were religious in nature. There was an ornate cross on his forearm and a scripture on the opposite one, at least she thought it was a scripture.

"Well, well, well, how you do my little pretty?" he crooned, looking Rebecca up and down, then noticing Elizabeth. "Oh, what's this precious morsel of meat you've brought me, Beck?"

"She's not for sale Maximus, off the market completely, she's doin' God's work and still packin' her v-card." Rebecca walked in and gave the young man a kiss on either side of his cheek, and turned to Elizabeth. "Sister Christian, this is Maximus, my pain-in-my-asses."

"It's Anderson not Christian," Elizabeth stammered. "Sister Anderson. I mean... I am a Christian. I believe in Christ, but it's definitely Anderson," she indicated her name tag realizing too late it drew Maximus' eyes directly to her breasts.

"Mo-lasses," his smooth voice drew the word out slowly, emphasizing his southern drawl. "You certainly a purdy little thang to still be carrying a v-card." As he spoke, he looked at Elizabeth like no man ever had. In fact, she could feel the back of her ears get hot.

"Mo... um... Molasses?" Elizabeth squeaked out, avoiding Maximus' eyes.

"Sugary, sweet honey. Sugary sweet," his smile, the deep masculine voice, it all made Elizabeth more aware of herself than ever before. Her entire body tingled from her head to her toes.

Chapter Seven

As Gaius pulled out from the mall parking lot, Sassy Sami was looking back at him from the passenger side of his old Toyota truck. "Bet those pups took it out of you, didn't they girl?" She rolled her head at him with that goofy grin on her face. "Let's grab a bite to eat, what'da ya say?" Sassy Sami snuffed and shook her floppy ears. "I'm going to take that as a yes." By the time they got home, Gaius had finished his fully loaded burger, and Sassy Sami had finished her two plain dollar burgers. Sitting in the drive-way, he sent Toni a text,

> *Hey T. Comin' by tonight?*
> *Planned on it. Everything okay?*
> *LOL, Yes, everything is fantastic! See you soon.*
> *Fantastic? Wow! Should I grab dinner?*
> *Nope, already ate with my new favorite girl!*
> *OMG! Can't wait to hear all about it! C U soon!*

Gaius smiled to himself. That was just the reaction he was hoping for. He led Sassy Sami into the house and unclipped her leash, and she immediately began sniffing her new surroundings before jumping into Sue's chair and curling up into a tiny ball. "Well, alrighty then. You know which truck is mine and you know which seat isn't taken... you're a little smarty, aren't you?" he flopped onto the couch, and the dog snuffed and sighed. Gaius opened a beer and took a long draw from it. *Only five-thirty,* he thought. *I have time for a little nap.* He took another drink from the beer and set it on the coffee table in front of him before putting his feet up. It seemed as if he dozed off for only a second when Sassy Sami leapt off the chair and started barking fiercely at door. Gaius jumped up, knocking his half empty beer over. As it foamed, the dog was barking even more aggressively, and he noticed the hackles had raised on her neck. "Hey, hey, hey, chill out girl, easy!" he shouted, running to the kitchen to grab a dish towel.

Toni walked in and stopped in her tracks, starring wide-eyed at the dog. "What the fuck Gaius!?" Toni's face was a mixture of astonishment and terror.

Gaius threw the towel over the spilled beer and knelt down by his new pet. Crooning to her, he said, "It's okay Sassy, it's cool. This is T, she's a friend. She's a good bitch, you'll like her. Easy girl."

"Did you just call me a bitch?" Toni inquired unimpressed.

"In a very doggie dog way, indeed, I did." Sassy Sami had stopped barking but was eyeing Toni with suspicion and keeping herself between the two humans. "I adopted a dog!" Gaius said proudly.

"Oh my gawd! Jesus, Gaius, what are thinking?"

Getting defensive he raised his voice, "Well, I was thinking I just lost my mom and I could use a faithful companion. And besides, it's not permanent yet. It's a temporary adoption, just to make sure she's going to work out. Her name is Sassy Sami, but I'm thinking of changing it."

Toni held out the back of her hand, the universal don't-bite-me dog gesture. Sassy Sami sniffed twice then licked. "Eeewww... Dog kisses, gross!" He knew she was acting more indignant than she felt. "Well, it wasn't the dinner date story I was expecting, but I suppose this is a good thing. She seems like a good dog. What's up with her boobs? Does she have pups?" Toni asked as started scratching the dog behind the ears.

"They are teats Toni, and yes, she just had a litter of twelve."

"Holy shit Gaius, please don't tell me you adopted them all." Toni looked genuinely frightened.

"Yea, they're all asleep in mom's room," he tried his best to feign sincerity.

"You're such a bad liar."

He smiled broadly at her. "Like I said, I'm not under any obligation, if it doesn't work out, I just leave her with the vet when I take her in to be spayed next week."

"You'll keep her." Toni said, grinning and rubbing the dog's big block head. "Pitbull?"

"American Staffordshire Terrier if you don't mind." It was Gaius' turn to feign indignation this time.

"Yea, that's what I said, Pitbull." Toni shot back with a wicked grin on her face. "This one is a keeper for sure, what a sweetheart." The dog was on her back, eyes closed enjoying the attention. "That barking just now was just her doing her job, wasn't it girlie? She'll deter anyone with that deep menacing bark, you know, dogs and kids, they know good people from bad, they can tell. Fail safe for sure, she'll keep the real bitches away from you, won't you Sassafras? How did it go with 'she's not my type' little Miss Sprint hottie?"

"Gonna change her name, but not to Sassafras. Where on earth did that come from? You're too funny." Gaius looked at the pure bliss on the dogs face as she reveled in the one-on-one attention. "As for the mall girl, well... she really isn't my type. A two-minute conversation with her was all I needed to see that. Too much make-up, too phony and she smokes. Ew."

"I smoke." Toni said frankly.

"And I wouldn't date you either. Damn girl, please," he winked at her and she smiled back, still rubbing the dog.

"What was the name the pound gave her? You said, but I don't remember."

"Sassy Sami, I guess she's mouthy from what the lady at the rescue says."

"Yes she is! You heard that reception I got, mouthy as fuck. Does she answer to either name better than the other? Sassy or Sami?" Toni inquired.

"I have no idea." Gaius confessed.

"In my experience, dogs name themselves," she got up and walked from the living room to just inside the door of the kitchen. "Sami, Sami girl, come." The dog rolled her head and looked up at Gaius. "Ok, let's try Sassy. Come Sassy, come, here Sassy." The dog laid at Gaius' feet, looked up and yawned. He and Toni exchanged an amused look. "Sassafras." Toni suddenly said. The dog sat up and looked at Toni, cocking her head to one side.

"No," Gaius said, "that's a retarded name. Don't call her that."

"Sassafras, come," Toni said once more, and the dog got up and sauntered into the kitchen. "Retarded or not, she comes to it. You can call her Sass for short, a dog needs a good one syllable name. Don't you, Sass? And her pound name was Sassy, so she's probably used to it already, a little anyway," she said rubbing the dog's neck as the dog leaned into the woman, grinning ear to ear.

Gaius sighed. "I'm not crazy about it, but... it does sort of fit her. Look at her smile. You're something else!" he said, in a no nonsense, strict tone. The dog stood up straight and arched her back like a cat. Her back legs got stiff, and she started snorting and baring her teeth, side-stepping and snuffing.

"What the fuck?" Toni started to laugh. "She *is* mouthy! Plus, I think she likes her name. I think she just told you off too. Didn't you girl, you just told him to fuck right off didn't you?" Toni crooned to the animal like a baby. "Got everything you need for her? Food, a bed, leash, treats?"

"Well, so far she likes mom's swivel chair. It's as good as any place for her to sleep, and I don't sit there so it's fine with me. She curls up in it like a cat. I'll use a pan for water and a Tupperware bowl for her food. She had cheeseburgers with me tonight."

Toni arched one eyebrow as she looked at him inquisitively. "Cheeseburgers?"

Over the weekend, Gaius became more and more smitten with the grey pitbull. By Sunday, he was sure he would keep her. She made him smile, and smiling was definitely something he needed more of.

In the Monday morning mail, the life insurance check came. He had been expecting the letter, yet it felt like it came out of left field and struck him in the face. He started to cry, and it turned into a full on bawl as he held the two hundred and fifty-thousand-dollar check. "Oh mom, I love you, I love you, I love you! I'd trade this money ten times over if I could just have you back!" He wailed and cried and felt foolish, childish even. The dog suddenly began to howl low and deep, sounding as pained as Gaius felt. Sass seemed to know what Gaius needed, and as his crying subsided, she came to him and dropped her head into his lap with a heavy sigh. Gaius reached down and stroked her neck and head. "Thanks Sass, I needed that," he wiped his face with his sleeve and grabbed his phone to text Toni.

Coming by tonight? Got the $$$. Not sure how I feel about it.

The life insurance? Talk about bittersweet. Oh honey, I'm sorry.

Feels like blood money. Would rather have my mom.

Me too. Love you buddy, so does that mutt of yours. Hang in there.

She doesn't like mutt. American Staffordshire terrier is what she prefers

LMAO. See you about quarter after six, I'll grab dinner.

TY. Don't know what I'd do without you.

You're Welcome! C U soon.
FYI-Sass doesn't eat onions or tomatoes.
Custom takeout orders for a dog? WTF?
She's not a dog, she's a little person in a dog suit, with
a sensitive stomach.
Ok, I get it. LOL! No onions or tomatoes.

It was a quarter after six, and like clockwork, Toni showed up with an extra-large pepperoni and pineapple pizza with extra cheese and thin crust. Gaius selected the biggest piece, put it on a paper plate, and placed it on the ground for the dog, he got a second plate and grabbed himself a slice. Toni poured two glasses of Coke from a two-liter bottle and set them on the table. Sassafras woofed down her slice and looked expectantly at the two humans.

Toni glanced over at Gaius. "So, you got your walking papers, huh? What's next for you, my dear?"

"Walking papers?" Gaius looked confused.

"The check. Quarter million dollars?" Toni raised an eyebrow at him again. "What'cha gonna do?"

"I don't know. Stay. Go. Go where?" he sighed deeply. "You trying to get rid of me, T?"

"Yes," She said playfully. "I was just thinking you might be happier if you got out of this house for a while, there's a lot of memories here. I know you said you weren't ready to put the house on the market, but you could pay the mortgage from anywhere, especially now that you have that fancy shmancy iPad of yours, and a big fat check. It's the twenty-first century, everything can be done online nowadays. Fly, be free my child!"

"Pleasant, Utah is only about a nine-hour drive." Gaius said off handedly.

"That's like the third time you've brought that place up. Yea, nine hours isn't too far. Far enough to feel like an adventure, but close enough to come back if you wanted. You know, if things didn't turn out like you wanted them too," she took a bite of pizza.

"Well, it's too late for that," he retorted. "Mom's dead. That's not how I wanted things to turn out."

"I know honey, I know, but it is what it is and your mother would want you to be happy. To see some of this big ole world, fall in love, get a bit crazy and *be happy*! I'm certainly not telling you how long or how to grieve, I'm just stating what I *know* Sue would want. I know in my heart, G. She would want you to move forward, she would want you to seek happiness, whatever that looks like." As if to emphasize Toni's point, Sass made a confirmative whine, stretched and walked a few steps to the table where they were sitting.

"Are you ready for a big adventure Sassafras? Or do you just want another piece of pizza?" Gaius smiled and scratched her big head. "This mutt makes me smile!"

"I didn't think she liked being called a mutt." Toni glanced at them both, grinning to herself. "I'm glad though, you definitely need to smile more, kiddo."

"Honestly T, I didn't think losing her would affect me like it did. I thought I was tougher than that." Gaius sighed and put his head in his hands.

"Oh honey, it's your mom! Losing anyone is hard, but losing your mom, that's super tough. Grieve and feel bad, that's the normal reaction, G." Toni took another bite of pizza and spoke, while chewing, "This place could use some sprucing up, how about this..." She swallowed her food and continued. "How about you put some of the money into a home improvement fund. While you're gone, I'll hire some contractors to get this house back in tip-top shape. If and when you put it on the market, it'll be marketable and you could potentially get your money back and then some. And if you keep it, it will look different and help the pain of the memories stored here. Thoughts?"

Gaius rubbed his face and ran his hands through his hair before speaking. "I think that's a sound plan, T. Let's go to the bank tomorrow, I'll put some money into an account with both our names so you can have access to it. Put some of the other money into a checking account I have access to and part of it into an account I don't have access to, like a short term CD or something, that way I won't blow through it. I mean, two hundred and fifty thousand is a lot of money, but realistically, it could get spent real quick, you know?"

"Oh honey, you're a wise one, you are," Toni agreed. "Let's plan on spending some time with each other tomorrow to put the rest of your plan together."

"Cheers! Here's to the 'The rest of the story!'" Gaius exclaimed enthusiastically.

"Here's to you Gaius Kinza Stewart, and the rest of *your* story!"

Chapter Eight

Rebecca moved deeper into the house calling to Hattie leaving Maximus and Elizabeth alone in the living room. "Sugar, sit," he said, moving a pile of papers off the couch and placing them on the floor by the wood burning stove. "Wanna Wii bowl?"

"A wee bowl of what?" her voice sounded squeaky.

Maximus roared with laughter. "It's a video game, a Wii console, you've never heard of one? You've never played Wii?"

"Oh sure, sure," she giggled nervously, wondering where Rebecca had gone.

Maximus was up and turning on the TV and console and finding controllers for the game. He created a guest character that slightly resembled Elizabeth and named her Sister Christian. For the bowling game, he typed in MX for himself and SisChris in her name spot. He went first and got a strike. As he sat, he said, more to himself than anyone, "I've still got it."

Although Elizabeth knew what a Wii was, she had never played and had a hard time making her character release the ball at the right time. When she finally figured it out, it went directly into the gutter.

"Oh snap, you ain't never played this, have you gurl?" he bounced off the couch and came up behind her very close, placing his hand over hers, she could feel his shirtless body behind her. "This is how you do it." With his hand over hers, he swung their arms back and forth as if warming up to bowl. Feeling his hard body behind her gave Elizabeth an unusual fluttering in her stomach. "Ready?" he said, and lined up her hand with the head pin. Their arms went back, and as they came forward Max said urgently, "Release the button, now, now!"

She did what she was told but a bit late, so the ball didn't have much power behind it. But it appeared to be going straight. It hit just left of the head pin and five pins fell.

"Well done little lady, my turn," he went and not only swung his arm, but walked forward and lunged deeply as he released the ball. It curved slightly and earned another strike. "Your turn, step back here so you can get some power behind that ball," he put his arm around her waist and walked a few steps backwards just as Rebecca reappeared in the living room.

"Whoa, whoa, whoa buddy, let her go. I told you she ain't available."

"Aw shit, Beck, party pooper. Always gotta rain on my parade," he let go of Elizabeth. "You're up, might as well go."

Elizabeth walked towards the TV like she had watched Max do and released the button just right. The ball went straight and hit the pins center, knocking down nine. "Thanks", she said and handed back the controller. "That was fun."

"Ya' get one more shot to pick up."

Elizabeth glanced at the TV then at Rebecca. "Go for it, kid," she said. "But hurry, don't want no one coming to look for us."

Elizabeth moved over about a foot and did the same thing, the ball rolled straight and she picked up her spare. "Yea!" she said, and spun around facing the two.

Rebecca did a little golf clap. Elizabeth noticed Maximus' eyes were looking lower at her bottom. His eyes snapped up to meet hers and raised his hand for a high five. "Good job!"

"Gotta get little Sister Christian back, Maximus, sorry. We don't want the mission president to send out a search warrant." Sister Armstrong motioned to the door with her head.

"It was very nice to meet you," Elizabeth said. "Do we want to offer a prayer before we go?" Rebecca and Max exchanged a look and they both shrugged as if it didn't matter to them one way or another. "Okay," Elizabeth said, back into her Sister Anderson mode, she bowed her head and began, "Dear Heavenly Father, thank you for allowing Sister Armstrong and my paths to cross today with brother Max and..." She stumbled on the other name. "Hat. We are grateful for their willingness to open their homes to us and extend their friendship. We pray that you watch over us as we return to our homes, guide us and keep us safe. We say this in the name of Jesus Christ, amen," she opened her eyes and saw Max was watching her, his big brown eyes were bright, staring directly into hers, a coy smile playing at the corners of his mouth.

"Okay, that was lovely Sister, let's get going." Rebecca shuffled Elizabeth to the door and they made a hasty departure. They heard the door close behind them, but Elizabeth felt Max's eyes on her as the hustled down the sidewalk. After walking in silence for a few minutes, Rebecca said, "Maximus sure had eyes for you, girl! Have you ever been with a black guy before?"

"What?!" Elizabeth exclaimed. "*With* how? Max is only the third black person I've ever met. I mean, technically... what do you mean?"

Rebecca laughed heartily. "Oh boy, I forgot, you really do still have your V-card. Oh girl, damn. How old are you?"

"I'm not sure what you're talking about, but I'm almost twenty-two."

"Twenty-two and a virgin? C'mon. Get real." Rebecca looked hard at Elizabeth.

"Um, yea, of course I am. I can't believe you'd think..," she could feel her ears turning red. She looked at her feet as she continued to walk.

"It's cool, kiddo. There's nothin' wrong with waitin' for the right guy. Don't think I could do it, but different strokes for different folks as the saying goes."

They walked a few more blocks in silence then Elizabeth said to Rebecca, "You never finished telling me about Elder Nelson and how you ended up in Kentucky."

"Oh, there's not much else to tell. I did the lessons, the first few in the alley. The Elders stopped in almost every day at first. Brought me a bit of food, a new pillow. They helped me find a flop house so I could get straight, off the shit. Somehow they were able to get the church or someone to pay for the rehab. The whole time, I thought if I could pull my shit together, maybe cute little Elder Nelson would look my way. The more sober I got, the less he came around. Eventually, he confessed to me he had a girl at home and they were engaged to be married when he returned. I felt too committed to not go ahead with the baptism. The girls in the rehab house were also involved with the church, so it just made sense."

"How'd you go from Schmitty to Armstrong?" Elizabeth asked.

"Had to make a clean start, literally begin a new life. I liked the idea of being first alphabetically, and wanted a tough sounding name. Armstrong fit the bill on both counts. You know Lance Armstrong, live strong, etcetera. It just fit. I mean, I didn't have cancer or anything, but you get the point. When I moved here I changed it legally, left my old life behind completely, became a new woman." They walked and said nothing for a few minutes. Rebecca continued. "I needed to get out the city, for real! By the time I got clean, I had saved up about a hundred and eighty-five bucks, and a ticket to Columbia was only forty-nine dollars. That would leave me over a hundred dollars to get started somewhere else. Nashville was sixty-nine dollars. I sometimes wonder how my life would have turned out if Kentucky wasn't the blue light special of the day," she chuckled as if there was an inside joke Elizabeth didn't understand. "When I got here, I went and found the local ward. You were right about one thing, Mormons are Mormons anywhere you go, so I knew they'd help me. The bishop recommended I stay with a little widow that was struggling. Her husband had recently died, and her kids had families of their own and didn't have time to stop in on a daily basis, so, that became my new flop house. Sister Barney was her name. I did light housekeeping and cooking in exchange for my room and board. Eventually, I found a job, moved out on my own. Here I am."

"Well, you're still active in the church, right?"

"Active enough." Rebecca grunted. Once they were back to the Jolley's they joined Sister Paula and Sisters Jolley plus the mission president.

"How'd it go?" The mission president asked.

Elizabeth couldn't meet the mission president's eyes. She just looked down at her feet. Thankfully, Sister Rebecca Armstrong answered. "It was just lovely, Brother! We had a great and very spiritual afternoon. Sister Anderson was amazing and said the loveliest prayer when we wrapped things up. The spirit was so strong, we almost lost track of time. I can't wait to do it again. What did you say earlier, we could do this weekly?" Everything about Sister Armstrong's demeanor and voice tone was so perfectly in line with the objective of the splits, how could the Mission president disagree.

"Same time next week good for everyone?" he looked around anxiously as everyone began to nod in agreement.

The same time the following week, all the women convened at the Jolley's. Sister Jolley fed them all a hearty meal before they went. "To give them strength and sustenance so they may stay pure and wholesome," she had said when she blessed the food. Elizabeth had to admit, it was good. Even though she wasn't crazy about Sister Jolley or her daughter, the food in their house was always decent. As they went their separate ways in pairs, Sister Armstrong slipped her arm into Sister Anderson's. "We'll be making the same stop at the same family's house again this week. What's the first lesson the missionaries officially teach?"

"The first visit is usually about establishing trust with them. Getting to know them, you know."

"Well, we've already established trust!" Rebecca laughed. "What's next?"

"Recognizing the spirit." Sister Anderson was excited about teaching the lesson and getting back on track with her temporary companion.

"Okay! Let's go establish some trust and recognize some spirits!" Rebecca was almost giddy as they walked back down Third Street. Hattie answered the door this time, and Elizabeth was surprised to see how pretty and slender she was. She looked as young as Rebecca. For some reason, Elizabeth had expected an old woman or someone not nearly as attractive, perhaps she has just assumed Maximus was Hattie's son, therefore would be at least her mother's age. Rebecca introduced her as Sister Christian, but this time, Elizabeth didn't correct her. It didn't seem important.

Max jumped off the couch when the three women entered the living room. "Yay!" he exclaimed. "We can finish that bowling game we started last time. So good to see you again Sister Christian."

"Oh no you don't," Rebecca called out. "You're pushing reset and we're having an all-out tournament this week. There's no Brother Mission President to contend with, and we all know what they say about mice playing while the cat is away."

She smiled wickedly as Max restarted the game listing himself first and SisChris next. She noticed he had refined her doppelganger and changed the hair to be long and straight instead of the ponytail hair style she had picked out. She also noticed he had made her eyes a bit bigger and her nose a bit narrower. It actually looked a little more like her than it did the week before. Elizabeth couldn't help but notice he had put sexier clothes on her character. Now her cartoon was wearing a short pink skirt and a traditional bowling shirt that was a matching pink and black, as well as bold pink lipstick and stylish shoes. Next, he added Rebecca which he listed as TheBeck.

"You playin' sis?" Max shouted to the woman that had gone into the kitchen for drinks.

"Sure." A voice shouted back from the kitchen, and Max added Hat at the bottom of the score card. Hattie brought out a large pitcher of sweet tea and a platter full of meat, pickles and cheese. She went back to the kitchen and returned with a loaf of Wonder bread and a small jar of mustard, a butter knife and a half eaten bag of Ruffles. Maximus went first and left his frame open, missing one pin on the spare pick up. Rebecca started making herself a sandwich, popping one of the small pickles into her mouth.

"What?" Elizabeth cried. "You've not been practicing since I've been gone?"

"Just givin' ya' a head start, little Missy," he replied. In no time, the first game was done and Rebecca had won, with Max second, Elizabeth third and Hattie last. "Ready for the final elimination game?" Max asked Rebecca, spinning his controller in his hand.

"Oh, I'm good Mr. Max. Why not have Sister Christian here take my place in the finals, and I'll go keep Hattie company if you know what I mean," she gave Max a meaningful look and walked down the hall into Hattie's room without knocking.

"Just me and you, kid," he said as he restarted the game with just two players. About the third frame, Elizabeth smelled something she had never smelled before. The only way she could really describe it was sickly sweet. She looked around to see if Max was alarmed in any way, but clearly he wasn't. He was enjoying beating her badly on this second game.

"You sure take your Wii bowling seriously." Elizabeth joked with him.

"Oh yea," he replied, "but I like the golf better." The smell was overwhelming now, and Elizabeth glanced down the hallway. "You want some of that, just go on down and tap on Hat's door. I don't think she'll mind." Max said off handedly.

"Some of what?"

"What them gurls all indulgin' in down in Hat's room. You want some, just go on down. I'll wait out your turn."

"No, I'm good." Elizabeth answered a little anxiously and took her turn bowling. During the last frame, Rebecca came out of the back room giggling to Hattie. Her eyes were red and glassy. "Are you smoking heroin?" Sister Anderson blurted out.

The two women looked at each other and burst into fists of laughter. "Heroin?! What the fuck?" Maximus looked at Elizabeth then at the other two before also joining in their laughter.

"Heroin is not funny!" Elizabeth was fully shaken now and completely out of her element.

"Well, she got that straight," Hattie snickered. "Heroin is not near as funny as the Original Gangsta. Shit, where did you find her, Beck?"

"That be some sweet OG, sister, no doubt about it. Not smack!" Max was wiping a tear from his eye. Elizabeth could feel her whole face turn red as she turned to Sister Armstrong who became silent, the color draining from her face.

"Aw shucks girl, it's just a bit of weed. Nothing to get your panties in a knot, or Jesus jammie's...whatever they're called." Rebecca looked genuinely regretful. "I'm sorry Sister Christian, I was out of line."

"Yes you were! Are!" Elizabeth was flustered. "And its Sister *Anderson*!" she shrieked. Maximus and Hattie had stopped laughing and were both looking between the two missionaries with grins on their faces.

"Our lesson this week was to be on recognizing the spirit." Rebecca said, turning her attention from Elizabeth to Hattie. "Outta respect for Sister Christian, I just wanted to mention that."

"*Anderson*!" Elizabeth shouted a second time.

"Well, Sister Sweet Cheeks, just you breathe." Max's deep voice was smooth and sounded soothing. "Ain't nothin' happened here today that's gonna send you down below. You want to feel the spirit, recognize God, you come to my church this Sunday at nine-thirty. Then I'll come to yours. What time it start? That way, you ain't gonna get in any trouble wit' anyone. You still be doin' God's work, ya hear me? Ain't nothin' happened here. Nothin', ya hear me?"

His voice was putting her under a spell and calmed her down tremendously. She stared into his eyes and felt almost hypnotized. Snapping out of the trance, she said, "We should go." Elizabeth left little room for an argument. They gathered their things and made a hurried exit.

"Nine-thirty in the morn on Sunday, Sister!" Max roared at them as they hurried down the sidewalk. "You won't regret it, Molasses. Beck, you know where we meet, drag her along."

"I can't believe you were smoking marijuana!" Sister Anderson hissed at Sister Armstrong when they were well away from the Johnson's house.

"Well, I can't believe you were alone playing video games with a young black man, Sister Anderson. That's breakin' rules too. You know it, I know it. You certainly don't want me to tell Sister Jolley all about your bowling lesson with Mr. Maximus hot body, do you? No, you don't." Rebecca answered her own question and kept on talking. "Trust me. You don't want no one to know you spent a few hours like a normal young adult, playin' video games and sippin' tea in the same way I don't want anyone knowin' I puffed a bit of a jay with my best friend like a normal young adult myself. C'mon, Liz don't tell anyone, do us a both a favor, keep your trap shut. Please. Besides, it's been scientifically proven, marijuana has medical properties. It beats Prozac, at least for me. I *am* sorry if I made you uncomfortable, please though, please don't say anything."

Elizabeth had heard that several states like Colorado and Washington were making marijuana legal, but that didn't make it right. They walked back to the Jolley's in silence. As they said their final farewells for the evening, Rebecca turned to both Elizabeth and Paula. "So, I'll pick you up about nine in the mornin' on Sunday, okay?" Elizabeth nodded, Paula raised one eyebrow and looked between the two women.

Chapter Nine

Gaius ended up sleeping on the couch more and more, it was comfortable enough. Sassafras licked his hand a little after dawn, just a gentle nudge to be let out. He groggily got up and opened the back door so she could take care of her doggy business. Leaving the door open, he flopped back down on the couch and rubbed his forehead, should he get up or go back to sleep? The dog reappeared by his side with a grateful look on her face, he swore her expressions were so humanlike. He put his hand on her big head and scratched as she leaned into him, appreciative for the attention. "Well Sass?" he said out loud, "What'd ya think we should do today?" The dog yawned her indifference. Gaius got up and put a pot of coffee on. It had been a while since he was up this early and he might as well take advantage of the extra couple hours. Grabbing a yellow notepad and pen, he sat at the kitchen table with his cup in hand. He titled the paper 'shit to get done' and underlined it. He wrote 'bank accounts' at the top of the list and added 'thrift store', 'Autozone', and 'Petsmart'. The last entry was 'clear out the house'. Beside that he drew a little sad face. What was he going to do with the rest of the stuff in the house? Sue's personal belonging were gone, but the rest of the house was full of... stuff. Next to the sad doodle face, he wrote a question mark and circled it.

After his coffee he got motivated. He found a box and began to empty the contents of the cupboards and drawers into it. The last cupboard he opened was full of coffee cups. He recognized several from trips him and his mother had taken. That was her thing, coffee mugs from their travels. He started removing them from the cupboard until he found one that said "Grand Canyon" and had a picturesque scene of the desert wonder of the world on it. Memories flooded back to him. The road trip with his mom, how old had he been? He could feel the tears sting his eyes as he set the cup on the table. Taking out more and more cups and glasses, he began to feel as if this cupboard were an optical illusion, how in the world could all these things fit into that one small cabinet? The last cup he pulled out had pictures of him playing baseball in the seventh grade printed on it. Most were faded from the dishwasher and years of wear, he figured she put it on the top shelf as an attempt to preserve the photos. As he set it on the kitchen table, he noticed something in it. Another fifty twenty dollar bills bound with a single rubber band. Tears ran down his cheeks. His mother was *still* taking care of him, even after her death. He pocketed the thousand dollars and opened the next cupboard, his tears starting to subside.

After going through the entire kitchen, Gaius placed just two items next to the coffee mugs on the table: an apple slicer and a small pocket knife. As a kid, the only way he would eat apples was if his mother would slice them with the round looking utensil. The pocket knife said 'Yosemite' on it and had reminded him of another vacation they had gone on when he was a bit older, thirteen, fourteen he guessed. Everything else in the kitchen could be donated. He wondered if there was anything Toni would want and as he put the kitchen items into two cardboard boxes which he hauled to the bed of his truck. He went into the living room. All the furniture was so old and worn out. Looking back, he realized his mom had never really splurged on herself, but instead saved her money to take him on trips. *Christmas is for stuff, but birthdays are for travel.* She had said to him year after year when they had planned their annual outing. Some years it was the Grand Canyon, Yosemite or Yellowstone, other times, they had stayed closer to home, Aspen, Denver or Durango. Once they had even ventured as far south as Chaco Canyon in New Mexico. Feeling the wad of bills in his front pocket he also realized she had saved her money, not squandering anything that wasn't absolutely necessary.

"Screw it," he said aloud. "It's all got to go." Sass had made herself comfortable on Sue's old swivel chair and looked up at him with a worried look and made a little whine noise. "Oh you can keep the chair, Sass, don't worry, geez," he started boxing up the nick-knacks and hauling them to the truck until there was nothing left in the living room except Sass's chair, the couch which was his make-shift bed and a half dozen framed pictures he wanted to keep. Looking at the pictures, he decided to take them out of the cheap and old frames they were in, he could preserve the pictures in a folder and put them with the important documents Toni had brought over days ago.

The third photograph was the 8x10 of him as a baby. As he took the back of the frame off, he saw an envelope and recognized his mother's handwriting. 'Kimball Smith, 425 E. 700 N. Pleasant, Utah 84018'. Their address was printed as the return address, it was unopened, stamped 'return to sender'. Behind it was another letter with unfamiliar writing on it. He took out the letter and a scrap of yellowed newspaper fell to the floor. He began to read the swirly script as he bent to retrieve the article clipped from the paper. As he glanced at it, he realized it was his dad's obituary, he started reading the letter again.

"Sue, stop with this nonsense. I do not know what you think is so important that you keep writing to Kimball, but please, please stop! Heavenly Father has called him home. He is no longer walking this earth but is in Our Lord's arms. There is a reason God needed him so soon, it's not up to us to question His reasons. War is sad. It is unfortunate accidents happen, even in situations they should not. Either way, he is gone. There is no relationship that needs to be rekindled. I'm not trying to hurt your feelings, Sue. There is nothing more to say, you can only imagine the devastation of our loss, there is nothing else here for you. I'm asking as nicely as possible, please stop writing. Stop calling. Please, stay out of our lives. We pray that whatever you and Kim had has become a priceless memory for you, but again we do not need to share that as your relationship with him went against everything we believe in. I ask you graciously to honor our wishes and not to contact us again. I'm sorry. Best of luck with your life.

Mary R. Smith"

Gaius' grandmother? Looking at the date, it was summer of 1992. Picking up the unopened letter, he held it just a few seconds before opening it and reading his mom's handwriting. There was a wallet sized picture that matched the 8x10 he had just removed from the frame. It said on the back in his mom's neat print, Gaius K. ten weeks. Gaius replaced the letter and picture into the envelope and set it with the other pictures from the frame. At least he knew she had tried, and perhaps that's why she had held onto this unopened letter all these years, proof she had tried. Pleasant, Utah. That was the destination. 425 E 700 N. Pleasant, Utah. Finishing the task at hand, he put the empty frames into a box that was heading to Goodwill.

Once the truck was sufficiently full, he headed out to donate the items. He pulled up into the donation line first, emptying the bed of the truck before going in to find the homemade vase. After looking in the household items and not seeing it, he found an employee and asked about it, explaining the story as briefly as possible. Without missing a beat, the employee directed him to a glass case with the more expensive items in the thrift shop. A different employee greeted him and asked if there was anything she could help him with. Blushing just a bit, he retold her his story of inadvertently donating a handmade budvase that most likely was made by his father, who died when he was an infant. "It's a two toned blue with a little white daisy."

The counter employees face lit up as she walked to the farthest glass counter and opened it with a key from a set worn around her wrist with a bungee type bracelet. "Is this it?" She produced a six-inch tall slender blue vase that did indeed have a ceramic white flower on the front and was two toned blue, the glaze blending the colors, making the white of the flower seem even brighter. She walked it back to Gaius, he turned it over to find the initials KS and the year, 1991.

"Yes!" He said, grinning broadly and noticed the price tag on it was twenty-eight dollars. "Do you think I could get a discount? I just brought in a bunch of stuff and another bunch last week when I accidently donated-" He was cut short.

"Honey, you just go on and take it, so glad it hadn't sold already, it would have gone on sale on Saturday and been marked down. I'm glad you found it," her warm smile comforted Gaius, he nodded his head and sincerely thanked her. As he exited the store, looking at the vase, he did feel somehow connected to it. Even if the only two things he had from his father was this vase and the Polaroid picture Toni had brought over. The picture of his dad was blurry, he was looking down at his mom, his mom staring into the camera. She was in perfect focus, perhaps his dad had just walked into the shot, or something. All he could tell was he had dark hair and was smiling at his mom like Gaius had never seen anyone smile at her.

Dammit Mom, why did you have to leave me? The sting of his tears hit his eyes. *No, no, not going to cry* he thought to himself, *unless they are tears of joy*. Joy from finding some missing piece of his life he thought would otherwise be forever lost. As he climbed into the cab of the pickup the tears began to roll down his face.

Chapter Ten

By the time Toni showed up that evening, Gaius had completed everything on his list. The kitchen was empty. The living room had only Sue's old chair with the dog still curled up like she hadn't left her spot all day, the couch, the tall antique lamp and the coffee table. In his room there were only six boxes with the personal items that were worthy of holding onto.

"What's going on here?" Toni asked, setting a paper bag of burgers and fries onto the coffee table in the living room. Sass sat up nonchalantly, yawned and took notice of the food.

"Well," Gaius began, "it's time, T. I gotta go."

Toni sighed and looked at the floor as Gaius handed her a burger from the bag. "Shoo dog!" She said a little too harshly, "I get the chair if there is only one." Sass hopped to the floor and looked expectantly at Gaius. Toni was trying to eat like everything was fine. "I got Sassafras a burger too, it should be in there, no tomatoes, no onions." Tears were brimming at her eyes.

"Oh T... fuck, don't cry. You were the one that encouraged me to go, remember? It's what my mom would have wanted?" Now they both had lumps in their throats and tears in their eyes. Gaius sat the rest of his burger onto the wrapper on the table, Toni held hers in her lap.

"Baby, I know, I know," she sniffled and sighed. "Lost my bestie and now you. I'm just a selfish bitch, that's all. Hate the thought of you gone, hate the thought of you staying."

"Yea," he sighed heavily. "I know the feeling. So here's the good news. First, I found another thousand dollars stashed in the kitchen." Toni looked up and she smiled slightly.

"Well that *is* good news."

"And I found the vase at Goodwill, the one with KS on the bottom, I really think my dad made that for my mom. The lady at the store let me have it since I donated the rest of my household belongings. They were asking almost thirty bucks for it, can you believe that?" he smiled and laughed a bit, the tears subsiding. "Oh, and the check!"

"The check," she repeated, trying to match his smile.

"I put a hundred and seventy-five thousand in a long term CD, it's supposed to make a little money over eighteen months, who knows, either way, I can't get to it for a year and a half. I put forty-five thousand into an account with you as a secondary debit card holder. If you don't mind T, could you find a contractor or something for this house? Like you said, it needs a serious make-over. I don't know if I want to sell it or not, but I do know for sure, if I sink forty or so grand into it, I'll get it back in spades if you get my drift."

"Wise beyond your years, G." Said Toni, stuffing a bit of her burger into her mouth.

"With the last thirty thousand I opened a regular checking savings account, for my big adventure! Plus, I have almost seven of the nine thousand cash my marvelous mama left stashed around the house, so if I play my cards right, I should be able to live on the cash for a bit and let the money just sit, you know?" he started to get excited and his voice changed gears, "Oh, and I found an address and a letter from my grandma, my dad's mom." Toni's eyes opened wide and her eyebrows shot up. "Plus Kimball K. Smith's obituary." Gaius continued. "Mom said all my life how much I looked like my dad, I never realized it until I saw that picture of him, the one they used was in his military dress blues," he took a folder from the side of the couch and retrieved the slice of worn newspaper and handed it to her. She looked and nodded.

"Oh my gawd, you sure do," she said, "especially in the black and white of the newspaper, dang... I'm sure she saw him every time she looked at you. Survived by his parents, William and Mary Smith of Pleasant, hmmm..." She handed the clipping back to him and he took out the two letters setting them on the arm of the chair where she sat. She finished her burger, wiped her fingers on a napkin and picked up the letter from Mary first, skimming over it.

"The one marked return to sender wasn't opened until I found it, but there's the same return address on both envelopes, my baby picture was in it too, it's in the envelope. I gotta hand it to her, she really tried."

Toni picked up the paper with her best friend's familiar handwriting on it and felt Sue's presence through that written page. Tears stung her eyes as she read. The letter had all the raw emotions a young mother could feel. Sue confessed she had kept Gaius, had tried to reach him several times and was overwhelmed with the responsibilities that came with being a single mom. It also professed her love and regret. "Damn, I can hear her voice in this letter. Wasn't opened, huh?" Toni asked, setting it down on her lap and picking up the wallet sized photo, a single tear rolled down her cheek. "You were always such a cute little shit, too bad your dad and his family never got the chance to see that," she smiled and put the letter back in the envelope and handed it all back to Gaius. "So that's your lead, Sherlock? A letter that told your sweet mother to go away? May she rest in peace, *your* mother, not his, if that bitty is even still alive! Seriously G, just to be clear here."

Gaius could see rage flicker in Toni's eyes if only momentarily. "It's cool T, don't get your panties in a knot," he snickered. "It's not really good old granny I'm going to look for, it's her kids. Bet'cha I have kin out there somewhere, brothers, sisters, aunts, uncles, cousins, Mormon's have big families, right? That's the religion with the multiple wives too, right?" His eyes get wide, he cocked one eyebrow and made a quizzical look with his lips.

Toni laughed. "G, you gotta point, it wasn't their fault your dad knocked up your mom and their wicked parents wanted nothing to do with you, you're absolutely right! If you don't expect much from it, you won't end up disappointed." Toni nodded and looked at Gaius, "It's a good plan to start in that town in the address, kiddo. What else you got?" She smiled but her eyes looked sad.

Chapter Eleven

Saturday night, Sister Anderson could hardly sleep. What had she gotten herself into agreeing to meet at the Baptist church the next morning? Up early, she found her smartest looking skirt and cleanest blouse. After a shower she actually did her hair with the curling iron instead of the consistent single pony tail she wore. Sister Cooke was suspicion but said nothing. Over cold cereal for breakfast, after blessing the food, Paula asked, "What's up today, you never did say."

Elizabeth avoided her eye, "Well, while trekking the other day we met a family that invited us to their service and agreed to come to ours later in the day. Sorry I assumed you'd want to go, experience a different culture, you know..."

She trailed off and Paula nodded slightly. "Ok, I'm game. It's only an hour, right? We'll still be on time for Sacrament meeting?"

"Of course, Sister, wouldn't miss it." Elizabeth smiled warmly even though she had a deceitful feeling in her stomach. She was looking forward to seeing Maximus more than Sister Rebecca.

Promptly at nine o'clock, Sister Armstrong pulled up in a sleek looking eighties model Buick, it was orange with a white top and definitely didn't look the twenty plus years old it was. Rebecca got out as Elizabeth and Paula stepped out of the little house they shared, compliments of the church. "Well now, don't you look pretty." Rebecca said to Elizabeth. Sister Paula crawled into the back seat while Rebecca and Elizabeth got in front and buckled their belts. "We gotta be gittin' on down the road ladies, this church is a ways away," she put the car in drive, did a three-point U-turn and headed towards the highway, going south. Elizabeth noticed the ring on Rebecca's right hand was no longer the gold CTR ring she had worn previously but a gold and black ring with a cross on it and a red stone in the center, it was much flashier than the plain gold one she had on the day before. They drove in silence for ten minutes before Rebecca turned some music on. The local classic rock radio station came on.

From the back seat, Sister Cooke said, "I think we're out of our territory way down here."

Rebecca answered as Elizabeth had no idea what to say, "Sister, we're following the spirit, going where God sends us. I believe the holy ghost spoke directly to Sister Anderson here while we were giving our lessons the other day at the Johnsons', seriously, you should have been there, it was very moving, very spiritual." Elizabeth glanced sideways at Rebecca and the two women caught each other's eye. "The Johnsons' will be joining us at our ward later this afternoon, I believe they are ready to take the next step in exploring the idea of baptism."

Sister Paula didn't say anything after that but continued to look out the back window. They hadn't baptized one person. Elizabeth knew the idea of baptizing a whole family would keep Paula interested. Rebecca steered the big car into a huge parking lot. Both Elizabeth and Paula were in awe of the grandness of it. The sheer size was intimidating and there was a three story high cross in the front, casting its shadow over the front door. Sister Anderson tried to picture their Savior on that cross, it was so huge. He wouldn't have even been noticed way up there. As the three women climbed out of the car, Elizabeth noticed some of the Baptist women were wearing pants! Others were dressed to the nines, in ultra-high heels and bright red lipstick with low cut blouses, while others dressed similar to Sister Cooke and Anderson, but bit more stylish and with brighter colors. Sister Cooke leaned into Sister Anderson and whispered, "We're almost the only white people here, are you sure it's cool?"

"Of course!" Elizabeth answered a little too loudly and a little too enthusiastically.

Rebecca smiled warmly at them both, "Ready for an experience of a lifetime ladies?" She winked at Sister Anderson and smiled wickedly at Sister Cooke. They walked in as if this were the most normal thing to do on a Sunday morning. The Pastor welcomed them and shook their hands warmly as Rebecca introduced them. Other members came up to introduce themselves and enquired where they were from and why they were here. Rebecca answered all their questions, stating simply it was like an exchange program but for churches. The people nodded as if that made complete and total sense. Everyone was very friendly and kind. It felt like a meet and greet, almost a party atmosphere.

"Y'all be sure to stay after a bit fo' some coffee and sweets."
A large black woman in a sharp blue and white dress with a
matching hat said to them. "That's when ya' really gits to know
folks, we're so *glad* to have you here!" She smiled so broadly,
"Thanks fo' comin', we just love newcomers." With that
remark, she turned and started talking to another woman in a
similar dress but purple, her hat just as elaborate as the first
woman's.

"Becca Boo!" Maximus sauntered up from behind the girls,
wearing black jeans and a smart looking button up shirt with a
fine purple and blue paisley pattern. The top was pressed and
clean, he was clean shaven as well, sporting a gold chain with a
diamond studded cross dangling from his neck, his shoes were
so shiny they gleamed. He was smiling like the Cheshire cat as
they turned to greet each other. "Didn't think you'd come," he
said looking directly at Elizabeth. She had a hard time meeting
his eyes, his voice seemed to unnerve her, so she just nodded
and looked at her shoes, Paula looked between the three of
them not saying anything.

"Hat saved us some seats?" Rebecca enquired. "I'm sure
we can all scoot a bit."

Maximus's eyes never left Elizabeth. "Well Sister, don't
you look lovely today?" he placed his hand on the small of her
back as he led her into the large room with dozens of pews.
The look on Sister's Paula's face was somewhere between
disgust and envy. Elizabeth allowed Max to lead her as she
took in the enormous room. In the front there was a life sized
Jesus hanging on a larger than life cross, a thorn crown on his
head, painted blood running down his face, his expression
pained and sorrowful. His hands and feet were nailed with real
nine inch nails, large stained glass window accented the scene
perfectly. There was a choir of about two dozen members to
the right in matching royal blue gowns and white collars. A
pulpit loomed large over the front row. On the left side of the
pulpit was a small group of musicians attending to their
instruments.

The congregation was getting settled into their rows of
pews and Elizabeth looked around the big room. She couldn't
believe or even guess the number of people that were in
attendance. For the first time, it made sense to her why the
Mormon neighborhoods were broken down into wards, they
would also need a church this large to accommodate everyone

if they all came to worship at the same time. She also realized there was every color of skin, more shades than she had realized existed. Making a mental note of the diverse skin tones, she started putting them in 'lighter' or 'darker' than me categories. A thought came to her, if she were able to line everyone up in order of skin tone, from dark to light, the shades would be so difficult to distinguish, there were that many, the colors would go from dark to light so gradually, it would take hundreds of people. She could see the flesh colored rainbow in her mind. Elizabeth looked at Rebecca and noticed she was sliding into a pew next to Hattie, then Max slid next to her and left a couple feet for Sisters Anderson and Cooke to squeeze in. Looking at her own arm next to Maximus' she wondered how many people would be between them in the human rainbow. The contrast between their skin was sharp.

As the congregation settled down, the Pastor stood at the pulpit. "Good morning brethren! Thank you for coming on this beautiful morning!" Suddenly he sang, "God is good." And the people sang it back. He sang, "Lift our voices, God is good." And the people sang louder. "Praise God, Praise Jesus!" The crowd sang, some said hallelujah, some said amen. The pastor finished singing and said, "Let us pray." The room was silent for a moment, then the Pastor raised both his hands above his head and spoke in such a loud voice, that the microphone was only necessary for those in the very back and rafters to hear. "Holy, holy, holy God, thank *you* for this day, thank *you* for this perfect life! Oh holy God, bless those today that have come to worship you, for it is *you* who we love, it is *you* who saved us, who gave us this beautiful life…"

Elizabeth could hear around her people saying "hallelujah" and "amen" throughout the opening prayer. She had her head bowed, eyes closed, with her arms folded across her chest. As she listened to the Pastor Praise God, she opened her eyes slightly out of curiosity. To her left, Sister Cooke was seated and poised about the same way she was, eyes tight, arms folded. As she turned her head to the right, her eyes met Max's. He was smiling, his eyes sparkling in amusement. She looked past the handsome grinning man to her friend, Rebecca. Her eyes were closed but her face was turned upwards to the sky, one hand raised above her head, the other in a tight fist over her heart. Elizabeth's eyes went back to Max. He was still watching her, still smiling. Caught off guard and not knowing what to do, she shrugged her shoulders. Maximus's grin turned to a full toothy smile as he shook his head slightly, "Oh sweet, sweet gurl, you gotta know, there ain't a right or wrong way to pray," she had a hard time concentrating, Max whispering to her, his smooth, hypnotic voice, his full lips close to her ear, the close proximity of their bodies. Just then the crowd said in unison "Amen."

The Pastor began making general announcements and surprised Elizabeth. "We also want to take a minute to welcome some special guests here from Utah and Idaho," he motioned where they were sitting with his hand, and continued. "We are all children in God's eyes, we are all one family, one heart... Welcome Sisters." Again, throughout the crowd came "Hallelujah", "Amen" and "God is good." Elizabeth found herself nodding and looking at those that were looking at her, Sister Cooke was looking at the ground, a sour look on her face. The choir sang, the small band leading the way. The sermon resumed. The preacher said on several occasions, "Can I get a witness?" And someone would say "Praise God" or "Amen." Many people were standing and reaching their hands into the air. The Pastor asked who was ready to accept the Lord into their hearts, so they may be reborn. Many hands went up.

Elizabeth was so swept up in the energy of the room, her own hand began to raise. Sister Paula jammed her elbow into Elizabeth's side and when she turned to look at her, she shook her head vehemently. Elizabeth put her hand down and looked at Maximus and Rebecca. Rebecca's hand was raised above her head and her eyes were closed. Maximus was looking at her and laughed. Fifteen new people repeated the words the pastor said and became reborn, accepting Jesus in their hearts, they sang another song. The words of the songs were projected onto a screen that had descended from the ceiling, "Going Up Yonder" was the name. It was catchy and upbeat. Some clapped with the rhythm, many swayed with their eyes closed, hands lifted to the heavens. The next part of the sermon was about acceptance, accepting all of God's children, about accepting God into your heart, letting go of hate and stereotypes. The Pastor read from the Bible, quoting from the Old Testament, Romans 15:5-7. People clapped, commented and raised their hands and voices into the air. "May the God of endurance and encouragement grant you to live in such harmony with one another, in accord with Christ Jesus; that together you may with one voice glorify the God and Father of our Lord Jesus Christ. Therefore, welcome one another as Christ has welcomed you, for the glory of God."

Elizabeth was moved, the energy, the praise God's, the halleluiah's all of it. They all sang again, jubilantly, with happiness. The Pastor asked if anyone else needed to be saved, and a few people came up and the Pastor blessed them, laid his hands on their heads and prayed. *They do that at my church too*, Elizabeth thought, *well, the laying of hands and praying part.* There was a closing prayer, another song, and it was done. People began filing from the worshipping room to the just-as-large gathering room for coffee and pastries.

Elizabeth felt earnest and flush. Happy and surrounded by warm affection. She certainly wasn't expecting this type of feeling from that type of assembly but here she was, feeling the spirit, feeling the raw emotions, flushed with excitement, tears brimmed her eyes when Rebecca hugged her. Maximus' smile was bright and uninhibited. Sister Cooke looked stiff and uncomfortable but followed. As they shuffled out of the chapel and into the larger meeting room, Elizabeth couldn't help but feel like a rock star. Person after person came up to their small group and introduced themselves, some hugging them, some shaking their hands, all of them inviting them back and thanking them for coming. Everyone seemed to know Hattie and Maximus as well. Everyone was friendly, chatty and kind. Coffee and boxes of doughnuts came out of nowhere and were handed around. Laughter was everywhere, children played and munched doughnuts while their parents and grandparents caught up on the latest happenings of their families.

Max sauntered up to Elizabeth and asked her when they needed to leave for her hour of worship. *His voice is like silk,* Elizabeth thought. Sister Cooke looked anxious and answered him before Elizabeth could. "We can go anytime." Sister Paula snapped, "And our church service isn't just an hour, it's three hours and yea, we should probably go soon, you know, don't want to be late," she looked uncomfortable as she glanced between the three of them.

"Three hours?!" Max's eyes got wide as he looked directly at Elizabeth.

"Well, you don't have to stay for the whole thing, Sacrament is only an hour," she was flustered as she stammered on her words.

"It's cool, brother," Rebecca to the rescue, "I've got you anytime you need to get home. Are we ready?" She looked at them and smiled warmly. Sister Cooke was bolting to the door with the other three hustling to keep up.

Chapter Twelve

As they approached the car, Sister Anderson got in the back, followed by Sister Cooke, Maximus took the front and had a diagonal view of Elizabeth. As they drove in semi-silence, he snuck glances at her, grinning and winking from time to time. The light conversation circled around the weather and the best and most economical restaurants in the area, it moved to the best way to eat grits, with salt and butter or brown sugar. Elizabeth was barely listening, replaying the church service she had just attended in her head. No wonder they were having a hard time getting people to hear their message, the local church was exciting, loud, and exhilarating and the spirit was hard to deny. She had felt it stronger than she had in weeks, a renewed sense of her faith. Elizabeth was so excited to share her faith, her service and her beliefs with Maximus.

Rebecca pulled the big car into the church parking lot, "Ok folks, Sunday school, take two," she laughed and Elizabeth noticed the ring on her right hand was again the gold CTR ring. As the two sisters climbed out from the back seat, Elizabeth noticed the look on Max's face was similar to the look Sister Cooke had at the Baptist church. *Sure we're okay* his eyes seemed to say.

Sister Anderson smiled reassuringly and Rebecca slipped her arm into Max's. "Are you ready for this?" she whispered to him as they all hurried to catch up with Sister Cooke. Elizabeth was painfully aware that Max was the only black person in their gathering on this Sunday. People parted, giving them plenty of room as they stared. Conversations stopped as they approached. Sister Cooke was now about ten feet in front of them chatting with her peers as if nothing was out of the ordinary but she could also see the distasteful looks on the others' faces. The bishop was greeting his followers in the lobby, shaking their hands and smiling. When Sister Cooke approached, his mouth fell open as he saw jean clad Maximus in tow with the three ladies. The Bishop shook Sister Cooke's hand, then Sister Anderson's, he acknowledged Sister Armstrong with a stern but friendly look then he did something that shocked Elizabeth, he completely snubbed

Max, as if he were invisible. Sister Anderson touched the bishop's arm intending to introduce them, but the bishop turned and began to speak to the next people as they entered. As they filed into the chapel looking for a place among the pews with seating for four, Elizabeth noticed others spreading out taking up more room than needed. Not once did anyone slide over and offer them a seat, in fact, it felt as if they were being ignored.

Sister Cooke saw the Jolley family in one of the first few rows and apologized as she separated from their little group to join them. It seemed that everyone was avoiding Sister Anderson and Sister Armstrong's eyes acting as if they were invisible. And *no one* looked at Max, if they did it was more a look of distain than a welcome. Finally, they found three folding chairs in the overflow area that had been opened up behind the chapel. The accordion style doors separated the gymnasium from the chapel and were only opened when there was a full house. Rebecca shrugged and sat first, the other two following suit. The bishop stood up and went over the itinerary of the service for that morning noting the page numbers from the hymn books for the musical numbers and mentioning the speakers' names that would be talking that morning as well as making an announcement regarding the blessing of a new baby born to one of the local families.

The bishop introduced the member that was offering the opening prayer and Sacrament service was on its way. After the prayer, the bishop again took the pulpit and made some local announcements regarding the boy scouts service project and congratulating one of the sisters for becoming the new primary president. He invited the family members of the infant boy to come forward for the blessing. Max craned his neck to see what was going on as approximately eight men, including the bishop formed a circle around the new father holding the baby boy.

"It's a naming ceremony." Rebecca whispered into Max's ear loud enough for Elizabeth to hear. She thought about it for a moment and realized it *was* a naming ceremony although she had never thought about it like that before. They had always just called it blessing the baby, and every LDS child was blessed with their father and other relatives who held the priesthood. The next speaker was an adolescent girl that was clearly very nervous. She read a long poem from a large book about families being forever and the importance of going through the temple, she read from the Book of Mormon, quoting a few scriptures. Finally, she finished by bearing her testimony that she believed the church was true, she knew Joseph Smith was a true prophet and professed her love of her church publically, "And I say these things in the name of Jesus Christ of Latter Day Saints, Amen." The congregation echoed, 'Amen' uniformly.

The first hymn was sung and the priesthood blessed the sacrament bread and water. The deacons took their trays and started up the isles passing the salvers to the end worshipers, they each took a bite sized piece of Wonder bread, popped it into their mouths and passed it to the next person. As they made their way back to where Elizabeth, Rebecca and Max were sitting, Rebecca leaned in to Max and whispered, "You should probably skip this part, don't want you to be condemned to hell, these folks take the body and blood of the son of God *very* seriously." Sister Anderson took her offering and passed it across Max to Rebecca and observed Rebecca passed it along without taking one herself. Elizabeth noticed there were several people peering over their shoulders watching them. Rebecca was right, as if they haven't already condemned Max just for the color of his skin, they would certainly denounce him all together if he participated in their sacred sacrament, and why hadn't Rebecca consumed hers? Elizabeth was starting to feel conspicuous among those she had considered friends just this morning. The water or 'blood of thy Son' was passed out and the same ritual, all of this took place in silence and the only noise that could be heard was from restless children.

A second hymn was sung and a man looking to be in his fifties got up to speak. Elizabeth recognized him from past weeks and knew him to be kind and loving from her experience. As he began his talk, his eyes traveled to the farthest part of the chapel where the trio sat. His three-minute speech was all about his beliefs that this was the one and only true church, and how grateful he was to God. He continued, "In the Book of Mormon, dark skin is a sign of God's curse, while white skin is a sign of his blessing. When the Lamanites displeased God, because of their iniquity, the Lord God did cause a skin of blackness to come upon them." *Is it my imagination or is this man talking directly to Maximus?*

Elizabeth thought. "It's known", the man continued, "when those Lamanites became Christians their curse was taken from them and their skin became white unto the Nephites. This is from 2 Nephi 5:21 and 3 Nephi 2:15," he looked down as if he were consulting notes. Surely this was Elizabeth's imagination, this wasn't really his message. He wasn't really speaking directly to Max, he couldn't have been. Another question floating in Elizabeth's mind was if this was the talk the man had prepared or if he was improvising due to Maximus sitting in the back. The local man finished his talk with the same closing words, he would like to bear his testimony, he knew this church was true and he believed that the leaders of the congregation were indeed called by God to be in the positions they were. He finished by saying the same words the young woman had said, "And I say these things in the name of Jesus Christ of Latter Day Saints, amen."

Again, the crowd repeated the double syllable word. Without a sound, the man left the front of the church as two women walked up, the first took her place at the piano. The second woman opened a violin case and adjusted the strings slightly. They began to play beautifully together, the music filling the room with heavenly, hypnotic, music their tune getting stronger towards the end as their confidence built. As they finished, Maximus jumped up and began to applaud animatedly. "That was amazing!" He said to the young women.

It took only a few seconds before everyone had turned to stare at him, the violinist turned a bright shade of red and both girls hustled back to their respective seats as Max nodded and sat himself. Elizabeth had never seen a black man turn red, but Maximus blushed from the crown of his head all the way down his neck, Rebecca placed a reassuring hand on his knee. From Elizabeth's vantage point, it looked as if Rebecca was stifling a smile. There was another hymn sung, the closing prayer said and sacrament meeting was over. As the people began to file out, it seemed obvious that those that were not avoiding Maximus, Rebecca and Elizabeth were impolitely staring at them. Sister Cooke rejoined them at the back of the meeting room and announced she was heading to her Sunday school class and encouraged Elizabeth to join her. The look she gave her companion was almost pleading.

Rebecca placed her hand on Max's arm and said to Elizabeth, "Don't worry about us, I'll get Max home safe and sound. You have a great rest of your day and let's talk again soon, okay? It's been fun."

Rebecca hugged Elizabeth, Max nodded and smiled at her. "Maybe not fun, but real interesting," he said grinning, his silky voice making Elizabeth weak in the knees. "I do hope to see you again sooner than later," Maximus added, slightly bowing towards Elizabeth as he and Rebecca bid their goodbyes. The pair headed for the door as the rest of the ward shuffled off to their classrooms to continue their Sunday worship.

Sister Anderson watched them leave and turned to head down the hall to her Sunday school lesson. She swore she heard a boy of about four years old say to his mother, "Mama, did you see that, we had a nigger come to our church for a visit, he looked really, really, *really* dirty, didn't he? That's why they're the black people huh, mama? Cuz they're dirty."

"That's right, son." The mother's deep southern drawl accentuated the t sound in the word right making the word into almost two syllables. Elizabeth stopped and stood there, stunned as she watched the woman take her son to his Sunday school lesson.

Maybe her imagination hadn't been running wild.

Chapter Thirteen

Gaius was packed. There were only a few boxes he was planning on taking plus his mother's chair for his dog to sleep in. He carefully wrapped the pottery in a small box and wrote 'fragile' on the outside. When and if he found his grandparents, he wanted to ask about the vase with KS 1991 on it and see if they knew where the others had come from, especially the birds in their love nest. The rest of his childhood memories and the few items of his mom's he wanted to keep were safely stored in the attic, out of the way for the contractors that would be coming. Toni would be by after work to say her goodbyes and he would be leaving the next morning as soon as he woke up.

He had told her he wasn't going to have a set schedule but would instead just 'go with the flow'. Gaius had map-quested the general directions to Pleasant, Utah, bungeed the chair and boxes into the bed of the pickup, and loaded a small cooler full of drinks and snacks. As far as he was concerned, he was ready. The couch was still in the living room with the coffee table, his mother's ashes in the urn sat as a centerpiece. He had instructed T to get rid of couch, and table when the work began. The lamp was his great grandfather's and Toni had said she would make sure it was safe.

Sass walked around the empty house looking for her chair to curl up in, she had an anxious look on her face. "Don't worry, girl." Gaius said reassuringly to the dog, "I wouldn't leave you behind, you're my main squeeze." The dog made a whining noise and shook her head, her large floppy ears making an agreeable flapping noise. "That was a 'yes' you want to go, right Sass?" he rubbed her head and she leaned into him.

Toni showed up at a quarter after six as she did almost every night since his mother had passed. Tonight she suggested going out to eat, since it was their last night to see each other for who knew how long. He looked at the dog as she suggested they take her with them. "The weather is nice enough, we could sit on the patio at Stromboli's." Toni suggested. As they walked to her car she asked, "Did you see the front page of the Chronical this morning?"

"No. Why?"

"The Salvation Army said they found a, and I quote, significant amount of money in an item that had been donated, did you go through everything good before dropping it off?"

Gaius shrugged. "I thought I did."

"Yea, weird, I thought I was pretty thorough too," she agreed. They piled into her car and she pulled out into the street. "The article said if a person could identify it, they would return it. If I was a betting person, I would bet it was fifty twenty dollar bills wrapped in a single rubber band."

"Yup." Gaius agreed, nodding. "Actually, I found another thousand going through the kitchen stuff, I must have just missed one. The one donated made a total of ten grand. So if I let them keep it, it's like the ten percent a church would take. Right?" he laughed, "I'm glad they got it, they can keep it. My little *mamacita* would like that."

When they got to the restaurant, they found a place on the patio and a young waiter came out and took their order. After a few beers and a couple all meat calzones, Toni looked away, Gaius noticed there were tears brimming in her eyes. "C'mon T, let's not do that", he said looking away himself.

"Gonna miss you is all," she took the last swallow of her beer and picked up the bill the waiter had set on the table.

"Oh no you don't," Gaius protested and snatched the paper from her hand. "I've got this, or shall I say, Mom's got this one," he pulled a wad of cash from his pocket and counted enough out to cover dinner and a generous tip. "Let's go Sassafras."

Toni put her arm around him as they walked back to the car. Once back at the house, their goodbyes became awkward. "I'm not even coming in." Toni said, "Be safe, that's all. And have fun and call when you arrive, let me know what you find out about your new family, and..."

He laughed and held his hands up, "Okay, okay." Suddenly his smile fell. "Oh, wait one second!" He dashed into the house grabbing the silver and black urn off the coffee table and kissed it quick before taking it back outside. "Can you take care of mom while I'm gone?" he asked, a lump forming in his throat.

"Got it, no worries buddy," she hugged him fiercely and took the urn.

"C'mon Sue," she said placing the urn gently into the passenger side and buckling the belt around it. "I can't say goodbye more than once, gotta go kiddo."

"It's a 'see you later', not a 'goodbye'" Gaius countered. He leaned over and hugged her one more time, "Thanks for everything, for real. I couldn't have gotten through this without you."

"What are friends for?" she smiled wanly. "Now go get some sleep so you can get an early start tomorrow, you've got my number, email and address, keep in touch dammit!" She forced a smile.

"Sounds good, and will do, will do..." His smiled had returned. Gaius and Sassafras walked slowly back to the house, turning to wave as Toni put her car into reverse and pulled away. The dog looked up at Gaius, the anxious look had returned to her face. *Weird how dogs seem to know what's up,* he thought. Meandering through the empty house, he briefly thought of just getting in the truck and driving as far as he could right then at nine o'clock at night, but he thought better of it. Stretching out on the couch, he looked at his dog and patted the cushions for Sass to join him. After jumping up she circled three times and plopped on the end where Gaius' feet were and sighed heavily. "I'll second that." Gaius mumbled as he started to doze off.

It seemed he had been asleep for just a few seconds when the feeling of prickly pins and needles in his feet woke him. The dog and the young man had switched positions in the night. As they had laid together, the dog had started curled in a tight ball at one end of the couch with Gaius stretched out, now it was him that was curled tight into a ball and the dog was stretched out with her block head resting comfortably across Gaius' ankles, restricting the blood flow to his feet and causing the numb feeling. "Hey", he groaned, "please tell me how such a small dog can take up so much room," he yawned and looked through the window to see the outline of the eastern mountains, the sun getting ready to make its appearance. Looking at his cell phone, he saw it was only 545a.m and there were two new texts from Toni from late the night before.

> *Hey G, just one more well wish from me. Call anytime you need anything, drive safe, don't talk to strangers & no hard drugs, lol. Love you*

Stay away from fast cars & fast women, advice that just came to me. Probably your mom channeling through me from heaven, right? XOXO

Gaius looked at the pitbull who had re-adjusted herself to accommodate for her ankle pillow disappearing. "C'mon blockhead," he said as he scratched her shoulders, she made a resisting noise and opened her eyes, not looking at him she slid off the couch and stretched. "There's not even coffee here Sass, we might as well get going," she huffed indifferently, and he let her out to the back yard. Gaius went to the bathroom and brushed his teeth packing the toothbrush and paste into the backpack. "Let's do this thing," he said more to himself than the dog. After a quick stop at McDonalds, Gaius merged onto northbound I-25. The sun came up to the right of him and the dog curled up into a tight ball and went back to sleep. "Some company you are," he said and adjusted the stereo to an old eighties station. It seemed the disc jockey's prattle went on forever, finally they played a tune from Night Ranger.

"Sister Christian oh the time has come,
and you know that you're the only one to say..."

Toni's ring tone. A wave of sadness washed over him, was he making a mistake going to Utah? What was he doing? Who was he looking for? What was he running from? The song continued,

"Where you going,
what you looking for..."

Gaius was lost in thought as the miles started to roll by. Sassafras slept peacefully. When Gaius turned west onto the I-70, the sun moved behind them and his thoughts again went to his mother. *What was that thing she would say when things were going good? It was like a prayer or something.* He thought to himself, tumbling the words together like pieces of a puzzle. "May the road rise to meet you and the wind stay at your back, the sun on your face... or was it the sun to your back and the road rising to the wind?" The dog yawned and sat up, looking at him, blinking awake. She made a little whining noise and shook her head. He continued, "I remember now doggy dog, 'May the road rise to meet you, may the wind always be at your back, may the sun shine warm upon your face and the rain fall softly on your fields and until we meet again, may God hold you in the palm of his hand.' What'd ya' think, Sass? Was that it? Probably some ancient Pagan

Proverb, yes?" She made a noise somewhere between a snort and a yawn, staring at him intensely. "Irish blessing you say?" he looked at the dog briefly as her attention turned from him to the road with a look of satisfaction. Sometimes he imagined she was a person under some spell, forever cursed to be a dog instead of a human being. Sass yawned. Gaius re-set the cruise control. "Miss you, mama. Wish me luck," he said softly to himself as he lifted the paper cup toasting the sky.

Chapter Fourteen

"Are we going to do splits this week?" Elizabeth asked Paula, trying to sound casual about it. Since the Sunday before last, '*The* Sunday', Elizabeth hadn't seen Rebecca or heard Maximus's smooth, silky voice. Not wanting to appear eager but also genuinely hopeful, she continued cleaning the small kitchen in their apartment, preparing for the day and acted casual. Since the Baptist-exchange-program as Paula had dubbed it, their days had gone back to what they had been. Trekking, community service, scripture study and worship, attached at the hip with her companion, there wasn't much additional time for anything else.

"Umm..." Paula drew out the syllable, "I don't think so, we should ask the Mission President though, he would know." Elizabeth nodded and continued her chores. Later that morning while Paula was writing a letter to her mother, Elizabeth was reading the Book of Mormon. Her mind kept wandering to Maximus's smooth dark complexion, *about the color of rich dark chocolate* she had thought more than once. She had tried to picture their hands entwined, the contrast of the colors of their skin. She didn't want to believe the scripture from the book of Nephi had racial slurs and was skimming over it, trying to concentrate but distracted. *Surely even if the original text had said those things, the church had to have updated it, right?* Elizabeth remembered a story her mom had told more than once about how proud she had been in the late 70's when black men were given the right to hold the priesthood. *How old was her mom? How old was she in the late 70's?* The math wasn't making sense to Elizabeth, *how could it have been so recently black men were able to hold the priesthood, how was it the original Book of Mormon claimed it was a curse to be black?* She saw Maximus' smile and beautiful eyes in her head, *not black, brown, beautiful brown, in fact why do people even call it black? The color of Max's skin isn't black at all.* Her mind was reeling and she was feeling giddy, confused and lost in thought all at once when the sound of a text came in on the phone the church had provided for them.

Paula jumped up and grabbed the phone as if she were expecting someone. "Oh wow, look at that," she said reading the message. "It's the Mission President, what a coincidence, we were just talking about him earlier. That's really weird." The tone in her voice and the way she was nodding her head gave Elizabeth the impression Paula was reading a script. "We're supposed to go to the church tonight a little before relief society meeting, I guess we need to set up chairs or something." Paula avoided Elizabeth's eye.

"Okay." Elizabeth responded. The moment felt weird. Fake. Scripted.

They arrived at the church at four p.m. and met several other sister missionaries from their area. Elizabeth noticed three new sister missionaries and realized it was about that time, where they switched with a new companion and the 'greenies' became experienced and the new ones got seasoned for the next cycle. Elizabeth realized there was an odd number and hoped splits would be recommended for the more experienced missionaries so she could see Rebecca, Hattie and mostly Maximus. The sister's began setting up chairs and preparing food for the evening's lesson.

The mission president came in and was greeted warmly by all the young women. "Hi Sisters!" He went around and shook hands and hugged many of the missionaries as if he were a celebrity. "Sister Anderson, could I speak with you, in private, a moment, please?" His smile reminded Elizabeth of a shark and she suddenly felt uneasy. They walked down the hall to the bishop's office where Elizabeth was surprised to see the bishop sitting behind his big desk. He stood when they walked in and shook their hands and motioned for them to sit in the twin black chairs positioned in front of him. "Sister Anderson" the bishop began warmly, "looks like you're about ready to go home." It was a statement, not a question.

"I've got about another month or so, sir," she responded politely with a tight smile on her lips.

"Actually, about eighteen days is all." The mission president spoke for the first time since the door to the office had been shut. Elizabeth did the math in her head, that wasn't right, she had at least another month, maybe more.

"We've got some new missionaries fresh out of the MTC and for some reason, there was an odd number sent to our area." The mission president was now talking faster and more animatedly. "If it's alright with you, we're going to wrap up your mission a few days early and get you home in about a week." Both men were smiling at her in a way that made her feel strange.

"Um, I'm good," she said.

"Good as in good to go, or good as in good to stay?" The bishop asked pointedly.

"I'll stay my last month, there's no reason to rush home, it's not like I have a guy at home waiting for me or anything like that. School doesn't start until the fall, I'm not employed," she laughed nervously.

"No? Well..." The two men looked at each other and the mission president continued, "It seems like you may have a guy here." Elizabeth felt her mouth go dry and her hands get moist simultaneously. "We've had a few, um..." The bishop struggled to find the right words, "um..."

"Some incidences have been brought to our attention, Sister Anderson." The mission president continued for the other man. "There have been some, well... complaints about the family you've been teaching with your splits with Sister Armstrong, if that's even her real name. We, uh, we, uh..." The mission president was at a loss for words, the bishop picked up where the other man hand left off. Elizabeth was beginning to feel as if she were being set up and brought down at the same time.

"There are allegations of misbehavior with a member of the opposite sex as well as a suggestion of drug use." The bishop was now talking with authority. "We've got two general options here Sister Anderson. If we were to file a formal complaint to the General Authorities, they would terminate your mission and you go home tomorrow."

"What?!" Elizabeth was beginning to panic, "This isn't fair, no one has even asked me *my* side of the story."

"So you admit there is a *story*? Please Sister Anderson, fill us in on all the story details so we can make our decision as to what to do with you!" The mission president's voice had increased in decibels and gone a half octave higher.

"Nothing. Nothing has gone on!" Elizabeth's voice also sounded as if it were altered by the situation. "You said there was another option, two you said, what is my second option?"

"Exactly what we just talked about, we have you transfer to the missionary office for the remainder of the minimum number of days for you to successfully complete your mission, about a week. Then we send you home as if none of this ever happened and we all get on with our lives." The silence in the room became heavy as Elizabeth realized the two men were waiting for her speak.

"I've done a good job," she said, "I'm a good missionary and a good representative for this church. I have a strong testimony and feel seriously like I'm being persecuted against because I brought an African American to our Sacrament meeting."

"No, no..." The bishop interrupted her, "That has nothing to do with anything, members of the other race are always welcome here." *Other race?* She noticed he also smiled like a shark. "There have been very serious allegations about the relationship you have with Mr. Johnson and Sister Armstrong. When you were paired up with her, we were all hoping your faith and spirit would move her to get off the fence when it comes to picking a place to worship, we all know there is only one true church."

"We just hope her influence hasn't been..." The mission president and the bishop exchanged looks, "We just hope," he began again, "that you still feel temple-worthy, that the events with Sister Armstrong hasn't left you, um... compromised in any way, do you understand what I'm asking?"

Elizabeth felt her face flush and the back of her ears get hot, "Thank you for your concern, both of you, I appreciate it, but I assure you, the splits I did with Sister Armstrong were completely spiritual and the Holy Ghost was within our hearts and protecting us at all times. They were some of the most spiritually moving lessons of my entire mission experience to be honest. The Johnsons are a fantastic family. Sister Armstrong is an amazing young woman, her story is very inspiring."

"Oh, we're very familiar with Rebecca Armstrong's story, Sister Anderson," the bishop sighed. "So, beginning on Monday, you'll report here at eight, you'll be answering phones and doing some light filing. We'll make arrangements for you to fly home the following Saturday."

"Will I still be staying at the little house with Sister Cooke?" Elizabeth enquired.

"Yes, yes, of course, Sister, it wouldn't make sense for you to move for just a week. Sister Cooke's new companion will be

Sister Lopez from Odessa, Texas. She'll be moving in, so you'll all be a bit cramped for a day or two but you ladies should manage just fine."

By the time Elizabeth got out of the meeting with the bishop and mission president, many women from the ward had shown up with more food for the evening. Elizabeth could see Paula was already bonding with the newbie, Sister Mia Lopez. For the moment, she opted to avoid them. She hated gossips and could hardly imagine what Paula had told the mission president. The meeting went by quick, as they cleaned up and put the chairs back in the big closet, Sister Jolley approached Elizabeth. "Everything okay?" she asked, a condescending fake sincerity on her face.

"Peachy." Elizabeth said back, smiling tightly. So maybe it wasn't Paula that had gone to the bishop after all, maybe it was Sister Jolley. That made a little more sense, but not much.

"We're you able to get with the bishop before Relief Society?"

It *was* Sister Jolley. No one else had known she had a meeting with the bishop except Paula. "Yes, Sister, I did, it was very enlightening!" Elizabeth matched the fakeness of Sister Jolley's tone. The two ladies' eyes met and Elizabeth noticed Sister Jolley's narrow slightly before she looked away. Elizabeth surprised herself by saying, "Thank you for your concern about my well-being, I appreciate you taking such an interest in my life."

"Well, I just didn't want to see anything horrible happen to you, *those* people are unpredictable. You know what I mean." Sister Jolley answered.

Give someone enough rope, and they'll hang themselves, an old saying Elizabeth's grandfather had taught her, at this moment that statement couldn't have been more accurate. *Those people?* Elizabeth thought bitterly. Suddenly, she despised Sister Jolley. "Actually Sister, I don't know what you mean, please explain it to me." Elizabeth Anderson folded her arms across her chest and stared at the older women expectantly.

"Well, if you don't know, I'm not going to be the one who tells you, I don't gossip."

Sure you don't Elizabeth thought. Sister Jolley busied herself with her purse and didn't look at Elizabeth again.

"Ready to go?" Sister Paula asked with an excited look on her face, Mia looked nervous and uncomfortable, but she supposed that's how she looked seventeen months ago.

"Sure." Elizabeth followed them to the little car the church had provided and asked Paula if she wanted to drive.

"Um, yea, I guess."

"Well, I'm leaving soon, you should get used to it." Elizabeth said as she climbed in the back of the Honda Sonata.

As Paula pulled from the church's parking lot, the cell phone chimed that they had received a text. Paula reached for it, but Elizabeth was quicker, "Not while you're driving Sister Cooke, keep us all safe," she laughed as she opened the cheap flip trac phone. It was Rebecca.

> Hey Sis A, u ok?
> Yes/no IDK. Was reported I'm seeing M in an inappropriate way.
> LOL! He wishes!
> They're sending me hm. Leave next week.
> NO WAY! Ouch, they don't mess around?! That sux.
> O it's not like that. Almost done anyway.
> Wrkng @ church office, come by. Save this number 8017563401 hm landline.
> Ur peeps still have a landline?
> LOL, yes. Keep in touch. You've been the highlight of my mission, thanks. Tell Max bye too, he made the last few months bearable.
> He's some fine eye candy for sure. U take care. TTYL.
> That's not what I meant!
> LOL, yea it was!

Elizabeth deleted the entire thread. Once they got home, they had to figure out who was sleeping where. Elizabeth agreed to take the couch. "I'll start packing my things tomorrow and you can unpack at the same time, it'll be fun and we can all get to know each other." Elizabeth was beginning to get excited to leave now that it was set in stone. After the girls said their evening prayer and thanked the Lord for the opportunity to have each other in their lives for this short time while serving Him, they all went to bed. The cell phone was in the kitchen on the charger and as Elizabeth laid down, she heard the familiar ding of an incoming text. It was almost eleven, who would be texting that late? It had to be

Rebecca. She got up and went into the kitchen retrieving the text without unplugging the phone.

Hey Sister Christian, it's M. You still on the air?

Max?

Yes, how many other M's you got textin u?!?

LOL, you make a good point.

Take care sweet thing, was hoping to say bye in person but it doesn't look like that's going to happen.

I know, right? U take care 2. UR a special man & I'm glad to have met U.

Aw, u 2 sweet, sugar. B good and if u can't, call me.

LOL, will do. Bye Maximus. Take care of yourself.

U 2 XO

For the second time that day, Elizabeth deleted an entire conversation thread. Afterwards she realized she should have gotten his number. She should have gotten Rebecca's too, at least she gave Rebecca hers. *Bummer* she thought as she made herself comfortable on the sofa, *I hope they keep in touch, they will be the only ones I miss.*

Chapter Fifteen

The drive took Gaius a little longer than anticipated due to a couple long stops and one missed turn. Sass was great the whole trip. As Gaius pulled into the little town of Pleasant, he passed a sign that read, "Welcome to Pleasant, where it's more than pleasant." Shortly after that, he passed the customary green sign that said Population: 667 Elevation: 6,430. He crested the last bend in the road and he got his first glimpse of Pleasant, Utah.

For a moment, he thought he might have stepped on the set of a western movie, or into a real live ghost town. There was a C-store gas station, a church, a hardware store, it was old fashioned enough to still call itself a hardware store, an old Dairy Keen burger stand, Domino's Pizza with a sign that read 'carry-out only', two schoolhouses and a municipal building. He thought there may be more and kept driving along the main street a few miles before he realized that was the whole town.

Don't blink or you may miss it, he heard his mother's voice in his head. After doing a three-point U-turn he started to wonder where he would stay. It never dawned on him there wouldn't be all the available chains like Hilton, Holiday Inn or even Motel 6. As he drove back into town from the opposite direction he noticed a city library and a sign that read Carpenter's Post with a smaller red sign underneath that read VACANCY. It was an old fashioned motel where the doors to the rooms were mere steps from the vehicle parking. Gaius pulled in the parking lot and got out, stretching. Sass followed and began to sniff around to find a place to pee.

"Hey there!" A woman's voice called, "You should probably put that dog on a leash, pitbulls are known to be aggressive, we wouldn't want anything bad to happen, you know what I mean? I mean, I'm sure your dog is a nice dog, I'm just sayin' everyone round here knows everyone including their dogs, I just don't want any problems, you get it, right?"

Gaius snapped his fingers and motioned towards his vehicle and Sass jumped back into the open door of the truck. "She's a good dog, wouldn't hurt a fly, but whatever you say. Do you work here?"

"Yea," she said and popped her gum noisily, nodding.

"You take pets?" Gaius asked.

"What kinda pets?" she continued to chomp her gum.

"The dog."

"Yer dog? Yea, we take dogs, you gotta have him on a leash though, all the time." The woman continued to snap her gum loudly, "If you need a room, come on in, we're seriously the only place in town," she turned and walked back into the door marked 'office'.

"She's a she." Gaius said after her and heard the tinkling of a set of bells as the door swung closed. He looked around, there didn't appear to be anything for miles and the way the cold wind was whipping around him, he guessed the altitude sign was right and they were well above the mile mark. Well, he'd come all this way he might as well stay at least one night. If things weren't a bit rosier after a good night's sleep he'd head on back to Colorado and help Toni paint the house. Plan B wasn't so bad. Thinking about the house reminded him of his mom. The now familiar sadness washed over him as he wished for the millionth time she was still alive.

Gaius heard the little bells and looked up as the woman walked back out of the door carrying a clipboard with a paper attached. "It's fifty-eight bucks a night plus tax, comes to about sixty-five. If you want to do a whole week and are paying cash it's four hundred bucks, get ya' a nice little discount," she handed the clipboard with the check-in information on it.

The wind blew the paper and Gaius had to hold it down as he scanned over it. "Not sure how long I'm staying really, don't even know if I want to stay tonight..." His voice trailed off as he kept his eyes on the paper.

"Dude, listen to me, there *isn't* any place else to stay, don't you get that? This is it. It's still March so don't even think about sleepin' in your truck, its freakin' cold at night!"

"Okay, fine." Gaius scribbled his signature on the bottom, "I'll pay cash when I check out tomorrow."

"Okay by me," she said taking the clipboard from him. "Gotcha in the pet room all the way to the back, there's a place he, I mean she, can do her business. Clean it up though, okay, please, I hate dog doo-doo, for real. If you need shampoo and stuff like that, there's a C-store on the other end of town, 'bout a mile east." Gaius had remembered seeing it when they came in, he tried to remember if there had been a beer sign in the window. He had brought his own shampoo but a cold beer of any kind was sounding good. The woman reached in her pocket and pulled out a key on a single ring with a small placard attached that said 1010. "All the way to the back," she said again, "your room is really ten, we thought it sounded fancier if there was four numbers so anyway, you're just room ten, it's the last one."

"Got it." This woman was beginning to get on Gaius' nerves. He hopped into the driver's seat and started the engine to pull to the back.

"I'm Ruby!" The woman yelled to be heard from inside the running truck.

Gaius rolled down the window part way. "Nice to meet you Ruby," he put the truck in drive.

"Gaius Stewart, right? Can I call you Guy?" she asked smiling wide at him.

Pulling towards the back of the motel, he said out the half rolled down window, "No." The motel rooms were in one long line, at the end there was a little park for kids with a set of swings, a slide and a couple of rocking horses. *Used to love those things when I was a kid.* Another smaller fenced off area was obviously used for the dog bathroom, there was a fake fire hydrant and a small bench on the worn lawn. Room 10 was actually nicer than Gaius had imagined. It was set up like every other highway motel room Gaius had seen, but at least it was clean.

Sass sniffed all around and jumped up on the bed and did her customary circles before plopping down and sighing heavily. "Well don't get too comfortable my furry friend, I don't think we're staying too long, but you're good where you are for now." Sassafras whined and yawned, then curled up for another nap. Gaius got his backpack and briefly wondered how safe everything would be in the bed of the truck. Looking around, he thought to himself, *there isn't anyone around to steal anything.* He took a long shower, dried his hair, and put on clean jeans and a fresh tee shirt. As he sat on the edge of the bed, he opened the bottom drawer of the night stand. There was the familiar Gideon's Bible. It looked like it hadn't been opened once since it was placed in this drawer. Gaius closed that drawer and opened the top one to find the smallest phone book he had ever seen. He picked it up and turned it over in hands, it was only five by seven and not even a half inch thick. Thumbing through it to the S's, he ran his fingers down the small page to Smith, the first one was 'Smith, B.M. 425 E 700.'

Grabbing his cell phone, he hit the call button twice knowing Toni was the last person he dialed, who was he kidding, she had been the *only* person he had called in months.

She picked up on the second ring. "Hey kiddo!" Her voice sounded light and carefree, but he knew she was worried about why he was calling. "Everything alright?"

"Yea, yea, of course, just getting settled into the *only* motel in the town, guess I should be grateful they had a room. Seriously T, this place is right out of a Dean Koontz novel, it's friendly and a bit creepy at the same time," he paused and continued, "There's a phone book in my room about the size of the address book on your desk and I found a Smith with the same address but it's a different first name, B.M."

"B.M? As in Bowel Movement or Bad Mom or Bitchy Mormon? Same address? I think you've found your wicked grandmother," she inhaled, and exhaled loudly and Gaius briefly wondered if it was a joint or a cigarette.

"Yup, looks that way. As sketchy as this place is, I'll probably just come back tomorrow. I don't know, nothing feels right."

"Of course it doesn't," Toni retorted, "it doesn't feel right because it's not what you know. Don't come running home just yet."

"Oh, this coming from a woman that shed tears when I left?" Gaius didn't know whether to laugh or cry.

"That was just me being a selfish old bitty. You stay put for at least a week, at least enough time to do a drive by on the address and scope the town out."

"I won't need a week for that, T," he set the phonebook down and ran his free hand through his damp hair, "I think I could get a tour of this place in about fifteen minutes and be good, talk about the middle of nowhere. I'm sure they named it Pleasant to cover up the fact it's *not*!"

"Yea, I kind of figured," she said and suddenly she cried, "Bill and Mary!"

"What?!" Gaius was confused by Toni's sudden shift in conversation.

"B.M, Bill and Mary, wasn't the name of the survivors on the obituary William and Mary Smith? Bill's short for William, seriously G, I think you found them in thirty seconds. That town *must* be small," she took another drag of whatever it was she was smoking.

"Yea. Way," he scratched the dog's head. "You're probably right, T. I've been cooped up in the car all day, haven't eaten and need a beer. I'll drive around a bit and see if I can find this address and... I don't know, then what? Hi, I'm your grandson that was supposed to be an abortion, nice to meet you?"

"Yes, *yes*! Say that, just like that or how about, I'm the fetus you wanted to murder." Toni delivered the line with the all the drama of a forties film starlet.

"You're too much, T. Too much!"

"Well kiddo, I've gotta run. Keep me in the loop."

Gaius found he didn't want to hang up, he wanted this connection with Toni, Colorado Springs and his lost mom. "Your incredibly busy schedule?" he said teasingly.

"Actually, yes," she giggled like a school girl. "I'll tell you all about it next time, but I'm late, you know how I am about being late." This he was familiar with. Toni was *never* late. The call center she worked at, the same one his mom used to, was a stickler for attendance. The end result was an overactive sense of time and an obsession with punctuality. Sue had been the exact same way. The now familiar feeling of loss washed over him as Toni rushed her goodbyes and disconnected.

Chapter Sixteen

The three sister missionaries were to meet at the church first thing Monday morning. After arriving, the mission president encouraged Sister Paula to take Sister Mia trekking for a few hours while they got Sister Elizabeth settled into her new position. Elizabeth could tell the two young women had already started to bond, their friendship taking quick shape. Too bad for them, they would only be working together a few months, it was the way of the mission.

Reminiscing about the last year and a half of her life, she found she felt good about it, but also a little disappointed. It seemed the mission wasn't as glamourous as she had dreamed when she was a child. She hadn't baptized a soul. That being said, the people she had met, the good companions, the bad ones, the families she taught lessons too, the ward members, Rebecca, Max and Hattie, *especially Rebecca Max and Hattie*, were all blessings in her life. It was good she would finish here, working side by side with the leaders of this ward. Elizabeth was a little apprehensive about going home because she hadn't decided if she would go to college or look for a job in the little town. She was away from her family now, but she wasn't really on her own. The church always made sure they ate and had a roof over their heads.

Elizabeth was so lost in thought she hadn't realized Rebecca had come in and walked within a few feet of her, "Hey Sister Space Cadet, what's up?"

"Sister Armstrong!" Elizabeth was so surprised and happy to see her friend, she jumped up, and hugged her tight.

"I've only got a minute, just wanted to pop in and say hi and bye." Rebecca smiled warmly at Elizabeth. "Oh, and bring you this." In her hand she had a pink gift bag adorned with white ribbon. "Don't open it until you're alone, especially not here."

"Oh, my, gosh!" Elizabeth said in horror, "There's nothing illegal in here is there?"

"Sister Christian, my, oh my how you crack me up. *No,* there's nothing illegal in there, just something I thought you may… oh I don't know, it was a spur of the moment, I-think-Sister-Christian-needs-this spontaneous purchase Maximus and I made when we were hangin' at the mall last weekend and talkin' smack about you." Rebecca winked and she looked earnest as a full smile lit up her face. Elizabeth was struck by how beautiful her friend was. How had she never noticed it before? Could this have been the first time she saw Rebecca with a sincere and genuine smile?

"Max picked me a gift?" Elizabeth found the words stuck in her mouth.

"Oh yea, Max picked it and I helped find the right size. I guessed. Hope it fits, hope you wear it. There's a letter in there too with my address and a note from Max, I know you missionary types like to write folks letters, so if you feel the spirt move you to put a pen to paper, keep us in mind."

Elizabeth hugged her friend again, "Love you, Sister."

"Love you too, Liz. Take care and keep in touch, okay?" They smiled at each other and Rebecca turned to go, just as the bishop came in.

"Sister Anderson, just who I was looking for," she heard the shark in his voice before she saw it in his smile, his voice made the hair on the back of her neck stand up.

"Bishop, good afternoon." Elizabeth's voice was even and emotionless.

"Will you see me in my office," she wasn't sure it was a question or a command but followed him. The bishop closed the door behind them and motioned for her to sit in one of the chairs that faced his big desk. "Well, it looks like there is no reason to keep you hanging around here, since your time is about done, your last companion has been reassigned, there isn't any pending business, I'd like to congratulate you on completing your mission and schedule your exit interview and plane ticket home as soon as you're ready," his eyes were cold and matched the smile.

"Well... um..." She was at a loss for words. "Technically, I'm not supposed to go home until the end of April, but it's not even the end of March yet, I'm a little confused."

"Oh don't be." The bishop refuted, "It's actually a break a lot of young women in your position pray for, getting to go home early while remaining in good standing with the church and your records will be noted that you successfully completed your service. There's nothing to be confused about young lady, you've served Our Lord and Savior to the best of your ability, completed your time, touched many lives, I would imagine," his voice faded as if he were reminiscing and said, "Should we do your exit interview tomorrow? You could be on the flight back from Nashville to Salt Lake City on Wednesday."

She wondered if there was a question she was supposed to answer or if it was just his way of telling her what she would be doing. Elizabeth could feel the anger rise inside of her and for what, she wasn't sure. It wasn't like she was being punished. The bishop and mission president were being as nice as she had ever seen them. She had not been reprimanded nor given any warning or counsel about her suspected unmerited behavior. This conversation had actually left her more confused and she let the resentment do the talking. "Why wait bishop? Why not do the exit interview right here, right now? I bet there is a plane leaving tomorrow from Nashville to Salt Lake, there's no need to lollygag!" Her voice was sharp, sharper than she had intended, but it was too late now, the words were out.

"Well sister, since your flight was booked with a seven-day advance notice, it can't be changed, therefore you'll be going when you were scheduled, and as for the exit interview, I'd like the mission president to be here for your review, for *both* of our benefit." The bishop's words were clipped and sharp. "You have a service project to complete tonight with Sister Jolley and one of the other Relief Society ladies, then tomorrow morning will be your exit interview, follow up phone calls to your contacts and have a strategy meeting with Sister Cooke and her new companion so you can pass along any leads of baptism you may have, if there are any," he mumbled that last part almost to himself, "then you'll need to pack later tomorrow night and we'll have a car arranged to take you to the airport on Wednesday first thing."

She could feel her lips drawing together tight as her face grew flush and her hands involuntarily made fists, the flight had been booked days ago. They had planned to get rid of her without her knowledge. This sneakiness really irritated her. This was not how she had planned to go home, at this point however; she was grateful to be getting away from this ward and especially the bishop.

"Yes sir." Elizabeth said through clenched teeth, "are we done now?"

"Indeed we are." The shark smile was back. "Please see Sister Jolley for your last service project. Thank you, Sister

Anderson. It was a pleasure getting to know you and I look forward to our exit interview tomorrow."

I bet you do.

Chapter Seventeen

Elizabeth found Sister Jolley sitting on the couch in the foyer with a woman in her mid-twenties a boy and girl of about three ran around. The young woman held a chubby baby boy of about six months that looked black or mixed race. The two women stopped talking and turned to look at Sister Anderson as she appeared from the hallway. "Well, speak of the devil." Sister Jolley said and turned to the other woman. "Jill, this is Sister Elizabeth Anderson, the one I was telling you about, and she's the missionary that will be assisting you tonight with your kids. Sister Anderson," the older woman turned to face Elizabeth, "Jill needs some help with her little ones tonight and perhaps some, you know, um... housework help, obviously she has her hands full!" Sister Jolley motioned towards the hyper toddlers.

"Sure." Elizabeth said, smiling, "Are the other sisters coming too?"

"No." Sister Jolley replied, "You can handle it alone, can't you?"

"Sure. Of course, it's just usually we do all our service projects together," she couldn't recall the last time she did something without having one of the other sisters with her. Perhaps she was looking at this hasty departure all wrong. It was starting to set in. She was leaving. Elizabeth was able to refocus on why she was there in the first place. As the primary hymn went, "I hope they call me on a mission, to teach and preach and pray like missionaries do."

Refocused and recharged, she smiled at the two women and declared how happy she would be to help with the children and house for Jill. They climbed in the old green Buick. As they pulled out of the church's parking lot, Jill announced she would have to swing in and grab her oldest daughter at the day care.

"Usually she sits up front where you are, but we'll put her in the back and she can hold one of the twins, it's no big deal at all. Really," she pulled into a strip mall parking lot, and Elizabeth saw one of the businesses was called 'Lil Busy-Bodies'. *Weird name for a daycare*, Elizabeth thought, *what do they teach them, how to gossip?* Jill threw the car into park and hopped out saying in a thick southern accent, "Be right back."

Elizabeth turned to look at the three kids in the back seat, they were all staring at her with their little mouths half open, drool dripping from one side of the baby's lips, none of them making a sound. In only a minute or two Jill reappeared with a girl of about five years old and she was obviously really upset about something. As they got closer to the car, Elizabeth heard Jill say "...now you're just gonna sit in the back like I told you and hold your little sister 'til we get home! Ya' hear me?"

"No!" the child screamed, "I get shotgun, that's why I'm the oldest, so I can ride shotgun!" The girl had her mother's southern belle accent.

"It's ok," Elizabeth said, climbing out of the car, "I can squeeze in the back."

Jill looked pointedly at Elizabeth's backside. "I doubt it girl, no offense." Jill looked back at her daughter. "Now *I mean it*, Abigail! Get in the back and hold your sister like I told you to. *Do it now!*" Jill swatted the girl on her bottom as she climbed in, the child immediately started to howl as if she were hurt and cried like a wounded animal until they pulled in the driveway. Her tone immediately changed.

"I want a pop." Abigail said determinedly.

"Coca-Cola, Coca-Cola", the twins began to chant in unison, even the baby's eyes looked like they lit up.

"Y'all hush now!" Jill screamed at the back seat, the older boy and Abigail started to cry. Once they pulled up to the house, the young mother got out and grabbed the baby and headed up the walk-way while Abigail and the little girl climbed over the front seat and out of the car. Elizabeth tried to unbuckle the car seat for the little boy but she couldn't seem to get the latch to let go, the child continued to cry.

"Mommy! Mommy! Mooommm!" He began to kick at Elizabeth, making it even harder to release the restraints of the car seat. Elizabeth looked back at the house, Jill and the other three kids had disappeared inside. Finally, the clasp released and she was able to free the toddler, the boy climbed out of the car, yelling hysterically for his mother. Elizabeth followed the boy up to the doorstep and picked him up and set him on the top stair, the kid was already screaming, why not hurry up the process to get him inside? Elizabeth went to open the front door but found it was locked. Weird. She knocked and rang the bell, the toddler was on the verge of a complete meltdown. The knob twisted, and twisted back the other way, Elizabeth grabbed it and pushed open the door knocking Abigail on her rear end. She began to holler for her mom. The two kids creating a stereo effect with their crying while the rank smell of the house reached Elizabeth's nostrils.

"Shut up!" Jill yelled over all the crying, packing the baby on her hip, "You kids shut up, *now*! If you don't, I swear, I'll give you something to cry about! Now move it!"

The two kids scrambled for the living room where the other toddler was watching SpongeBob. Jill started giving Elizabeth orders. "So just preheat the oven to four twenty-five, then throw some fish sticks in when it's hot, they take about twenty minutes. So right before they're done, there's some craft cheese slices, put them on almost all of them, the baby don't eat cheese yet, when they're done, just holler. You may have to wash a cookie sheet for the sticks, I'll be in the living room with the kids, let me know if you need anythang," her accent was accentuated as she sauntered to the living room.

Sister Anderson began to notice her surroundings. The house was filthy. It stunk like soured dish rags and rotting food. The kitchen sink was piled high. Every flat surface was heaped with dirty dishes or empty fast food packaging. The garbage was overflowing and the stove looked like it hadn't been cleaned all year. Elizabeth set the oven and peeked in to make sure there wasn't anything inside that would burn. She was glad she did because there was a cookie sheet with half of a pizza on it. Elizabeth threw the pizza on the trash pile and washed the cookie sheet, then got the fish sticks out and arranged them. She filled the sink with soapy water and by the time the fish sticks were ready to have the cheese put on them, she had the majority of the dishes done and the counters and stovetop wiped down.

As she surveyed what was left to finish the kitchen, it dawned on her this was the first time she had been alone in... how long? Technically she wasn't alone now, Jill and the kids were just down the hall, but seriously, how long had it been? Almost a year and a half. She reminisced about her mission, the good times, the frustrating times, the bad times, the times she felt the Holy Ghost the most. Maximus's dark skin and beautiful eyes came into her head as she remembered the Sunday at his church, how handsome he'd looked and how the spirit had filled her that morning and then dissipated that afternoon at her own services.

Elizabeth arranged the fish sticks on the serving plate in a big heart, filling it in with the extras. She took it into the living room and before Elizabeth could even suggest a blessing, the kids grabbed the food with both hands and shoved it into their mouths. Jill didn't even look up from her smart phone as she said, "Hey, you got the kitchen, right?"

"Um, sure?" Elizabeth said, and added, "You're welcome." As she walked back into the kitchen to finish cleaning up she thought, *Yea, I'm ready to go home.*

A few minutes later Jill appeared at the doorway of the kitchen holding the baby boy and asked her, "You don't mind watchin' the kids for a minute while I run uptown to help an old friend, do ya?" her tone had changed. Jill had a broad smile on her face. "I'll only be a minute or so. Maybe an hour," she handed the baby to Elizabeth and turned to go to her room.

"Did you adopt this little angel?" Elizabeth asked Jill as she was walking away from her. Jill spun around wide eyed.

"Oh no! He's mine. My granddaddy fucked his nigger slave way back in the day and that gene just pops up every now and then."

"So, you're partly African American decent?" Elizabeth looked confused at the blonde haired, blue eyed Jill and thought about the three toe-headed children in the living room, all with blue eyes and fair skin.

"No, no, no... of course not, that was my granddaddy's negress, we don't know what happened to her kin."

"That's genetically impossible." Elizabeth said, looking at the baby very closely for the first time. His eyes were light, grey-blue, his skin not that dark, it was the tight curled black hair that gave the baby's origins away. Jill spun to walk to her room saying over her shoulder, "Ain't nothin' impossible in the south, suga'."

Elizabeth was thinking over everything she had ever known about genetics as she began her task. She hesitated to put the baby in the filthy highchair, but didn't see anywhere else to set him while she finished the dinner dishes and swept the floor. She cleaned the highchair tray, scrubbing it to a shine and got two ice cubes from the freezer and put them in the tray. The baby touched and explored them, putting one in his chubby hand and to his mouth. Elizabeth began to sweep the floor. After twenty minutes both ice cubes were melted and the kitchen was clean, or at least a lot cleaner than when she arrived. The baby was giggling with delight as he smacked the water in the tray. She needed a mop. Instead of being nosy, she thought she would just go ask. "Jill?" Elizabeth started to walk into the young mother's room. "Do you have a…"

She was cut off by a panic stricken voice. "Wait, wait, I'm poopin'!" Jill yelled and slammed the master bathroom door shut. Elizabeth smelled the now familiar sickly sweet marijuana smoke, it made her think of Rebecca, Maximus and Hattie. "I'll be out in a few minutes." Jill said through the door, still spraying the air-freshener.

Elizabeth decided to put her efforts into cleaning the highchair instead of the floors. The baby laughed as she made different animal sounds and cleaned around him. After another ten minutes or so, Jill reappeared freshly showered with fresh make-up applied, hair done and tight jeans on, she looked like she was heading to happy hour not to rescue a forsaken friend.

"Gittin' baptized the week after next. Wash away all my sins, you know? Figured I best get all my wild out now, right?" She winked at Elizabeth and continued, "Put the baby down with a bottle at eight, the twins, eight thirty and the let Abby stay up 'til nine or nine thirty at the latest."

Elizabeth glanced at the clock, it was 7:11 p.m. "I'm supposed to be back to the house by nine, it's my curfew so to speak."

Elizabeth was trying to get Jill to look her in the eye but the young woman was making an effort to avoid eye contact. "Oh, don't worry 'bout that, I'll tell Sister Jolley, you don't have to worry, besides, ain't you leavin' for home the day after tomorrow? Ain't nobody gonna care about what time you git in tonight honey, *nobody*." With that, she walked to the front door, car keys in hand, waving goodnight to the children in the living room, they hardly acknowledged her as she left. Elizabeth stood there, not knowing what to do, she didn't even have the TracPhone. Sister Jolley knew where she was and Jill said she would also tell her. The thought didn't actually give her any comfort. The kids were too little to leave alone, and now it was more of a moral obligation for Elizabeth. What if she left and something happened to them? With that she went into the living room smiling, "Anyone want to play a game?"

It was ten after midnight when Jill staggered into the living room, smelling of liquor and cigarette smoke. Elizabeth had incorporated all the kids to help her clean the whole house, bargaining a later bedtime if they helped out. She had been nostalgic about it, remembering when she used to make a game of clean up with her younger sisters. Jill didn't seem to notice.

After the kids had gone to sleep, around ten, Elizabeth reveled in the quiet and alone time she had. It was nice to sit on the back porch and listen to the noises of the small neighborhood settling in for the night. Now the young mother was home, Elizabeth was anxious to get home herself. Elizabeth told Jill how nice it had been to meet her and wished her well. Jill offered Elizabeth a twenty-dollar bill and slurred the words, "Shank You." Elizabeth declined the money at first, but decided it didn't matter, she was heading home soon anyway so when Jill insisted, Elizabeth didn't argue and slipped the twenty into her skirt pocket.

It was late, or early depending on how a person looked at it. She walked back to the small house where the other two missionaries slept and snuck in as quietly as possible, feeling a twang of guilt for some reason. She hadn't done anything wrong, still something didn't feel right. Elizabeth slipped off her shoes and settled onto the couch fully clothed. It seemed she laid awake for hours before finally drifting off, her mind whirling over her exit interview with the bishop and mission president, what she would tell her parents, how she would get home, who she should call first. Maybe Tish would come get her, Salt Lake wasn't that far away. She was grateful for the twenty Jill had given her worse-case scenario, she could take the train to the bus stop and the bus almost home, certainly that wouldn't be more than twenty bucks. Finally, her eyes started to feel heavy and she dosed off.

Chapter Eighteen

The C-store did, gratefully, sell beer and wine coolers. As Gaius checked out, the forty something clerk filled him in on the laws of the land when it comes to the alcohol sales. "No sales on Sunday so be sure to stock up Saturday night. There's not a state liquor store out here. You're stuck with beer and wine coolers. For the hard stuff you've got to go to Provo. It's about an hour and a half away. Their hours up there are screwy so be sure to check before you leave. You don't want to go all the way up there and find out they're closed," she prattled on while double bagging the six pack of Corona in paper. "So anyway, welcome to Pleasant, you'll love it here!" Her smile was so genuine and she seemed so sincere that Gaius wanted to believe he would, but from what he had seen so far, he just wanted to go home.

Just to be friendly, he asked, "Do you happen to know the Smith's?"

"Mary and Bill or Rose and Rudolph?"

"Excuse me?" Gaius was surprised by her answer.

"Mary and Bill Smith or Rose and Rudolph Smith? They aren't related, it depends on which Smith's you're looking for."

"Mary and Bill? I think... Um, yea, I think Mary and Bill," he found he was lost for words.

"So sad about their son you know, worthless war. So dumb you know, people killed over stupid stuff, great people, just gone, so sad. I knew Kim, we went to school together. Goodness, it's been twenty or so years already since he was killed. I can't believe it, the way time flies. You know, you kinda look like Kimmy. Did you ever meet him? I can't remember the year he was killed; you were probably a little bitty at the time," she continued without giving him a chance to answer or comment. "He was a good guy, one of the last good guys if you ask me, so sad for sure. I don't think Mary ever got over it, seriously, I think all of her health problems are all related to losing her boy. And thank God for Bill, bless his heart, what would she do without him?"

"Yea." Gaius looked at the floor.

"People can die from a broken heart, I believe it," she handed Gaius the bag of beer and gave him his change and continued the one sided conversation. "Great meeting you, my name is Vicki. Here every day 'cept Sundays and I only work every other Saturday, if you need anything I'm around though, don't think I caught your name."

"Gaius Stewart", he said. "Nice to meet you too, Vicki, thanks," he walked out of the store and saw Sass had moved over to the driver's seat of the pick-up, grinning and looking like she would drive away if she had the keys. Gaius snapped a picture and sent it to Toni with a text.

> *Pleasant tour over, ready to drive G home. Love, Sass. You're a dog, not a pussy. Suck it up, buttercup. TTYL Love ya' XOXO*

Smiling and shaking his head, he got into the driver's side as Sass moved to the passenger side and the beer rode between them back to the motel. Settling onto the bed with the dog, he drank a couple of the beers and dozed off.

The next morning, Sass woke Gaius needing to go out. Gaius followed her sleepily into the fenced area for dogs and sat on the bench. He looked around and was in awe of the beautiful sunrise. The sky turned from purple to pink to orange then yellow gold. Sass had done her business and sat at Gaius' feet as he watched the daybreak sky show. Inspired by the grandeur and beauty of the sunrise, he took Sass to the C-store to get a cup of coffee. "Hi Vicki," he said coming in and waving.

"Hi Mr. Stewart," she answered, "My apologies, I don't remember your first name."

"Gaius, like Gaius Baltar from Battle Star Galactica" He usually didn't use this reference because most people had no idea who Gaius Baltar was nor even heard of Battle Star Galactica, but Vicki was that right age, she might.

"Okay, BattleStar Galactia Gaius, got it," he didn't think she got the reference and he suspected she'd forget his name, but it didn't matter. Making his coffee sweet and creamy he thought about how to approach Vicki about where the Smith's lived. As he went to the counter he casually said, "Remind me how to get to seven hundred north. It's been a while since I've been in town."

"Oh, super easy sweetie, just remember state and central is zero," she held up her left arm, "This is State Street." Holding up her right arm said, "This is Central," she crossed her forearms in an x. "Where they cross are where all the numbers start, so if you go east on state, you have first, second, third east, if you go south on central, same thing, one, two, three south. What's the address? This town's so small, no way you'll get lost."

"425 East, 700 North" he said, a bit shyly.

"Oh yea, the Smith's! We talked about that yesterday, sorry, I've slept sense then," she smiled and shook her head slightly, "My memory isn't what it used to be. Anyway, we're on third east and state right now, if you go east to four hundred, turn north, which is gonna be a left, then just keep going until you get to seven hundred north, if I recall, their house is the second one on the right past the intersection of four hundred and seven hundred, got it or should I draw you a map?"

"Naw, you don't need to go out of your way for me, I'm sure I can manage, east to four hundred, left on seven hundred, no problem. Thanks, you rock," he paid her for the coffee and headed out. Sass was curled in the passenger seat and didn't even look up when he climbed in, placed the coffee in the cup holder and started the truck. "Not much of a morning girl, are ya' Sass?" She snuffled, sighed and otherwise ignored him as he backed out of the C-store and went east.

Just like Vicki had said, it wasn't hard to find. The house was a simple two story, red brick home, split level with double doors and flower pots on the porch. The yard was well kept. There was storage building in the back, it was as tall as the house. There was a four-foot chain link fence looped around the entire property. Dormant lilacs ran along the north fence waiting patiently for spring. A relatively large tree stood in the front. The mailbox clearly read 425 E. and below that, Smith.

He turned left at the intersection, swung the truck in a U-turn and parked near the curb with a clear view of the house, trying to look inconspicuous. Sipping his coffee, he wondered what his next move was going to be. Seriously, how was he going to do this? Just walk up the sidewalk and ring the bell or stalk them until a 'casual encounter' happened and he was able to introduce himself that way.

Lost in thought, he didn't realize a man had come from the side of the house and was walking down the driveway carrying a couple of flags. Gaius noticed as the man attached the American flag first and ran it up the pole partially, then attached a black flag below the National one and ran them both together until they were at full mast. The black one had the POW/MIA insignia, both looked worn, sun-faded and old. Gaius watched the man, it must be Bill. He looked the right age and even from a distance Gaius could see a little bit of a family resemblance, or was he just hoping there was. Bill Smith came out of the little gate, looked in the mailbox and retrieved a couple pieces of mail. He sorted through them as he walked back to the house, disappearing from view. Taking a long drink of his coffee, Gaius started the truck and returned to the hotel and called Toni. "Hey T."

"Hey kiddo, what's up? Everything okay?"

"Yea..." He didn't know what he wanted to tell Toni or what he was hoping she'd tell him. After a brief pause, he continued, "I saw my grandpa, well, I think it was him."

"No way!" Toni exclaimed, "You weren't kidding when you said it was a small town! Did you talk to him? What are you going to do?"

"Um, that's why I'm calling you, what do you think? Should I just walk up to the door and lay it on the line, or should I stalk them until we run into each other?"

"Hmm... You said it was a small town. I don't know, my knee jerk thought is to just walk up to the door. But then if I think about it for five seconds, I really don't know. What would you say if you casually ran into them? No, no, I think you should control the situation, go to their door. What'd ya' got to lose, buddy?" he heard her exhale, and she rambled on. "Lay it on the line, that's what you're there to do, right?" he sighed because he knew she was right. "Good luck, kiddo. Keep me posted," she said warmly as she disconnected.

Chapter Nineteen

It seemed to Elizabeth she had just closed her eyes when there was a pounding on the door. As she woke she realized it was morning, early morning. She got up and went to the door as she heard Paula go into the bathroom. She opened the door to find Sister Jolley and the mission president. "So you made it home, huh?" Sister Jolley said in an accusatory manner.

"Of course", Elizabeth replied. "Where else would I have gone?" She was confused.

Sister Jolley rolled her eyes indignantly, "Don't play coy with me, you little trollop!"

"What?! What did you just call me?" Elizabeth was now wide awake and finding she was getting angry and feeling defensive and wasn't sure why, a knot formed in her stomach.

"Now, Sister Jolley, we haven't heard Sister Anderson's side of the story." The mission president was speaking.

"What side of *what* story?" Elizabeth was becoming irate.

"There was an accusation..." the mission president trailed off as Sister Jolley interrupted.

"Do you really think we're stupid?" Sister Jolley looked as angry as Elizabeth felt. "People *saw you*! You and Jill, just drinkin' it up, dancin' down at the honky tonk. Lord knows what else! *and* I happen to know you weren't home last night, I stopped in to check in on you ladies, and your companions said you were out doing 'service work', Service work? *Service work*!? Is that what they call it now days, you know the rules, you know you don't go and do service alone, you know what time curfew is, but yet, you feel as if those rules don't apply to you, you should be *ashamed*!"

Elizabeth looked at all the faces of those around her, Sisters Paula and Mia had joined them in the living room and were standing directly behind Elizabeth still in their pajamas. She realized she was still wearing the skirt and blouse from the night before. The two older women were looking at her up and down, smugly.

Composing herself, she said curtly, "Sister Jolley, it was *you* who sent me on that service project, that babysitting-housekeeping hell, I would have happily skipped it had you not insisted I be there," her lips squeezed tight together as she forced herself to stop talking. *Sister Jolley set her up. She did this on purpose to make a scene,* Elizabeth thought to herself, the sinking feeling in her stomach getting worse.

Playing on the dramatics of the moment, Sister Paula innocently said with a pout in her lips, "When you stopped by last night, we thought you knew where she was. Sister Jolley, we had no idea she wasn't where she said she..."

Elizabeth snapped her head around to meet Paula's eyes. "I was *exactly* where I was supposed to be last night," Elizabeth's words came out in a hiss.

"You look as fresh as a daisy, young lady, up all night?" Elizabeth looked down at the clothes she was still wearing from the day before. Sister Jolley continued, "There were *witnesses*! People *saw* you!" The older woman looked condescendingly at Sister Anderson. "And Jill's oldest, little Abby, swears *she* babysat last night, and you left with her mom about eight when the baby went to bed."

"That's crap! She's *five*!" Was all Elizabeth could manage to say.

"Are you calling her a liar?" Sister Jolley's face was beginning to turn red from her anger.

"She's five," Elizabeth repeated. "And the baby didn't go to bed until closer to nine."

The mission president shook his head slightly and sighed heavily, "Sister Anderson, would you gather your belongings, please, I'll be back in about an hour to pick you up."

"Gather my belongings? I'm not sure I follow you."

"Pack your stuff, you're going home," he replied matter-of-factly, as he walked back out, leaving the three girls standing there with Sister Jolley.

"Serves you right!" Sister Jolley jeered at Elizabeth.

"What? I didn't do anything wrong." Elizabeth said as Sister Jolley slammed the front door behind her and stormed out. "So... What was that all about?" Elizabeth said as she turned to her companion. She folded her arms across her chest and looked at the two girls.

"I have no idea," Sister Mia answered at the same time Sister Paula snapped.

"Where were you last night?"

"At Jill's, babysitting, I thought that's what I was supposed to do, Sister Jolley sent me there, that's it, cleaning their stinking kitchen, babysitting the herd of her rug-rats. I've never been in a bar or honky tonk, or whatever they're called, good grief, what in the world, this is ridiculous," she ran her hand through her hair and sighed.

"Well, I guess that's what you get for hanging out with those black people." Paula's voice was patronizing, "You know how the old saying goes, when you lie with dogs."

Elizabeth's eyes narrowed as she glared at Paula. "What are you freaking talking about, sister?"

"Well, nothing..." Paula was stammering on her words and would no longer meet Elizabeth's eyes. "I'm just sayin', niggers are trouble."

Before she even realized what she was doing, Elizabeth shoved Paula so hard, she staggered backwards and fell on her rear end. Sister Mia Lopez's eyes grew wide in alarm. Elizabeth pointed a finger at Paula, "Don't you *ever* disrespect human beings like that, you bigot, you racist! Is that what our Heavenly father would want? What about equality? What would Jesus do? Have you forgotten the golden rule? Loving your neighbor? What is your *freaking problem*!?" Elizabeth was screaming now, feeling her composure start to slip. Sister Mia was holding her hand over her mouth looking terrified.

"What's *your* problem!?!" Paula's face was red with outrage.

"What's yours?" Elizabeth countered, "That you're a prejudice pig?" With that, Sister Paula picked up one of Elizabeth's shoes from the floor and hurled it at Elizabeth. She easily stepped out of the way as the shoe hit the door.

Mia gasped as sister Paula returned to her feet. "You heard the mission president, gather your things and get the freak out of here, you freaking *freak*!" Paula was screaming. Mia stood there silently, mouth agape, not sure what to say or do.

"You're the freak, Paula. Get with the times for heaven's sake! You're a bigot and a liar and a fucking hypocrite!" As the four-letter f-bomb fell on everyone's ears, the room went silent. In utter frustration, Elizabeth stormed into the bathroom and slammed the door.

"She's a disgrace," Elizabeth heard Paula tell Mia as she turned on the water for the shower. As she showered, she started to calm down. She still wasn't sure what the ladies were talking about and who in the world was seen the night before with Jill, but either way, she was done; ready to go home. The exit interview popped into her head. Certainly they would send her home with an honorable mission ending, right? She hadn't *done* anything, there was no reason *not* to send her home with her file stamped, 'complete'. As she did the math in her head, she realized she had only been gone sixteen months, three weeks and four days, how short could the mission be cut and have no one notice? By the time Elizabeth had finished showering and doing her hair the other ladies had started making breakfast, there was a heaviness to the air, but the conversation was almost normal. Elizabeth ignored them. She found her big suitcase and started stuffing it full with the few outfits and shoes she had. She had a smaller back-pack that she put personal mementos in. After finishing packing she was still mad, but resigned to whatever the mission president had in mind, she sat at the breakfast table, served herself and took a bite of the eggs. Both of the other girl's stared in horror at her.

"What?" she asked.

"We were waiting on you to bless the food." Mia said meekly.

"Oh crap, sorry, I thought you already had, my bad." Elizabeth dutifully set her fork down, crossed her arms and bowed her head as she listened to Mia give a quick blessing of their meal. After breakfast, Elizabeth cleared the dishes from the table and started running the sink water to wash them. It seemed to be an unwritten rule that whoever cooks are exempt from cleaning up. The other two sisters had gotten out their scriptures and started to read. Just as Elizabeth was wiping off the counters and table she heard a car in the driveway. Thinking it was the mission president she grabbed her backpack and suitcase and walked out the door, not saying anything or even looking back.

"It was nice meeting you, Sister Anderson," Sister Mia called after her, "good luck with your life."

"That little skank will need all the luck she can get" Paula chimed. Elizabeth felt the hair on the back of her neck stand up and thought, *takes one to know one*, but kept her snarky comment to herself and slammed the door.

As she approached the driveway, she finally looked up and was surprised to see Maximus leaning coolly against Rebecca's big orange Buick. "Well good morning Sister Christian," His voice was so deep and sexy, Elizabeth thought to herself; her stomach did a flip just hearing him. "You sure lookin' fine this mornin','' he continued, "Sauntering out here with your bags, what a surprise, we elopin'?" His broad smile lit up his face.

"It's sister ..."

"Anderson," they said in unison, and laughed together.

"Oh my sweet sugar, girl..," he smiled at her, the combination of his voice and those beautiful eyes that seemed to be looking through her made her brain swim and her vocal cords go soft. "Where I come from, if some'un give you a nick name its cuz they have a special place in their heart for 'em. See. That's all girl, you touched my soul," he looked at her suitcase. So, ya' headin' out?"

"Apparently" she said, a little too sharply. "I guess everyone's upset with me for sleezing around honkytonks, chasing wild men and getting drunk last night!"

"Well that upsets me too," he cooed, "I can't believe you'd do any of that stuff and not invite me." He smiled at her coyly.

"Right?!" she laughed nervously.

They shared another awkward moment and Max said, "Take care of yourself, girl. Keep in touch, Beck knows how'da reach me. I meant what I said, you touched my soul," he put his hand to his chest, "You gave me hope there's real folk out there, real nice folk, like you... Nice folk like you, with a real nice ass," he winked at her and grinned. She blushed and looked at the ground. "You're clueless ya' know" he continued.

"Clueless? About what?" she enquired still not looking at him.

"'Bout how lovely you are. Seriously girl, from the inside out, you're gorgeous! Fucking gorgeous with a capital motherfuckin' G."

Elizabeth felt her face flush red as she mumbled, "Thank you."

"Now imma gonna git on down the road before I cause you any more grief," he held out his hand for her to shake.

Glancing at it, and looking directly into his eyes, Elizabeth threw herself into his arms and hugged him. "You're amazing Mr. Maximus, so grateful our paths crossed," she breathed in his scent. Maximus released her slowly, his smile was sad. "Be a good sugar, and if you can't, call me, promise?" Elizabeth nodded wordlessly as he got in Rebecca's car and put it in reverse just as the mission president came around the corner. Max smiled and tipped his head towards him in a friendly acknowledgement.

The mission president pulled into the drive and unlocked the passenger door. Elizabeth climbed in and threw her backpack into the back seat. Wordlessly, they pulled out. Elizabeth noticed the suitcase still sitting on the lawn. *There's nothing in there I can't live without* she thought as they drove to the church. When they arrived, she saw the bishop's car and Sister Jolley's mini-van.

"Bet you're excited to be gettin' on home." The mission president remarked off handedly as Elizabeth climbed out of the car and retrieved her backpack from the backseat.

"Yea, whatever." Sister Elizabeth Anderson said over her shoulder. She hadn't felt that flippant in a decade. She really was ready to be gone from this place. Maybe not excited to be going home, but definitely excited to be leaving here.

Chapter Twenty

The next few hours seemed dream like to Elizabeth. The bishop had informed her that Sister Mia had called to tell them she had left her suitcase on the front lawn. Elizabeth said she didn't care and suggested donating the drab clothes to the ward, surely someone could use them. She knew she would never wear any of it again.

As everyone made themselves comfortable in the bishop's office, Elizabeth noticed Sister Jolley walk by the opened door. She smiled into the office and said, "Thank you, Bishop." And continued to walk down the hall, the bishop gave Sister Jolley his best shark smile and nodded. As he closed the door and settling into his chair behind the big desk.

"Well." The bishop said looking at Elizabeth. "I'm not sure where to start," he looked down at his notes and continued. "Sister Jolley has brought to my attention you had a little going away party last night. Sister Cooke confirmed you weren't home last night until..." He glanced down at his notes again, "Actually, she wasn't sure what time you got in. She did mention that you physically assaulted her this morning and Sister Lopez backed up that accusation. I'm in somewhat of an awkward position Sister Anderson, as you can see. Um..."

Before he could continue, Elizabeth said, "Physically assaulted her? She threw a shoe at my head! That's it? You aren't even going to ask me what happened?! You know, *me*, Sister Anderson? The person that is being falsely accused here."

"What happened last night?" The bishop and mission president asked at the same time.

"Nothing!" Elizabeth exclaimed. They looked at her blankly, waiting for her to continue. "I babysat, I cleaned the house, I made dinner, I did what I thought was my final service project. Jill said she would be only an hour but she didn't come back until after midnight. What was I supposed to do? Leave those children alone?"

"Hmmm..." the bishop softly said. "Sister Jolley came to me this morning with this," he opened his iPhone and tapped a few times, and turned it towards Elizabeth so she could see an open Facebook page. It was Jill's. There were several new pictures posted from the night before, time and place stamped so there was no confusion. There were obviously no pictures of Elizabeth but on several of the posts there were statements and comments such as "Cheers Sister Anderson, good luck!", "Safe travels Elizabeth, great meeting you." And the most disturbing, "If you ever get back this way, Sister A, let's finish what we started." A comment from someone she didn't even recognize.

"This doesn't prove anything," she said scrolling through the posts, and handing the phone back to the bishop.

"No?" The bishop re-pocketed his device and stared at Elizabeth. "It seems like there is plenty of proof here. And with Sisters Mia and Paula's verification of your fist fight this morning. Lots of evidence."

"Fist fight?" she said with a mocking tone. *Evidence I'm being set up*, Elizabeth thought and reminded herself not to fall into the victimhood trap.

"Well, I don't know what to say about Paula's bigoted and foul mouth or fictitious Facebook posts. Anyone can say anything or be anyone on the internet. That's not proof of anything," she reminded herself to say as little as possible, she was nervous, her hands were moist with sweat and her mouth moistened like she may throw-up.

"This is true." The bishop said flatly, the shark eyes upon her. "You've done a good job up to last night, and this morning. Wouldn't you agree, brother?" The mission president nodded his head. "To give you the benefit of the doubt," the bishop continued, "we do want to be able for you to complete your mission on a positive note and want everyone involved to feel good about the decision. From their account, it appears you are the one with the foul mouth, Sister Anderson. Do you want to tell us more about what happened between you and the other sister missionaries this morning?"

Elizabeth was slow to answer, weighing her words carefully. It was their word against hers, two to one right off the bat. "Sister Paula is prejudice against black people," she began, "I took offense to the bigoted and hateful remarks she said and we had words. I think Heavenly Father's love encompasses black people as well as white people. Sister Cooke does not share this belief with me."

The bishop and the mission president exchanged pointed glances, neither of them saying anything for several seconds. "I see." The bishop finally spoke, "I think what the best solution for everyone would be is to have you return to your hometown as soon as possible. I spoke with Southwest Airlines this morning and they have agreed to let you fly stand-by home today. The agent said you shouldn't have a problem getting on. They were very accommodating. Is there someone you can call to pick you up at the Salt Lake International Airport tonight?"

Elizabeth's mind raced, Tish was the first person to pop into her head, but she wasn't a hundred percent sure of her cell phone number. "Yes", she replied to the bishop without hesitation.

Taking the land-line phone from him, she dialed the number. Sure enough, Tish's voice came onto the voice mail, "You know what to do. You know when to do it, that's right, hang-up and send me a text!"

Elizabeth heard the beep and she begin to speak. "Hey Tish, it's me. I'm on my way home, can you come get me tonight in Salt Lake? I'll be on..." The voicemail mono-toned speech gave her a menu, "If you are satisfied with your message push one or just hang up, to re-record, push four, to delete, push seven." Elizabeth hung up. "What's my flight information?" she asked the bishop.

"Well, we're not exactly sure, as I said. You'll be stand-by, with the hour time difference. Should be about seven-thirty or eight tonight. Are we good here?" The question was to the mission president.

"I think so," he answered, "Shall we close with a prayer?"

"Of course," the bishop bowed his head and began, "Our dear Heavenly father..." Elizabeth didn't hear the prayer because her mind was spinning on how she was going to get home. Salt Lake was over two hours away from her home town, hopefully Tish will hear her voicemail.

Standby on Southwest was uneventful. She had to change planes in St. Louis, but caught both her connections without incidence and landed in Salt Lake. She walked out of terminal one and looked down the one-way road searching for Tish. The air was so dry. She forgot how dry Utah was or perhaps she didn't realize how humid the south was, either way, it did feel good to be back. She walked back into the terminal and approached the ticket counter. The lady smiled sincerely at her as Elizabeth asked if she could use the phone. The customer service agent smiled and handed Elizabeth her personal cell phone. "Here you go, sweetie, just use mine."

"Thank you." Elizabeth replied as she keyed in Tish's number.

It went to voicemail. She hung up and dialed again, again it went to voice mail. In desperation, she sent a text.

Tish, its Elizabeth, I'm in Salt Lake, call me at this number.

"No one is answering." Elizabeth explained handing the phone back over the counter to the Customer Service Agent. "I don't know what to do, I have very little money and haven't eaten all day except for peanuts and a smoothie in St. Louis."

"Where's home?" The agent enquired.

"Pleasant." Elizabeth replied.

"Oh wow, that is a ways away. Hmmm... you can take Trax all the way to Provo now, don't know what to tell you from there, honey. If you're friend calls back, I can tell her that's what you did if you want." The agent's expression was of true concern. Not seeing any other alternatives, Elizabeth nodded and walked to the street to look for the shuttle to take her to the train station. She only had thirteen dollars. Following the signs, she stood where they directed her to wait. Before the bus arrived, the Southwest woman appeared beside her. "Hey, I'm glad I caught you. Your friend called back and she said she'll meet you in Provo at the train station in her Dad's Volkswagen." Elizabeth thought of the older mint green Jetta. "Also," the agent continued and handed Elizabeth a brown paper bag, "I got you a little snack for your trip. I hope everything turns out okay for you, Sister Anderson." Elizabeth remembered she was still wearing the name placard.

"Thank you," she replied humbly, "You have no idea how much I appreciate it." Elizabeth felt tears sting her eyes. The agent hugged her and told her everything would work out for the best and she was sorry for her loss. Confused, Elizabeth asked, "My loss?"

"Oh my goodness, I'm so sorry. You didn't know?" The agent's expression was of pure shock, "I pulled up your record locator and read the notes the Tennessee agent put in. I hoped you wouldn't mind, I was only trying to figure out how to get you from Provo to Pleasant before your friend called back. The notes said your mother's father had died and that's why you were coming home early. I can't believe you didn't know. It must have been very recent, I'm so sorry."

Elizabeth's mind whirled, her maternal grandfather had died when she was in Junior High from a brain aneurysm. Confused for only a moment, she realized the bishop had obviously lied to the airline to get her gone one day earlier without paying the upgrade. "Thank you, yes, yes, I did know he was gone, it's been a long day, I'm sorry," she stammered on her words. She wanted to announce the bishop had lied and he was a fraud, but she also didn't want to look as if she were being vindictive or fraudulent.

"Oh no, I'm sorry." The agent's clear blue eyes looked at Elizabeth pitifully as she handed over the bag of snacks, "Here's your bus, good luck."

"Thanks again." Elizabeth said and climbed on the shuttle bus for the short ride to the Trax station. She tipped the driver two dollars and used the ten to buy a one way-end-of-the-line ticket to Provo.

Once settled in, she opened the bag of goodies from the agent. There was trail mix, an apple, a Snickers bar and a bottled water. She opened the Snickers bar just as the conductor came through checking tickets. "No food or drink on the train, Miss. Please put that away," she took another bite and stuffed the rest into the front zipper of the backpack. Elizabeth noticed the pattern of the conductor after a couple stops and was able to sneak the rest of the candy bar and trail mix before she got to her destination. As she stepped from the train she noticed her friend leaning casually against the VW with two pieces of paper in her hand. When Tish spotted Elizabeth, she held up the two papers, one said 'Welcome', the other said 'Anderson', she flipped them around and they said 'Sister' and 'Home'. "Oops", Tish said laughing and turned them right so they said, Welcome Home, then turned over said, Sister Anderson. She threw her arms around her friend and roared into Elizabeth's ear, "I missed you!" Letting her friend go and walking around to the driver's side she said, "Would have had better signs if I had had more notice. What's up with you? Wasn't expecting you back 'til next month. Everything okay?"

"Yea... I guess." Elizabeth yawned, "It's a long story."

"Welp," Tish said, "we have over an hour drive home, spill it."

Chapter Twenty-One

Gaius talked to Toni almost everyday now to report his stalking activities. If the flags were up at 425 East, he kept driving, if they weren't he took his place kitty corner and waited for his grandpa to come out and raise them. He had observed they had a baby blue Lincoln Town Car in the driveway plus and older Chev in the back. Occasionally he noticed a little black poodle at the feet of the old man. The way it moved gave Gaius the impression it was old and may not see very well. After that morning ritual, he went back to the motel and looked forward to the next morning. If someone had told him six months ago he would be stalking his paternal grandparents in a little, insignificant town in central Utah he would have thought them crazy. *Crazier things have happened* he heard his mom's voice in his head.

During a phone call with Toni he had confessed he was feeling braver about approaching his grandpa. He had seen him five of the seven days he had driven by. The plan in his head would be to put Sass on a leash and casually walk by when he saw the old man come out to raise the flags. "Like Nike says, just do it." Toni had said on Friday night.

"Okay, okay, yea, I'm doin' it, T", he sounded like he was trying to convince himself. "I've only got two more days in the motel and so if I do it tomorrow, depending on their reaction, I'll either head back to Colorado Springs, or pay for another week at the motel, what do you think?"

"I think you sound as nervous as a whore in church," Toni laughed.

"Well I'm *more* nervous than that!" Gaius laughed right along with her. "I'll call you tomorrow, same time, same great station."

"Sounds great, G. You've got this," she said reassuringly. "Love you."

"Love you too, bye," he hung up. This was it, he was going to do it. All he needed was a leash for Sass, the motel employee had told him every time she saw him to put the dog on a leash, but he hadn't, now he had an excuse to. Dialing the front desk, he inquired about a PetSmart or pet supply store close by.

"You needing something for that pitbull of yours?" the woman asked.

"Um, yea..." he forgot how full of questions the woman was. "I thought I'd get her a leash like you suggested."

"Oh yea, you know, never mind, now I know that dog, I think you're right, I don't see her being aggressive. She's a sweetheart. It's not necessary for us, you know, the closest pet supply place is in Provo. No need trudging all the way up there just for a leash. You're checking out day after tomorrow, aren't ya'?"

"I think so." Gaius responded slowly. "I'm not exactly sure what I'm doing."

"Well, that room's available if you need it another week, you just let us know. We'll take good care of you, in fact, I hope you've enjoyed your stay. Do you need anything?" her exuberance was overwhelming.

"Naw, I'm good." Gaius replied. "Thanks though." And he hung up. Spotting his leather belt on the floor, he called Sass to him. "We could make this a leash, couldn't we Sassafras?" he asked the dog as if she would respond. Gaius undid her collar and threaded it through the belt buckle and re-attached it around the dog's neck. He could hold the notched end, wrap it around his hand in fact. Feeling the excitement in his stomach, he realized he was going to meet his grandparents.

The next morning, he woke before the dog. Looking for the least wrinkled and cleanest outfit he had, he donned jeans and a blue and green snap button long sleeve plaid shirt. Paying close attention to his hair, he groomed and primped in anticipation. *Maybe I should shave,* he thought to himself, *no time*. He didn't want to take a chance of missing the man. Hurrying to the C-store, he came in smiling to Vicki as she rang up another customer.

Once the patron had left she said, "Good morning, Battlestar Galactica. Good to see you." She had taken to calling him that, he was sure it was because she couldn't remember his name.

"Hey Vic," he said as he added sugar to his coffee, smiling he walked to the counter and started counting change.

"Well look at that, there's Bill and Mary Smith. Isn't that who you asked me about the other day?" Gaius froze afraid to look, afraid to meet Vicki's eyes. He slowly turned to the right and sure enough, there was the blue Lincoln and Bill was helping Mary out of the car. His grandma Mary was a bitty thing. She looked like she was shrunk into herself. Wrinkled and small she looked twenty years older than Bill. His heart started beating fast and he could feel the sweat break out on his palms as he heard the double glass doors open.

"Good morning Sister Smith!" Vicki said very loudly as if the old woman was deaf. Mary Smith's head raised and she smiled and her gaze moved to Gaius and their eyes met. He wanted to smile, he knew his face looked petrified and even pained, but he didn't move, he just stared at his grandmother.

"Good morning, Vicki." Bill boomed.

"Kimmy?" Mary's voice was confused and soft. She began to cry, "Oh my Lord, I can't believe it, Kimmy, my boy. I knew you'd return; I never gave up hope. When the military told me you were missing in action, I always knew you were still alive. I always knew you'd return. The Lord works in mysterious ways, praise Him, thank you God for bringing my son home," she had shuffled over to him and threw her frail arms around his waist, tears streaming down her face. "I always knew you were alive," she whispered into his ear.

Gaius stiffened not knowing what to do. Slowly he raised one arm and put it around the small woman, hugging her gently. His and Bill's eyes met.

"I thought ya' all knew each other." Vicki said confused, looking at Mary embracing Gaius and then at Bill who stood just as frozen as his grandson, their eyes locked on each other.

After an awkward moment, Bill rushed to his wife apologizing to Gaius, "I'm so sorry, my wife has confused you with someone else. My sincerest apologies. She has Alzheimer's, she's mixed up. I'm so sorry," he put a protective arm around Mary and started to steer her back to the front door. "So sorry, again. C'mon sweetheart, let's get you back home."

"What's going on, Bill? Its Kimmy, can't you see that? I've prayed, we've prayed, here he is! He's alive! What are you doing? I don't want to leave; I want my boy. He's here, we believed, everything is going to be fine and it is now. Kim. Son," she was struggling against her husband, trying to turn back, tears streaming down her face, her words running together to the point she stopped making sense.

Just as they reached the doors Gaius blurted out, "I'm Sue Stewart's son." Bill's head jerked around, his eyes wide.

"Who?" Mary asked, "Whose son did he say he was?" her eyes looked at her husband pleadingly. She was obviously confused and very emotional. Bill and Gaius continued to stare at each other. The younger man noticed tears welling up in the old man's eyes as his mouth silently said 'no'.

"Sue Stewart," he repeated. Gaius continued forcing the words from his mouth, "I guess she worked with your son Kimball one summer, or something like that, back in the early-nineties."

"Oh," was the only syllable Bill could breathe.

"Yea." Gaius replied.

"Could you come by the house?" Bill enquired. "We're at 425 East 7th."

"Okay." Gaius answered before Vicki had the chance to. "When?"

"At your earliest convenience." Bill's voice was solid, almost sharp. He led his wife out of the store and to the car, opening the door for her. She looked exhausted, drained.

"Should I just follow you?" Gaius asked. He had followed them out the front doors. He felt as if he were slipping into shock.

"That's fine," Bill said over his shoulder as he got his little wife into the front seat and buckled her in like a child, tears were welled up in her eyes. "Oh dear, I forgot the milk, that's why we came down here, we need a quart of milk to make lemon poppy seed muffins," Bill said looking between his wife and the doors of the convenient store.

"I'll grab it, no worries," Gaius volunteered.

"This your truck?" Bill said indicating the beat-up Toyota.

"Yup," Gaius looked at his feet.

"I've seen you around. The dog's friendly?" Bill asked.

Sassafras had moved over to the driver's side and was watching them with her goofy grin on her face, "Yup, super friendly."

"Yea, okay, you can bring the dog too, don't forget the milk. See you in a few," Bill looked at Gaius as if he were a ghost. "Fourth and seventh, we're the second house on the right. It's a red brick home. Looks like we've got some catching up to do," he walked around to the driver's side and got in.

"Sorry about upsetting Mary," Gaius stammered.

"No worries, it happens, she'll forget before we get home. Alzheimer's is a horrible condition, or, in this case, maybe a blessing." Bill started the big car and put it into gear. "See you soon," he pulled out of the parking lot.

Gaius returned to the store and got the milk, taking it to the counter he had a hard time looking Vicki in the eye. "Oh my God, you're the Park Service girl's kid, aren't you?" The look on her face was pure shock. "For real, you look *just* like him! There is definitely no question. We all just thought she got an abort..."

Gaius cut Vicki off. "My mom's name is Sue. Sue Stewart and yes, she worked for the Park Service here in Utah in the early-nineties, and yes, she got knocked up by Kimball Smith and yes, she didn't get an abortion and yes, I'm the Smith's grandson," his jaw tightened at the last part, his hands made fists, *calm down*, he thought to himself.

"Dang." Vicki said ringing up the milk and his coffee.

Fully back in control of his emotions, he said, "Sorry, Vic if that came out a little sharp, I didn't mean it to sound so callous. I'm feeling a little overwhelmed, seriously, sorry."

"So that was the first time you've met them?" Vicki said incredulously, "Wow, heavy stuff. Good luck, keep me posted. Wish I could be a fly on the wall, no doubt, overwhelmed sums it up. Wow. Wow. Wow. Go easy on Mary, she hasn't been right in her head for years," her voice had taken on a nervous tone.

"Will do." Gaius said flooded with mixed emotions, "Keep this on the DL, okay? Please? I don't want to be the hub of gossip for this town."

"The DL?" Vicki had a quizzical look on her face.

"Down-low, between us, I know it'll be hard, you knowing Kim and all, um, my dad, uh, yea, you know what I mean... I'm sure in a little town like this, this whole situation could be headline news."

"For sure," Vicki agreed, "I get you, no problem, I won't say a thing to anyone, I promise."

"Thanks." Gaius said and he turned and left the store. Before he pulled out of the C-store parking lot, he sent a text to Toni.

Plan B = casual encounter. Update tonight. On my way to their house! Wish me luck.

The drive to 425 East 700 North seemed ten times longer than it had when he still felt invisible. Gaius knew he wouldn't hear back from Toni right away. She was at work and at the call center an employee didn't take a personal call unless it was official break, even in an emergency.

Again, the mixed feelings. On one hand he was thrilled to have found a connection to his dad but on the other hand, this family had done nothing to help his mother raise him. She sacrificed so he could have. Child support or even emotional support would have been nice. *Everything happens for a reason*, his mom's voice in his head again *I wouldn't change a thing*.

After parking the truck and attaching the belt to Sass's collar, Gaius grabbed the milk and went to the door, it opened before he could knock. Bill cracked the door just enough to grab the milk and promptly closed it again, leaving Gaius standing there confused. He turned and started walking back to the truck when the door opened again.

"Meet me in the backyard." Bill said just loud enough to catch Gaius' attention and the door closed again.

Sassafras yawned and shook her head, causing her ears to flap loudly. "Tell me how you really feel, Sassy-pants." Gaius said to the dog and led her to the backyard. There was the older truck that caught his attention. He thought it may be a '68. As he started walking towards it the kitchen window slid open and Gaius heard Grandpa Bill whisper loudly,

"Not this part of the backyard, back over by the carport. I don't want Mar to see you. I've got her calm and I think the memory at Vic's store has past." The window shut as quick as it opened. Gaius was a little taken aback as he walked back from where he came, the back door opened just a crack, Bill's loud whispered voice said, "Mind moving your truck over where you were parked the other day? Thanks." Bill quietly shut the door.

Gaius was feeling more and more confused. As he climbed in the truck with the dog, he said out loud, "Maybe we should just go back to Colorado, girl. What do you think?" The dog huffed and put her head down indifferently. After Gaius moved the truck, they walked back to the Smith's house, opening and closing the gate as quietly as he could. Slipping through the carport and turning into the backyard, he suddenly found himself face to face with Grandpa Bill. It was as if they were looking into a time lapse mirror.

"I'm speechless." Bill said first.

"Um... yea..." Gaius was having a hard time forming his thoughts let alone words. They looked at each other until it became uncomfortable.

"You can let your dog off the leash if you want. She can't get out if the gate's closed, and Boo-boo is in the house. He's so old, he wouldn't remember how to play. Mar's watching the Today show. When it goes to commercial I need to run in there and occupy her until it comes back on. We have routines and as long as we don't mess up those routines like this morning, we're good," he glanced through the kitchen window into the dining room to see his wife sitting at the table watching the show, drinking a cup of tea. "Her mind's been gone a while now, the doctor's say it's Alzheimer's but I'm not so sure it's not just plain defense against what happened to our boy, repression I think is what they call it. The government never did recover a body so we've been in limbo for decades thinking... Oops, there's the commercial, I'll be right back," he hustled through the sliding glass door that led into the dining room and sat down across from her, engaging her into a conversation about the show, sipping on his own cup of tea.

Gaius took the belt off Sass's collar and she gratefully rolled on her back in the grass making grunting noises that sounded more like a pig. He looked through the window into a neat and clean house that appeared as if it was last updated in the late eighties. *Is that wood paneling?* He thought, trying to get a closer look. He realized the show was back on and Bill was heading back out the sliding glass door. "We've only got a minute, there's more dang commercials than minutes of the show," he said annoyed. "Lookin' at you, don't think there's any reason for a paternity test," he sighed heavily, "How's your mom?"

"Dead." Gaius was moving from guttural noises to single syllable words.

"Oh no, I'm sorry to hear that. She was a lovely girl, young to have passed already? Early forties, right? Was it an accident?" Bill seemed genuinely interested.

"Cancer." Gaius had moved up to two syllable words.

"What a shame." Bill shook his head and looked at his shoes and repeated, "What a shame."

"Is it?" Gaius was starting to get his thoughts together but they were having a hard time getting from his head to his mouth.

"Yes, it is a shame when young people die. I'm genuinely sorry for your loss. You've got to understand something. It was never your mom I didn't like, it was the whole situation. They were young, your mom wasn't a member of the church and didn't have any desire to be, I've often thought if we could have converted her, gotten her baptized, she could have been a member and, well... maybe the temple, who knows, things could have turned out differently," his eyes looked sad and the raw emotion betrayed how old he really was. "It was really our only prerequisite," he continued, "we wanted our son to be married in the temple to a member of the church, sealed for all time and eternity, you know, an eternal wife. We didn't think it was too much to ask, but your mom said no. She wouldn't even consider it. She had her own ideas, she was set in her ways. Gotta run, it's a commercial again. Mary gets agitated if I'm not in there for the commercials." Bill slipped back through the sliding glass door and Gaius tried to eavesdrop in on their conversation. Although he couldn't hear them, he observed how tender Bill was to Mary. Reaching out to take her hand, getting her another cup of tea, kissing the top of her head.

It's the little things that are important, his mom's voice again, *and the big thing, that thing called love.* It had never dawned on Gaius that his mom had been given an ultimatum. Smiling to himself and thinking about her, he remembered there was no faster way to piss off Sue Stewart than by giving her an ultimatum. Telling her there were no choices made her dig in her heels even more.

Bill slipped back out when the show returned. "That's the last of the ads, the show will be over in just a few minutes and the lemon poppy seed muffins will be ready," he heaved another sigh, "It's the same thing every day, bless her heart. If we keep the routine the same we can somewhat regulate her behavior, it's been a labor of love for sure. How long can you stay? I would like to talk some more," he hesitated and looked back through the window. "This is going to sound crazy, but I have an idea. How good are your acting skills?"

"Acting?" Back to double syllable words.

"Well, if you can convince Mary you're Kim and act completely casual like this is the most normal day in the world, she just may not lose it. You know, come in and eat a muffin, call her mom 'n normal stuff, you know? That way, we can talk and I can still keep an eye on her. She can't be left alone for any length of time, not even ten minutes." Gaius noticed a cloud of exhaustion over Bill as he said those words. "She should take a nap here in a few minutes, hard to say though, she was pretty agitated this morning, but I think she's pretty much forgotten the whole incident," he looked in the window again and Gaius could see the love in Bill's face, exhausted or not. "And if it doesn't work out and she flips again, just go. Most likely she'll forget within the hour."

"Okay." Gaius followed his grandfather into the dining room through the sliding glass door, his stomach in knots.

Bill and Gaius slipped in through the sliding glass door. Bill said in a rather loud voice, "Son, you want a muffin and some tea?"

"Sure." Gaius said on an inhale of breath as Mary slowly turned her head towards the two of them. There was a long moment when it seemed to Gaius there was no air in the room, no one breathing.

"Good morning, Kimmy." Mary said and turned her head back towards the television.

"Morning." Gaius said in one exhale. *Back to two syllable words*, he thought. His and Bill's eyes met as Bill handed him a warm lemon poppy seed muffin on a small white plate. Bill turned and got a matching cup and began making a cup of tea. Gaius glanced around and spotted a large portrait of Kimball Smith in full military dress-blues. He wore a serious expression on his face, his hair cut military style. It was the same shot that was in the obituary but in color and much larger. With the exception of the jaw line, and Gaius' shaggy hair, the resemblance was uncanny. Gaius' face had a slightly softer shape his eyes a little more round.

Bill noticed him looking and said softly, "He certainly looked sharp in that military uniform." Gaius looked at his grandfather and noticed his eyes brimming with tears. "So many things I wish we could have done differently. Would have done differently." The tears fell and Bill turned towards the sink and began to cry quietly, his shoulders shaking ever so slightly. Gaius felt a lump in his throat and his own eyes burned with the threat of tears.

"Kimmy, you comin' to church with us tomorrow?" Mary asked all of a sudden, without taking her eyes off the TV.

"Um, yea," his voice sounded strained and not his own. Bill blew his nose and turned back to Gaius. The younger man could see the pained expression on his grandfather's face. They looked at each other and Gaius shrugged. He didn't know what to say.

"Mar, you wanna lay down, try and nap? The morning news is almost over, there's just sports left." Bill suggested this to his wife as if it were the most customary thing to do after the news.

"Yea, I guess," she pushed herself to her feet and shuffled down the hallway, it seemed to Gaius there were lights that had gone off in her eyes. Bill was following her to their room. Gaius began to eat his muffin and drink his tea. He glanced out the sliding glass door and observed Sassafras lying in the sun on the cement. When he looked back to the TV, he noticed the little black poodle lying in a small dog bed next to the armchair Mary had been sitting in. As if it knew it was being observed, it raised his head and looked at Gaius through glassy eyes. After about five minutes, Bill returned, offered Gaius another warm muffin, and sat at the kitchen table.

"She'll nap now until around two." Bill said taking a bite from of a muffin, "It's like taking care of a perpetual child. Seems unfair for someone's mind to go like that," he said while chewing.

"I bet." Gaius almost smiled, not about what Bill was saying but about his one and two syllabled answers. "It's sad." *Oh my god, I just did it again*, he thought.

"So, what brings you to Pleasant?" Bill enquired.

"You." Gaius became serious as his eyes met his grandfather's. "Mary."

Bill took a bite of his muffin and chewed thoughtfully without saying anything. After an awkward silence he sighed. "Don't know what to say to that," he shook his head slowly and turned back to Gaius "Not sure I caught your name, can't keep calling you Kim."

"Gaius." And he took another bite of muffin.

"Okay, well Guy, like I said before, I'm not sure..."

Gaius interrupted him, "It's Gaius, not Guy."

Bill chuckled, "Okay, call me William," he slowly shook his head again, "So Gaius, I'm still not sure what you're after. Mar and I don't have anything, no money, no more family, she's lost her mind already, our health isn't the best. We have a daily routine and that's about it. There isn't much to us, and I'm still a bit confused why you sought us out, what you're expecting to accomplish." Bill finished his muffin and washed it down with the tea.

It was Gaius' turn to sigh. He looked out at the dog lying in the sun. "I don't know, William." The words continued to elude him, what was he supposed to say? Gaius turned to face the old man and shrugged. "Guess I should be going then," he got up and put the tea cup by the sink and the paper napkin next to it, when he turned around, Mary was standing in the doorway.

"Sacrament meeting starts at one o'clock, Kim. We'll see you tomorrow," she turned and trundled back down the hall.

"Um..." Bill began, "You've got to know it's nothing personal. I don't even know you, I wouldn't know where to start a relationship with you. I don't know what good it would do to even entertain the idea. I know you look a whole lot like my dead son, and Gaius, that hurts, it hurts to look at you. It hurts to think how things could have been different, but they're not," he sighed. "I'll be right back." Bill hustled down the hall after his wife and returned in moments.

It was his eternally optimistic and forgiving mother's voice in his head, but the words that came out of his mouth were his, "There's nothing to say about the past, there's nothing to say about the future, there's nothing ensuring we even have a future, all we have is right now. *This* moment. You, of all people, should know how quickly the mind can be lost, how quickly *life* can be lost. If you don't want me in your family, that's fine. I'll go. I hold no grudges, William, but to be honest, looking at your circumstances, knowing what's up in my life, it seems we need a bit of each other."

They stared at each other for what seemed like a very long moment. The older man broke the silence, "I was kidding about the William, please, call me Bill. Only my mother called me William, and even then, only if I was in trouble. Church starts at one tomorrow, if you're interested. Its Mary's only real social outing except for when we have to run to the grocery store. The service means a lot to her. I'm not opposed to getting to know each other a little, Guy, I just can't promise we're going to be the happily-ever-after family you're hoping for."

"Okay Bill, I have no expectations, only got two more nights at the motel and I'll head back to Colorado. It's no big deal," he paused and said, "Actually, I take that back, it *is* a big deal, meeting you and Mary, seeing Kim's house, the town where he grew up, the whole thing has fascinated me and appeased something that has been missing in my heart my whole life. I'm not asking for a commitment to me, or for you to even acknowledge who I am. I'm curious. Curious about who my dad could have been. And..." He hesitated, "I *wasn't* kidding, call me Gaius."

On their second day in the motel, Gaius had managed to get his mom's old swivel chair out of the back of the truck and into the motel room where Sass had been sleeping on it on a regular basis. Gaius did a load of laundry and ironed his only button up shirt with the iron in the motel room. He used one of their wash cloths and shined up his shoes a bit, they didn't look new but they looked better. Gaius heard the noise from his cell phone indicating a text had come in. It was Toni.

OMG! On break, can you talk? I've got 8 minutes.

Instead of texting her back, he just hit the button twice and called her, she answered on the first ring.

"Oh. My. GAWD!" She exclaimed, "What happened? How'd it go?"

He could hear she was eating something, one of his pet peeves, people eating while talking on the phone. He remembered the other rule of the call center, no food on the sales floor and knew she was multi-tasking and watching the timer so she wasn't late clocking back in.

"Nothing much. How are things?" Gaius deliberately paced his response, knowing Toni was chomping at the bit to hear all about it.

"Spill it, G. Details, baby, details."

"Well... Grandma Mary has a pretty severe case of Alzheimer's and thinks I'm her son. Grandpa Bill is an ornery old cus that doesn't really see the point of having me in their life. Either way, I'm going to church tomorrow with them."

"Holy shit." Toni was flabbergasted. "It's a good thing your mom is cremated or she'd be rolling over in her grave about now. The Mormon Church? Wow."

"Yea, I'm going to do it, if only for an hour or so. Cause a ruckus in this little redneck town then head back home on Tuesday."

He was now multi-tasking, talking on the phone and putting the iron and ironing board back into the motel's closet.

"Home here?" she asked. "Oh no, about that. G, you can't come home right now, I've got contractors working on the floors, and they're tearing out that old linoleum in the kitchen and the carpet in the bedrooms and replacing it with wood flooring throughout the whole house. Now's not a good time to head back, there's no place for you to stay. Your place is a huge construction zone right now." Gaius could hear the panic rise in her voice. "I want the house to be perfect and beautiful and wonderful when you get here, I need a few more weeks."

"Sure, okay," he replied, making a mental note of some of the National Parks he wanted to see, or maybe he'd spend a few days in Moab.

"Gotta run, G. I'll call you later."

Gaius could hear Toni's timer going off, he disconnected and glanced at the clock. One o'clock, he had twenty-four hours to get ready for church. Walking with Sassafras on the short belt leash, he wandered down the main street and found a hair and nails salon open. A haircut was probably in order.

Chapter Twenty-Two

On the drive home, Elizabeth was going to eat the apple the airline agent had given her but, Tish swung through a late night drive-up. As they drove into the night, Elizabeth told Tish about her mission. She explained how Sister Jolley had set her up and how Paula had been so narrow-minded and bigoted and how poor Sister Mia was caught in the crossfire. Elizabeth rambled on about Rebecca and Maximus, stating they would be the ones she missed the most.

"What are you going to tell your ma?" Tish asked.

"I'm not sure yet," Elizabeth answered, looking out into the night. "In fact, I'm not even sure I should go home tonight. Can I spend the night at your place? I forgot my suitcase and the only clothes I have are what I have on. Maybe I could show up at the house tomorrow before church or something. Or maybe sneak in while they're at church and surprise them when they get home."

"You forgot your suitcase? In Kentucky?!" After a brief pause Tish suddenly smiled wickedly, "Oh, I know. How about if you just go to church tomorrow and be like 'hey mom, what's up?'"

Elizabeth laughed but as the idea sunk into her head she began to think it was the way to go. It was already going on midnight, she was tired. "You got something I could wear?"

"Sure." Tish said. "You're gonna do it, aren't you?"

"Well, it beats knocking on the door now, it's freakin' late. It beats getting up early and confronting her before church. Let's face it, we may get less questions if we're at church already, right? My folks aren't going to make a scene in front of the rest of the ward. Yea, I think you're right, it's the best option."

"Tomorrow's the first of April, April Fool's Day. You could just play it like you were trying to be funny, you know, 'ha-ha, here I am.'" Tish's expression was comical, her eyes wide and her smile rivaling an evil clown's grimace.

"Oh my goodness, Tish, you're frightening!" Elizabeth giggled, "It'll be testimony Sunday, a nice distraction. Did you tell your dad why you needed the car?"

"Um, yes and no..." Tish's face grew serious, "I told him I needed to run to Provo, to help out a friend, but didn't say who the friend was or what kind of help, so... no. I'll make huge brownie points with my mom if I go to church tomorrow. And quite honestly, seeing the look on your mom's face would be worth going. You've got to practice your evil clown smile, though do it like this," she made the grimacing face and made her voice sound robotic, "Hi mama, I love you, I love you."

Elizabeth laughed. "I missed you, girl! Dang, you make me laugh." They were approaching the outskirts of the small town. "Sidewalks are all rolled up, place is shut down this time of night, looks exactly the same... I can't say I missed it, but," Elizabeth sighed, "I don't know Tish, I didn't like where I was any better. Maybe the tough thing is just growing up, regardless of where you are. Kinda sucks, I'd go back to being ten anytime."

"Yup." Tish turned left to go down her street. "Barbie's and monkey bars. It's where it's at! I want to leave here so bad, but I don't know where I'd go or what I'd do. Maybe we should look into UVC and become roommates, or something."

"Maybe. Yea. Something. My mom wants me to apply at BYU; she said I'll have a better chance of finding a good husband there." Elizabeth sighed and shook her head. Her long, emotional day was catching up with her and her eyes suddenly became heavy at the prospect of a clean bed. "Let's sleep now and figure it out later," she grabbed her backpack and followed Tish down the basement stairs to her room.

"Take the bed, I'll sleep on the couch in the TV room." Tish hugged Elizabeth, and grabbed a pillow from the bed, "Glad your home, bestie."

"Thanks. Love you." Elizabeth stripped down to her garments, flopped onto the bed, and was asleep in less than a minute. She woke to the stirrings of the house. Curled in the duvet from Tish's bed, she laid there listening. It took her a minute to remember where she was. The room was dark and she had a feeling it was later than she thought. The door opened slowly and Tish tip-toed in wrapped in a towel with a second towel on her head, her phone was turned on flashlight mode and she set it down quietly so there was a little light for her to find her clothes. When she turned and saw Elizabeth looking at her, she jumped, "Creeper!"

Elizabeth smiled and threw the blanket over her head. "Guess I gotta get up."

"If you want to make sacrament meeting, it starts in an hour."

"What?" Elizabeth said, suddenly wide awake, "I thought you said last night we're in the last time slot and sacrament doesn't start 'til one."

"I did, and its noon." Tish said letting the towel drop while finding a matching black bra and panties.

Elizabeth watched her with a certain amount of envy, the delicate underwear, so pretty and sexy. "I need to wash clothes, crap, there's no time," she grabbed her backpack and emptied it on Tish's bed. "I've got nothing," she saw the gift bag from Rebecca and Maximus and peeked in. "Oh my goodness!" Elizabeth could feel the flush of her face as she took the lacy underwear out of the bag and held them up for Tish to see. They were light pink and a boy's cut for full bottom coverage.

"Cute!" Tish exclaimed, "Where'd you get those?"

"My friend, Ma..." She stumbled on her words as she corrected herself, "Rebecca, Sister Rebecca Armstrong picked them for me. I think I told you about her last night, the recovered heroin addict."

"Well, she's got good taste in panties. Isn't that kinda weird though, another woman buying you underwear?" Tish was looking at Elizabeth with an expression that clearly said, are-you-really-telling-me-everything?

"Um..." Feeling put on the spot, Elizabeth stumbled on her words, "Did I mention Maximus to you last night? I don't remember."

"The hot black guy with the sexy voice? Yea, you mentioned him." Tish's eyes danced, Elizabeth saw her friend's enthusiastic curiosity even in the weakly lit room.

"Well..." Elizabeth could feel her face flush and was grateful for the dimness.

"Maximus bought them for you?" Tish's eyebrows flew up and her mouth dropped open in an exaggerated expression of surprise.

"Um... They were a gift from the two of them, I just now opened it for the first time. I'm as shocked as you are." Elizabeth slipped them over her garments and looked in the mirror.

"No offense but that looks ridiculous." Tish said, clad only in her bra and thong panties. She was surveying her friend in the mirror, "Try them without the garments." Elizabeth was torn, on one hand, the garments were sacred, given to her after she went through the temple and before she left for her mission. On the other hand, they needed to be washed and she had to admit, Tish was right, the lacy panties looked ridiculous over the top of the long underwear. "Go shower, I told my folks you were here but not to tell your parents." Holding the phone flashlight under her chin, Tish slowly rotated her head towards Elizabeth with the grimacing evil clown smile on her face, "It's a surprise," she said in the robotic voice, then switched the bedside lamp on and laughed at herself.

"You're a weirdie." Elizabeth said as she took off the panties and grabbed the towel from the floor to wrap around her and headed to the bathroom. The shower felt glorious! It was hot and the water pressure was good. Elizabeth thought about the shower in the last missionary house she lived in, the water just dribbled out and it was always damp when she got out. She felt grateful to be back in the dry west and smiled to herself. Once showered she could smell the garments were needing a wash worse than she originally thought. She slipped the panties from Maximus on and fastened her bra. It didn't smell as bad as the garments since she had been wearing it on the outside of the sacred underwear. Wrapping the towel round her she slipped back into Tish's room. She could hear the ruckus upstairs from the other kids in the house. She supposed, like her own younger siblings, they were all becoming teenagers and young adults.

"Sexy!" Tish exclaimed, eyeing her friend.

"Yea, that's the look I'm going for, coming home early from my mission without a good excuse, surprising my parents, 'hey everyone, look who's back?'... sexy... yea..." Elizabeth shook her head and laughed to herself. "What do you have I can wear?"

"Welp..." Tish was going through her closet, extracting a few hangers, "since you're *not* going for sexy, I've got this long hippie skirt, so no one will notice you're not wearing the Jesus jammies. For the top I've got a few sweaters. How cold is it supposed to be today?" She handed the clothes to Elizabeth and picked up her smart phone, opening the weather app. "Mid-sixties. Here, wear the blue one, it will go better with the skirt and shoes, plus, it'll really make your eyes pop! Can I do your hair and make-up?" Tish was smiling.

"Yea, okay, let's hurry so we're not late, do you have a slip? This skirt is a kind of see-through."

"Just this black one, throw it on. I've got the flat iron heating up. Let's doll you up, sweet-cheeks." Within minutes, Tish had Elizabeth looking like she was ready for a night on the town.

Chapter Twenty-Three

Gaius had a hard time falling asleep that night, when he finally did, he dreamed of his mom. Before she died, she had told him she would come visit in his dreams. She had explained to him her mothering would not stop just because she left this planet. In the dream, he was running late and had to pick her up from the doctor's office. When he walked in there was a blonde-haired receptionist and she smiled at him and said, *'We're so glad you're not late. Your mom is with you already, in here.'* And she touched her hand to her heart. *'She loves you so much.'* The door to the back office opened and he turned his head to see a young version of his mom standing there in the doorway, wearing a white long flowing dress, a glowing light behind her. She didn't say anything but Gaius could hear her in his mind, *'I'm not in any pain, son. You don't have to wait for me to be happy. Don't be late. Go on foot through the forest, that's important. Go on foot through the forest."*

"I'm sorry," he mumbled, half awake and half asleep still. As he became conscious and remembered where he was, the sting of tears pained his eyes. It was as if she had been in the room with him, the dream seemed so real. Being away from their house had helped, but he still missed her every day. *Go on foot through the forest*, he got up and picked up his cell, he realized it was only a quarter to seven. The dream, there was a message here, he knew it. *Go on foot through the forest*, his mom had often used a dream interpretation website and he typed the address into the phone. When the site came up he searched for *go on foot through the forest.*

He read what the site produced.

Foot: your dream may be unconsciously asking you to reconsider the direction your life is going, questioning what your life is based on. An ancient Chinese proverb, 'All great journeys begin with a single step.' Your dream may be advising you to move forward, one step at a time.

Forest: The forest is often a symbol of the unconscious. Its animals and birds can be symbols for the instincts and emotions. This may represent exploring the world of the unconscious mind. A forest in a dream may represent you are searching for a breakthrough in your waking life.

"Okay mom, I think I get it, thanks. Miss you so much," he quietly said to himself, swallowing back the lump that had formed in his throat. Sassafras was sound asleep on the swivel chair. He might as well get up, he thought to himself as he threw back the covers and headed into the bathroom. Gaius heard the dog get up, stretch, yawn and shake her head. Once he was finished in the bathroom, he came out and noticed Sassafras at the door, ready to go take care of her own morning business.

"Let's go, girl," he said and followed her out. The morning was brisk but not too cold, the sunrise beautiful. *It's the first of April*, he thought to himself, *I can't believe she's been gone over a month*. The dream came back to him, *Go on foot through the forest*. It dawned on him there was another message, *don't be late*. With that thought in mind he walked Sassafras and took a shower, got dressed and observed himself in the mirror.

The haircut had left a slight tan line along his hair line, *it will take a day or two for that to fade*, he thought. Recognizing his father's face now in the mirror, he realized his haircut really accentuated the family resemblance. He hadn't cut it short enough to be military, but he had shorn it up significantly. Sassafras went to the door with him as he got ready to leave, he was really early, but had nothing else to do.

"Come on, girl, I'll ask Grandpa Bill if you can stay at his house while we go to church." Sass's tail wagged with enthusiasm at the prospect of a car ride, regardless of where they were going. He pulled into the Smith's driveway and let the dog and himself through the gate.

The old poodle dog, Boo-boo, was at the back porch and started to bark, the sliding glass door opened and Mary stepped into the sunlight. "Oh Kim, I thought you were going to church with us today," she looked crestfallen at him.

"Of course... mom." The title felt so false on his tongue.

"Well you can't go like that, jeans aren't allowed, you know better," her voice was stern and she looked very disappointed. Bill stepped out behind her and put his arm around her shoulders. "He's wearing jeans, that will never do," her eyes welled up with tears as she spoke to her husband.

Before Gaius could say anything, Bill answered his wife. "He's not ready for church yet, honey. It's still early, don't worry, he'll change before we leave." Bill steered Mary back inside to a chair at the table. Gaius followed them in. "You are early son, but right on time." Gaius noticed the table was set for two, there was a plate full of crispy bacon, another plate of French toast and a bowl with scrambled eggs.

"Have you had breakfast?" Mary asked. Gaius shook his head as he sat at the end of the table while Bill got another plate and utensil setting. Feeling self-conscious, Gaius didn't move towards the food or engage in conversation. Bill folded his arms and Mary clasped her hands in her lap and they both bowed their heads. Bill began,

"Our Heavenly Father, thank you for this meal we are about to partake in. We ask thee to bless this food so it may strengthen our bodies and minds. We ask for forgiveness, Father for those we have sinned against and pray they may know our actions were pure and without ill-intention. We pray those that we may have hurt find forgiveness in their hearts so they may be released of the burden they carry and know your love and our love. We thank thee for this beautiful day, we thank thee for the prophet and those before him, we thank thee for all of the blessing thou has bestowed upon us. We say these things, humbly in the name of Jesus Christ, amen."

"Amen" Mary said clearly and louder than her usual tone. Bill began serving his wife and passed the dishes to Gaius for him to serve himself. He noticed there was really only enough for two, so he took as little as he could, leaving as much for Bill as possible.

"Go ahead," Bill said.

"No, it's okay." Gaius replied "I'm really not that hungry." Which he wasn't, he was truly feeling nervous and uncomfortable. He noticed Bill didn't make more or eat at all. After breakfast, Bill asked Mary if she wanted a nap, Gaius remembered him saying routine was important. She feebly agreed and Bill followed her down the hall and tucked her in, returning to the kitchen in a matter of minutes. Gaius had gathered the dishes and put them by the sink, finding a dishcloth, he wetted it and started to wipe down the table when Bill returned.

"What's your pants size?" Bill asked as he started to load the dishwasher.

"I don't know." Gaius answered, caught off guard a little. "Twenty-Eight I guess."

"About a thirty, thirty-two-inch length?"

"About." Gaius responded.

"We only have about an hour before we got to get Mary up and ready to go, her nap is going to be cut short today. C'mon, follow me, let's see if we can find some slacks for you," he went out the sliding glass door and headed across the back lawn, Gaius followed.

Once they reached the large garage, Bill retrieved a key that was hanging by a cord near the door and unlocked it. The place smelled musty and old. Bill went to the stairs in one corner and started up them. Once upstairs he opened another door, inside was an apartment with a bed, nightstand, dresser and posters on the wall. It struck Gaius immediately, this was his dad's room. Bill opened the closet and started flipping through the hangers, extracting a pair of black slacks, "Try these," he said and tossed them to Gaius. Gaius held them up in front of him, holding the waist where it was supposed to be.

"These look okay," he said looking at them a little closer, it was obvious they were decades old, but they were business slacks. How out of fashion could they be?

"Okay, let's get them cleaned up. Follow me." Bill started walking back out of the small bedroom and noticed Gaius looking around at the posters and artifacts hanging on the walls. Bill paused in the doorway, "This was his room," he said quietly. "I avoid the place mostly, sometimes though when I miss him so much it hurts, I come out here and sit and pray and remember him. Sometimes I can hear him trying to comfort me, other times I can almost smell him. He was a beautiful child of God. He was a wonderful young man." Tears had welled in the old man's eyes. "Twenty plus years and I still miss him every day."

Gaius could relate. "It's a nice room." It was all he could think of to say.

They exited in silence and walked down the stairs to the washer and dryer at the bottom. After Bill had cleaned the slacks, Gaius tried them on. They were a little too big, so he had to wear a belt and roll up the cuffs. They looked good enough, at least that's what Bill had said. It didn't take long for Bill to help Mary get ready. They all piled in the Lincoln town car and pulled away, leaving the two dogs to guard the house, or sleep in the sun, whichever seemed more pressing.

Alice Anderson had been sitting in the same pew at church for almost two decades. The second row from the front on the far right was the perfect spot for her then-growing family and they gravitated to that location each week. Now it was just her, Daniel and the two youngest girls and the wooden bench seemed big. Sometimes other ward members had joined them when there wasn't any other place to sit but for the most part, it was the Andersons' area.

It was testimony Sunday and spring was breaking ground everywhere, that combination explained the small number of worshipers this morning. She heard Brother Smith's voice, greeting the other members and knew he was walking his demented wife to the front row. Poor thing had gone mad when her son died. Alice hadn't really known them but remembered when their son had been killed while serving in the military. The town was small and losing a young local boy was big news. If she remembered right, she was pregnant at the time with Paul, her second son. Zeb was about five, Elizabeth was just a toddler. Lost in thought she didn't really notice the young man escorting the old woman to the front row. A hand touched her shoulder and she heard Brother Smith's voice, "Good morning Anderson family, great to see you on this fine Sabbath."

The girls and Daniel turned and responded with similar greetings. Alice smiled up at him as he moved past. Her eyes glanced towards the Smith's unofficially designated seats on the front row. It was then she saw the young man. Confusion curled her brow as she stared at him. It was like she was seeing a ghost. Even though she didn't know the fallen solider she remembered his handsome face in the newspaper. This boy looked like him, frozen in time, even his slacks and denim shirt looked like a flashback from the nineties. She couldn't help gawking. Daniel nudged her in the ribs. She turned to look at him startled, and noticed his face also had a quizzical look. Their eyes met and he looked over her head to the other ward members. Slowly she turned her head to follow his gaze and noticed the majority of the crowd in attendance were also staring and whispering between themselves. Alice looked back at her husband and she shrugged slightly. The organist began to play a prelude, the sign for everyone to take their seats. On the front row, Mary sat smiling with her eyes closed, holding Bill's hand with her left hand and the stranger's hand with her right.

They sang the opening hymn and listened to the bishop's announcements, and testimonies began. Alice glanced at her husband and daughters. She couldn't remember when the last time one of her family had gone up to the podium on fast Sunday. All of a sudden someone was sliding in to sit next to her, the entire family shifted to make room for the new-comers and Alice looked up and recognized Patricia. Confused, she looked at the young woman who had slid into the pew next to her. *Elizabeth?*

"Hey Mama A." Tish said in a loud whisper. "Brother Anderson, good to see you."

"Elizabeth?!" Daniel exclaimed as he leaned over Alice awkwardly to hug his daughter, then greeted her friend "Tish. Good to see you too!" He leaned over farther and gave her knee a little squeeze.

"What are you doing here?" Alice whispered in Elizabeth's ear.

"Happy April Fool's day."

Chapter Twenty-Four

Gaius hadn't said a word since arriving at the church. He knew the other people there were staring and talking about him. The little town was answering a whole bunch of questions about his life and for now he would enjoy the moment, holding his grandma's hand and listening to the people 'bear their testimony.' Gaius had never heard of this nor seen the ritual. One by one, different people would get up to the microphone and say approximately the same speech. They wanted to bear their testimony, they knew the church was true and they were thankful for their families, religious leaders and finally, their religion. They finished with 'I say these things in the name of Jesus Christ, amen.'

Behind him, he heard loud whispers and movement. Turning, he saw two young women, about his age, sliding into the pew across the aisle from him and one row back. He watched as they put their heads together and talked with the family that had already been sitting there. The older woman, the mother probably, looked surprised and worried. The older man, the father, wore a genuine smile and his eyes had lit up when he saw the girls. The younger girls looked disinterested.

The woman speaking said the final sentence of her testimony, "And I say these things in the name of Jesus Christ, amen."

Gaius was still watching the family from across the aisle when his attention was redirected to the front by Bill's voice, "Oh no, no, no." Apparently, Bill had also been distracted and was looking in the same direction as Gaius and while they both had their heads turned, Mary had gotten up and taken the spot behind the microphone. The bishop had gotten up to help adjust the height for Mary, just as Bill had bounded up the three steps of the stage. She began speaking, and Bill took a seat looking a little panicked.

"For God so loved the world that he gave his one and only Son, that whoever believes in him shall not perish but shall have eternal life, John 3:16," she looked over the congregation, "Many times over the years I have thought about those words and the sacrifice that our Heavenly Father made for us," her eyes welled with tears and her voice cracked with emotion as she continued, "Losing a child is the most horrible thing anyone could go through, terrible beyond words. Something no one should have to endure, a person should bury their parents, not the other way around," she paused and Gaius wondered if she was finished, she looked at the faces of her neighbors and continued, "I would like to stand and bear witness today that I know this church is true. I'm grateful for an eternal life, I know I will see my son one day, the day I meet our Heavenly Father's son, Jesus Christ, our Lord and savior. I love my husband, Bill. I'm grateful for his patience and the love he has for me. I'm so grateful for strong leaders like President Monson and our local bishopric. I say these things in the name of Jesus Christ, amen," she turned and took a seat next to her husband, still on the front row facing the ward. Mary, the bishopric and everyone seemed to be staring at Bill, waiting for him to do something. He got up and straightened the microphone to accommodate his height.

"Good morning, brethren, sisters. I don't recall a time I've stood before you to bear witness of my testimony so being prompted by the spirit, or by my wife, here I am." There was a slight chuckle throughout the room. Bill looked at his feet and seemed to gather his thoughts. "Mar's right about one thing, parents shouldn't have to bury their children. Losing Kim..." The raw emotion sprung to Bill's face so quick it took him by surprise and he stopped speaking for a few seemingly long seconds. "They say God doesn't give a person anything they can't handle and I know losing our boy changed us, it..." Overcome with emotion again, he took the Kleenex the bishop offered him and shook his head, "I'm sorry," he said in a small voice, "I know this church is true. I love this ward, Pleasant is our home and it always has been and always will be. I'm grateful for our neighbors and friends, the bishopric, I'm grateful for the love and support everyone has shown me and Mary. I'm grateful for the experiences I've had as I know they have made me who I am today. I would especially like to say to the young people here to engage in life. Time flows fast. Enjoy your youth, enjoy each day as it is truly a gift from God. Carpe Diem as the Roman poet Horace would say." Gaius and Bill's eyes met, raw emotion seeped from his grandfather's face. "My last piece of advice from an old man is to learn the art of forgiveness and practice it on oneself. Humbly, I say these things in the name of Jesus Christ, amen."

"Amen." The unison voices repeated.

Bill walked to Mary and assisted her down the steps, Gaius stood and helped his grandparents back to their seats looking up and through the crowd as he did. It seemed most people weren't paying much attention to them, many people had started crying while Bill was speaking and were dabbing their eyes. Gaius' eyes scanned the room and he saw the two girls that had come in a few minutes prior. The one on the outside gave him a thumbs up when their eyes met. He looked at the next young woman and she nodded at him and smiled shyly, breaking eye contact to look down at her hands. *Weird*, he thought, *she looks a little like the girl in my dream this morning. Were they running late? Was that part of the message? Don't be late, or was it about someone else running late?* He continued to observe the family. The parents of the group were looking forward at the stage area as the next speaker began their public testimony. The hour-long meeting was almost an hour and a half. Many members were inspired to get up and give their thanks, bear their testimony. Some were emotional, others sounded almost robotic.

The bishop made an announcement that Sunday school, Priesthood meeting and relief society would each be shorted by ten minutes to make up for the additional time in sacrament meeting. Gaius could see Mary was exhausted. She said she was hungry. Bill assured her there was food when they got home. Many church members spoke to them on their way out, shaking Gaius' hand as well as Bill's. Some hugged Mary and told her they would stop in and say hi sometime. Finally, they reached the car and Gaius got in the back while Bill buckled in Mary. As they pulled out of the parking lot, Bill said, "We used to stay for the other classes, but when the time slot changed and church interrupted Mary's naptime routine, we just started going only to sacrament."

"It's cool." Gaius replied. "Thanks for inviting me Mary, um... I mean, mom," his and Bill's eyes met in the rearview mirror. Mary's head was bobbing sideways. She had already fallen asleep.

"I haven't seen her that lucid in years, Gaius," Bill said, "her testimony today was nothing short of a miracle." After a moment of driving in silence, Bill continued, "How long did you say you were going to stick around Pleasant?"

"I don't know," Gaius responded honestly, "I'm taking things one step at a time," he thought of the dream as he said it.

"Well, I'm going to throw something out there and you decide what is best for you and get back with me. Listening to Mar today made me realize she knows you're not Kim. I would love to see more of what we saw today, not to mention, I could use some help. Son, it's exhausting taking care of her. Here's what I propose, we can get Kim's old room cleaned up and you can stay there so you don't have to pay for the motel plus you've got your own space. Leave anytime, no obligation."

Gaius' mind was spinning. The dream this morning, this conversation, attending church today, the whole thing seemed surreal. "I'll let you know," he managed to say as they pulled in the driveway.

As they got out of the car, Bill said, "It's fast Sunday today, so I won't be eating. I'll make Mar a little snack. I'm sure our Lord will forgive her but what I'm trying to say is let's talk tomorrow, I'm drained. Mar's exhausted." Gaius got the hint, he called Sass as Bill kept talking, "There's a little diner up the way a bit, on the north side of town, it's the only place open on Sundays. I'm sure you could get a good meal there this afternoon. Their food isn't half bad and they have breakfast all day. Let's talk again tomorrow." Bill held out his hand for Gaius to shake, Gaius slapped it, back slapped it and made a fist for a bump. Bill smiled, "Youth is wasted on the young," he made a fist and they bumped them together, then sideways hugged each other.

"See you tomorrow, Gramps." Gaius said climbing into the cab of his truck, Sassafras jumped onto his lap and moved over to the passenger side.

Chapter Twenty-Five

After Sacrament meeting, the crowd dispersed into their Sunday school classes. In the foyer outside the chapel, Elizabeth, Tish and Alice stood after more enthusiastic hugs and hellos from the family and a few friends. "What happened?" Alice whispered into Elizabeth's ear, loud enough for Tish to hear it but no-one else.

"What do you mean?" Elizabeth didn't look directly at her mother, but instead looked to the ground and past her down the hallway.

"When you were little, I always knew I was about to be lied to whenever you answered a question with a question." Alice's tone was light enough to be playful, but sharp enough to mean business.

Elizabeth met her eyes. "Nothing, really," she looked around, although they were alone in the lobby area she didn't feel like getting into it right here, right now.

"Why are you home early? Why aren't you wearing your garments?" A fellow church member had come from the bathroom and was heading to the classrooms. Recognizing the women, she stopped and said hello and welcomed Elizabeth home. Alice's tone changed dramatically, in fact, her whole demeanor had changed as she spoke to the ward member. The words, tone, and body language all of a sudden beamed. After the lady walked away, Alice's expression changed again, she returned her icy stare towards her daughter. "So, again I ask! Where are your garments and what are you doing home early?"

Sighing, Elizabeth answered, "It's a long story, Ma. I lost my suitcase, I got in super late last night. Let's talk after church. I'll help make dinner, is the key in the same place? I really want to unpack and get settled in."

"Well I didn't know you were coming so soon. Your room has become somewhat of a storage area. I put the treadmill in Paul's room and some of my sewing stuff and quilting frames in your room."

"Paul will be home about Halloween time. We've got the summer to figure it out." Elizabeth could feel the hair on her neck prickle, her mom was more concerned about Paul's return than her daughter standing right in front of her. She bit her tongue. Elizabeth and Tish exchanged a glance. "So, mom... am I going to be able to get into the house? I think Tish and I are gonna dip out right now and I'll see you in a few hours?" The last part of the sentence was deliberately formed as a question, Elizabeth wanted her mom to still think she was making decisions for her kids, regardless of their age.

"Dip out?" Alice sighed resigned. "Yes, the key is where it's been the last decade if the house is even locked, I'm sure the back door is open. I really wished you would have called Elizabeth." Another sigh. "Plan on a sit-down with me after church. I want some answers, young lady. Nice seeing you, Patricia, be sure to tell your folks we said hello." Alice never did start calling Tish by her nickname. A sit-down to Elizabeth was the equivalent of a lecture from her mother, Alice had used the term before and they had never ended well. Either way, Alice went down the hall to her classroom and the girls exited the same side door they had come through.

"I'm starving." Tish said.

"It's fast Sunday, I can't eat until tonight." Elizabeth answered with no enthusiasm, she was hungry too.

"You're killin' me here." Tish whined "I'm going to Blondie's for a late lunch, they are the only place open today, please come with me. If you don't want anything, you don't have to eat, but if you do, I'll buy so you won't be breaking two rules." Another rule of the Mormon Church is that they don't spend any money on any Sunday.

"Ok." Elizabeth caved, knowing she would order biscuits and gravy with a side of extra crisp bacon. Blondies served breakfast all day. Perhaps she could skip dinner and still stay with the one meal rule. It dawned on Elizabeth that her mom may be a bit crabby this afternoon because of being hungry. They took the large corner booth and ordered. As they were talking casually about nothing in particular the young man that was with the Smith's walked in. Elizabeth noticed he was cute. How did she miss that? "Hmmm... you're right, he is a cutie," Elizabeth said, "I didn't notice before."

"Are. You. Serious." Tish raised one eyebrow and looked hard at her friend, "That was the *first* thing I noticed," she wiggled her fingers towards Gaius in an almost wave. He saw the girls and smiled. "I'm inviting him over," Tish said softly. Before Elizabeth could object, Tish had turned her waving fingers around and was now motioning him towards them. Gaius said something to the hostess at the counter and started walking towards them. Tish's smile spread across her face while Elizabeth glanced at him and back at Tish.

"Hey, I recognize you two." Gaius said warmly as he walked to the booth. Tish slid around to the middle and made room for him to join them. "I like the way you two go to church," he said still smiling.

"Excuse me?" Elizabeth said, finally looking directly at him.

"Well you guys rolled in late and bailed early, that's my kind of church meeting," his smile was disarming and Elizabeth found herself at a loss for words.

"My kind of church meeting too," Tish answered, smiling broadly. The waitress, brought the girls their food.

"Good afternoon," Gaius said, looking at the waitress's name tag, "Frida. How are you today?" he upturned the coffee mug and smiled at her.

"I'm fine, thank you," she answered, not looking directly at him, "Can I get you anything?"

"Sure," he said, "a cheeseburger and fries."

"With everything?" she added.

"Yup," he answered.

"Hey Elizabeth, almost forgot, welcome home." Frida said. She turned and walked back to the kitchen.

As Gaius added sugar and cream to his cup, he said, "I like my coffee like I like my women, hot, light and sweet. I'm joking, well, kind of..." He laughed quietly to himself at his own joke. Elizabeth smiled and thought about Maximus. If she drank coffee would she like hers hot, black and sweet? Tish was in full blown flirting mode and laughed a bit too loudly. She started eating her breakfast burrito. Elizabeth looked at her, cleared her throat and folded her arms.

"Oops, my bad, sorry Sister Anderson, we forgot to bless the food," Tish set her fork down, put her hands in her lap and looked at Gaius with a half-smile playing at her eyes.

Elizabeth prayed quickly and almost inaudibly, "Our dear Heavenly Father, thank you for this food we are about to eat, we pray that it may strengthen and nourish our bodies. We say these things in the name of Jesus Christ, amen," she looked up as she picked up her fork, both Gaius and Tish were staring at her, smiling. "What?"

"You go girl." Tish said stuffing some egg in her mouth. Gaius took a swig of his coffee. "So, who are you and where'd you come from?" Tish asked turning her attention to the young man.

"I'm Gaius Stewart. I hail from Colorado Springs," He held up his coffee mug in a mock salute, "and you ladies are?"

"Tish Ingersoll, I'm 'it' only backwards, get it? I.T, T.I?"

"Or Treasure Island or Turquoise Iguana." Gaius said smiling back at her, enjoying the Tish name game. "Or Totally Intelligent or Too Ironic."

"Right?" Tish giggled.

"And you are?" Gaius turned his attention to Elizabeth.

"Elizabeth Ord Anderson." Did she really just say her full name like a four-year old would? *Ugh*, she thought, *so much for first impressions*.

"Lizard? Really, how cool!" He said whole-heartedly.

The girls stared at him with confused looks on their faces. "Didn't you just say Elizabeth *Ord*? Liz Ord, lizard."

Elizabeth was almost twenty-three years old and had never put her name together in that way. "I go by Elizabeth, not Liz," she could feel her face flush.

"Fair enough, I go by Gaius, not Guy, so... respect," he saluted her with his coffee mug again.

"I'm so going to call you Lizard." Tish said playfully finishing her breakfast burrito. Elizabeth shot her a look. "So, what brings you through Pleasant?" Tish continued.

"Oh, I don't know. I may not be passing through. I may be settling in. I could be Pleasant's newest most eligible bachelor," he answered, grinning, directing his gaze to Elizabeth.

"What are you nuts?" Tish was flabbergasted, "Kids moving out of here in hoards and you're wanting to move in?" She shook her head. "Pleasant is not as pleasant as it sounds."

"You are correct there, but I've never been one to follow the crowd," he answered.

"Oh, a rebel, I like that," Tish said, her grin somewhere between normal and evil clown. Frida returned with the cheeseburger. "Elizabeth just got home from her mission," Tish volunteered.

"A mission of what?" Gaius inquired.

The girls looked at each other with an amazed look on their faces. Had they ever met someone that didn't know what a mission was? "It's where you go to another city or country and teach the word of the gospel, pass out the Book of Mormon to those interested, and then, hopefully, baptize them." Elizabeth explained.

"Where'd you go?" Gaius sounded genuinely interested.

"Kentucky," Elizabeth answered through a bite of the biscuits and gravy.

"And you baptized a lot of people?" he asked stuffing another bite of his burger into his mouth.

"Oh, no. Women don't hold the priesthood, but we gave a lot of lessons and the elders followed up with the actual baptisms. I'm not sure how many we actually converted, it was a good experience though. I'm glad I went," Elizabeth finished, not sure if she was trying to convince Gaius or herself.

"How long were you gone?"

"About a year and a half."

"Cool," he said, swirling some fries through ketchup. "Was it fun?"

"It was..." she hesitated, fun wasn't exactly the word she would have used. "It was... interesting."

"Did you like the south?" he enquired.

"It was okay," Elizabeth said, "I wasn't crazy about the humidity, but overall, it was a pretty place, especially during autumn."

"Yea, I agree. I've only been to New Orleans and Texas, so I don't have a lot of southern exposure, but from what I've seen, I wasn't so impressed."

"I went to Florida when I was a kid," Tish interjected, as to not be left out of the conversation. Neither of them replied, just continued to eat.

"You should try some fry sauce," Elizabeth suggested. "Have you ever had it before?" she got Frida's attention and asked for fry sauce.

"What's in it?" Gaius asked as he dunked a wad of fries into the ramekin.

"Mostly mayonnaise and ketchup. Every place is different. Some places put lemon or sea salt in theirs. Sometimes there are secret recipes and only certain people know what the secret ingredient is," Tish explained.

When Frida returned to see if they needed anything else, Gaius motioned to the sauce and asked, "What's in this stuff?"

"Mayo, ketchup, little salt and a shot of lemon juice," she replied clearing some of the dishes.

"So much for Blondie's secret recipe," Elizabeth giggled.

"I don't think it was ever a secret," Frida said walking away from the trio.

"So, shall we all meet here again next week, same time, same place, same great channel?" Gaius questioned the two girls.

"We've got church," Elizabeth snapped.

"I'll be here," Tish beamed, dipping her chin slightly and flashing Gaius her sexiest smile.

Chapter Twenty-Six

Tish prattled on about Gaius the entire five-minute drive from the diner to her house. Elizabeth ran in to grab her garments. She had rinsed them out in the shower and hung them on the towel rack to dry, hoping to be able to slip them on before returning home, but no such luck, they were still too damp. She shoved them into her backpack and ran back up the stairs where Tish was waiting for her. "Who you texting?"

"I'm not, just updated my Facebook status to 'hoping to be in a relationship.'"

"Ha-ha, you're funny," Elizabeth climbed in the passenger side of the car and sighed.

"You okay?" Tish asked.

"Yes. No. I don't know," Elizabeth could feel the tightness in her throat, "I guess I'm just nervous."

"About your sit-down with your ma?" Tish put the car in reverse and backed out of the driveway.

"Crap Tish, I could have walked home," Elizabeth said, changing the subject. "Geez, for months I walked everywhere and I'm home less than twenty-four hours and got you chauffeuring me around."

"Aw shucks, I missed you. So glad you're home. Let me know if you need anything, be tough with your folks, hang in there," Tish pulled into the Anderson's driveway, threw the car into park and turned to hug her friend. "You beat your family home. Go in and clean something. That always seems to put your mom in a good mood."

"Good call." Elizabeth grabbed her backpack, and walked to the backyard knowing the back door would be open. She threw the garments in the dryer, at least she would be wearing them when her family got home. She went upstairs to her room. Her mom hadn't been kidding when she said she had made it somewhat of a storage room. Quilting frames, batting, fabric, boxes of old jeans and hand-me-down clothes were lined up along the walls. The sewing machine was on top of her dresser and spread across her bed was a variety of patterns and project books. She sat on the bed and picked up a framed picture of her and Tish from the nightstand. They were just kids in this picture, fifth or sixth grade. Tish was posed like a supermodel, her head thrown back, eyes closed, Elizabeth was looking at the camera all teeth and a smattering of freckles. *Those were the days*, she thought.

Elizabeth heard the car pull into the driveway. *That wasn't very much time to clean anything*, she thought to herself rushing back to the laundry room to grab the underwear and bound back up the stairs. Once back in her room she stripped down to the pink panties. She hesitated before deciding to keep them on. She pulled on the garments and re-dressed in Tish's clothes as she heard the front door open and her family spill into the house. Putting on an award-winning smile, she walked down the hall to greet her little sisters.

Jozette moved by her saying, "Welcome home, Sis."

Giselle threw her arms around Elizabeth and said sincerely, "I missed you. Hope you don't mind, I used your room for a bit, before mom decided to make it her sewing room."

"Not a problem," Elizabeth replied, "glad to be home. Love you." Elizabeth kissed Giselle on her cheek, both younger girls disappeared into their room. They were so grown up to Elizabeth, these little girls she helped raise, where did the time go? She entered the kitchen and threw her arms around her dad.

He hugged her tight and kissed her, "Glad you're home, honey." Then walked down the hall to his room, removing his tie and jacket as he went.

Alice was removing items from the fridge and turned to preheat the oven. "Here's some peppers, make this salad for me, please," she said, stacking peppers with a head of lettuce and few whole carrots on a cutting board and sliding them across the counter to Elizabeth. "None of us have eaten all day, so we're going to have dinner a little early. I did this casserole yesterday; it just needs to cook." Elizabeth took the cutting board and began slicing the peppers. "So, can you explain to me in a hundred words or less why you're home before Mother's day?"

"Um, probably not," Elizabeth kept her eyes on her task at hand. "I will tell you, it was nothing bad. A misunderstanding of sorts, I guess. Plus, there was a fresh batch of missionaries from the MTC and the accommodations for us were cramped. I don't know what to say Mom, it just worked out better if I came home now, no harm, no foul."

"Well you know I don't like being caught off guard. Showing up at church today, well it was like something from a bad dream." Alice was prepping the casserole and taking out dishes from the cupboard to set the table.

"Oh, c'mon Mom, it wasn't that bad, most the folks I talked to just thought it was time I returned. No one keeps track of these things."

"According to you!" Alice snapped. Finally, their eyes met. Alice's jaw was tight, her lips pressed hard together.

Elizabeth found herself counting to three before speaking, she didn't want to sound defensive or engage in an argument with her mom right before dinner, or anytime for that matter. She hated arguing with her mom. "I'm sorry, but I'm home, like it or not."

Elizabeth managed to keep her tone even and maintained eye contact with her mother. The oven dinged it was heated and ready for the casserole. Alice looked away and put the food in the oven and called down the hall, "Girls, we need help setting the table, please." Both girls and their father reappeared, all had changed into sweats or jeans.

"I'm going to go change my clothes, be right back," Elizabeth announced. Once she was back in her room with the door shut, she sighed audibly and started pulling open dresser drawers trying to figure out what she could wear. Finding a pair of black sweats and a baseball style white tee shirt with red sleeves, she noticed everything fit her a little loosely. Looking in the full-length mirror, she decided she must have lost some weight while in Kentucky. That thought surprised her since everything she had eaten in the last year was deep fried or covered with cheese. Returning to the kitchen, she noticed her mom slicing a loaf of French bread and her sister tossing the salad, the other folding cloth napkins, her dad heated a couple cans of corn in a saucepan on the stove. She smiled to herself and thought, *it's nice to be home.* Even though she had already had her one meal of the day, she was going to eat with her family. Heavenly Father would understand.

Chapter Twenty-Seven

After Gaius left the diner he headed back to the motel to let Sassafras out, while he waited on the bench for her to do her business, he sent Toni a text,

Can you talk? Within seconds, the phone rang,

"Hey buddy, what's up?" she said cheerfully.

"You off today?" Gaius inquired.

"I am," she said, "Shift bid this month is a 715 start with Sunday, Monday off."

Gaius laughed and shook his head, "After all these years, you still can't get weekends off?"

"Oh sure I can, but not with such an early start time, seriously, I could come in at nine-thirty and have weekends off, but who wants to stay there 'til six?" Toni answered. "I'd rather just get up and get it over with, you know what I mean? And I don't care about working Saturdays. What's up with you?"

Gaius smiled and thought of his mom and her monthly shift bids, the trades, the giveaways. Sometimes she had even paid people to pick up her shift when he was sick or had school events. Often on Christmas or Easter, she would work for other agents and let him go snowboarding or camping with friends, stating she felt good about working for those that wanted it off because they believed it was a special day, as a single mother, she also enjoyed the extra money.

"So, what'd you decide to do?" Toni asked, "You comin' home? Do I need to get the contractors out of your house?"

"Umm... I don't know what I'm doing yet," Gaius replied hesitantly. "Good old Grandpa Bill gave me an offer I'm not sure I can refuse."

"Oh did he now?" he heard Toni draw on a smoke, as happy as she sounded, he assumed it was weed.

"Yea he did," Gaius answered, "he showed me Kim's old room, no one's been in there for decades, probably since he died, and told me I could stay there rent free as long as I helped out with Grandma Mary."

"What does that old bitty need help with?" Toni huffed into the phone a little sharply.

"She's old."

"Oh, for hell's sake, G! She's not *that* old!" He could hear Toni getting agitated on the other end.

"Maybe not physically, but her mind's gone, Toni. I think she has Alzheimer's or dementia or something like that. I don't know, she's not right though, she's not right in her head." Gaius sighed, "She thinks I'm Kim sometimes, sometimes she seems to know exactly who I am. Sometimes she looks like the lights are on and no one's home and other times, she's as sharp as a tack."

"So, a room huh?" Toni's voice was laced with sarcasm, "A room *in* their house?"

"Not exactly in their house, it's a room above their detached garage, I would have some privacy, be able to come and go as I like," he wasn't sure who he was trying to convince, her or himself. "Sass would probably love it, their yard is fenced in and they have this old poodle dog she seems to like."

"Listen honey," Toni said, "I don't know what to tell you. It's not money, you could afford the motel another week or two."

"I know that!" Gaius' snapped a little quicker than he had intended it to, "I get it. I have choices because my mom is still taking care of me." Tears stung his eyes and a lump formed in his throat at the memory of his mother, but he managed to say, "My mom always taught me, choices are good."

"This is true, your mom always believed if there was a way to do it all...do it *all*!" Another inhale of smoke and a slow exhale.

"It's why I called her the make-it-happen mama-cita, indeed Toni."

Toni laughed remembering her friend. "I miss her."

"I do too." There was a moment of silence on the phone and Gaius continued, "I think I'll check it out, what do I have to lose? Oh, and I forgot to tell you, I met a few new friends at church, girls, well, kind of women, they're my age."

"Oh my gawd, I forgot, you went to church!" Toni laughed. "How did *that* go?"

"It was a little weird, but cool." Gaius thought about the church meeting, "It was something called testimony Sunday, it was strange but honestly, no stranger than any other church. In fact, in some ways it was tamer than some of the other religions I've seen."

"Yea, probably." Toni said thoughtfully. "I don't know much about the Mormons, they are occasionally in the news, but not often and not for horrific deeds like raping little boys. Glad you had fun, you going back? You said you met some Mormon women? Cute women? Ladies or hot chicks? Details boy-o, details!"

Gaius roared with laughter, "Hot chicks that happen to be cute Mormon women."

"Well it sounds just lovely," Toni said. "Sounds like you're making friends and getting along nicely. Maybe you should stay put, give me a few more weeks getting the house put together for you. I've got painters and plumbers coming by, you won't even recognize the place when you get back."

"Then I probably won't want to sell it," Gaius replied, half-jokingly.

"Hopefully you'll want to settle back down here in good old Colorado Springs, I miss you, kiddo. Gotta run."

"Sure," Gaius said and he swore he heard a knock at Toni's door. Hanging up, he flopped down on the bed realizing he was still wearing his dad's pants. He rubbed his hands over his thighs thinking at one point in time his father had worn these same pants probably to attend the same church. *Had he ever gotten up to bear his testimony?* Gaius thought. *Was he wearing these pants? Did he sit in the same pew and hold Mary's hand as he did?* With these thoughts filling his head, he dozed off and slept soundly through the night.

The next morning, Gaius decided to just do his normal routine. Mainly because he wanted a cup of coffee, but he also wanted to talk to Bill to see just how serious he was about Gaius moving in. He walked into the C-store and greeted Vicki.

"Well if it isn't the talk of the town!" Vicki said dubiously.

"Whatever do you mean?" Gaius said innocently, not looking at Vicki.

"Oh, whatever do I mean?!" She was beside herself as she continued, "You tell me to be on the DL, the down-low, remember? You said 'keep this between us, Vic', did you not? Then you show up at church with Mary Smith on your arm! There is nothing that is DL about that! You created the biggest spectacle this town has seen in twenty years! I thought you wanted to be anonymous?" she was out of breath she was so worked up.

"Well... yes and no." Gaius stirred his coffee, "It just happened, I didn't plan it. I don't want the whole town talking about me, but yet..." His words trailed off and he didn't know what else to say.

Vicki seemed to pick up right where he left off, "But yet, that old lady needs you, doesn't she?"

He sighed heavily. "Yea, she does," he finally looked directly at Vicki as he snapped the plastic lid on the coffee cup. "And I need her and Bill, it's a two-way street." Gaius put the $1.16 on the counter.

"So, does that mean you're gonna hang out a bit?"

"For a little while. Bill said I could stay in Kim's old room," Gaius answered. He picked up his coffee and headed to the door then paused and turned to finish the conversation. "Gotta get me some cleaning supplies and paint, no one's been in there since he died."

"Oh, I'm sure not," Vicki said sadly, "no doubt about it. Horrible them losing their only kid," she sighed. "Neither one of them have been the same since."

"It's rough losing someone you love," Gaius said, sipping his hot coffee. Vicki had just confirmed what he already expected. Kim had been an only child.

"You're awfully young to have lost too much, to know that kind of pain, I mean, no offense," she smiled at him as if she wanted to spare him of ever having to feel such hurt.

Looking at his shoes, not wanting to appear as if he were just fishing for sympathy, he said, "Well, I'm an orphan, a twenty-one-year-old stray."

"Wow. You're so young," Vicki said, "I didn't think about that, I'm sorry to hear about your mom, you're right, that really sucks."

"Thanks," Was all Gaius could say.

"Good luck, have a great day, you deserve it," Vicki was all sincere smiles.

"See you tomorrow. Same time. Same great station," Gaius said as he exited. Pushing Sassafras into the passenger seat he drove north towards seventh. When he got there, he parked in front of the house noticing the two flags run up the flag pole. Bill had already performed his morning routine. Gaius opened the gate and let Sass through and followed the dog, closing the gate behind him. As he was walking up the drive, he saw Bill standing at the end waiting for him, he also heard Boo-boo yap his greeting. Sass was always happy to see Boo-boo and immediately flopped onto her back, exposing her belly for the old dog to sniff and explore.

"Mornin' son." Bill said. "You made a decision on what you want to do?"

That was quick. Gaius searched the old man's face wondering if he really had a preference on Gaius' choice. It seemed Bill had given him mixed messages over the last few days. On one hand, Gaius felt like Bill wanted to get to know him, in other ways, Bill may just be looking for a live-in sitter for Mary, a cheap hired hand to help out. Either way, he nodded his head and said, "Yea, I'll hang out a bit. Can't promise anything long term, you understand. My house in Colorado is getting worked on and the contractors are going to need more time to finish up. I can't commit to that long because I don't know how things are going to turn out, but..." He sighed, "But I think a month is a good starting point for relationship building, agreed?"

Bill pursed his lips together and nodded one time. Gaius wasn't sure this was a good or bad sign. "Well boy, we gotta lot of work to do then." Bill said turning and walking to the garage as the two dogs played briefly and curled up in the shade like two old pals. The two men went up the stairs.

"Kinda thought you might stick around so I started cleaning the place a bit. Maybe you should go through some of the clothes, some may fit and some may even still be in style. I'm washing the bed linens, swept the floor, how much stuff you got over at the motel?"

"Not much, a couple boxes of books, a backpack full of clothes and an old chair."

"A chair?" Bill enquired.

"Yea, an old swivel chair of my mom's" Gaius answered and Bill nodded once. He noticed the closet had been emptied and a large pile of clothes were on the stripped bed.

Seeing Gaius looking at the clothes Bill said, "Most these clothes have only been worn a couple times. Church clothes don't really go out of style, you may find something interesting here. We can just clean and take these posters down or leave them up, doesn't matter. Whatever you don't want, we'll box up and label them Kim's room and put them in the attic. This is a project I've been meanin' to do for twenty years, just ain't never got around to it."

Gaius picked up the jacket that laid on the top of the pile. It reminded him of his mother's jacket he had given Toni, aviator style, brown leather. He slipped it on to check it out for size. It was a little big, but not too much, he certainly wouldn't have wanted the next smaller size. He replaced the jacket onto a hanger and returned it back to the closet. He continued to go through the clothes, carefully checking each pocket before deciding whether to keep the item or get rid of it. In the third pair of pants he found a folded piece of paper. There was a game of dots that made squares. In each box, there was the initial K or S. At the bottom was printed 'I can't believe you buy into this BS!' Below that was a smiley face and different writing that said 'I love you anyway'.

Looking a little closer at the writing he wondered if his mother had drawn the smiley face. It looked as if it were made with much heavier pressure, like the K's on the game board. Perhaps this was a note they had passed... in church? Had his mother gone to the ward to make an effort to pacify the Smith's? She probably had explored the idea. Was she pregnant with him at the time? His thoughts whirled in his head thinking of the ultimatums thrown at her by Bill and Mary. He looked at the paper again and briefly thought, maybe this wasn't his *mamacita's* perfect print writing. He didn't care and refolded it, putting it in his jeans pocket. Gazing at the posters, he decided the only one that had to go was the large picture of Jesus. He carefully took it off the wall and placed it by the clothes he didn't want. Gaius opened the top drawer of the nightstand and rummaged through the contents. Towards the bottom he found a small journal. Only the first three pages were written on.

> *Dear Heavenly Father, Dear Earthy Father and Mother,*
>
> > *I don't understand why you are so against love. I realize you are disappointed in my actions and I know I've participated in premarital sex. I am not denying it. This I know is wrong and I'm willing and able to repent for my sin but I do feel like it is unfair for you to ask me to give up the woman I love and my unborn child. You have told me my entire life that you know what is best for me, but do you? Really? Do parents always know what's best? I love Sue and she loves me and just because she has not been baptized,*

you reject this love. Because I'm a loyal son and I love my church and our Heavenly Father, I will break it off with her and join the military as you both have requested. As you said, Parents Know Best and obviously in your eyes, I'm still a child. Perhaps the Army will change that.

Gaius could feel the emotion in his father's writing. The next letter was written to his mother. Tears flooded his eyes and he sat on the bed and read.

Dear Sue,

Please know I will love you always. Regardless if our child is a boy or girl, if you keep it or find another family for it, I know our love is true and I know our baby was conceived in love if not in marriage. I am sorry. I am sorry we met at the time we did because of the pain and heartache I've caused you. This was never my intention. I am an accountable person, Sue. I will not blame this mess on my parents or my church. I am a man divided, my love for the church and my love for you. It makes no sense why both these great loves can't fit in my life as they both fit comfortably in my heart. I know you will respect any decision I make but you need to know, our separation was never due to a lack of love. I love the idea of us being a family, I love the idea of us raising our child and who knows, maybe one day going through the temple or at the very least, getting married. Since this cannot be, I will sadly say goodbye.

I love you to the moon and back.

The words his mother had said to him his entire life, I love you to the moon and back, came from Kim, his father, the man that loved his mother, who wanted to be with her. He knew his mother had never seen this letter, it had been hidden in this little notebook. Would it have made her feel better to know Kim loved and wanted her? Bill had returned carrying a box of cleaning supplies. "Got Mary down for her nap." Bill said and noticed Gaius' emotional state. "You okay, son?" he hustled over and sat next him, placing his arm around Gaius' shoulder.

"Yea, yea, I'm fine," Gaius said closing the journal, "can I have this?"

Bill removed his hand from Gaius' shoulder and placed both hands on his knees. "Yea, you can have it. There have been a couple times over the years I've wanted to destroy that journal, burn it, at the very least rip out those few pages but I didn't. There was always something that told me to just leave it," he shook his head and a sadness washed over his face. "Yes, I want you to have it. There are more blank pages than written on ones, maybe you can continue writing in it, tracking your days and life." Bill got up from the bed and started picking up the cleaning supplies he had hastily dropped. "Is this the stuff you don't want?" he asked indicating the pile of clothes and picture of Jesus. Gaius nodded. He put the book on a little shelf in the closet. In silence the two men started cleaning and bagging the items in the room. There was very little conversation between them as they finished the task at hand.

Gaius loaded two bags of Kimball's clothes and two boxes of other items into the back of the pick-up. Bill opened one box and let his hands touch each of the items, his eyes clouding over with tears. Extracting a small silver medal attached to a red and white ribbon, he said, "I'm going to keep this. Kim won first place in his eighth-grade track meet. It was a good day for him, both Mary and I were there and it was as if he wanted us to see how fast he was, how far he could jump." The tears were streaming down his face. "Although the team didn't place, it was a junior high highlight for Kimball." Bill opened the second box. The first thing he noticed was a Book of Mormon with Kim's full name etched on the top front cover in gold. "I'll keep that too," he said, swiping it out of the box.

"If you don't mind," Gaius continued, "I would like to have some of the pictures in his room scanned, some are Polaroid pictures and a few are of my mom."

"You don't have to have them scanned, son, you can keep them." Bill said looking at the medal in his hand. He opened the gate for Gaius and Sassafras ran out from the back yard.

"No" Gaius exclaimed, "You stay, stay!" Sassafras looked panicked and ran around the truck barking wildly. "Well, I guess I'll take her, I think she has an attachment disorder," he let Sass jump on his lap and make herself comfortable in the passenger seat, "It's cool, Gramps, we won't be long." Gaius backed out of the driveway and Bill shut the gate behind him. *I hope I'm not making a huge mistake*, Gaius thought, looking in the rearview mirror at Bill and Boo-boo. He knew in his heart he wasn't committed to this man or the confused woman inside but he couldn't go home, not just yet. What's a month?

He wasn't kidding when he said it would only take a few minutes to pack the items at the motel. Gaius observed the confused and flustered look on the dog's face. "Don't worry, girl. We're just moving… again," he stroked her head reassuringly.

After securing the things in the back of the truck he walked around to the office to check out and pay his final bill. Ruby was there and expressed a disappointment when he told her he was checking out. Enthusiastically, she said, "I saw you at church yesterday with the Smith's. Are they kin? You kinda look like them, well, their son, may he rest in peace. You look a lot like him in fact. He was older than me in high school, but I remember him, handsome fella."

"Yup," Gaius said, "and thank you. Bill and Mary are my grandparents, their son that looks like me is my dad."

She smiled and gave him his change. "Ohhhhh…." The way she drew out the sound, he knew she knew exactly who he was. She avoided his eyes as he turned to leave. "Kim was a good man," she said to Gaius' back, "It's a shame you never got to meet him."

Gaius turned at looked at her, she raised her eyes to meet his. "Thank you," he said, "I'm sure he was."

"Good luck with the Smith's," she said cheerfully, "hope to see you around. Pleasant grows on a person after a while."

"You'll see me," he called over his shoulder. "I'm going to stay with my kin for a bit."

Chapter Twenty-Eight

Elizabeth had made herself comfortable in the basement. Her mind wandered. The next item on her to-do list was figuring out storage space. Making room may be as simple as moving stuff from one place to another. After a sound sleep, she woke to the normal noises of her sisters getting ready for school. Elizabeth kissed her mother good morning, grabbed a bowl and spoon, and sat down at the table to have cereal with Jozette. She noticed her little sister's eye make-up looked awfully black and her hair, overly straight. Giselle joined them and Elizabeth noticed she had the same look.

"So happy to be home." Elizabeth beamed at her sisters. She couldn't believe how old and young they looked at the same time. High school for her had seemed like ages ago, her five-year reunion already coming up the following year. "Bet you guys are glad school is almost out, what do you have two more months?" Neither girl answered her. Elizabeth realized they both had head phones in and were listening to music. She smiled and signed 'I love you' in American Sign Language.

Giselle, laughed and said, "Love you too, sis." The girls finished their breakfast, dutifully took their bowls to the sink and rinsed them and headed out the door, hollering their good-byes to their mom as they went. Alice asked Elizabeth if she wanted some orange juice, both women sat at the table.

"I think I'll move downstairs, have Zeb's room." Elizabeth said casually.

"That will take some serious work." Alice replied.

"Right?!" Elizabeth said and asked, "What *is* all that stuff? Have you turned into a hoarder, mom?"

"No" Alice said smiling and shaking her head, "it's just a lifetimes worth of things, not just my life time, but your dad's and all five of you kids."

"What are you going to do with it?"

"Give it to you kids," Alice said, her tone insinuating, 'duh'.

"So you don't mind if I go through it, categorize it and get rid of some?"

"Not at all, honey, in fact, that would be great."

"Can I use the Ford?"

"Of course, dear. Love you," her mom smiled, kissed the top of her oldest daughter's head, and left Elizabeth to her soggy cereal. She straightened up the kitchen, then grabbed a few large garbage bags and headed to her room. Flinging the doors of the closet open, she drug out all the shoes. She grabbed her black and white 'Chucks' and her swanky black high heels, whatever she wore one or the other would match. The rest of the flip flops, sneakers and sandals went into the bag. Elizabeth continued through the closet and dresser and put more than half of the clothes into the bags.

Looking at her bed, she realized there were a few stuffed animals. She reminded herself of her age. Goodness, stuffed animals! She threw them into the bags. She remembered when her dad had won the pink bear holding the red heart for her at the state fair when she was still the only girl in the family. She was Daddy's Little Girl for so many years, and *bam*, two little sisters but she treasured the memories of those days. She was going to keep the little pink bear despite being an adult now. She fished it out of the bag and placed it in the closet.

Pulling into the donation lane of the Deseret Industries, otherwise known as the D.I, she noticed Gaius' truck with the goofy dog sitting in the passenger's seat. When it was his turn, he threw the truck into park and jumped out to help the store worker unload the boxes and bags from the bed of the truck. Elizabeth noticed he was smiling and talking animatedly to the female employee.

Is he a flirt, she thought, *or a charmer? Or just a nice guy?* She knew Tish would be bummed to have missed this encounter. As the last box was removed from the truck, he lifted the tailgate and noticed Elizabeth. Gaius' smile got even bigger as he walked toward her truck. She rolled down her window as he said, "Hey little Lizard, what's up?"

"Don't call me little lizard," she replied coolly, and smiled. "Guy."

"Okay", he laughed, "Hey big Lizard."

"Ha ha, you're not funny," she narrowed her eyes at him, "not funny at all."

"Sure, I am," he grinned at her, "So, how about if you call me G, and I can call you Lizard. G is not just the first initial of my first name, it is a special nickname given to me by my aunt Toni, who was my mom's best friend in the world. So you call me G, I call you Lizard, deal?" she stared at him, working at keeping her features neutral. "Seriously," Gaius continued, "Lizard is the coolest nickname *ever*, if my name was Liz Ord, I would absolutely, without a shadow of a doubt, go by Lizard."

Finally, she laughed. "Okay, G! Since you put it that way. But you're the only one, not Tish, no one else."

"Ok, Liz Ord," his smile was infectious.

The thrift store worker had approached Elizabeth's passenger side. "Was it just the bags of clothes and shoes?" she asked.

"Yes." Elizabeth replied, "Thank you!"

"Do you need a receipt?"

"No thanks." Elizabeth turned her attention back to Gaius. "We've got to move, there are people behind us. Meet me at the front of the store."

"Right." Gaius said. He hustled back to his truck and drove it to the front. They parked so the driver's side windows were next to each other.

"I'm moving into my dad's old room today," he said.

"Wow, weird. I'm moving into my brother's old room today." There was a moment of odd silence. Elizabeth suddenly became self-conscious, realizing she was wearing sweats. Her hair was pulled back with a bandana, and she didn't have any make-up on at all, she wasn't even wearing a bra.

"So yea, you want to come help me and I'll come over and help you, four hands are better than two and the time will go faster if you're not alone, what do you think?" His words came out in a gush, but she smiled and nodded.

"I've got to run home real quick. You're at the Smith's on 7th?" she asked.

"Yea," he replied a bit taken back.

She saw the confused look on his face, "It's a small ward," Elizabeth smiled, "See you soon." Elizabeth drove home as fast as she dared. Her parents had always said, 'never drive faster than the speeding ticket you can afford' and right now she was broke and couldn't afford *any* ticket. She swung into the driveway and bounded up the stairs to her room and changed into a pair of worn jeans, white tee shirt and a grey and black cardigan. With the weight she had lost, the clothes hung just right, the pants not tight enough on the legs to show the lines of the garments. *Why am I suddenly worried about that*? She thought while brushing her hair out and applying a little lip gloss and mascara. She never could figure out all the eye liners and fire engine lips, it wasn't her. Looking at herself in the mirror she thought the outfit looked a little school girl, and decided on two braids for her long hair. Her hair desperately needed a trim, she had only one cut since leaving over a year and a half ago. It looked better in the braids.

With haste, she drove to fourth and seventh but noticed Gaius' truck wasn't there, so she kept driving. She went around the block and thought about Tish. Pulling into a park, she sent Tish a text.

What's up?

Still sleep, call u ltr

As dark as it was down there, Tish could probably sleep all day. Elizabeth pulled back out, and drove around the block noticing Gaius still wasn't there. *Had she misunderstood him? He had invited her over, right?* Going around a fourth time, she noticed Bill Smith standing at the gate, leaning on his elbows, he motioned for her to stop.

"You're the oldest Anderson girl, aren't you?" he smiled and looked grandfatherly.

"Yea."

"You been gone so long you don't remember your way around town?" he asked a sheepish look on his face.

"No," Elizabeth was feeling as if she had just been caught doing something she shouldn't have.

"Well, I just seen you drive by three times, you lost?"

"Um, no sir," she was suddenly embarrassed, "I was looking for -"

"Gaius?" he asked, interrupting her, the sheepish look suddenly looking devilish. "Come on in, we've got poppy seed muffins just coming out of the oven. Gaius had to run to the hardware store, said you'd be by," she parked and got out, he opened the gate for her. As they walked into the house, the little black dog came out and greeted them, the barking getting Mary's attention. She turned to see the young woman.

"Who are you?" The old woman asked.

"I'm Elizabeth."

"I don't know you! You should go right now!" Mary yelled. "Bill! Bill!"

"No, no," Bill rushed to Mary's side. "This is the Anderson girl, you remember them, Alice and Daniel. This young woman, Elizabeth, is their daughter, you know her. You do, Mar."

Mary's eyes met Bill's. "If you say so," she looked so confused, and frail, her red-rimmed glassy eyes going back and forth between Bill and Elizabeth. The timer went off for the muffins and Bill got to his feet and put oven mitts on, he extracted them from the oven setting them on a rack to cool. Mary moved to the table, Elizabeth sat across from her. "Who are you?" Mary enquired of Elizabeth.

"Elizabeth." Elizabeth and Bill answered in unison. Mary looked confused, Bill set a warm muffin on a little plate in front of her and a steaming cup of tea.

"Would you like some tea?" Bill asked Elizabeth.

"Yes, thank you," she replied. He sat a cup of Earl Gray tea in front of her and a muffin on a matching plate.

Mary continued to stare at Elizabeth, and asked again, "Who are you?"

"Elizabeth?" This time her name came out as more of a question.

Bill smiled at Elizabeth. "Thanks for humoring her", he said then got himself a tea and muffin and joined the women. Just as he sat, Gaius appeared in the back door.

"Hi family!" Gaius exclaimed enthusiastically, "I've always wanted to say that, and now I have, felt so good, I'm going to say it again. Hi family!"

Gaius, after grabbing a muffin, plopped down in the last chair available and took a bite. "Best lemon poppy seed muffins I've ever had," he said chewing. Smiling at Elizabeth he added, "Hello my little Lizard."

Mary shouted, "Her name is Elizabeth!" Everyone looked at each other and suppressed their smiles.

"Yes, it is, Mar," Bill said just as jubilantly.

After tea, muffins and lively conversation, Mary announced, "I'm tired."

"Well Mary, you should be, it's that time of day." Bill got up and put his arm around her, helping her down the hallway. Gaius and Elizabeth cleared the table and they retrieved paint supplies and a bag full of chocolate brown and turquoise sheets from Gaius' truck. Grabbing one can of paint in each hand, Elizabeth started up the stairs with Gaius behind her.

"I noticed you changed out of your work clothes," he said.

"What do you mean?" she answered with a question. What did her mom recently tell her about answering a question with a question?

"Well, when I saw you at the thrift store, you looked like you were in work mode, ready to roll up your sleeves and dig in," he paused thinking about how to continue, "but now... um... don't get me wrong, you look great, just not dressed for gettin' grubby."

"Oh, these old clothes, no they're grubbies, I'm in work mode," Elizabeth did lie after she answered a question with a question, this was the nicest outfit she had except church clothes.

"Well, I just didn't want to get paint on your cute..." his words faded as she noticed him looking at her rear end. "Your cute... um... jeans. Yea, I don't want you to get paint on your cute jeans," he stuttered aware he was just busted checking out her ass.

"What are all the sheets for?" she asked dumping the bag out on the bed as he found a screwdriver and started removing the screws holding up the closet door.

"For the obvious little Lizard, I need sheets. But first I'm going to make a closet door. I can't stand these accordion style ones, then I'll make a couple little throw pillows and curtains so it all matches. This was a trick of my mom's when I was little. We would go to yard sales and buy sheets that kind of matched and she would make pillows, curtains, duvet covers, whatever with the sheets." The first door came free from the frame. He handed it to Elizabeth. "Can you carry this out, just leave it on the landing and I'll take it down to the truck when I get the other one off."

"I've got it," Elizabeth said, taking it from him and heading out of the room. She got to the truck and placed it in the back, before she could get back, Gaius was heading down the stairs with the second closet door.

"Thanks, you rock. Would you mind taping off the floor boards and door casing? If you can do that, I can follow with the paint brush." The room was done in a dark wood paneling with the trim painted dark brown. Gaius continued, "If we paint the trim white and clean the paneling really good with this," He held up a large container of Pledge lemon oil, "I think the whole room will look new. I didn't spend a lot of money because I'm not sure how long I'm staying, but I think with a little bit of effort, it will look grand."

Bill appeared in the doorway with what appeared like a walkie-talkie in his hand. He set it on the night stand and explained, "Gaius, I need to run to the grocery store, I only have about an hour before Mary wakes up, if you don't mind just listen in on her, if she wakes before I get back, just one of you go sit with her, probably you, son. She seems to know who you are a bit more."

"Is that a baby monitor?" Elizabeth asked recognizing the knobs and speaker.

"It is," he sighed. "I love that woman more than anyone knows but the only way I can get one minute to myself is to listen in on her, it's like taking care of a small child. I don't want her to wander off or hurt herself."

"No worries, Gramps, we got this." Gaius said smiling.

Bill noticed the supplies, "Thanks for your efforts in getting this room cleaned up and back to a usable space. I really appreciate all your help." Elizabeth noted the pain in the old man's face as he turned to leave. "Thanks again, I'll be right back."

Gaius picked up a gallon of paint and began to shake it vigorously as Elizabeth opened the wide blue masking tape. She bent over to start applying the tape above the floor boards when she distinctly felt Gaius' eyes upon her. Glancing at him from her bent over position, she became suddenly aware of herself and felt her face flush. Elizabeth straightened up, turned around and sat down, demurely smiling at him the whole time.

"Who knew you were such a distraction," he said, returning the smile and resuming shaking the paint can.

They worked in silence for a few minutes.

"So, what's your sign?" she asked, and cringed inwardly. It had sounded like a pick-up line from a horrible 80's movie.

"Oh," Gaius sounded surprised. "Are you into astrology?"

"No, not really," she looked up at him and smiled, "In fact, I'm not sure why I asked you that, just conversation, I guess."

"Well my little Lizard, I'm glad to see you're not so gullible that you would fall for hocus pocus, fortune tellers, but for the record, I'm a Taurus. If you go by what the astrologers say, that means I'm steady and reliable, creative and crafty, loyal and moody, which I'm not saying I'm not, but I bet those could be Leo traits too," he had begun to paint the inside of the closet with the roller.

"So you don't think there's anything to it?" Elizabeth asked."

"I don't know, Liz."

"Liz? Another nickname?" she rolled her eyes and smiled.

"No, Liz is short for Lizard, duh..." He regarded her with a don't-be-stupid look, smirked and giggled to himself. "So anyway, I think religion and astrology and all of that BS is much more simple than we make it. For example, back in the day, before Jesus' made up birthday, when Aries appeared in the sky, people knew it was time for their little lambs and goat kids to be born. Of course the weather was getting warmer, winter was obviously wrapping up, those were other obvious signs... When the stars changed to Taurus, it was time to breed and birth the bulls and cows, besides a person's sheep were already done and it's still too cold to plant the garden. All this was just a way of life."

"Christmas?" she said, completely distracted from her task by the conversation. "Did you just call Christmas, Jesus' made up birthday?"

Gaius laughed, "No offense, Elizabeth, but yes, people celebrated the Winter's Solstice long before Mr. Christ was around. It's a special day, when the sun starts moving south again, but it's nothing more than basic astrology." Secretly, she liked when he called her Lizard better than Elizabeth, but she didn't say anything about it. He continued, "Pagans used to decorate trees each year as an offering to the sun so the days would become longer again. They placed offerings, gifts, under them, but they didn't chop them down or anything like that, it took the Christians adopting that tradition and twisting it all up."

"Pagans?" she asked and resumed placing the masking tape above the floor boards.

"Yes, Pagans," he grinned, "Country dwellers that aren't committed or baptized into a specific religion." As he said those words, he heard his mother say them in his head, a moment of sadness washed over him. "Anyway, it's like those folks back then had to have words to live by, you know? The Astrological signs were born from there and morphed. Somewhere along the line, someone messed it up for financial gain. Ancient capitalism-"

"Bill," the voice was quiet at first, then a little more urgent, "Bill?!"

"Be right back." Gaius beamed at her, the moment of sadness gone. He bounded down the stairs and headed to the house. Elizabeth busied herself finishing taping off the floorboards and door molding. She started painting with the open paint as carefully as she could as to not get paint on her, she probably should have kept her sweats on instead of changing into the jeans. Since it was just the closet and the floor boards, the painting went fast and by the time Gaius returned, she had more than half of it done. "Lookin' good, my little Lizard, and the painting doesn't look too bad either," he flashed her that infectious smile.

"Ha, ha," she said back, "Thanks. Only have around the door and the one stretch there on the floor and we're done with the painting."

"I'm going to make the curtains with the sheets, I wonder if Grandma Mary has a sewing machine?" Gaius said, more to himself than to her.

"Well, if she doesn't, we do." Elizabeth added. "My mom has all that kind of stuff."

"Cool, do you think your mom would let me borrow it?"

"Let's just take the measurements of the windows and I'll do it. Ma has all the whistles and bells. It would be easier to do it there, not kidding," Elizabeth said thoughtfully.

"Okay," Gaius grinned as he threaded the sewn edge of the flat sheets through a tension bar. "Ta Da, closet doors," he said dramatically.

"They look good. We can polish the paneling too. This place is shaping up!" he said appraisingly.

Elizabeth surveyed their work. He was right, it did look good, much better than it had that morning when they had started. "So, I'll do the curtains tonight. Let me take those two sheets, did you want throw pillows too?"

"If you want to," Gaius said, a little sheepishly, "I don't want it to be a hassle or anything."

"It won't be," she answered, a little too quick.

"How about if I come over to help you with your room?" Gaius said, you could sew and I could paint, or whatever," he smiled encouragingly at her.

She laughed, "Oh, my room won't be as simple as yours, but I could use the help." As an afterthought, she said, "I'm going to invite Tish too, six hands are better than four." Elizabeth knew Tish liked Gaius, maybe this would be a good way for them to get to know each other, and get the room cleaned out a bit quicker so she could move in.

"This is true," his words sounded a little crestfallen, but it could have been her imagination. "I'll be over about ten tomorrow or is that too early?"

"No, ten's good," she answered, mentally checking when everyone should be gone from the house. Hopefully her mom would be busy. She took the two flat sheets and the paper with the measurements. "Ok," Elizabeth said, suddenly feeling awkward.

"Ok," Gaius said back, they looked at each other and after a pause both started talking at once.

"See you tomorrow."

"Thanks for all your help," Gaius followed her down the steps and opened the gate for her.

"You're welcome," she answered, grinning, "If only my room was going to be as easy as yours, you don't know what you've gotten yourself into," she could feel her face break into a full-blown smile. "My room currently looks like a storage unit, seriously, boxes floor to ceiling, crap everywhere!"

Their eyes met. "You're really pretty," he said.

"Thanks," she looked down and her stomach balled into knots. *On one hand, he's so cute and sweet, but on the other hand, Tish is my best friend.* "See you tomorrow." Elizabeth got in her truck and put it into drive. It only took her five minutes to get to her house, she had glanced at her phone when she pulled into the driveway. One missed call from Tish, two new texts. Elizabeth hit the icon for Tish's number and the phone began to ring as she walked into the house and put the keys back in the key bowl by the door. She headed up the stairs to the room with the sewing supplies.

Tish answered the phone, "Hey Chica, what's up?"

"Just making some curtains for your lover-boy." Elizabeth smirked to herself, knowing the few hours she had spent with Gaius would get a rise out of Tish.

"*My* lover-boy? Are you talking about Gaius?" The confusion in her voice was palatable. "You're making curtains for... Gaius?"

Elizabeth burst into laughter. "Tish you're so freaking cute! *Yes*! I'm making curtains for G," she tried out the nickname subconsciously. It felt nice. "When I texted you this morning it was because I ran into him at the D.I. We've been hanging out," she wanted the last sentence to come out emotionless, but even she could hear the excitement when she said it.

"What?!" Tish shouted. "O.M.G! Seriously, you didn't say anything about him this morning, I would have gotten up... What did you two do? Did he ask about me?"

"Cuteness Tish, you are full of cuteness," Elizabeth laughed. "How did I get so lucky to get a bestie as cute as you?"

"Why did you just answer my question with a question?" Tish said flatly.

Elizabeth laughed, "I'm going to move into Zeb's room, wanna come help me move some stuff to the garage tomorrow morning about ten-ish?"

"Yea, okay," Tish sounded suddenly bored.

"Gaius said he'd be here about that time too, so..." Elizabeth trailed off.

"So wear cute jeans and make-up! Gotcha, Sista! Woo-hoo! Can't wait! I've never been so excited to clean," Tish's voice was full of enthusiasm.

"You crack me up. See you tomorrow."

"Kisses."

"Kisses," Elizabeth disconnected. She rummaged around for a pair of scissors and measuring tape and started work on Gaius' curtains. As the afternoon turned to evening, her family returned from school and work. Alice had popped her head in and was pleased to see Elizabeth working on a project. She asked her if she needed anything and told her when dinner would be ready.

It was well after midnight when Elizabeth finished the pillows and curtains. She was exhausted and her eyes hurt, but it would be worth the extra effort to see Gaius' face light up. She fell asleep with thoughts of him on her mind and a smile on her face.

Chapter Twenty-Nine

Elizabeth got up a little before dawn the next morning. She sent a text to her brother, Zeb.

Taking over your room, anything you want to keep?

The return text came almost immediately. She should have known he was up and getting ready for work.

LOL, sis. Hasn't been my room since T and I got hitched. Good luck.

Smiling to herself, she slipped on her shoes and walked to the backyard towards the shed and thought about her older brother, Zeb. She had nothing but good memories of him.

Opening the shed, she saw she would be able to create a ton of room for the boxes in Zeb's room with just a little organization. Elizabeth went to work stacking, organizing and sorting the shed as the sun rose and her family woke and went off to their daily routines. Her mom came out and brought her a granola bar. "Don't forget to eat, sweetheart," she said, handing the snack to Elizabeth. "Looks good in here, but... why are you cleaning the shed?"

"Mom," Elizabeth looked directly into her mother's face. "I'm taking over Zeb's room. I believe I told you this days ago."

Alice sighed, "You did, but what does that have to do with the shed?"

"Where am I going to put all that crap?" Elizabeth asked exasperated.

Alice's answer came out defensively and caught them both off guard. "It's not crap! Do *not* throw anything away until I've gone through it," her eyes almost had a desperate, pleading look to them.

"I won't, ma. Just don't turn into a hoarder, that's all." They held each other's gaze for a few seconds, "Tish and G are coming over to help. Is that cool?"

"G?" Alice looked questioningly at her daughter.

"Yea, Gaius. Um..." she gathered her thoughts and avoided her mother's eyes. "Gaius... um... Smith? But I don't think that's his last name, he was with the Smith's on Sunday at church," she hoped adding that he was at church would leave a favorable impression on her.

Her mother sighed, "Tish is coming too?"

"Yea, she has a weird crush on him, or something. You know how Tish is," Elizabeth answered, sweeping the now cleared floor.

"Well, that's good. Enjoy your day, darling. Loves," Alice turned to leave.

"Thanks mom, love you too," she was surprised her mom hadn't said anything about having a boy at the house. Elizabeth found a dolly in the garage and started moving the food storage containers. At ten o'clock she was lifting a five gallon, sealed, bucket of rice onto an identical bucket of pinto beans in the corner of the shed when Gaius pulled up. She had a clear view of him from the door and watched as he looked into the rearview mirror. He combed his fingers through his hair and checked his teeth for bits of food. He climbed from the truck and she emerged from the shed, simultaneously, her cell phone received a text.

"Hey my little Lizard!" He said, his face fully lit up in an ear to ear smile.

"Hey G. Where's Sass?" she asked, removing her phone from her pocket and glancing at a text from Tish.

Overslept, OMW

"She's being lazy and stayed at my grandparent's house, looking out for Boo-boo and Mary. You know she's a working dog now."

"That's cool," Elizabeth acknowledged. "Tish is running late, surprise, surprise," she replaced her phone in her jeans pocket. "Ok, so check it out," Elizabeth said indicating the shed. He glanced in there and back to her. "Here's the challenge if you're up for it," she paused for dramatic affect. "We're going to take a ton of stuff that is currently, comfortably, sitting in a fifteen by fifteen bedroom and miraculously make it all fit into this four by six-foot shed space. Got it?"

He winked at her, "Got it."

She got the emptied dolly from the shed and muscled it out the door, he grabbed one side, she grabbed the other and they rolled it back to the house, shoulder to shoulder walking in long, lazy arcs, winding their way back to the house, neither saying anything until they reached the basement. "This is it." Elizabeth said, showing him the filled room and the little progress she had made.

"Wow," he said, surveying what needed to be moved, "this *is* going to be a magic trick."

"I think if we break it down to chunks, it'll be more manageable." Elizabeth said, her eyes scanning the disarray. "The food storage, to the shed. Anything that says 'Zeb' on the outside of the box needs to go to the truck. I'll take whatever to him later today or tomorrow. Anything that says 'Paul' can be moved to the room next to us. The boxes marked for me, let's just drag them to the family room and I'll go through them at my leisure. Giselle, Jozette's stuff, out to the shed... um..." Elizabeth could feel Gaius looking at her, she turned to meet his eyes.

"Have I mentioned how pretty I think you are?" Gaius said, looking her directly in the eye.

Blushing she looked at her feet, "Yea... I think you said that yesterday. Thank you." Gaius started to move towards her, one hand reaching out towards her waist. *Holy crap, he's going to kiss me!* She thought, almost manically.

"Elizabeth..." Tish sang her friend's name, each of the four syllables a different note, as she bounded down the stairs, the pressure of the room suddenly deflated by her presence.

Gaius and Elizabeth turned their attention to her and physically moved away from each other. Tish's eyes went from one to the other sensing the moment of awkwardness. "Good morning," she sang each syllable of that too and smiled radiantly at Gaius.

Overslept, my butt, Elizabeth thought, gauging her friend's appearance. Tish looked gorgeous! Her hair and make-up done perfectly, her outfit said 'let's work, or play' and her blouse showed just the right amount of cleavage. Elizabeth had always been a little envious of her best friend's perfect size C breasts. Hers were small, not even a B cup, cleavage wasn't an option. She hated wearing a bra though and sometimes didn't, and never slept in one as so many of her friends and companions did, *so there were upsides to being flat chested.* "Okay!" Elizabeth said in full blown cheerleader mode, "Let's get to work," she looked at Tish.

"Party pooper," Tish pouted at her friend.

"Takes one to know one," Elizabeth answered, turning on her iPod and plugging it into the portable speakers sitting on the entertainment center.

The three of them started moving boxes from the room, Gaius went up the stairs and retrieved the dolly and began moving the rest of the food storage to the shed, stacking the five gallon buckets as high as he could. Elizabeth and Tish drug boxes to the family room and Paul's room and together they carried some of the heavier ones up the stairs. The iPod kept them motivated while they worked.

About one o'clock, they surveyed what still needed to be done. The room looked like a room again, but the family room looked like a storage unit had puked in it. There were nine large purple, plastic bins stacked neatly by the bottom of the stairs, six of them said Christmas on the outside, three said Easter.

"You should probably leave the Easter ones out." Tish suggested, "Its next weekend, isn't it?"

"Or the weekend after that." Elizabeth said, "I'm not sure actually, but yea, probably a good idea. Let's move them to the garage."

"Easter is the first Sunday after the first full moon that follows the Spring Equinox. That's why it changes every year." Gaius said, looking at the girls.

"Huh?" Tish grunted and almost defensively said, "Easter is the celebration of Jesus' resurrection."

"Sure," Gaius said grinning at her, "that explains the rabbits and eggs for sure."

"Why are you so difficult?" Tish asked.

"Why are you so gullible?" Gaius retorted, starting up the stairs, backwards, with two of the Christmas boxes on the dolly, he slowly pulled it up. "So as the ancient fable goes," he began, his face becoming animated as if he were telling a story to children, "long before Christians took over these sacred holidays' celebrations, there was Eastre and the marvelous egg. So, the egg was a sacred symbol among the Babylonians. They believed a massive egg with a big 'ole rabbit painted on the side fell from the heavens into the Euphrates River. And the town's people are all, what's up with this egg? And it starts to break open and Eastre is hatched. She's all 'hi, I'm the Goddess of Spring and the rabbit is my totem animal'."

The girls looked at each other and giggled over Gaius' girlie goddess impersonation. They had reached the garage. Elizabeth spotted a ladder they would need to put the bins in the rafters. "I'm not buying it." Tish found herself becoming more and more defensive of a religion she worked at avoiding. "I'll stick with the truth, ever heard of the Bible?"

"Tish, Tish, Tish..." Gaius was shaking his head. Elizabeth glanced over her shoulder and noticed Gaius was starting at her backside as she climbed up the ladder. "Let's save the Bible conversation for another time, shall we? For the record, I don't believe any of it. It was written by a bunch of men two-thousand years ago, it's been translated and re-translated nearly to death. As for the resurrection story, have you ever heard of Attis, the Roman god of about two hundred B.C?" Tish shook her head and he continued. "So Attis," Gaius said, returning his eyes to Tish, "was believed to have been born from a virgin mother, on December twenty-fifth. Sound familiar?" he handed a box up the ladder to Elizabeth, "It was believed he died and was resurrected every year during the first week of spring, not just once, but every year! Horus was the same character in the Egyptian religion, born from a virgin mother, died, came back to life. Do the research, most religions aren't that different, maybe in name, but not in idealism."

Elizabeth started to climb back down. Gaius said, "Just stay there. Tish and I will go get another couple boxes. C'mon," he said, putting his arm around Tish and directing her back to the basement steps.

As Elizabeth witnessed the innocent act of affection, she felt a twang of jealously in her stomach. *Can't be*, she thought to herself, *I'm not attracted to Gaius. Him and his crazy beliefs and ideas, sure he's cute and all, but...* When he appeared back in the doorway carrying a much lighter bin, her face involuntarily broke into a smile, *Okay, maybe I'm more attracted to him than I want to admit.* She took the bin from him before he walked out saying, "Be right back."

"I'll be here," she called at him.

Gaius looked back and up at her as he left, his whole face smiling. Her heart melted as her stomach flipped. Moments later they were back with the last of the Christmas boxes. He left the two girls there and went back to get the boxes marked Easter. Tish was able to lift the lighter of the two boxes up to Elizabeth.

"He likes you," Tish said quietly to Elizabeth as she passed the purple bin to her friend. Elizabeth scrunched up her face and shook her head, placing the bin next to the others. "Yea, he does," And added with a Chinese accent, "you one lucky lizard."

Elizabeth laughed as Gaius reappeared with the dolly and two of the three Easter bins stacked on it. "Hey you two, you're not supposed to have any fun unless I'm here, ya' hear?" he grabbed the top bin and effortlessly handed it up to Elizabeth, smiling, then did the same with the second one. Tish walked down the steps to get the last bin marked Easter.

Gaius met her as she crested the upper floor. "Good job, Tough Stuff!" He said smiling. They each grabbed one side of the bin and walked it to the ladder in the garage. As they handed it up to Elizabeth the lid came loose. A few items slipped out. Elizabeth watched as Gaius and Tish steadied the box before more items could tumble and set it on the garage floor. Tish picked up two stuffed rabbits and a couple of baskets. "Hey, I've got one of these," Gaius exclaimed holding up a painted nest, "mine's painted a little different though."

"Really?" Elizabeth was genuinely surprised, "I think my mom made it in a ceramics class before she got married to my dad and had us; it's old. There are two little birds that go inside too."

"Yea, yea…" Gaius was nodding his head. He set it back in the bin, "mine too, male and female."

"Probably." Elizabeth answered even though Gaius hadn't really asked a question. Tish had repacked everything and was securing the lid. They lifted it to Elizabeth, she slid it into place and barely had enough room to turn and get her body positioned to climb down the ladder.

"What's next?" Gaius said, rubbing his hands together.

Elizabeth looked around before she answered. "Um, I think that's as far as we're going to get today, my mom's gotta go through that stuff," she indicated a pile of boxes and bags that had been placed together, "I'll vacuum and move my mattress down here, at least that."

"That carpet is nasty with a capital N!" Tish said, looking over the floor covering.

"Yea." Elizabeth sighed the word, "it's pretty gross."

"Would your folks get mad if we ripped it out?" Gaius asked, looking from one girl to the other.

"On that note, I'm gonna dip out." Tish said, moving to Elizabeth to hug her.

As their heads came together, Tish whispered, "Don't have *too* much fun." They looked at each other and Tish squinted her eyes and flattened her mouth into a quasi-dirty look, then broke into a full-blown smile, "Love ya', bestie."

"Love you too. Thanks for all your help today, I owe you."

"Bye Guy," Tish called, already climbing the stairs. She corrected herself, "Gaius."

"See ya' later, Tough Stuff," he called after her, then to Elizabeth, "What do you think?"

"About tearing the carpet out?" her eyebrows shot up in a surprised expression. "Are you serious? I don't have any money for new carpet, like seriously, I have no money," he had gone into the now empty room and pulled up the carpet in one corner.

"There's just cement under it," he tapped the corner of the carpet back down, "Let me think on this one, you ask your parents if we can pull the carpet, we'll figure it out together," his eyes were locked on hers. Her cheeks blushed.

"You're pretty," he said, smiling shyly.

"You've said that already," she also smiled and looked down, breaking their eye contact.

"And I'm going to keep saying it until you believe it yourself," he walked toward her and slipped his arms around her waist. She stiffened just a little not sure what her reaction was supposed to be, her knees literally felt weak.

"Look at me," he said softly. She looked up at him as he continued, "You're more than pretty, you're beautiful, from the inside out." Gaius bent his head to kiss her, she moved away and pulled from his embrace. "Sorry," he mumbled, it was his turn to look at his feet.

"It's..." she didn't know what to say, "It's... um... I don't know. Tish is my best friend."

"What does Tish have to do with anything?" he asked looking at her. Her silence said more than word ever could. "Oh no, no... no... Tish is a cute girl, has a great body, I'm not saying anything bad about her. Seriously though Liz, she's not my type."

"She does have a great body," Elizabeth agreed. "Awesome boobs, don't you think?"

"If one was into boobs, yes, she does. I however am an ass man," he winked and said, "You know Gaius, he's an *ass*, man," he laughed at his own joke. She did too.

"I can't jeopardize a twenty-year friendship for a guy, um... a man, I've only known a few days. She means a lot to me. Honestly don't know what I'd do without her."

"But she's not my type." The magical moment lost. "Awkward," he joked in an attempt to lighten the mood. "Subject change, did you get around to my curtains? I mean, it's no big deal if you didn't, I just..."

"Oh-my-gosh. Yes! Follow me," she started up the stairs with him right behind her.

"Man, you do have a nice ass."

"Gaius!" She laughed and shook her head, picking up speed, rounding the landing and headed up the second flight practically running. Elizabeth had the curtains hanging from a small rope, tacked against the wall, they were tied together in the middle with a turquoise bow creating an hourglass shape. They looked amazing, he saw the pillows she was holding, one in each hand. "I made two big ones and two round smaller ones that just accentuate, you know," she looked at him, searching for a reaction.

"Wow. Seriously, wow. I don't know what to say, these are... Wow!" Gaius looked truly impressed, he looked at every small detail she had added. "Mom's were never this fancy. Thank you."

That one look was worth staying up late, she thought to herself. "Your welcome. Thank *you* for all your help today, couldn't have done it without you, for real, wouldn't have happened. Grab the pillows, I'll grab the curtains." After loading the items into the cab of Gaius' truck, he climbed in and left the door opened, looking at her, not knowing what to say.

"See ya' Sunday at Sacrament?" she asked.

"Hopefully before that," he answered. "Thanks again, my beautiful little Lizard. By the way, where does Ord come from?"

"It's my mom's maiden name," she said, grinning at him, "well, for sure I'll see you Sunday and perhaps before," his smile made her knees weak, again. She watched his truck disappear and felt joyous, light, giddy. *I could fall in love with this man*, she thought as she floated back to the house.

Chapter Thirty

The week was uneventful. Elizabeth scrolled through her Pinterest and caught sight of a really cute outfit. It was a short black skirt and simple peasant style blouse with darts in the front and three ornamental buttons on one side of the scooped neck, the outfit was tied together by a stretchy belt with a silver buckle.

Giselle still hadn't moved into Elizabeth's old room. The sewing machine was still set up on the desk. There was much more room since Elizabeth had moved her twin-size bed to the basement. She started to dig through the boxes of fabric and patterns. She found an older vintage style pattern with a little modification, she could make it look a lot like the picture but long enough to accommodate her garments. She found the perfect black fabric too, a polyester blend that her mother had probably used to make a Halloween costume of one kind or another. There was also several yards of a white, gauzy material that would work for the blouse. Opening the box with buttons, she found three little silver and pink ones that would work perfectly, they were smaller than the ones on the Pinterest site, but they would look great.

Over the next couple days, both Tish and Gaius had sent texts to her, but she had returned their texts with *busy*. Tish was curious.

Busy doing what?
Sewing.
Sewing what?
You're so nosy.
As long as it's not a wedding dress, we're good.
It's NOT a wedding dress! LOL! TTYL

The skirt was the easiest item she made, the blouse turned out to be much more difficult. She added a lacy slip to the inside to hide her garments. Once she tried it on, she admitted how nice it turned out. Elizabeth also found a pattern for a summer jumper with spaghetti straps. She wouldn't be able to wear it. She decided to make it anyway since there was a perfect print fabric for it. She could always wear a half jacket over the top, or give it to one of her little sisters, she found a light denim material and started to make a short-sleeved button up blouse with simple white buttons and stitching, cutting the sleeves just slightly longer than the pattern.

On day three of not seeing Elizabeth, Tish just drove over to her house and walked in. It had been years since she knocked, no one did, everyone just walked in at the Anderson house. She called out her friend's name. "Elizabeth... Are you upstairs or down?"

"Up, in my old room." Came the answer.

Tish took the stairs two at a time and went into Elizabeth's childhood room. "Wow." Was all she could say walking into the room, there were scraps of fabric and thread everywhere, paper patterns were lying on the desk with scissors and straight-pins.

"Check it out." Elizabeth said proudly, holding up the skirt and blouse together as an outfit.

"Holy cow! You made this?" Tish asked.

"Yea, and this too," she showed her the jumper.

"Wow, wow, wow, can I have this please?!" Tish was already pulling off her shorts to try on the one-piece outfit. "This is so freakin' cute! You saw it on Pinterest, didn't you?" she had wiggled into the clothes and was re-tying the top to accommodate her breasts.

"It looks really cute on you," Elizabeth commented, "I wasn't sure how I was going to pull it off with my—"

"With your Jesus Jammies." Tish said playfully. Elizabeth shot her a dirty look. "By the way... You're good, this doesn't look homemade at all," she was admiring herself in the full length mirror on the back of the door.

"Thanks," Elizabeth acknowledged, "I'm wearing the other outfit to church on Sunday."

"Still trying to steal my boyfriend are you?" Tish teased.

"Maybe... Maybe you're not his type," Elizabeth treaded lightly, not meeting her friend's eyes.

"And you are?" Tish had one hand on her hip and her head cocked to one side.

"I didn't say that," Elizabeth stammered.

"And just what *is* his type?"

"I don't know," Elizabeth said, regretting bringing it up. How could she tell her best friend it was Gaius himself that had said Tish wasn't his type? How could she tell her best friend Gaius had wanted to kiss her?

"Never mind, you're right, I have no idea what his type is."

Tish sighed dramatically, "I hate to be right all the time, kiddo, but I was, I am…" Elizabeth waited. Tish took her time to finish, "He likes you, just like I said when we cleaned out Zeb's room, and here's the kicker, *you* like *him*!"

"I don't know," Elizabeth avoided her friend's eye.

"Oh please!" Tish whined, "You didn't make your hot new outfit to impress me. Admit it, you like him." Elizabeth could feel her face start to flush, she nodded. "It's cool." Tish went to Elizabeth and slung one arm over her shoulders and turned her so they looked together in the mirror at their reflections. "We've been through thick and thin missy, and no dumb dude is going to come between us. Go for it, he's yours, you have my blessing. Be happy."

Elizabeth turned to her friend and kissed her on the cheek, "You're the best."

"Well, I wouldn't go that far, but I am taking this outfit."

Chapter Thirty-One

Elizabeth had managed to avoid Gaius throughout the rest of the week. She had been coy about his texts, answering them but not being too wordy or inviting. In reality, she didn't know *how* to be around boys. She still thought of Maximus on occasion and wondered what he was doing, Wii bowling? The thought of his voice still made her pulse race. Really, the few visits to their house had been the only time in her life she had been alone with a man. *How pathetic*. She thought.

Sunday morning, Elizabeth tried on the new outfit, twirling she made the hem of the skirt bob up, exposing her garments. Being in the basement by herself gave her a new boldness. She stripped off the garments and put on the lace pink panties, and left her top naked. Her hair was loose, not combed, just a little bedhead. She moved to make the skirt move again, the lace panties barely peek-a-booed out. Elizabeth placed her hands over her bare breasts and moved her torso back and forth with more force.

Fall Out Boy's 'My songs know what you did in the dark' began playing on her iPod. She was lost in the music and watching herself in the mirror, it was hard to believe the sexy, lean woman in the reflection was her, she moved her head more so her hair swayed. Moving with the music, she danced, half naked, uninhibited, rubbing her hands up and down her torso. It felt so foreign to be... sexy.

"Elizabeth! Breakfast!" Jozette's pubescent voice screeched down the stairs, and the spell was broken.

Elizabeth suddenly felt chagrinned, embarrassed. Ashamed. "Be right up," she croaked, grabbing her garments. Taking off the skirt, she put the garments back on, and her pajamas over them and hurried up to breakfast, still feeling heat in her cheeks. She sat with the family and hoped her dad didn't call on her to say the blessing.

A few blocks away, Gaius' grandfather served him a biscuit, two strips of bacon and some scrambled eggs. Gaius opened the bread and made a breakfast sandwich, then clasped his hands in his lap and waited for the prayer before he started eating. It hadn't taken him long to get used to this custom in the Smith's home. Bill noticed the breakfast sandwich and smiled at Gaius, "Kim used to do that," he said gently. He bowed his head and prayed, blessing the food and thanking God for Gaius.

"Amen." All Gaius could think about was seeing Elizabeth. She had been busy all week since their cleaning adventure. He had gone to the thrift store and found some khakis and a short-sleeved shirt, after washing and ironing them. The outfit definitely looked better than what he had worn last week. He had really been hoping for something a little more in-style. Shopping at a thrift store in Pleasant, Utah, his options were limited.

Church started and ended on time this week. When Sacrament meeting was over, the young adults converged in the foyer as the rest of the churchgoers found their way to their next meeting. Gaius reached Elizabeth before Tish did. "You're pretty," he whispered, she looked at her feet, "more than pretty, beautiful."

Tish approached them as several other churchgoers moved down the hallway. "Blondie's?" she asked, her eyes moving from Gaius to Elizabeth and back to Gaius.

"Thought you'd never ask." Gaius smiled at Tish and they both turned to Elizabeth.

"I should probably go to Sunday school."

"Yea, there are a lot of things I should probably do, for real, a *lot*, but..." Tish took her friend's arm and started walking towards the door, "A girl's gotta eat!"

Gaius followed, enjoying the view. Once they were in the parking lot, Tish looked at Gaius, "Yours or mine?" she asked, Gaius looked confused. "Vehicles, do you want to take your truck or my car?" Gaius shrugged. Tish continued in a Gypsy accent, "Your beauty is blinding, so much so, the man cannot even speak," she turned to Gaius and said normally, "Let's take yours, then my folks may still think I'm here if my car's here, capisce?"

"Capisce," Gaius repeated. He couldn't keep his eyes off Elizabeth. She looked so put together this week. Her clothes fit her perfectly, and complimented her figure. The skirt was shorter than last week and showed a little leg. She was wearing make-up, but it wasn't overly done. Gaius had never seen her hair down. She always had it pulled into a singular ponytail, or two long braids. Today it was flowing off her head, down her slim neck and poured over her shoulders in a golden sheath.

His heart raced just being near her. Gaius was glad Tish insisted on sitting next to the door putting Elizabeth in the middle for the short ride to the diner.

Frida greeted them and retrieved menus from under the cashier's podium.

"Sunday, Fun day." Tish sang ambling over to the same booth from the week before. Elizabeth followed, "After you my dear." Tish said in an English butler accent.

Elizabeth laughed and climbed into the semi-circular booth, Gaius noticed Frida taking a long look at Elizabeth's backside. "You look nice today, Elizabeth." Frida said, handing each of them menus, "I mean, you look nice all the time, but today, you look especially nice."

"She *made* her outfit!" Tish shouted, obviously impressed, "By hand."

"No, really?" Gaius exclaimed.

"Wow, impressive, totally." Frida said, "Your hair looks nice down like that too, I don't remember you wearing it like that before." Turning to Gaius she asked, "Coffee?"

"Yes, please," he said turning over his cup.

"I'm getting the same thing I had last week." Tish said.

"Yea, I'm getting the same thing, too." Elizabeth said.

"So, if I remember right, breakfast burrito for you, Tish? Biscuits and gravy for you, Elizabeth? Bacon, extra crispy. Cheeseburger and fries for you, young man?" Frida was smiling as she took the menus from Tish and turned to Gaius.

"Throwing a curve ball at you, Frida, my friend, I'll have the B.L.T."

"You have an advantage because I'm wearing a name tag, I'm not sure we've officially met."

"I'm Gaius" He said, full faced smile, offering his hand for her to shake.

"As in Baltar of Battlestar Galactica?" Frida asked, offering him a firm handshake.

"Kind of. Um… I'm not a doctor and I've never explored the final frontier, but yes."

"You're getting Star Trek and Battle Star Galactica mixed up," she said flatly and added, "Fries with the B.L.T?"

"Yes, ma'am." Gaius added sugar and cream to his coffee and stirred.

"Look, the Sunday paper!" Tish held up the periodical. "Wonder what my horoscope is this week," she opened the paper and began reading. "Sagittarius: When you notice miracles, more miracles will happen. Don't be surprised if there is a new adventure taking you far from home. Your dreams are within reach. Woo *hoo*!" Tish whooped, "I'm ready for a new adventure."

"What does Scorpio say?" Gaius asked, a half-cocked grin on his face. Elizabeth shot him a questioning look.

"Okay, Scorpio: A change of scenery would be good for you. Life is like a slate, able to be cleaned at will. Look at your life as if it were brand new and let the old fade away. Oh my, gosh!" Tish exclaimed, "That's so right on, it's crazy!"

"What does Taurus say?" Gaius asked without additional comment. Tish looked at Elizabeth, shrugged and read. "Your career may be the only thing keeping you sane. When others argue, don't play into it. Take care of yourself before you can take care of anyone else." When she was done, she asked, "Who's a Taurus?"

"I am," Gaius grinned.

"Who's a Scorpio?"

"My mom," he said grinning, "who is deceased, let me remind you. I'm sure that change of scenery is really working for her. Those things are junk, they could apply to anyone, no one reads all twelve of them so, something will fit in your life. Like with the Taurus, the last line, take care of yourself before you can take care of anyone else, really? That applies to everyone! For real. Lizard here is a Leo, read hers."

Tish obliged, "Leo: A new love may appear unexpectedly, unlike any partner you've ever had. Be open to dreaming your own dream, when you do, you will inspire others."

"Well bingo! You're pretty damn inspiring, Lizard." Gaius said grinning. "And I sure hope that new love appears to you sooner than later," he winked at Elizabeth as Tish refolded the paper and placed it on the bench beside her.

"Why'd you tell me you were a Scorpio?" Tish said.

"I didn't, just asked you to read Scorpio. I'm telling you, they all apply to everyone, or not, seriously, it's just a load of B.S."

Frida appeared with the food. "What sign are you?" Gaius enquired.

"Leo." Frida said setting the plates before them.

"Liz is too," Gaius beamed, "according to today's horoscope, you'll be happy to learn that a new love like none you've ever had may appear unexpectedly."

Frida didn't comment, just smirked and nodded. Elizabeth side-stepped the horoscope issue and moved her attention to her food. They all began to eat. After several bites, Elizabeth remembered they hadn't blessed the food. Should she say anything? She had also started eating, instead she listened into the conversation Tish and Gaius were having about the history of the zodiac signs.

"Yea, the Leo in the sky would warn the people to watch their children and animals because the lions of the area were looking for easy food. Its summer, it's hot, not a lot of game to hunt. The Virgo is the celebration of the harvest. Libra is about selling their products and produce."

"The scales!" Tish interrupted.

"Yes." Gaius smiled, "The scales, time to sell the fruits of your labor. The Scorpio in the sky meant to keep your boots upside down as to not offer them as comfy beds for the scorpions."

"Really?" Tish was enthralled with the conversation.

Gaius nodded and continued, "Sagittarius was the time to hunt game, deer, elk. Capricorn was the time to gather around the fire and tell stories, I mean, c'mon, it's the middle of winter, right? What else were people from thousands of years ago going to do while sitting around trying to keep warm?"

"It kinda makes sense," Elizabeth said looking at Tish.

"It's just weird how accurate those horoscopes can be," Tish replied.

"Nawww..." Gaius drew out in a long breath, "People will believe what they hear and see; that's all. Astrologers, psychics and televangelist bank on people like you, Tough Stuff."

"You don't believe in psychics either?" Tish asked.

Gaius shook his head as he ate his fries. "People are people. They aren't too hard to figure out, especially if you pay attention, you know, watch a person. If you want to label that psychic, well... I'm psychic enough to know Frida wouldn't go out with me," he swirled the last fry over the last of the ketchup on the plate.

The girls exchanged a look that seemed to ask *would he go out with Frida?* When she returned to the table Gaius smiled and asked. "What are you doing next weekend, Frida?"

She looked confused and looked to the girls for help. They just stared at her. "Workin', probably," Frida answered.

"Maybe we could get together when you're off. My schedule is totally flexible," he smiled at her, a look that melted Elizabeth. She wished he was asking her out and smiling like that. Frida looked again at Tish and Elizabeth in confusion, they both shrugged.

"Are you kidding?" Frida put a hand on her hip and stared directly at Gaius. He shook his head and looked very sincere. "Thanks, but, no. I'm actually in a committed relationship," She said, "um... you're super cute, I bet Tish or Elizabeth here would love to go out with you. Tish you should take this fine looking young man on a tour of our beautiful little town." Frida smiled at the three of them and continued to clear the table. "Can I get you guys anything else?" They declined needing anything at that moment. Frida assured them they could take their time; it was a slow day.

Once she was out of earshot, Gaius grinned at Tish. "Told you, but it's not because I'm psychic, it's because I'm observant. My guess is she would be more interested in one of you two than me." Gaius had a mischievous look on his face.

"Frida? Gay?" Tish's eyebrows were raised in surprise.

"Girls are lesbians, boys are gay." Elizabeth said almost inaudibly.

"Hmm, who knew?" Tish said taking a drink of her iced tea. Elizabeth shot her a dirty look.

"So, want me to give you a psychic reading, Elizabeth?" Gaius said, a playful smirk on his face.

"No, thank you kindly." Elizabeth had a hard time meeting his eyes, "Perhaps you should be psychic with Tish." Elizabeth knew Gaius was up to something. She did not want him to make her feel naïve, or ignorant.

"I thought you said you didn't believe in psychics." Tish was wary now.

"I believe everyone is psychic, and no one is psychic. Here take my hands, I'll show you," he reached across the table for Tish to take his hands. Gaius bowed his head and closed his eyes, Tish looked at Elizabeth, she shrugged. Tish bowed her head and struck a similar posture. After about five seconds, Gaius sat up, his eyes wide. "Tish, I'm getting something!" A look of genuine concentration spread across his face as he continued. "You feel so trapped in this town, your parent's are pressuring you to go to school or..." He paused for dramatic effect. "Find a man? But you feel like you're too young for that, you just want to enjoy your life. It's a big world out there, you want to explore it, see places and meet people. You feel too young to settle down or make lifelong career choices. Your family doesn't understand you and they don't understand why you don't connect with them more but you feel you have nothing in common with them. If you had the means and the support, you'd leave this place tomorrow and never look back." There was a moment of silence, Gaius suppressed a grin; his lips tightening as he tried his best to keep a straight face. Tish looked at Elizabeth, shook her head, and threw her arms around her and began to cry. Gaius was confused, the laughter quelled. "What's wrong?" he asked. Elizabeth looked over her friend's shoulder at Gaius, bewilderment across her face.

Tish's episode began to subside. She blew her nose loudly. "Oh. My. Gosh. Totally, Gaius, wow..." Tish choked out, "no one has ever described me so well, been able to verbalize the way I feel. I don't know how you just did that, but... wow... I don't know what to say."

Gaius' eyebrows knitted together and he stared in astonishment at Tish, Elizabeth had her arm protectively around her friend. "Uh, I don't know how to tell you this, Tough Stuff, but I made all that up, I was totally pulling it out of my ass based on the little bit I know about you."

"What!?" Elizabeth gasped. "Are you serious?"

"Jerk?!" Tish declared.

"C'mon, now. Don't be mad. I did it just like professional psychics," Gaius began to explain, "I used educated guesses. I watched your body language. I kept it vague, like the horoscopes. Unlike professional psychics, I didn't charge you a bunch of money. I am sorry I made you cry though, that was purely unintentional."

"You butthead!" Tish cried, "Why would you do that to me? You suck!"

Elizabeth nodded, "Yea G, that was a crappy thing to do."

"What'd I do?" Gaius questioned, "For real, I didn't say anything Tish didn't already know about herself. Why would you get mad at me for that? So, I was only trying to make a point. Millions of people pay billions of dollars to have scam artists do what I just did. Guess. Psychics are nothing but overpaid actors, except they don't actually contribute *anything* to society, they're scammers. It's the same with the horoscopes, it would be okay if it were free, but most folks can't afford to pay for information they already know. A therapist would be better. Seriously, imagine what that money could do used in a positive context, like say free psychological therapy for those that need a stamp of approval," he looked at the girls, their faces blank. "Or education or the arts, or dog rescues, or park and recreations, or financial help to single mothers. Seriously, like *anything* else!"

"Well, thanks for telling me what I should have already known about myself," Tish had thoroughly composed herself. "I guess you're right. Who am I kidding, anyone who knows me, knows my frustrations," she giggled to herself, the mood at the table lightened. "Sorry I got so upset, you really did nail it."

"Looks like my keen perception was right-on on the Frida front too." Gaius tilted and nodded his head towards the counter where a young woman was sitting. The waitress was being fed a French fry by the young lady, the two of them looking deeply into each other's eyes. It was obvious from the look on Frida's face, she was smitten.

"Isn't that Laurie Rasmussen?" Tish asked. She recalled bumping into Laurie at the grocery store. Her cart was scant with a few Valentine's Day items, a bouquet of flowers, chocolates and a card. "Now that I think about it, she seemed a little embarrassed when I asked her if she was seeing anyone. She said yes, but it was no one I knew, and I said, 'really? I know almost everyone around here, what's his name?' and she said 'Free' and then corrected herself as if she didn't know the name of her own boyfriend and she said 'Fred, Freddie.' And that was it. But it was Free at first, you don't think she's... I don't believe it, seriously, I've known Laurie my whole life. Gay?"

"I think we *all* have a 'gay meter', you know?" Gaius said quietly. "C'mon, we've all looked at someone the same sex and thought, 'damn, that's hot'. Yup, I think everyone's a little gay...or lesbian in this case."

The trio stared in silence at the two young women. It was obvious to Gaius just by the easy way the two made each other smile they were in love. Eventually Frida noticed them, "Can I get you guys anything else?"

"No, we're good," Gaius said smiling and put the money on the table for the tab and tip. Tish had stood and started walking to the exit as Elizabeth climbed out of the booth.

"Wouldn't have believed it if I hadn't seen it with my own two eyes," Elizabeth said softly to Gaius.

"Tune in next week," Gaius said in a mock 1940's style television announcer's voice, "same time, same place. Same great channel," he smiled wide at Elizabeth and offered her his arm.

"Tune in weekly to the Sinners' Club!" Tish said enthusiastically as she banged open the front door with a flare of gusto and strolled out, the other two arm in arm behind her.

Chapter Thirty-Two

After church on Sunday, the Anderson family pulled the bins of Easter decorations from the garage rafters. Alice walked over and popped the lid off one of the boxes while Jozette opened another one. Alice extracted the birds nest and held it up for her daughters to see. "Look, I made this, years ago before I had Zeb. Another lifetime ago," she laughed humorlessly.

"Gaius said he had one similar but it was painted different," Elizabeth interrupted, "I wonder where he got it."

"The one he has is probably Sister Smith's. She was the teacher. In fact, she taught the relief society and the boy scouts ceramic classes for years!"

"No kidding," Elizabeth pondered this new discovery.

"Oh yes, Sister Smith was quite a talent in her day."

Each of the girls grabbed a bin and followed their mother into the house. By dinnertime, the contents of the three bins were distributed throughout the house and yard.

Elizabeth thought of the information Gaius had told her about the history of Easter. The Mormon religion was relatively new. Easter seemed to be around much longer, the Catholics celebrated it and that religion was centuries older than the Mormon's. "Wonder why we decorate with rabbits and eggs?" Elizabeth asked as much to herself as anyone else in the room.

"Easter is all about our Redeemer as we celebrate His triumph over death each year," Alice said whimsically."

But what about the eggs and rabbits? Elizabeth thought. Perhaps Eastre was the explanation and Gaius was right. The house phone rang and Jozette reached it first, after a moment, she called her dad.

"It's for you? No idea who it is," she said, handing the receiver to her father.

"Hello," Daniel chimed. He listened for some time and continued, "Well, I'm sure it was a misunderstanding." Another long pause. "I don't understand; it doesn't sound like him," his brow furrowed in frustration. "Another missionary? Said what?" The color had drained from his face and his hand shook slightly, "Okay bishop, I'm sure you and the other leaders know what is right. I'm sure you've reviewed the evidence and have..." More silence, "Yes, yes, of course. Okay. Thank you. Yes, yes it was nice to talk to you too. I will, bishop, thank you. Goodbye," he hung up and turned to Alice.

"What? Is everyone alright?" her eyes wild, searching between him and her daughters.

"It's Paul," Daniel's eyes were moist. He was fighting a flood of emotion.

Alice's eyes grew wide, "Is he okay?"

"Yes. No. He'll be home tomorrow," Daniel explained. Tears sprung to Alice's eyes. "There was an incident, involving another missionary, um a..." Daniel stalled for words, "um... I don't know the whole story. I'm sure it's wrong, I'm sure it's lies and someone has something out for him, but..." Alice's tears started to come more rapidly as Daniel continued, "Bishop said that it has become more and more common with missionaries nowadays, the way society in general is becoming more and more... sinful... there's a possibility he may be excommunicated, I guess that's happened to other missionaries in his same situation."

"For what?" Alice implored. "What situation? What are the accusations?" her voice was washed-out and she took a deep breath to calm her nerves.

"There was..." Daniel started but was momentarily overwhelmed with emotion, he continued, "There was-" Daniel stammered. "It involved, um...inappropriate conduct."

"Excommunication? What could have been so bad?" Alice asked as Daniel put his arms around his wife.

"We need to hear the whole story," Daniel comforted. "We need to hear Paul's side before we can make a judgement on anything."

"Oh Daniel, this is terrible. What are people going to say?" she sobbed into his chest. Elizabeth turned away from her parents and rolled her eyes with flourish. *It's always about what other people are going to say,* she thought as she walked downstairs to her room.

Chapter Thirty-Three

Gaius rose early and made himself a half pot of coffee from a virtually new Mr. Coffee machine he found at the D.I. He figured it was worth the seven bucks since he didn't have to get dressed and leave the house to get his early morning brew. He used one of his mother's cups that they had picked up on a vacation to Texas. During the same D.I trip, he found a green Coleman cooler. He froze zip lock bags of water and put them in the cooler with his cream and sugar, as well as a few bottled waters and occasionally, a Coca Cola. It served as a makeshift fridge and also offered him his own private space while giving his grandparents their privacy. He enjoyed joining the older couple for their brunch and tea. After, while Mary took her nap, the routine often changed. Sometimes Bill went to the grocery store, or Gaius took Sass to the dog park. Their private conversations often diverted to the old truck in the backyard.

Gaius guessed right, it was a 1968. Bill had told him the story of getting it for Kimball when he turned eighteen, an indulging gift for their only child. He and his son had rebuilt the 327 engine together. Eventually they had the short-bed C10 truck painted red and white with custom pin stripes. Gaius could see at one time it had been a beauty. Idleness, age and the sun had begun rotting it.

During one of their conversations, Bill had asked Gaius if he could stay with Mary every Thursday so he could go to Provo to volunteer at the Missionary Training Center or do temple work, explaining he had to give it up when Mary started needing full-time care, but he had missed it terribly.

"Of course. No problem, Gramps," Gaius had said accommodatingly, although he had no idea how they trained missionaries or what 'temple work' meant.

The first Thursday Gaius was in charge of his grandmother was uneventful. Bill had slipped out while the Today show was still on. Gaius had followed their morning routine to the letter. While Mary napped Gaius began tinkering with the truck. He kept the baby monitor hanging from a belt loop. When she woke, he brought her to the back patio where she seemed content watching the dogs play. Observing her from the corner of his eye while he worked on the truck, he saw her swirl her hand around on the patio table and nod her head as if to a tune. When he asked her what she was doing she replied she was reminiscing about painting.

"Painting?" Gaius had asked.

"Yes," she answered, her eyes lighting up with the memory. "I used to love painting ceramics, in fact I used to teach ceramic classes at the community college, years ago."

"Really? Wait here, grandma. I have something I want to show you," he ran in to the garage and grabbed the box marked fragile. "I found these in the closet." Gaius said, opening the box. Technically, it wasn't a lie. He *had* found them in a closet, he just hadn't mentioned it was his mother's in Colorado.

First he took out the birds' nest and two birds. Mary's eyes lit up. "Oh my!" she exclaimed, "I haven't seen these in years! I thought they got sold in a yard sale." Gaius had unwrapped all three pieces and put them together on the table. Mary tentatively picked up the male bird. "When you do a piece like this, the glaze is applied by dry dusting a mixture over the surface of the piece you're working on or with salt or soda or, like with this bird, you can apply it with an airbrush," she picked the female bird up with her other hand. "Then you put it in a kiln at a high temperature…Years ago, the advanced class I taught did these three pieces so the students could experiment with a variety of glazes," she looked at the other pieces Gaius had extracted from the box, placed the two birds in the nest and continued. "The beginner classes did only one glaze, usually we did nativity sets, dipping them into the glaze and sometimes an over-glaze. Then there were the vases the intermediate classes made. These are ones I made, look here are my initials," she turned one of the vases over exposing the MRS 85, "The other one was before I started putting my signature one them," she picked up the vase with the KS 91 on the bottom. "Kimmy made this one when he took my class. This is such a great example of the effect you can get with a glaze over another glaze. The flower was a dipped piece he attached at the end, it combined two techniques. It was always one of my favorite pieces. You said you found this in the closet?"

He nodded. No need to tell her which closet.

Her face had a far-away look as if there was some piece of information regarding the earthenware she couldn't quite put her finger on. "I really thought these all got sold, years ago."

Gaius made grilled cheese sandwiches for dinner before Wheel of Fortune started. Thinking about Elizabeth, he couldn't wait to tell her about the pottery. He decided he would ask her to join him next Thursday for his grandma-sitting adventure, the thought made him smile. Three more days until Sunday, three more days to see her. Church wasn't really his thing, but he did enjoy walking in with his grandmother and walking out with Elizabeth and Tish. The diner lunch was a bonus. He was definitely enjoying the blooming relationship with the two girls. Thinking about their Sunday rendezvous, he also thought about the waitress; it even felt like a friendship was blooming with Frida.

Monday morning, he joined his grandparents for breakfast with his 'Everything's Bigger in Texas' cup of coffee. Bill's demeanor seemed a bit more rigid this morning, more on edge. Gaius' gut feeling was to just go with the flow.

"Son, have you ever heard of the Doctrine and Covenants?"

"Nope," Gaius said grinning, "but I bet you're going to tell me about it." He took a bite of muffin.

Bill looked anxious, "The book originally contained two parts; a sequence of lectures setting forth basic church doctrine, followed by a compilation of important revelations or covenants. Hence the name, Doctrine and Covenants."

"Okay," Gaius said cautiously.

"So as I was saying," Bill took a book of scriptures from the counter and opened it to a passage that was bookmarked and highlighted and handed it to his grandson. Gaius began to read.

> ...And, behold, this should be wine, yea, pure wine of the grape of the vine, of your own make. And, again, strong drinks are not for the belly, but for the washing of your bodies.
>
> And again, tobacco is not for the body, neither for the belly, and is not good for man, but is an herb for bruises and all sick cattle, to be used with judgment and skill.
>
> And again, hot drinks are not for the body or belly.

And again, verily I say unto you, all wholesome herbs God hath ordained for the constitution, nature, and use of man every herb in the season thereof, and every fruit in the season thereof; all these to be used with prudence and thanksgiving.

Yea, flesh also of beasts and of the fowls of the air, I, the Lord, have ordained for the use of man with thanksgiving; nevertheless, they are to be used sparingly; And it is pleasing unto me that they should not be used, only in times of winter, or of cold, or famine....

"Okay," Gaius repeated. He got the gist of what it was supposed to convey but was wondering where his grandpa was going with it, "What does all that mean exactly?"

"Well, son, it's the Lord's doctrine. Our bodies are our temples and keeping them pure and holy is what we strive to do. The word of wisdom is the guiding scripture for maintaining that purity. It's advising against the use of certain substances." Bill gave a hard look at Gaius giant coffee mug.

"So why do you drink Earl Grey tea?" Gaius said trying not to sound flippant or disrespectful.

"We drink tea to avoid body altering substances like caffeine-"

Gaius cut him off, "But Earl Grey tea has caffeine in it. It's black tea, that's where the *black* comes from, the caffeine. White or herbal teas probably don't have as much caffeine in them, but are still served hot," he took another bite of his muffin.

"That's not true," Bill stammered, "we get the caffeine-free kind, it's simply not true."

Gaius wondered if he was repeating that to convince himself. "Hmm... caffeine is a natural occurrence, it's not something added like a chemical, I'm sure there *is* caffeine-free Earl Grey, but I bet yours is just the regular caffeinated kind. I've wondered how Grandma Mary can go to sleep after a cup every morning, its mind boggling, maybe it has the opposite effect on her. I've heard of that happening. Anyway... caffeine, it's all natural." Gaius looked thoughtful and skimmed back over the highlighted page. "So you don't eat corn, rye or oats? We've eaten corn, and oatmeal is oats, right?"

Bill's expression was hard as he took the book from the young man.

Gaius ate more of his muffin. After a few moments, he added, "It's obviously not a you're-going-to-go-to-hell commandment if you don't follow it to the letter, more of a guideline to stay healthy. I think there is some room for interpretation here, Gramps. For example, it says grains may be used for mild drink, which could be referring to beer, and it specifically says it's okay to make, and *drink*, your own wine, sure for worshiping, but wine is wine. And..." He slid the open book back in front of him and re-read parts of the scripture to himself and continued. "Okay, like this part about using herbs in season could be talking about marijuana. It's as much of a medicine as tobacco, probably more. Pure tobacco also has medicinal qualities, oh and this line about those that remember to do these things will have health in their navel and marrow to their bones, well... duh... of course if you live a healthy lifestyle, you'll be healthy. Right? Truly, Gramps it sounds like good advice, but totally left to the reader's interpretation. And when was this written? My guess is couple centuries ago." Gaius looked up into his grandfather's face. Bill's mouth was set firm, his jaws tight, eyes narrowed, his forehead furrowed. "Alright, Gramps, my interpretation of this passage is to do things in moderation, don't eat a lot of meat, don't drink too strong of wine, nor smoke too strong of smoke, avoid things that don't contribute to your overall health and if you do that you'll be strong and healthy which of course is true because there is a scientific validity to taking care of oneself."

Without warning, Bill slammed his fist onto the table causing both Gaius and Mary to jump. "Do *not* tell me how to interpret my own scriptures!" he bellowed, "Do *not* tell me that cannabis and beer and caffeine are all acceptable based on *your* analysis! These scriptures were translated from God so it doesn't matter how old they are! It's God!" Mary's eyes had grown wide, they twitched between her husband and grandson, her mouth formed in a delicate 'o'.

Gaius didn't want to upset Mary and certainly didn't want to cause further distraught to his grandpa. "Well, it is sound advice, I'm sure it wouldn't hurt a person to live by those rules." In his mind he thought, *this could be the very first written documentation on living a healthy lifestyle, Deepak*

Chopra, seventeenth century style. He realized Bill was talking to him and began listening, trying to look interested.

"... they'll be here Tuesday evening about seven, we'll prepare dinner for them and you can start the lessons." Bill must have noticed the confused look on Gaius' face. "The missionaries, I've invited them over so you can do the lessons. I'm sure they will be able to answer all your questions and I'm sure it will be very enlightening and educational."

Mary's eyes crept to watch Gaius' reaction. He looked at her, and back to his grandfather. "Sure, I'll meet the missionaries." Church was now bleeding out of Sunday and soaking into his week. His first thought, how could he incorporate Elizabeth into it?

Chapter Thirty-Four

Gaius scratched Boo-boo behind the ears, and began cleaning the kitchen. Bill returned from helping Mary get ready for her nap and started helping. "Sorry if I came across gruff, Gaius." Bill apologized. "There's just so much to gain from opening your heart and learning about Jesus Christ. You are a child of God and He loves you."

"Appreciate it, Gramps. It's cool. I've gotta say, and I mean no disrespect, but... church is for sinners," his grandfather glared at him and looked as if he were about to say something. Gaius didn't give him the chance. "I'm a science guy though, just a warning."

Bill nodded once. "Have a little faith, son." They finished cleaning the kitchen, Bill sat to read his scriptures. Gaius headed to his room. He loved the way it had turned out and had to remind himself it was temporary. Elizabeth's curtains and pillows had certainly enhanced it. Even though it was hard to tell, Bill had seemed pleased too.

Picking up his phone from the charger, he was surprised to see the text from Elizabeth. It had come in only twelve minutes before.

> Hey G, busy?
> Hi Lizard! What's up?
> Some family stuff. Need help moving more boxes, lol!
> Np
> Awesome!
> Got a favor to ask you too.
> Sure. (?)
> I'll ask you in person. Be by soon, need anything?
> No. TY.

Popping his head in through the door, he asked Bill, "Do you mind if I leave Sassafras here for a bit? I'm going to go help Elizabeth Anderson again, she said they had some type of family something-something come up."

Bill nodded once. "Hope everything is okay, and yes, Sass is always welcome to stay here. I think she's good for Boo-boo, giving him a little friend. He has been so much more active."

Gaius looked at the two dogs laying together by Mary's empty recliner. "Thanks," he looked at the old man, reading his book of scriptures. Gaius cleared his throat. "I want you to know I appreciate you opening your house to me and that I wasn't dis-ing on your word of wisdom or anything like that. Your church is cool for you. Just not for me. And I certainly meant no disrespect to you, Gramps, like I said. I totally, agree, the word of wisdom sounds like great advice. We're cool?"

"It *is* great advice." Bill raised his eyes to meet his grandson's. "There's so much for you to learn, Gaius. I'm happy you're here, happy you've become a part of our lives, Mary's happy you're here. We're just so excited for you to learn about the gospel. This is a big part of our lives and we want to share it with you. I think you'll be glad you did." *There's so much for you to learn*, Gaius thought to himself. *Starting with factual, provable science, let's see, like biology, ecology, zoology, just to start with*. He bit his tongue. "Tell Ms. Anderson I said hello. Could you plan on staying with Mary on Thursday so I can volunteer at the MTC?" Bill asked.

"Sure thing, Gramps. See you in a bit."

Gaius pulled into the Anderson's driveway as Elizabeth appeared from the house, carrying a large laundry basket full of folded towels. Noticing she was walking towards her truck, he veered and opened the tailgate. She set the basket in the back.

"Hi." Just looking at her made him smile. Her hair was back in a ponytail, she was wearing a baggy tee shirt and black yoga pants. He could see the outline of some type of longer shorts under them. Maybe not as sexy as a 'whale tail', the distinct outline of a pair of thong panties, but to him, it was all Elizabeth so it was sexy enough.

"Hi," she smiled at him. "Thanks for coming on such short notice. My brother, Paul wasn't supposed to be back until later this year, but, surprise, he's home."

"Didn't you just come home early too?" he winked at her playfully. "I think I remember catching something like that at our first brunch at Blondie's."

"Yes, but not the same thing, well, kind of... I don't know, I didn't have inappropriate conduct with another missionary."

"Well, you should maybe think about stepping up your inappropriate behavior," his eyes bore into her and his smile was devilish.

She looked away and felt a little flush in her cheeks. "Um, okay, I'll get right on that," she rolled her eyes. "Anyway, I'm not sure what's going on with my little brother. He can be difficult, but my parents went to Salt Lake today to pick him up. When I got home, I had to take the train," she paused, "Well, in their defense they didn't know I was coming."

They went down the flight of stairs to the basement. After surveying the room and the living room, Gaius suggested rearranging the living room furniture to make room for the exercise equipment in the big common room. Elizabeth agreed, and they started to move the couch and entertainment center down the wall to free up the opposite side. There was an open box with 'boy's stuff' written on the outside, a stuffed ET doll had its head sticking out the top.

"Phone home." Gaius said impersonating the outer space alien.

Elizabeth laughed. "Funny. Do you think that's really what aliens look like?" she asked, still smiling.

"Do you believe in aliens, my cute little Lizard?"

"Well, yea. I mean, probably. That's a lot of space up there, our galaxy is only one. There are tons of other planets, you know? I mean, it makes sense…" Faltering on her words, she suddenly felt self-aware and knew he was watching her. "What do you think?" she asked and glanced up meeting his eye.

"You are right, there is a lot of space up there. Plus, it's the most scientifically plausible fairy tale. I would just love to think there were other lifeforms elsewhere. I don't necessarily believe they fly around in saucers spying on us or anything like that. Nor do I believe we are the result of an alien experiment. Have you heard that theory? That we were brought here by aliens like we're some alien kid's science project." Smiling, he went back to moving the free weights. "I always loved doing science projects," he added, completely lost in thought.

"Fairy tale?" she arched one eyebrow and watched him. He's so cute. She thought to herself, He's just so off base. How could anyone not believe in Jesus. Could he not feel the prodding of the Holy Ghost? Perhaps his way of thinking isn't wrong just different, right? It doesn't feel wrong. The spirit at the Baptist church didn't feel wrong either. Her heart swelled with the thought of that Sunday service, the electricity in the air, the music, the choir and preacher. She remembered how horrible the members of the local ward had been to her guests.

It made her flush with shame. Elizabeth was lost in thought. She hadn't realized Gaius had been talking the whole time.

"...like any other plant or animal life to grow and thrive, there would be only a few factors that needed to take place, water, oxygen, and time to evolve. Our galaxy is like billions of years old, so time is on its side. Its physics, you know, how the universe works and all."

"For sure," she agreed, "I love science." *Wasn't he just talking about fairy tales?*

"Oh man, me too!" His eyes lit up, "It was always my favorite subject in school."

"Science?"

"Yea, for sure. What was your favorite subject?" he asked.

"Seminary."

"What? Did you say seminary? I mean, in school, your favorite *school* subject."

"Seminary," she giggled. "It's offered here as an elective from seventh to twelfth grade."

"How is that possible, what about the separation of church and state?" he was flabbergasted.

"The separation of what?"

"The separation of church and state. One of the reasons our forefathers left England in the first place so they could have a secular government whose legislators would never be required, or permitted, to rule on the legality of theological views. History was my second favorite subject."

"I don't know," Elizabeth shrugged, "we have prayer at school, you know to open assemblies or sports events, bless the participants and stuff. A lot of students say a prayer in the cafeteria before eating."

Gaius shook his head. Their conversation turned to an easier subject, their favorite science projects in middle school. "I wish they taught more about evolution in school, it's fascinating to me, the way animals, people and plants adapt generation after generation to accommodate the change in environment. Have you ever read the book The Botany of Desire?" he asked.

"No, but I love to read, I'll add it to my reading list. What's it about?" Elizabeth was enjoying being alone with him, the expressions on his face when he didn't know she was looking, his tight muscles and the way they moved when he had to exert himself. *Chemistry is my new favorite science.* She thought.

"It's all about plants and the way they've evolved over the years," his voice was nice, not as deep as Maximus's but still masculine. "Apples, Tulips, Marijuana and Potatoes. That's what it's about, it's good, you'll like it. Did you know that McDonald's genetically alters the potatoes they use to make their fries, so they can get the consistent color and texture?"

"No kidding," she mulled over what he had just said, trying to remember how she was going to remember the name of the book. There was a moment of silence between them. "Weird. Pot, huh? I'll definitely check it out."

"You like the herb do you, Lizard? Wow, you didn't strike me as a stoner," his face showed genuine surprise.

"No," she laughed quick and loud as if that was the most ridiculous thing he had ever said, that *anyone* had ever said. "No, I just heard there are medicinal qualities to cannabis. That it has a bad rap."

"Oh, it has a bad rap! Not only in politics but big pharma. Okay, it's kind of one and the same, I mean seriously, think about it, if everyone that was on Prozac and Citalopram could just smoke a joint of bud they grew in their own back yard, well... they would go out of business. Politicians support keeping it illegal because of the private prisons and court fines. But the herb, it's good for what ails you," she smiled and didn't know anything about what he was talking about so it was probably better if she kept quiet. "I don't participate on a regular basis, but I've tried it. My mom ate some space cookies there towards the end."

Elizabeth felt the mood change and did her best to direct the conversation away from his mother, "Space cookies?"

"Sure, with pot in them. What do you call them?"

She laughed, "I don't call them anything. I've never seen one." Wanting to change the subject and keep the conversation light, she continued, "I like reading historical novels, they are like history with a twist. That was probably my favorite subject in school if we separate the church from state." Smiling, she stood next to him and put her hand on his shoulder affectionately, their eyes met. A heat rose between them. Elizabeth went back to the task at hand. They hauled some boxes to the shed and stacked them with the others. Due to all the added clutter, the small area had gotten very crowded leaving little room to move about. As Elizabeth turned, she lost her balance and fell into Gaius.

He grabbed her around the waist and pulled her close. "Are you okay?" A look of concern in his eyes.

"Yes," she said, "just clumsy," she looked at the ground, he put his hand under her chin and tilted it up towards him.

"You're so pretty," he said softly, their eyes meeting.

"Thanks," her eyelids lowered, but he was still holding her chin. Leaning in, he kissed her softly and lightly. Not knowing how to respond, her back stiffened, she pulled away.

"Sorry," Gaius mumbled, "I've wanted to do that for days and I thought you-"

"It's okay," she blushed heavily, "I'm just extremely inexperienced in these matters."

"Oh, I'm no Casanova," he smiled at her and made her look him in the eye. "You're not only pretty, you're smart and you're sweet. A rare triple combination in today's world."

"You sound a little like Casanova, the cynical version," she smirked at her own joke. "When we were texting earlier, you said you had a favor to ask me. What was it?" her pulse raced and her stomach flipped.

"Oh!" he cried, "That's right, I would like to request your company on Tuesday night for dinner," his smile was coy and a little mysterious. They walked out of the shed with their hands entwined.

"Are you asking me out on a date, G?"

"Um, not really, but maybe, kind of?" he continued, "Grandpa Bill is having the missionaries come over on Tuesday night, missionaries here in Pleasant, weird, right? Anyway, I thought it would be nice to have someone there with me, someone on my side."

Elizabeth suddenly felt a wave of disappointment wash over her, not wanting Gaius to pick up on it, she nodded a bit too enthusiastically. "Of course, no problem. The first lesson isn't really a lesson, it's more just getting to know each other. And what makes you think I'm on your side," her look was serious, arms across her chest, eyes narrowed.

"Well, you're my favorite Pleasant-ite, is that what you are, people from Pleasant? Pleasant-ites? Anyway, you're so smart, I would be honored to have your company."

"Smart?" she looked confused, he continued.

"Liz, it's a fact, when education goes up, religion goes down, it's all about being educated and smart people educate easier than dummies."

"I don't know about that," she began moving another box towards the bottom of the stairs. *What was he hinting at, that she was a dummy?* "Help me with this, please," she said.

"Oh Lizard, don't be mad at me. I didn't mean to offend." Quickly he hopped over to help her, his eyes were wide, remorseful. "Will you come? I don't want to upset my gramps either, but I can't stand the thought of doing it alone. I'm not good with religion. I need a favor from a friend."

"I'm not mad, G," she sighed. "You reminded me of the life I just left, I've only been home two weeks for cryin' out loud, *two weeks*, and I'm forgetting to pray at meals, skipping Sunday school, and, the worst part is, I'm not even feeling bad about it. I've been avoiding the bishop for my homecoming assignment, avoiding my mother, dreading my brother coming home, and on top of everything else, I'm kissing a hot -non LDS- man in my parents' shed. No, not mad at you, just disappointed in myself," she sighed, her shoulders sagged. "It's so much easier to just be told what to do, you know?"

He shook his head, "Maybe easier, but not near as fun." They looked at each other. She shrugged her shoulders. "Aw... my sweet little Lizard. You're so cute. Um... One question." Gaius took a few steps towards her and wrapped his arms around her waist. Their eyes met, he grinned, "Do you really think I'm hot?"

Chapter Thirty-Five

They finished organizing Paul's room. Gaius left in the late afternoon, as the shadows reached across the lawn, he kissed Elizabeth on the cheek and squeezed her hand before climbing in his truck. Her mind whirled and her stomach did flips as she thought about seeing him the following evening. She had never felt this way, not even with Maximus.

When Giselle and Jozette got home from school, they disappeared into their room. They said they had homework but there was something about the look in their eyes that didn't convince Elizabeth. She didn't say anything contradictory. Who was she to judge? She felt like a guest in her own home. It would take some time to readjust. Opening the fridge, she saw some leftover chicken and decided to make chicken salad. She began cutting the chicken into little chunks when she received a text. It was Gaius.

> *Roses are red, Violets are blue. I've not met anyone as Pleasant as you.*
> *LOL. You're cute. Thanks for all your help today.*
> *It is YOU that is cute! C U tomorrow.*

Elizabeth smiled to herself. How could a simple text exchange make her feel like she was floating? The memory of the kiss came back to her, even the soft peck on the cheek when he left, the way he held her hand, the way he looked at her. She couldn't get him off her mind. She made a chicken salad sandwich with a bagel and grabbed a magazine from the table. Once in her room, she said a quick blessing thanking her Heavenly Father for her food, family and life. Eating her sandwich and pouring over the fashion magazine, she was inspired to make more clothes. Some of the outfits in the magazine were horrible, hideous, others were sleek, stylish and feminine.

It was after ten when she heard her parent's car in the driveway and the three of them come through the door. They all went upstairs. She had left them a note that there was food prepared. Could it be true what Paul was accused of? She had heard their parents talking, the bishop had said it was consensual, but still? Did he have sex? What other inappropriate behavior that involved the word 'consensual' could get him excommunicated? What was he doing having sex on his mission, consensual or otherwise? She didn't want to think about Paul. Her mind automatically slid to Gaius, the feeling of his hands on her waist, the kiss, she kept thinking about that kiss. She thought of what she should have done, how she should have handled it. Kissing him back is how she should have handled it, putting her hands on either side of his handsome face and just planting her lips on his, that's what she should have done. A smile slowly played across her lips as she began to fade into sleep, visions of Gaius dancing in her head.

It seemed like only minutes when she was jolted awake by the sounds of her father yelling. She heard Paul snap something back, her dad roared, and her mother was crying. A few seconds later she heard Paul stomp downstairs. He went into his room, cursing under his breath. Elizabeth fell back to sleep thinking about her family and her future. She wanted Gaius in her life, but knew he would never settle in Pleasant, not in a million years.

The next morning, Elizabeth woke to the now familiar sounds of her family getting ready for their day. The breakfast conversation was tight. Nobody knew what to say. Daniel finished his toast and left. The mood at the table lightened considerably. Giselle and Jozette began to banter back and forth about a spring fling dance that was coming up.

"Your sister could help you two make a couple new dresses." Alice smiled warmly at her daughters. "That way you're assured no one else will be wearing the same thing."

"That's a great idea Ma, thanks." Giselle said, getting up from the table and kissing the top of her mother's head.

"Let's hit up the D.I today after school, we could get some fabric." Jozette offered.

"I've got plans tonight," Elizabeth announced to no one in particular, "Mom's got some cute material in my old room if you want to go through that box. There's some inspirational outfits in that magazine too."

"Did you say you have plans tonight?" Giselle's playful smile made Elizabeth blush just a little.

"Yes, I did," Elizabeth said proudly, "meeting some missionaries at the Smiths' for dinner tonight. Mind if I borrow something cute to wear?"

"Help yourself," her sister replied, smiling.

"Gaius is doing the lessons?" Alice's eyes shot up, "Well, isn't that nice. I'm so proud of him. Brother Smith is a good man and I'm sure he has been a good influence on that young fellow."

Elizabeth ignored her mother's comments and watched her little sisters leave for school. It was amazing that they were almost adults. Looking back towards her mother, she said, "It's amazing, those two, all grown up. What'cha gonna do when the house is empty, Mama?"

Alice sighed. "It's hard to say whether I'll cry or celebrate," she smiled despondently at Elizabeth.

"Probably a little of both."

"Yes." Alice agreed, "You're right. Celebrate first, cry later. Raising adults is much more of a challenge than I ever thought it would be, give me a roomful of toddlers any day."

"Really?" Elizabeth asked.

Alice sighed again, and Elizabeth noticed how her mom was starting to look her age. The softness of her skin, starting to sag, her hair, gray at the roots and her face covered with worry. "Oh Elizabeth. Where do I even start?" she shook her head, there was a hint of melancholy in her voice. Tears filled her eyes, but her voice remained steady. "Like this business with Paul. Your father and I have no idea what do about him. This thing he's been accused of, well... I don't want to get into it. I don't know why he's angry all the time, why he blames everyone else for his unhappiness. He's just so bitter. With a toddler, you just throw them in time-out."

"What happened?"

"Who knows." Alice shrugged. "One of the missionaries went to the mission president, said some things that implied Paul was... I don't know... Supposedly there's an eye witness," she sighed.

"Or someone with a serious grudge." Elizabeth suggested. "Of course, I want to give my brother the benefit of the doubt, who's the girl?"

Alice shrugged, stood and cleared the rest of the table, "The whole incident could shame our family's name for years to come."

"I wouldn't worry too much about that Mama, the Andersons are tough," she put her arm around her mom.

"I mean..." tears filled her eyes again, "people will talk," her voice came out in a whisper.

"Let them talk." Elizabeth said, giving her mom a reassuring squeeze.

"Let who talk about what?" Paul's voice boomed from the kitchen door.

Elizabeth's conversation with Paul was friendly and curt. The old rivalry seemed to flare immediately when Paul saw her with her arm around their mom. *He really is a butthead,* Elizabeth thought, but she didn't want him to be publicly shamed and certainly didn't want whatever was going on to affect her parents.

Alice had finished cleaning the kitchen and went to her room. Elizabeth went into the girls' room and opened one of the closets, thumbing through the clothes. She extracted a sexy little dress and held it up to herself in the mirror. It was tiny. Honestly, which of her sisters would wear this? As she went to put it back, she noticed a small baggie of white pills taped strategically to the inside of the racy garment. She returned the dress and looked around. Based on the twin beds, this was most likely Jozette's closet. She shut the doors and opened the closet on the opposite end of the room feeling a little uncomfortable, *what were those pills?*

The clothes in the second closet were definitely closer to her size and style. Elizabeth heard Paul's chair slide across the floor, he headed down the stairs. Elizabeth continued rummaging through her sister's closet and found a short sleeved, turquoise blouse that would look perfect with her black skirt. Extracting it from the closet, she headed to her room. Paul had put on some loud music with a bass that bumped the entire basement. Her mom's advice throughout her life had been to 'just ignore him', and that advice flooded her head as she went into her room and closed the door. After a moment's hesitation, she turned back and engaged the lock.

Trying on the blouse and the skirt, she admired the look in the full-length mirror. She noticed the blouse's v-neckline exposed the tops of her garments. Elizabeth realized her garments were becoming a hindrance in what she wanted to wear. There was talk of sacrifice when she received the undergarments, was this it? Being sexy? She thought about the cute one-piece jumper she had made. A memory flashed back to her from when they were in sixth or seventh grade. Her body was still a toothpick, but Tish was starting to get boobs. They were at a church summer festival at the local public pool.

The church leaders had insisted all the girls wear tee shirts over their swimsuits. Once wet they were heavy and she had slipped hers off. Before she knew it she was in the locker room getting a lecture on why 'Modest is Hottest'.

She tried on the blouse without the garments, it fit perfectly, showing just a hint of cleavage, hugging her body in all the right places. Maybe it was the way Maximus had looked at her in Kentucky or the way Gaius made her feel, but she wanted to be sexy. Looking at the magazine, she could see that modest was *not* the hottest, sexy was hot! Her body was youthful and firm, but...the commitment of the garments was sacred, they were to be a constant reminder of the covenants she took when she went through the temple. It was a rite of passage. They also were to protect her against temptation and evil. It was all a gentle reminder of her beliefs. Her mind filled with the teachings of her church. She would wear the garments and figure out a way to make them less noticeable under the form fitting blouse. Looking through a box of old jewelry, she found a turtle broche. It wasn't the exact color of the blouse, but strategically placed, it would hide the garments (and her cleavage) and not bunch under the flimsy fabric. Satisfied with the decision, she wondered what she could do during the next several hours that would take her mind off Gaius. It always seemed the more she looked forward to something, the slower the hands on the clock moved. She sent a text to Tish.

> *GM chica. What's up?*
> *GM! Not much, you?*
> *Bored.*
> *LOL! Welcome to my world.*
> *Tons to tell you. Come over, I'll cook for us.*
> *Is Paul there?*
> *Yes, but he's doing his own thing, he won't bother us.*
> *K*

Elizabeth realized there wasn't an emotional feel to texts, but the feel of that one letter, K, she wasn't sure if Tish wanted to be bothered by Paul, or not. She noticed Paul on the treadmill, shirtless. *Why wasn't he wearing HIS garments?*

"Hey bro, lookin' good," she smiled warmly at him. He was her brother whether she liked it or not, she should make an effort at least. "How are things going? Everything okay?"

Paul slowed the treadmill so he was walking at a brisk pace. "Mom didn't clue you in? I'm defective. In need of a psycho therapist. Gone mental," his winded breath made him sound creepy, each syllable coming out clipped.

"Wow, what happened?"

"Lies, terrible lies," the venom in his voice took Elizabeth by surprise. He sounded jaded. Elizabeth was caught off guard. He was cynical, harsh, his jaw set tight. Paul had always seemed a little angry, but this was just scary.

"Wow. Heavy," she didn't know what else to say so she changed the subject. "Tish is coming by and we're going to make some lunch around noon, if you're still here, you're welcome to join us," she was being hospitable and secretly hoped he would decline.

"Yea, if I'm around," he said, cranking up the speed on the treadmill again, "Thanks."

Returning to the kitchen, she found her mom going through the freezer.

"Thought I'd get a jump start on tonight's dinner," Alice announced.

"Cool, ma, just remember, I won't be here. I'm heading to the Smith's about five thirty. I'll eat there."

"You should probably bring something, a pistachio salad or Jell-O." Alice said, not turning to look at her daughter, "Here's some Cool Whip, I'm sure there is some pistachio pudding in the pantry, if you do a double batch, you can take some to the Smith's and we'll have some tonight too," she withdrew a frozen package of meat and set it on the stovetop.

"Okay," Elizabeth said. Her mom's idea of bringing something to the Smith's was actually a good one, neighborly anyway. The creamy pistachio salad would go with anything Brother Smith prepared.

"Could you peel these carrots for me?" Alice asked her daughter, retrieving the vegetables from the bottom drawer of the fridge.

"Sure. Tish is coming over for lunch, what should we make?"

"There's left over beans and rice from Friday, they need to be eaten."

"Okay." Glancing in the pantry, she saw an unopened bag of corn chips. *That'll work*, she thought to herself. Using the rice and beans, plus some grated cheese, diced peppers and onions, she made a humongous plate of nachos.

"Yum!" Tish said, walking in as Elizabeth extracted the plate from the oven.

"You look nice." Elizabeth said, eyeing her friend with a little suspicion.

Tish was dressed in a pair of sharp looking slacks and heels with a modest but stylish top, her make-up and jewelry accentuating the outfit perfectly. "Oh thanks." Tish replied off-handedly, popping a nacho into her mouth.

Paul appeared in the kitchen as if by magic. "Hey Tish. You're looking good my old friend, looking good!" He grabbed one of the chips off the plate and bit into it.

"Old?" Tish pouted at him, her mouth perfectly upturned.

Paul laughed. "A) you're older than I am. B) I've known you my whole life. C) you're dressed as if you're running away to Wall Street. It's an older look for you, that's all I'm sayin'," he took another cheese covered chip. "Wanna go downstairs and play naughty librarian and bad little boy?" he winked at her.

"Whot?" Tish answered in a heavy British accent, "You wot me to paddle yer bum?"

"Would you, nanny?" A wicked grin took a hold of his face. The sexual energy exuding between them was palpable. Elizabeth shot him a perturbed look, as Alice walked into the sudden silence.

She surveyed the young adults, "Patricia, you look lovely today. Do you have a job interview?"

"Naw Mama A, just out of clothes. I really need to do laundry. Our mom cuts us off when we turn eighteen. Says we gotta do our own even if we're still living there. She only has a few young 'uns left. Our house is a wreck anyway. Doesn't matter how many of us are there, laundry is a never-ending story. You know what I'm sayin'? Dirty clothes, they just keep coming and coming."

Elizabeth noticed Tish's chatter had a nervous edge to it. *What was up with her? Was it Paul and his nasty comment?*

"It's true," Alice added empathetically, "laundry is a never-ending chore. Tell your mom hello from me, I've got to run right now, we're doing a relief society craft project tomorrow. Sister Dunn and I need to prepare the supplies and go over the refreshment menu," she took a chip and ate it. "See you all later," she sauntered out leaving the three of them to finish their lunch.

When it was finally time to leave for the Smith's, Paul came up the stairs just as Elizabeth retrieved the Cool Whip salad from the fridge. He grabbed the keys for the truck, "See you later," he said over his shoulder as he bounded down the stairs.

"Wait!" Elizabeth cried as she sprinted after him, "I was going to use the truck tonight. I asked mom last night."

"So," Paul said, getting in and starting it.

"So?! Paul, stop. I have plans, I need the truck," Elizabeth could hear the whine in her voice, she hated when she sounded like that.

"What's going on, what plans? I have plans too. If you have a date, he should be picking you up, not the other way around." Paul's stare was hard, his lips firmly in straight line.

"I'm meeting a pair of missionaries at the Smith's over on seventh," she didn't feel the need to embellish on Gaius being there.

"Those geezers. Ya, I know where they live, hop in. I'll give you a ride over there. Text me when you're done and I'll come back and get you," he reached over and unlocked the passenger side. Flabbergasted and completely at a loss for words, she got in. Paul stopped in front of the Smith's home and Elizabeth got out, she didn't feel the need to thank him for the ride, she was still irritated. "Text me when you're done, I'll swing back by and pick you up."

"Sure. Whatever," she shrugged indifferently. No one could get under her skin like Paul. Elizabeth resolved to not let him get to her, at least not tonight. She let herself in the gate, carrying the container of pistachio salad and walked to the front door. After ringing the bell and standing there for what seemed like a long time, Gaius appeared from around the corner of the carport, his boyish grin made her knees feel weak.

"Hey," he said, "you're looking incredibly beautiful tonight."

"Um, thanks," Elizabeth answered, holding out the salad. "I made this for us tonight," she smiled as he took it.

"Oh, you didn't have to do that, Gramps and I made a great dinner, but thank you. I'm sure it's delicious," he slipped his arm around her waist as they walked into the back yard together. "C'mon in. The missionaries aren't here yet but are expected anytime." They went in through the sliding glass door. Sassafras and Boo-Boo came up to investigate the new comer, sniffing her shoes and legs.

Elizabeth scratched Sassafras behind her ears. "Hey good girl," she said to the dog. "And who are you?" Elizabeth bent over and gave the little dog a pet on his head too.

"It's Boo-Boo," Sister Smith said eyeing Elizabeth, "he's a good old dog."

"He sure is." Elizabeth agreed, alternating her attention between the two canines. The doorbell from the front door rang. Elizabeth could picture the two missionaries standing in the same place she did, looking expectantly at the wooden door. Gaius jumped up and darted out the sliding glass door, returning in less than a minute with them. *They all look so similar*, Elizabeth thought, *it's almost like you can tell how long they've been out by the dark rings under their eyes.* She read their name tags, Elder DeBuck and Elder Peterson. Brother Smith made more formal introductions all around, he called her Sister Anderson when it was time for her to be introduced. She wondered if it was because he couldn't remember her name or if he remembered she just returned from her mission.

The food was wonderful. Gaius and his grandfather had prepared traditional shepherd's pie with a green salad, topped with Thousand Island dressing and perfectly baked cornbread. Plus, a pitcher of iced tea and pink lemonade, known as the Pink Palmer. Once dinner was through, Gaius loaded the dishwasher while Elizabeth joined the missionaries and Smiths in the adjacent living room. The missionaries took the couch, the Smiths took their unchanging spots, Bill in his brown faux leather recliner, and Mary in her cloth covered one. Mary picked up her crochet and started looping the yarn over the single needle methodically. Elizabeth took the only other chair and wondered where Gaius would sit when he joined them.

Elder DeBuck was talking, "Thanks for having us in your home tonight, Sister Smith. The dinner was awesome, us missionaries always love a good meal. We really appreciate your hospitality."

"Where are you from?" Bill asked.

Elder DeBuck answered. "Calvary, Canada, sir."

Elizabeth had thought earlier she had heard a peculiar accent from the young man. Gaius walked in and surveyed the room, he walked over to where Elizabeth was sitting and plopped on the floor at her feet.

"And where are you from?" Bill directed the question to Elder Peterson.

"I'm from Billings, Montana," he replied, "love it up there."

Elizabeth thought of Rebecca. Didn't she say the missionary that baptized her was from a place in Montana? White Fish or something like that. "I've heard it's nice." Elizabeth said, smiling at the young man.

"You get to go fishing often?" Grandpa Bill asked.

"It's amazing." The missionary said to Elizabeth and turned to answer Grandpa Bill's question, "Oh every now and then. We're not regular fisherman, but we love the outdoors. My dad and brothers and I, we do the elk hunt every year, it's a family tradition. Good quality time together." Elder Peterson smiled and looked at each person in the room. "Now we're all together, I'd like to personally thank you for having us here tonight. Gaius, I understand you wanted to learn more about the Church of Jesus Christ of Latter Day Saints?"

Gaius shot a quick look to his grandfather. Bill met his eye, a slight smile played at the edges of his mouth. Returning his gaze back to the Elders, he nodded slightly and said, "You two kind of got boned, yes? Here you are in the heart of Mormon's Ville and you're trying to convert the one or two percent that aren't already baptized. Wow, talk about drawing the short straw," he sighed and offered them an apologetic smile. "So, yea, I guess I would like to know more about the Church of Jesus Christ of Latter Day Saints. It seems to make this whole town tick."

The missionaries began talking about Joseph Smith and his revelation and vision that lead to the formation of this particular branch of Christianity. Elizabeth had this lesson memorized, it was the first of ten lessons, and the one they gave the most. Often, they would only have one meeting with a particular family, after that they were mysteriously always busy the next several times they called. Elizabeth was only half paying attention, the other half of her attention was on Gaius sitting at her feet, almost as if they were a couple. The missionaries did a fine presentation for their first lesson and left the invitation open for the second lesson to be rescheduled. Bill was quick to invite them back again the same time next week. Just as they were getting ready to offer the closing prayer, Brother DeBuck asked Gaius if he had any questions from the lesson they had just given.

"Well, not exactly about the lesson you just gave, but yeah, I've got a hundred or so questions firing off in my brain. Did I catch you say you all are Christians, right? You believe in Jesus and all that jazz? Correct?"

"Yes." Both Brother DeBuck and Brother Peterson were grinning at Gaius and nodding their heads.

This is not going to end well. Elizabeth thought.

"So the whole Bible, not just your Book of Mormon, but the Bible, you believe in that, right?"

"Yes, yes." The Elders looked as if they were ready to bolt, lesson over, time to say goodnight.

"The Ten Commandments, Moses, right? We're talking about the same Moses, the carved tablets. *Thee* Moses." Gaius' tone changed slightly from interested pupil to sly fox. "What about the Thou Shall Not Kill commandment? Is that one in your world, Elders?"

"Of course," Elder DeBuck looked confused, but Elder Peterson suddenly looked a bit sharper, keener.

"Hmm..." Gaius said thoughtfully. "We all know my dad was in the military."

"May he rest in peace," Mary said from nowhere.

"Amen, Grandma, may he rest in peace. I wonder if he ever killed anyone." The room became still except for Mary's constant movement of her crochet needle. "What about you, Gramps? Didn't you serve in Viet Nam?"

Bill's eyes and jaw hardened, the furrow between his brows appeared as he answered, "I did indeed, son. There are exceptions to certain rules for the greater good of..."

Gaius interrupted him, his voice steady and resolute. "Of course, there are, just like exceptions when it comes to tea with caffeine in it. This is different though, of course. So. What's his excuse?" he motioned towards Elder Peterson and continued. "Do you hunt to feed your family?" Gaius questioned to the missionary.

"We eat the meat, yes," Elder Peterson replied.

"Fair enough," Gaius stood and the missionaries followed his lead. Elizabeth and Bill also got to their feet, a feeling of relief washing over the room.

"So, I'm going to give you guys a pass from being hypocrites, *this* time. You," he said looking to his grandpa, "get a pass because you probably were drafted and did what you were told. It's a sad deal, war. You," he pointed his finger at Elder Peterson, "get a pass because you don't waste the meat and because, quite simply, you don't know any better. It's a wonderful example of ignorance being bliss, wouldn't you agree, Sister Anderson." Gaius had never called her that. She nodded. He continued. "I'll be honest with you boys organized religion doesn't do it for me. I'm a science guy like I told my grandpa here before you all were invited over. I like things that are real, provable," his smile was warm and genuine, his voice firm. "As far as the church is concerned, I don't see it happening for me. As I've said before and will probably say again, church is for sinners. I'm not a sinner. Science is where it's at, I've got to be honest, I really enjoyed dinner and want to continue my temporary residence here, therefore; I'll go to church this Sunday, I'll agree to meet with you another week, but don't expect me to go much further with this charade," his gaze shifted to his Grandpa Bill, "I'm just not convinced and don't think anyone in this room has what it takes to convince me, not even Elizabeth, and she looks *very* convincing, wouldn't you agree, Elders?" Gaius looked at Elizabeth up and down in a most appraising way and looked back at the two young men.

Elder DeBuck blushed up to the roots of his hair.

"Yes, she does." Elder Peterson said a little too quickly.

"We good here?" Gaius enquired to his grandpa.

"I suppose," Bill mumbled. "I'm not going to go on with this anymore today." Tension began seeping into the room. Grandma Mary continued to crochet, Elizabeth stood at Gaius' side. He and Bill were staring at each other, looking as if they were sizing each other up, determining which man would make the next move.

Bill announced he was going to get Mary ready for bed. The Elders, Elizabeth and Gaius exited through the sliding glass door and walked out to the front. Once the missionaries left, Gaius and Elizabeth sat next to each other on the porch steps and leaned against the front door. The sun was setting behind them, but the light illuminated the clouds in the west with a dazzling pink and gold. Elizabeth leaned slightly into Gaius.

"No one uses this door anymore." Gaius announced. "Gramps said he had to change out the doorbell so it has a different sounding ring, so sad. Using the door triggers Grandma Mary's PTSD."

"How so?" Elizabeth asked.

"Apparently, when the officers come to tell you your kid got killed, well Gramps said it was just like in the movies. The doorbell rings, the parents answer, there are uniformed military people and they give you your kid's dog-tags." Gaius shook his head sadly, "Gramps said Grandma Mary just collapsed and howled like a wounded animal, he said she even kicked at the officers. Such a tragedy. Gramps said she's never been the same since, and they've never used this door since."

"Yea, that sucks." Elizabeth said and folded her arms across her chest.

"Are you cold, Lizard?" he asked slipping an arm around her shoulders.

Not when you're around. She thought, but muttered, "No, not really," she leaned into him and enjoyed the feel of his arm around her. Elizabeth enjoyed being around him, period.

"Hope Gramps isn't too mad at me, there's just not much else that really pisses me off than hypocrites," he sighed. "I get it from my mom, I think."

"I'm sure he's fine. I thought the whole thing went well enough and your food was amazing! Did you cook that?" she turned her head and beamed at him.

The worried looked evaporated from his eyes. "I made the shepherd's pie and corn bread," he said proudly and added with a wink, "ancient family recipes. I hope you're not mad at me either, Liz. Organized religion just hasn't added that much to society, in my opinion. In fact, I think it has drug civilization down, slowed progression. The dark ages, the days of the Christian massacres, Constantine, the whole messed up scene has set humankind back decades. God is just convenient to blame when things go wrong and praise when things go right."

"You really don't believe at all?" Elizabeth inquired.

"No Lizard, I don't," his eyes had a hint of sadness. "The Pagans may have had it right, they believed in nature, a person can't go wrong believing in nature, but…"

"I'll admit, I don't know anything different, but I can't imagine my life without my faith."

"Try." Gaius said suddenly with a boyish grin that started in his cheeks.

"What?" Elizabeth asked.

"Seriously," Gaius continued enthusiastically, "humor me. Pretend you've never heard of Jesus Christ, let that testimony of yours go for a minute."

She closed her eyes, a thin smile appeared on her mouth.

"Okay, you've blanked out your mind of all religious beliefs, right?" she nodded and opened her eyes. She would play along but there was no way she could just forget everything she believed, the church was ingrained in her.

"So, I'll be the missionary, okay?" he cleared his throat and removed his arm from around her shoulders. Gaius' voice took on the radio announcer quality she had heard him use before. "Hello Elizabeth, I'm Elder Let's-Pretend," she giggled. "I wanted to tell you today about my belief in an ancient cosmic Jewish zombie. Don't be scared, this is no ordinary zombie. This particular zombie can make you live forever but only if you symbolically eat his flesh and drink his blood. Also, telepathically you've got to tell him that you accept him as your master. When you do this, he will remove an evil force from your soul that is present in all of humanity. The reason for this evil force is because a woman made from a rib was convinced by..." He paused for dramatic effect, "a *talking snake*, so the talking snake convinced her to eat from a magical tree and this mistake she made caused all of humanity to be flawed."

"Jesus was Jewish?" Elizabeth asked with a tight smile on her face trying to play into his humor. She wasn't sure how to take this stab. On one hand, it sounded silly when he put it that way, on the other hand... Of course, he was just kidding. "You're a nut," she said, hiding a smirk, "where do you come up with this nonsense?"

"The internet, of course, silly Lizard, tricks are for kids. And who's the nut? The preacher or the convert?" His tone changed back to the radio announcer, "So now, all you need to do is to be dunked into a tub of holy water and you'll be saved, washed clean of your sins. Whatever they may be," his face constricted with a questioning look, and his normal voice returned. "I've always wondered about that, when people say Jesus died for our sins, what sins?"

"I never know how to answer questions with you." Elizabeth said, a little teasing in her voice.

"Honestly, with facts to back your answers is the best way to answer my queries."

"Well, it's hard to explain, but Jesus died so that we may live. Our sins against God are capital crimes and God himself our judge. When Jesus died on the cross, he took the punishment we all deserve so we could be with our Heavenly Father again," she noticed her tone had taken on her missionary lesson voice.

"It still doesn't make sense to me, Liz. What sins? I mean, I was born out of wedlock, but that wasn't *my* fault. I'm not perfect, but I'm no sinner. Never sinned so bad that the punishment would be someone dying on a cross."

"Well, it's like this," She heard herself say, "At the cross, God poured out His judgment on His son, satisfying His wrath and making it possible for Him to forgive us so we can be with Him again someday."

"Satisfying his wrath?" Gaius cocked one eyebrow. "For what?"

"Sins."

"Living isn't a sin. And why would I want to live with him someday? It doesn't make sense. Seriously, your god is kind of a dick, no offense." Gaius put his arm back around Elizabeth. "I'm still not convinced and you've still not told me specifically what kind of sins Jesus died for."

"Regular sins," she answered.

"Everything from speeding to manslaughter, huh?"

"Yup," she leaned her head against his shoulder.

"It's about faith, I suppose. I just *know* in my heart its true, Gaius. Jesus died so we may live to be with our Savior again."

"Sorry sweetie, still not convinced," he was enjoying her religious banter but more, he was enjoying her leaning against him. He could smell the conditioner in her hair, she had worn it pulled back in one long French braid. "Ever thought Jesus may have been a political advocate that the government put to death because they didn't want him to plant crazy ideas into people's heads?"

Leaving her head on Gaius' shoulder, she shook it, "No."

"Well, it could be true. Mary, you know, his mom not my grandma, she could have been telling him all along, 'Jesus, you're going to wind up dead on a cross if you don't watch your p's and q's.' It could have happened like that," he explained.

"No," she repeated, "He was the Son of God. He was special."

"No more the son of god than you or me," Gaius deliberately kept the tone non-confrontational. "No more special than you are," he kissed the top of her head. "Did you see the Mel Gibson movie? The Passion?" he asked. Elizabeth shook her head again. "It was horrible! I mean bloody wise; it was really gory. Seems to me, the men that strung up poor old Jesus were real dicks. So how much was a sacrifice to God and how much was just those men being caught up in the moment and being über assholes?"

"Never thought about it that way," she answered honestly.

"That's part of the problem with religion, Lizard. You're only taught one way to look at things and you're asked to believe them with no hard evidence. You're asked to put proverbial blinders on. If I may be so bold, you should check out another church," he suggested.

"I went to a Baptist Church when I was on my mission." It was a fact she was proud of.

"Wow, I bet that was enlightening," he said, a smirk playing at the corners of his mouth.

She turned her head to look at him before replying, "Can I tell you a secret?" she asked him in hushed tones.

"Yes!" He replied enthusiastically, "I'm an awesome secret keeper."

"Okay, cool. I've not told anyone this. So when I was on my mission, a black family invited us to go to their church. It was the most black people I've ever seen in one place, probably more in that one church than in this whole state, but there were a lot of white folks too, but anyway... I felt the spirt there." Elizabeth's voice had a whispered quality as if indeed, she was telling Gaius a deep, dark secret. "I haven't told this to anyone, please, don't make fun of me, but I was so caught up in the music and the people, the pastor," her eyes had a dreamy quality to them, as if she were seeing the service in her mind. "It was strange. You know?"

"I don't know, please, go on," he was smiling watching the color seep out of the clouds as the sun sank behind them.

"It was just..." Elizabeth stammered, she was at a loss for words.

"Oh, sweet Lizard, you've got to know, there ain't a wrong way to pray."

Elizabeth felt goose bumps go down her legs. Those were almost the exact words Maximus had said to her. She looked at his profile silhouetted against the fading light. "I know, I did, I felt the Holy Ghost so strong that day, in that church, not my own. It was different... weird, I can't describe it," she put her head back on his shoulder, her mind reeling with the possibilities that there may be more than one true church.

"Those folks believed their god was at their service too. Wanna know what I think about the Holy Spirit?" she nodded her head against his shoulder. "Well, if I were to believe in such things, which I don't, but if I did, I think my mom nailed it in her theory. The Holy Ghost is the Holy Mother."

"What?" Elizabeth's head jerked up as she turned to look at him.

"Okay, remember this came from my mom, she was a little witchy, but in a good way. She would always tell me the world worked in a Yin and Yang sort of fashion, male, female, dark, light, hard, soft, like that. Okay, so anyway, if god was the male there had to be a female, if god was the father, there had to be a mother. Obviously, Christ was the son. The idea would be to safeguard the mother, god's spouse or other half, whatever. Think about it, Liz. If you wanted to protect someone, how would you do it?" he asked, his eyes sharp and alive, dancing.

"Hide them?" her knee-jerk reaction came out as a question.

"Hide them, how?" one of his eyebrows arched up.

She shrugged, "I don't know."

He continued. "Don't name them. Liz, seriously, think about it. People use God's son's name as a swear word all the time. For real, if you want to protect someone, keep them hidden, like you said. Keep them *anonymous.* No one hits their thumb with a hammer and screams 'Holy Ghost', no, they say 'Jesus Christ' or 'God dammit' but if mama god had a name..," he drifted into his own thoughts.

"And the Holy Ghost has a still, small voice," she said as much to herself as to him. "Gentle, soft, like a woman. Like a mother." *What would my mom think if I bounced that idea off her?* Elizabeth thought sarcastically. "The Holy Ghost doles out advice," her mind was reeling at the thought of a female as part of the Holy Trinity. "It almost makes sense to me too," she said, still lost in thought. "Almost."

"Well, as much sense as any of it, Lizard," he put his arm back around her. "Let's be honest, none of it really makes sense."

Elizabeth was completely lost in thought. The idea of a hidden Heavenly Mother was spinning in her head. What was it about him that made her question everything?

Gaius was also lost in thought, he missed his mom. It would have been nice for her to have met Elizabeth. He needed to think about going back to Colorado too. As fun as this adventure had been, as good as if felt to have some closure and understanding about his dad's side of the family, as wonderful as it had been for him to have met Elizabeth, it was time. He needed to see what Toni had done with the house, figure out his next move. The mood fell into a comfortable silence as they both sat, his arm around her shoulders, her arm casually across his lap, her body leaning comfortably in the crook of his arm.

"What you thinking?" she asked quietly.

"About my mom," he answered truthfully, "I miss her. I think you would have liked her and her you. That whole Heavenly Ghost Mother thing, that was *her* theory. She had some out-there ideas! But the way she loved people… her different way of looking at life, it just made her into who she was. She was way ahead… The world would be a better place if there were more Sue Stewart's around, but when they made her, they broke the mold," his voice faded with the memory.

"Were you there when she died?" Elizabeth asked innocently.

"Yea." It came out in a sigh.

"What was it like?"

"What was what like?" he was confused.

"When she died? Sorry if it's too personal, it's cool." Perhaps she shouldn't have brought it up.

"No, it's okay," he took a deep breath. "If you've never seen anyone die of cancer, it's not a pretty sight. It got to the point we wanted her to die, she was miserable and only a shell of the woman she had been." Tears stung his eyes. "If she had been a dog, we would have put her down. Strange how people will do that for animals, put them out of their misery, but not humans." There was a pause, neither said anything. He went on. "To answer your question, it was a bittersweet relief when she took her last breath."

"Did you have your family there, with you?"

Gaius shook his head, the look on his face pained Elizabeth. "Ah Lizard, she *was* my family. Don't you get it? She was it. There *isn't* anyone else. Toni came by when she got off work, the hospice ladies came after I called them. I have no family, just her," his voice ached in her ears, the loneliness tangible. "I miss her so much." Tears stung his eyes.

Elizabeth put her arm around him, she leaned her head on his shoulder. For a few moments neither of them said anything, both lost in their own thoughts. It was Gaius that broke the silence. "Lizard, I'd like to see you again before Sunday's church brunch, is there anywhere I could take you on a proper date? This Friday is Friday the thirteenth, a magical day. We can go to town, dinner, a movie, whatever you want to do," his smile was charming.

"There's a temple tour going on Friday. Tish and I were talking about doing it, it goes all the way to Ogden, but we thought we'd stop in Salt Lake."

"A what?"

She giggled, the mood lighter immediately. "A temple tour. We start in Provo, then go to the Timpanogos temple in American Fork, over the point of the mountain to Draper, West Jordan's and right down town in Salt Lake, there's North Salt Lake and Ogden too. Or we could pop over Spanish Fork canyon to Manti, their temple is also beautiful. My older brother and his wife were sealed there. The Salt Lake one has been my favorite since I was a kid, it looks like a castle and its right in the heart of city, you can see the capital and there's a great mall there," her voice bubbled with excitement. "It's sponsored by the single's ward here locally, but there are single's wards all over the state doing it. It'll be like a temple tour singles social. There will be little events, guest speakers and stuff at each one, there's a whole schedule."

"Well, it's not the date I was hoping for but, I'm always up for a road trip. This one sounds like something I would never do on my own, so yea, count me in if it's okay with Tish."

"She thinks you're cute, I'm sure she'll be fine with it." Elizabeth smiled at Gaius and looked back to the sky. "The first star is out," she said, "Make a wish. Star light, star bright?"

He grinned and put his arm back around her shoulders. "That's the planet, Venus, but wish away, my dear."

"Okay." Elizabeth felt a slight blush across her face. "I wish... I wish..." She turned to look at him, his eyes were so blue in the fading twilight. He was so handsome. What could she say that she'd wish for, she didn't know herself what she wanted.

"You wish I'd kiss you," he said, a sparkle in his eyes that made them look as if they were dancing, his slightly crooked grin matching the rest of his expression.

Elizabeth's voice caught in her throat, she swallowed and nodded, her eyes falling to his mouth and he leaned in and kissed her. It was gentle, then a little more urgent as he put his arms back around her shoulders, her hands found their way to his back, neither of them noticed Paul cruise by slowly in the family truck.

"So, see you Friday?" she asked, pulling back enough to look into his eyes.

"Yes, Friday the thirteenth," he nodded and smiled wickedly, "You know about Friday the thirteenth, yes?"

She shook her head no.

"Before the patriarchal revolution, Friday the thirteen was celebrated as the day of the Feminine. It's a day all about women! Have you ever heard of the Frigg, the Norse Goddess of love and sex, creativity and fertility?"

She giggled and rolled her eyes. "No, I have never heard of Frigg, but I've heard that name used as a swear word."

"A Mormon swear word, how appropriate that in some cultures it means to copulate," he winked at her. "Beloved. That's what Frigg means," he placed his hand next to her face. "Beloved," his eyes studied her features. "What was I saying? Besides reminding you again that you are beautiful, so pretty. Oh yes, Frigg who was also very pretty. She was the highest ranking of the Aesir goddesses back in day."

"How do you know these things? And how far back in the day are we talking?" she giggled and leaned into him looking into the sky, watching the clouds move silently over the rising moon.

"I would say four or five hundred CE."

"CE like AD?" she asked.

It was Gaius' turn to giggle. "L, M, N, O, P," he wrapped his arms around her and they both looked up. It was a beautiful night. The clouds were high, the moon was waning.

"As for how I know these things," he sighed, "My hippie, witchy, weirdie mother with her Euro roots, she loved all the old folklores, and mythology. She swore she was a medicine woman reincarnated."

"You believe in that?"

"No. Like I said before Lizard, I don't believe in any of it. I believe..." He looked at her and continued, she met his eyes, the light from the moon was just enough to make out his features. "I believe this is it. We get one life, one shot. Our DNA was spliced together in a one of a kind fashion and live like you're dying. There is no tomorrow, only today," he bent and kissed her nose.

"So if the average age is seventy, you're saying that's it. You only get those seventy years? No before life? No after life? No next life? All time and eternity, all the space out there, that's it?" her voice was uncertain.

"Yup, that's what I believe. I would check the box marked Atheist if I was filling out a personal information form. Think about it though, Liz. If you only got seventy years, wouldn't it make you feel your life was more precious? More special somehow?"

She shrugged. "Maybe. I don't know, it's kinda depressing to think this is it, more precious or more insignificant? To think there isn't anything else? Our church believes this life is as bad as it ever gets, having a body, feeling pain and pleasure, it's a test and a privilege. When our Heavenly Father returns, those that are worthy will rise from the graves. That's why we don't cremate in our religion."

"So zombie style?" he grabbed her around the waist and nuzzled into her neck.

"No silly, everyone's body will be resurrected perfectly." Elizabeth relaxed into him. He made her head swim and she couldn't think. He kissed her again, she held his hand as they walked to his truck.

"Just my observation, but it seems like throughout history, it's always those that are promised an afterlife are the biggest assholes. You know what I mean? Those that don't get it. If you really believe this is the one and only shot you have and this is the one and only life everyone else gets it just makes life more extraordinary," he looked to the sky as he spoke. Elizabeth watched him. She had never thought about it like that, it just wasn't what she believed, way too sad to think this was the only go around, this imperfect life. Gaius dropped her off just down the street from her house, they said their goodbyes with more kisses. Elizabeth had never been in love but couldn't imagine feeling any better than she did at that very moment. As she floated into the house, she caught herself humming the opening song of a familiar church musical, 'It's My Turn On Earth'. *In fact, it was marvelous...*

Chapter Thirty-Six

The next few days flew by for Gaius. He did yardwork for his grandpa on Wednesday and stayed home to watch his grandma on Thursday. Gaius thought about Elizabeth constantly. He replayed the moments on the porch while the sun set. While grandma was down for her nap, Gaius texted Toni.

> *Hi T. Whatz up?*
> *Workin' everything ok?*
> *Yes, wonderful. Call me on break. Love ya.*
> *Will do buddy. XO*

He played with the dogs and surfed the dozens of channels of daytime television junk. The reality and talk shows were so dumb. How many people were really watching this garbage? The advertisements were even worse than the programming. *Pure crap*, he thought. Promptly at a quarter to three, Gaius' phone rang.

"Hi buddy!" Toni's voice chirped in the phone. "What's up? I've only got fifteen minutes."

"Hi T," her voice had made him smile involuntarily and he felt a flood of familiarity wash over him.

"The house is coming along nicely, you'll be happy to know, the painting is done and the floors will be done this week sometime. I hope you don't mind, I stuck with neutral colors in case you decide to rent it or sell it, we also have a little electrical we need to bring to code, but everything here is humming along. What's up in your world?"

"I met a girl," he blurted it out.

"Oh. My. Gawd!" She sounded surprised. "Wow! How? When? What's her name? How old is she? Details, details."

"Okay, okay. Remember the two girls I just met?" Gaius could feel his face drawn into a huge smile and knew Toni would hear his happiness on the other end. "She's one. Her name is Elizabeth. She's gorgeous! Smart. Funny. Mormon."

"Of course she is." Toni smiled in spite of herself. "I suppose we can't hold it against her."

"She's so sweet and innocent, it's endearing and cute. I'm not sure I'm the best influence on her and her folks will probably freak out when *and if* she tells them. It's not super serious, but..." His voice trailed off.

"But someone has snagged your attention. Good for you, G!" Toni said. "I'm sure she's something special to have turned your head, I hope to meet her one day. How's everything else? Are you still at the Smith's house? How's that been going?"

"Not bad. I'm watching Grandma Mary on Thursdays. She's asleep right now. Gramps is in Provo. He'll be home by dinner. We've got a routine going. It's better for Mary when we do. Sass is good, she has a buddy. His name is Boo-Boo. He's an old peek-a-poo, that's a Pekinese and a Poodle crossed. I had a visit with the missionaries, but I don't think I'll do that again, unless Elizabeth wants me too-"

"Missionaries, huh? Elizabeth, huh?" Toni was playful, her voice light.

"Yes missionaries. Yes, Elizabeth," he liked the way her name rolled off his tongue, the sound of it, the thought of her. "She was born and raised out here in nowhere Utah, second child of five, oldest daughter and just pretty 'n sweet, 'n smart..." He was at a loss for words on how to describe her. "She's amazing. I make her laugh and when she looks at me, well..." He sighed. "She lets me call her Lizard."

"Well then, she must think you're pretty special too. Lizard, huh? Elizabeth's too long, Liz is too short or what?" Toni questioned.

"Her middle name is Ord, it just flows." Gaius explained.

"That's a weird middle name." Toni said. "But I get it, Liz Ord, ha-ha, you're a funny kid."

"It's her mom's maiden name, and let's face it, it's no weirder than Kinza."

"You've got a point." Gaius could hear a beeping noise on her end. "Gotta run, hun. Keep me posted, send me a picture of you two, a selfie, or whatever they're called."

"Will do, T." Gaius smiled into the phone, "Love ya."

"Love you too, kiddo."

She disconnected just as Gaius heard Grandma Mary say in a sleepy voice, "Bill?"

Elizabeth's week wasn't so mundane. Paul was in and out, the air in the house seeming lighter and more breathable when he was gone. His energy and attitude were sharp and defensive. It seemed to Elizabeth he left right before their dad was supposed to get home and returned just after bedtime.

Elizabeth could hardly blame him for that, disappointing their dad was something none of the kids wanted to do, ever. She thought about the circumstances that led her to come home from her mission early and couldn't imagine coming home and being at the point of possible excommunication. The few times Elizabeth did see Paul, he looked at her with a mysterious smile. Not a friendly smile either, more threatening than the shark smile she had seen on the face of the bishop on her mission, more condescending than her mom's fake smiles, scarier than the freakish clown face Tish made.

Thursday evening over dinner Elizabeth commented to her parents that they would have the house to themselves the following night since all three of the girls had plans.

"Alone time." Giselle sang.

"We wouldn't know what to do with alone time." Alice said thoughtfully.

"I could think of a few ideas." Daniel said, winking at his wife.

Paul walked in at that moment and took a place at the table, grabbing a roll and several spoonsful of casserole.

"What are you doing tomorrow night?" Giselle enquired of her big brother.

"I don't know," he answered with a shrug.

"Well, all of us girls are going to be gone, so if you're not home, mom and dad could have the house to themselves," she took a bite of her dinner without looking directly at him.

"Where's everyone going? Ward party I didn't get an invite to?" he asked sarcastically.

"Spring Fling." Jozette said to no one in particular.

At the same time Giselle said, "High school dance, and Elizabeth is going on the single's ward temple tour."

"I'm sure there is plenty of room, son." Daniel added. "If you wanted to go, you know, it could be fun."

"At the high school dance or the single's ward temple tour?" Paul asked sardonically, his eyes cold.

"The temple tour, of course." Daniel answered a little taken back. "You may meet some nice young people. Kids with your same interests."

"Oh yea, the single's ward temple tour. Like the nice young adult Elizabeth met?" Paul's eyes were on Elizabeth. She kept eating and ignored him.

"Who did you say you were going on the temple tour with?" Alice asked.

"Were you talking to me, mother?" Elizabeth answered her mom's question with a question. "Um, Tish." Elizabeth uttered hastily and glanced at Paul. His face cracked into a broad, malevolent leer. "And Gaius," she added. *How did Paul know about Gaius?*

"Is that the Smith boy?" Daniel asked his daughter. She nodded in between bites of her dinner.

"Well, he needs some new friends too." Alice commented flatly.

"He looked pretty attached to Elizabeth when I saw them. Attached at the lips!" Paul jeered, his wicked grin had turned into an evil smile. Elizabeth immediately knew he had been spying on her. It was unnerving to think Paul was watching her every move. She gave him the dirtiest look she could and continued to eat. He continued his taunt. "So, let me get this straight, if I'm not around tomorrow that means all three of you little skanks and our mother dearest here could potentially all take a ride on the bologna pony express! Yee-haw!"

"Paul Matthew Anderson!" Daniel roared, "That's enough!"

Alice's face was contorted into a look of shock while Jozette and Giselle looked down at their plates. Elizabeth stared at Paul, her disgust intense.

"Kidding, kidding. When did everyone get so sensitive?" Paul asked, his attention returning to dinner.

Chapter Thirty-Seven

The next morning Elizabeth received a good old fashioned handwritten letter from Rebecca. She hurriedly opened it and read the short note.

Hey Sister A,

What's up? Miss you bunches! Hope this note finds you well, happy and healthy.

I've got some big news! Max and I are a 'thang'! Crazy right? It just happened one night and I couldn't be happier. He feels the same way (I hope, lol.) It's been nice and we have Hat's blessing (that's important). We've been talking about him moving in with me, I'll keep you posted. Been going to church with him, let's face it, the Baptist's really know how to shake and jive on the Sabbath! And the services are done in an hour, ha-ha, now you know my secret reasoning. Anyway... The way love feels! I couldn't be happier!

Keep in touch, I'll need a maid of honor eventually. Fo' real, gurl, I MISS YOU!

Write me back if you get the chance. I'd love to catch up. Take care and Happy Easter.

LOVE, Rebecca

Elizabeth re-read the note. She was surprised with Rebecca's good news and happy for them both. She thought of Maximus's eyes and that smooth, deep voice. *Rebecca and him will make a fine couple*, she thought, smiling to herself. *And if they ever have babies, they will be the cutest kids ever!* She found a paper and jotted a note back to Rebecca. Elizabeth wanted her friend to know she was happy for her new found love, she also included a note about her own love life and how enamored she had become with an attractive, non-Mormon. *Pleasant was the same but completely different* she wrote.

The temple tour didn't start until three o'clock and was supposed to last until nine p.m. Since Pleasant was over an hour from Provo, they decided to leave at one thirty.

Gaius agreed to pick them both up at the Anderson's. Elizabeth wore her hair in a single ponytail, she pulled it through the back of a dark green baseball cap. She also wore a dark grey baseball tee. She debated on wearing capris or jeans and in the end, picked the jeans. Tish showed up looking like a model in the outfit Elizabeth had made. She wore her hair down and had straightened it, her make-up and high heeled sandals completed the glamourous look.

"We'll probably be walking a lot today, those shoes gonna work?" Elizabeth asked her friend.

"I have a pair of flip flops in my bag, and a casual change of clothes, just in case." Tish replied. "Thanks for thinking ahead. You look cute, by the way."

"Aw, thanks." Elizabeth blushed slightly as she surveyed herself in the full-length mirror.

"Maybe you should try for sexy instead." In a flash, Tish had taken Elizabeth's cap off, taken her hair down and added eyeliner and lipstick to Elizabeth's face. She was rooting through Elizabeth's closet, pulling out a summer dress.

"Try this on."

Elizabeth changed into it, she could see the garments under the clingy fabric. "I don't know, I want to be comfortable," Elizabeth argued. "It's going to be a long day, I should go for comfort, not sexy."

She heard Gaius' truck pull up to the curb and exchanged looks with Tish. They both headed up the stairs. Alice had answered the door and was ushering Gaius in the house. "This will be such a great experience," she was telling Gaius, "have you ever been to Salt Lake City, or Provo?"

"Drove through Provo on my way here," he commented. The girls appeared in the kitchen doorway. Gaius looked at them. "Happy Friday the thirteenth," he said with enthusiasm. "Ready?" he asked, a curious look on his face. Elizabeth suddenly felt overdressed.

"Almost." Elizabeth said. "Be right back," she bounded down the stairs and changed back into her original outfit, brushed her hair up into the ponytail and affixed the cap onto her head. Grabbing a make-up removal wipe, she hurriedly ran it across her face, leaving a hint of the eyeliner and all the mascara. She added clear lip gloss. Checking herself in the mirror she thought maybe sexy just wasn't her thing. Hopping back up the stairs and into the kitchen, she was met by Gaius and Tish on their way out. He glanced at her, she thought she saw him smile. Tish had a quizzical look on her face, but said nothing. Elizabeth hollered her goodbyes to her mother as they shuffled out the door.

As he turned to look over his shoulder to back out, he whispered to Elizabeth, "You look very pretty," she grinned but didn't say anything as Tish pulled out her iPod and portable speakers. Before they got to the edge of town, Tish had the cab of the truck filled with the latest top forty hits. As they drove and sang and chatted, Elizabeth causally placed her hand on Gaius' knee. Occasionally, when he wasn't using both hands to drive or talk, he would place his hand over the top of her hers, their fingers lacing together naturally.

Just outside of Provo, they saw a billboard that had a picture of a family looking to the sky in horror as several jets flew over them leaving trails of white behind them. The message read 'Tell our government to stop poisonous contrails.'

"Gotta love fear propaganda," Gaius said, motioning towards the sign. "It's crazy to think some people believe the government is actually doing something to the jets to make them leave a poisonous jet-stream when the physics of the way jets operate clearly, *scientifically,* explains how the contrails are made. Ridiculous!"

"Scare tactics are the worst, for sure." Elizabeth said. "Seriously, just watch the news now days, fear, fear, fear. Even commercials are fear based. Drives me nuts."

Gaius glanced over at the girls and thought how different his life had become in only the last four months. His mom wouldn't have objected, in fact, she probably would have thought it was nice he was getting out and doing something, even if it was a temple tour with a couple LDS girls. "It's how things work, with the government, with the church, with education in some places, T.V, the media, if you tell people the same lies over and over again, they'll eventually believe them," he said with authority. "Look at the war after war this country gets itself into, the citizens believing everything the news feeds them, it's a joke."

"Is that why you tell me I'm pretty every time you see me?" Elizabeth asked innocently.

"Yes and no," Gaius answered.

Elizabeth's stomach lurched, maybe she didn't want to know if she had been duped these last weeks by him. He continued, "Yes, because I want *you* to believe it. The truth of the matter is I think you're gorgeous just the way you are. You don't need to doll yourself up, you're just naturally beautiful.

And you don't even realize it. No, I don't *just* tell you so you'll believe it. I tell you because I believe it, I see it, I know it because it's true."

"Aww, that's so sweet." Tish said.

The way love feels, Elizabeth thought of Rebecca's letter. Gaius took her hand and kissed it. A wave of emotion swept over her as her stomach did somersaults.

Chapter Thirty-Eight

"It looks like a giant cake." Gaius said, verbalizing his first impressions of the Provo temple. Indicating the gigantic white 'Y' on the side of the mountain, he said in a sing song voice. "I've got a really fantastic idea. Let's go up there. Up into the hills."

"Whoa there! Easy big fella," Tish said in her best Western accent and added in her own voice, "I'm not exactly dressed for a hiking adventure."

"Whose fault's that?" Gaius contorted his face at Tish, she stuck her tongue out at him.

Elizabeth laughed at them both as she took a flyer from a volunteer at a table. She scanned it over, it had the times listed for each temple's presentation and when the fireside chats would be. On the back was a game board, each temple on the paper had a place for a small ink stamp. The volunteer noticed she was reading the fine print under the game and offered him the stamp. It was the 'Y' logo for BYU in blue ink. There were nine temples represented on the paper. She glanced at Gaius and saw a look of concern on his face. As if reading his thoughts, Elizabeth said, "Don't worry, we won't go to all of them."

Tish took a selfie with the Provo temple in the background and asked Gaius to take one of her and Elizabeth.

"I need one for my Aunt Toni," he said, handing Tish his phone and wrapping his arms around both girls. "Smile and give her the thumbs up, Liz." Gaius instructed. Tish took several shots as she made a duck face. Gaius sent the best picture to Toni with the caption, *In Utah less than a month, already a polygamist, LOL!*

They stopped at the refreshment table and grabbed a bottled water. There were homemade cookies on small paper plates and Kool-Aid. Grabbing a plastic cup, he took a selfie of him and Elizabeth. He held the cup to his mouth and made his eyes wide, she raised one eyebrow and looked serious. He sent that one to Toni with the caption, *She's already making me drink the Kool-Aid!* They headed back to the truck.

"The mountains are cool, I mean, this whole place is beautiful." Gaius said, "Too bad the air quality is so bad, seriously, look at the blanket of nastiness. I can only imagine how wonderful this place looked back in the day."

"It's changed so much even in the last ten years." Elizabeth commented. "I remember when I was a little kid, there wasn't this many people here, it's like they just keep coming and coming. Like a migration."

"I know what you mean." Tish said. "I heard eventually the little towns will all blend together, even as far out as Pleasant is. It's hard to believe."

"Believe it." Gaius replied as he unlocked the truck. He got a reply from Toni,

She's beautiful. I knew from the first pix she was the one, she looks like your type, thumbs up here too. Have fun, kiddo. Go easy on the Kool-Aid.

He sent her a smiley face. "Where next?"

"Go north." Elizabeth instructed. "The Timpanogos temple is the next closest. It's in American Fork, the map says to take the five hundred East exit all the way to seven hundred North."

"Wait a second." Gaius said, "Those instructions sound familiar, like we're back in Pleasant. Gramps and Grandma live on fourth and seventh."

"All the towns are the same in Utah." Tish explained. "They're in grids. Instructions to go anywhere in any town in Utah will go something like; take the main street exit, go to the first light, turn right, go to the four way stop by the church, turn left, the house is half brick, half vinyl siding with a two car garage at the end of the cul-de-sac. Not kidding, welcome to Utah. It's a little boring but easy to find your way around."

When they arrived at the Timpanogos temple they noticed a choir of young adults getting ready to perform. As they approached the small crowd Elizabeth noticed Frida from the café. "Hey there." Elizabeth smiled and put her arm on the young woman's shoulder. Frida turned, and Elizabeth saw she was not alone. Laurie was standing just in front of her.

"Oh, hey." Frida said, a nervous smile flitting across her face. Her eyes darted between the three friends.

"Hi ladies." Gaius said, tipping his head towards them as if he were tipping a hat. Frida hugged Gaius spontaneously and smiled. "Good to see you! You look great in real life." Gaius said to her.

"Real life." Frida chuckled. "Good to see you too."

Laurie introduced herself officially to Gaius. She touched a very handsome young man on her arm, and introduced him to the group. "Shane, these guys are all from our ward," Laurie smiled broadly at him. "This is our new neighbor, Shane Thompson. Shane, this is Elizabeth, Tish and Gaius."

Shane was handsome. Perfect smile, his hair wavy and medium length. He took off his sunglasses and shook each person's hand. Elizabeth couldn't help but notice the unusual color of his eyes. Green or hazel with flecks of gold. "Pleasure is all mine." Tish purred when Shane shook her hand. Elizabeth noticed her friend held it for a fraction of a second longer when he tried to pull it way.

The choir introduced themselves as the 'Hymn Hummers' and began to sing. Gaius slipped his arm around Elizabeth. She looked around, she could tell from Frida's body posture she would slip her arm around Laurie if it were socially acceptable and Laurie was definitely not here with Shane. Elizabeth motioned towards them and whispered to Gaius, "Maybe it's good if Frida and Laurie have a man with them... Do you think Shane is...?" she didn't finish the question but Gaius knew exactly what she meant and nodded.

The Timpanogos temple itself was impressive, especially the stained-glass windows. It looked much newer than the Provo one. "Let's go camping and explore those amazing mountains. I love mountains." Gaius said into Elizabeth's ear. She nodded and put her arm around his waist, still enjoying the music. "I'm being serious," he whispered urgently. "I heart camping. It's like my most favorite thing to do, ever."

"Okay, okay, we'll go camping," she returned his smile and they listened to the rest of the hymn. Gaius clapped loudly when they were done, no one else did. Elizabeth felt embarrassed for Gaius, her face turned pink as she realized she should have told him no one applauded at these performances. Tish started to giggle and whistled. Many others began to clap and look around at each other, a little uncomfortable.

"Let's go." Tish said urgently, holding back from full on laughing.

"I need my stamp." Elizabeth called, jogging to catch up with Tish and Gaius. Once back to the truck, the three of them posed for a selfie with the temple and mountains in the background.

"When are we going camping?" Gaius asked as soon as they were back on the I-15 freeway.

"We're going camping?" Tish cried out in alarm.

"Camp-ping, camp-ping, camp-ping." Gaius chanted. Elizabeth began to laugh.

"You two are nuts," she said. "Draper, Jordan River and then Salt Lake."

"I'm not sure I can do it." Gaius confessed. "This place seems cool aside from the temples. There has got to be other, more entertaining, things to do around here. How much trouble will you be in if we don't go to them all?"

"None at all." Elizabeth said, "It's all for fun, just a social thing for singles. Gives everyone something to do."

"No offense, Lizard, but that's super sad." Gaius got into the carpool lane as he headed north. "Let's head right to Salt Lake, get something to eat in a real city," he suggested. "We have plenty of daylight, we'll still be able to see the temple."

They drove in silence for a moment. Tish said, "Shane sure is a cutie."

"I think you would stand a better chance with Frida," Gaius answered only half-jokingly. They arrived at the City Center mall and found food, then walked across the street to the Salt Lake Temple grounds. Elizabeth looked at the schedule she had gotten and commented the Tabernacle Choir would be singing at seven. They walked around the temple taking in the size and architecture of it.

"Look!" Gaius suddenly shouted, pointing upward. "It's the phases of the moon!" He started walking around specifically looking at the changing moon carvings on the granite stone. "There's the sun, and the big and little dipper, my favorite temple so far, this is awesome!"

"This one is my favorite too. Happy to see you get excited about something from the church." Elizabeth said coyly. "If I remember right, the moon phases are on all the temples," she was standing next to Gaius, they were looking up the spires, admiring the structural work.

"Say cheese." Tish called. Gaius put his arm around Elizabeth and smiled broadly, Elizabeth looked up at him just as Tish took the picture. The image captured the look of a woman falling in love. Gaius suggested they go on a little exploration while there was still light. They rode the Trax, Salt Lake's light rail system, and got off on a random stop.

Elizabeth said, "Do you hear that? It sounds like church bells." They listened and distinctly heard the sounds of church bells tolling. Gaius grinned and headed towards the sound. A few blocks away was a cathedral.

"Look, the Catholic church." Gaius said smiling, "the Mormons don't have a monopoly on the Utah belief system after all," he bounded up the steps and tried the door, it opened. Looking over his shoulder at the girls, he shrugged and went in, they followed. There weren't many people there since it was late afternoon on a Friday. Elizabeth was struck by the beauty of it. She had never seen such an ornately decorated church. The stained glass, the mosaic, the scenes of the saints and Virgin Mary, all around her she could see the stories of the Bible being told in pictures. In the center, behind the pulpit, was the scene of Jesus' crucifixion. She sat on the front pew taking in the sights of the stunning cathedral. Gaius sat next to her and their hands intertwined. She leaned her head on his shoulder and spoke very softly. "Thanks for bringing me here, it's beautiful."

"Not as beautiful as you," he whispered back.

"Thanks," she said, feeling a hint of blush come to her cheeks. "It's crazy to think about the people that built these buildings back in the 1800's. Our temple, this church, I mean really, they are both magnificent works of architectural art built in an era when everything had to be done by hand."

"It's true." Gaius agreed, looking around the massive chapel. "Gonna go find the little boys' room, I'll be right back," he kissed her cheek and strode out.

Tish was sitting in one of the side pews towards the front, her head bowed. Elizabeth wondered if she was praying and started walking towards her. She noticed Tish's cell phone, *probably playing one of her silly games,* she thought as she continued to walk observing the stunning woodwork. Towards the back were four little wooden booths. Elizabeth observed them for a moment and watched as an older man came out, a look of worry on his face. He moved to the front of the chapel, kneeled down and crossed himself then walked out of the side door. *It's a confessional!* Elizabeth thought to herself with glee. *I've always wanted to try one of these.* With the joy of a child doing something they hoped they wouldn't get caught, she slipped into the booth and closed the door behind her. Within seconds the divider slid open, there was a screen but she could see someone sitting on the other side. *It's just like in the movies!* "Forgive me Father, for I have sinned," she said. That was what she was supposed to say, right?

"When was your last confession, my child?" The soothing and comforting voice of the priest came back through to her.

"This is my first confession?" her statement came out in a question.

"Well my child, it is never too late to be absolved of your sins in the eyes of God. Tell me, what sins have you committed?"

Elizabeth paused. How far should she take this? Would she really be forgiven of her sins through this church, her transgressions wiped away clean like when she was baptized at eight years old or did she need to talk to her local bishop? She was due for an interview with the bishop anyway, they happened every six months whether she liked it or not. The priest must be used to momentary silence because he didn't say anything nor did he prompt her. She sighed.

"I'm ungrateful. Sometimes I take advantage of my parents." Elizabeth surprised herself by being honest. "I tell them what they want to hear, not necessarily what's really goin' on because I know if they knew, they wouldn't let me take their truck. I also tell them I'm at church, when I'm not. Lately, I haven't kept the Sabbath holy. Um... I think that's it."

"The things you are doing while you have your parent's vehicle or are not in attendance at services, are they illegal or immoral?" The priest enquired.

"No! Goodness, no," she paused, "Oh, and sometimes I forget to thank God before I eat, and I've not read the scriptures in weeks. And I didn't fast on fast Sunday."

"Fast Sunday? Where are you from, young lady?" The Priest asked.

"Pleasant."

"Hmmm... may I remind you of the third of the seven deadly sins," his voice was mesmerizing and soothing. "Sloth. Neglecting God is what you are doing when you engage in being slothful. Our lives are purposeful and by not concerning oneself with refinement and community support, we would not exist," he took a breath and a sip of water and continued. "Let me also remind you of the Ten Commandments. The third and fourth specifically. Do you remember them, my child?"

"Well, I'm sure number four is to Honor thy parents."

"Yes, the fourth commandment is to Honor Thy Father and Thy Mother. You are right, lying to them is not honoring them. They love you as our Father loves you," he continued. "The third commandment is to keep the Sabbath holy. By not coming to Mass and connecting with God weekly, you are not keeping the Sabbath holy."

"I'm sorry." Elizabeth said, a wave of guilt rushing over her. "I promise to repent. I'm sorry I sinned."

"God the Father of mercies, through the death and resurrection of His Son, has reconciled the world unto Himself and sent the Holy Spirit among us for the forgiveness of sins. Through the ministry of the Church, may God give you pardon and peace. I absolve you from your sins, in the name of the Father, and of the Son and of the Holy Spirit. Amen."

"Amen."

"Pray five hail Mary's, my child and go in peace."

"Hail Mary's?" Elizabeth asked. "Isn't one of the Ten Commandments to not put any other God before Him? I think that's the very first commandment, right? Thou shall have no other gods before me. Right? How will that work with the Hail Mary's?" The Priest turned his head and peered through the divider screen. Elizabeth looked hard, her eyes had adjusted to the dim light and she could see his facial features floating above the white square on his collar. He was younger than she had thought, maybe in his early thirties. Under the scrutiny of his stare, she blurted out, "I'm not even Catholic."

"Well, you *do* have some penance to do then, don't you?" The Priest said with a little laugh. "I should have known when you said you were from Pleasant you belonged to the *other* church." It struck Elizabeth that they always called their religion nothing more than 'the church', interesting to think about members of other church communities doing the same thing. "See your bishop. Reconnect with God. I meant what I said, respect your parents, church and community. It's what we *Christians* do, regardless of which pews we sit in on Sunday. Peace and God be with you, my child," she heard him laugh to himself as he slid the board back across the partition. *Glad I could make his day.* She stood and slipped out, a woman about her age with a nose ring and visible tattoos slipped in. Elizabeth saw Gaius and Tish walking out the doors at the back of the chapel and hustled to catch-up with them.

"Hey, where'd you go?" Gaius asked her as she approached.

"Confession."

"You didn't." Tish squealed.

"I did." Elizabeth said proudly, "and I enjoyed it. Feels good to be absolved of your sins, just like a baptism without getting wet."

"How many Hail Mary's did you get?" Gaius questioned, one eyebrow cocked and a smirk across his face.

"Five."

Gaius made a low whistling noise. "That's a lot." The trio stopped in the foyer. Rows of small tea light candles were lined against the walls. Some were lit, others were not. Gaius slipped a five-dollar bill into the donation box and lit one of the candles. "Miss you, Mama," he said as he touched the flame to an unlit candle. Elizabeth put her arm around Gaius' waist as they exited.

"Sir? Sir!" There was a woman's voice calling out to them. They saw a nun of about seventy, carrying a brown paper sack, rushing towards them. "The spirit moved me to bring this to you," she explained, forcing the bag into Gaius' hands.

"We don't need it, we're good." Gaius said, trying in vain to hand the sack back to the nun.

"We don't question God when we are moved to perform an act of kindness, we just move and get it done. God bless you, young people," she turned and with the agility of someone half her age, bounded up the stone steps and disappeared.

"Well, that was weird." Gaius said, opening the bag. "Looks like we got a bologna and mustard and two PB and J's, sandwich anyone?" The girls shook their heads as they started to walk towards the downtown area.

"Do you think I'll be in trouble with the bishop?" Elizabeth asked.

"Why would you be in trouble?" Gaius asked.

"I don't know, it was weird. I felt the spirit as if I was home in our church, but it was a priest and a confessional instead of a bishop in his office. Crazy, right?"

"Don't mean to burst your bubble, my little Lizard, but its people that create the energy, not god." They had fallen into step and walked into the setting sun. "Seriously, think about it, how else could Jim Jones have gotten hundreds of people to kill themselves? They must have all been moved somehow to commit mass Harakiri."

"Rock concert's move me." Tish admitted. "I mean you have a legit point with the throngs of people. I saw Carrie Underwood in the BYU stadium last year on the fourth of July, the energy in there was unbelievable; I was high on it for days after."

"The Baptist Church assemblies are like that, I felt the spirit there too." Since Elizabeth had already told Gaius this fact, it didn't feel too horrible admitting it to Tish too.

"As you ladies know, I don't believe in a god or a heaven, but..." He paused, gathering his thoughts. "If I *did* believe, I would think good people get into heaven and bad people don't, regardless of your faith. Seriously. Do you really believe folks like Mother Teresa or Gandhi didn't make it into heaven because they chose the wrong religion to represent?"

None of them spoke, absorbing and dissecting the question at hand. As they approached State Street they saw a young woman holding a sign printed on a piece of cardboard. 'Homeless and Hungry. Please Help.' At her feet were two children about five years old that appeared to be twins.

"What did that nun give us?" Elizabeth asked. "A bologna sandwich with mustard?"

"And *two* peanut butter and jelly sandwiches." Gaius said in astonishment. They approached the woman and children. It was obvious they had been living on the streets, the three of them wore dirty clothes. "Hi." Gaius said, flashing the mother his warm, handsome smile. "We don't have much to offer you, but here's a couple sandwiches and..." He reached his hand in his front pocket, extracting a few one dollar bills, and handed them to the young woman.

"Thank you, sir," she looked grateful as she slid the money in her pants pocket and took the brown paper sack. Gaius, Elizabeth and Tish turned south and kept walking.

"That was super strange." Elizabeth said.

"Weird for sure."

"You know what they say about God and His mysterious ways." Tish added.

The three of them hooked back up with the Trax and rode it west to another outdoor mall. This one was built from an old train station and was called the Gateway. They walked around, window shopping and enjoying a light conversation about the latest fashion trends.

Gaius bought the three of them a frozen yogurt as they wandered. They noticed a large crowd gathered at the edge of a park and meandered over. As they approached, they noticed two bald monks, dressed in dark reddish orange robes passing out bottled water and small boxes of non-perishable foods to the crowd that had assembled.

Elizabeth noticed the young woman with the twins. "Hi, we meet again."

"Oh, hello." The woman looked between the three of them.

"What's going on?" Tish asked.

"This is the homeless shelter." The woman explained, indicating the building to their left. "The Buddhist monks come this time every night and distribute food and water. We try and hit it up a couple times a week."

"Do you stay here?" Elizabeth enquired.

"No." The women said with concern on her face. "There's too many weird men that stay here. I shouldn't talk, but for real, Salt Lake has an abundance of weird homeless men. We go over on Redwood Road, there's a shelter for battered women, they take us in most nights. It's cool too, they have a kitchen, we can cook the food the monks bring us, most of it is mac n cheese and stuff like that. There's other women, kids. The people there make me grateful for what I have, you know? I'm healthy, my kids are healthy. We don't have some psycho man stalking us."

Elizabeth felt a pang of embarrassment in her gut. This homeless mother found reasons to be grateful and she felt entitled at her parent's home, entitled and privileged. There was always food, a bed, a shower, laundry and a car to borrow. Shame washed over her as she thought about the way she had acted when Paul wanted to use the truck and how put out she felt when her mother singled her out to help with dinner and clean up. She could definitely use a large helping of gratitude.

The monks finished handing out their boxes of food and were getting into their truck when Gaius approached them. "Hi," he said, smiling and waving to the pair in the truck. "We would like to help you. Do you accept donations?"

The two men looked at each other. The man in the passenger seat spoke to Gaius. "If you're serious about helping, come to the temple in the morning at dawn," he looked at the other man, still suppressing a laugh and rolled his eyes. Returning his attention to Gaius he continued, "We're on second west and first south. Are you a man of your word?" Gaius nodded without speaking, his brow knitted, a look of unease on his face. "If you are a man of your word, come at five a.m." The monk said. "Your friends are welcome too, be prepared to work. Community is very important for us, service to the community is of utmost importance. We are always happy for help. See you at dawn." They drove off.

"Five a.m.?" Tish looked incredulous.

"I've never been to a Buddhist temple, have you?" Gaius asked the girls as he slipped his hand into Elizabeth's. Her stomach did a flip. "Are you up for an overnight adventure?"

"Well..." She looked at him and Tish, a wave of giddiness washed over her. "You did say you are a man of your word, yea, I'm up for it. I've got no money to contribute though, none, zero."

"Yea, me neither." Tish added.

"I've got it." Gaius said. "A room with two beds will most likely be the same as a room with one."

"Where you gonna sleep if there are only two beds?" Tish asked.

"With my little Lizard, of course," he beamed at Elizabeth.

"I'll sleep with Tish." Elizabeth said, flushing scarlet red to the roots of her hair.

"No, you won't." Tish said, "You snore, she's all yours Gaius."

"We'll figure it out." Gaius said, teasingly.

They boarded the Trax and went back to the City Creek Center to get Gaius' truck. They found a room on Redwood Road close to the Buddhist temple. Gaius splurged for an upgrade and got a suite with one king sized bed and a fold out couch.

"We've got to call our parents." Elizabeth said.

"Thank you for the public service announcement, Liz." Tish said and sighed. "I'll go first," she dialed, waited a moment then, "Hey Mom. So Elizabeth and I are going to stay in Salt Lake tonight... Um, we don't need any money. We're doing a community service project early in the morning...It has something to do with the homeless, so...Gaius...Yea, but his name isn't Smith, its Stewart... Yes, of course, mother," her tone sounded a little irritated with the last remark. "Ah-huh...Yes... Okay, thanks. Love you too." Tish disconnected, "Next?" her eyes darted back and forth between Gaius and Elizabeth.

Gaius looked confused. "We're all responsible adults here, what are you all worried about?" he dialed his Grandpa's number. "Hey Gramps," he said, Elizabeth noticed he wore a nervous smile. "Could you feed Sass tonight and make sure she gets put in my room? I'm going to stay in Salt Lake." There was a long pause. "Yes, everything is fine," he repeated the same line Tish used with her mom. "We're doing a community service project in the morning, helping the homeless." Tish gave him a broad grin and two thumbs up. It was after all the truth. "Sounds good, Gramps. Yes, tell Grandma Mary goodnight too," he hung up. "That wasn't so hard, you two make me feel like I'm doing something I'm not supposed to."

"We're still figuring this adult stuff out." Tish explained. "Your turn, Elizabeth."

She sighed and got her phone out. Dialing the number, she hoped she got the voice mail. Paul answered on the third ring. "Hey brother." Elizabeth said nervously. "Could you tell mom I won't be home tonight?"

"Sure thing." Paul mumbled. "The girls are just leaving for the dance."

"I'm sure we'll be home by noon or so tomorrow."

"Okay, sis." Paul replied. "Oh, one last thing, be sure to wrap that rascal, if you get my drift."

"What?"

"Use a rubber," he hung up and her face flushed.

"Okay, now that's out of the way, I'm going to take a long bath." Tish announced. "I must have ESP because I packed an extra outfit. Anyone need the bathroom?"

Elizabeth and Gaius shook their head and Tish entered the bathroom. They could hear the water begin to run into the tub. Gaius looked at a text, it was from Toni.

Hey G, call me after six tonight. I have questions. Non-emergency.

"I've got to make a quick call," he said to Elizabeth, "Sorry."

"No worries" she said, eyeing the big bed. From behind her she heard him start to sing.

"Sister Christian oh the time has come... And you know that you're the only one..."

In astonishment, Elizabeth whirled around. He looked curiously at her and said into the phone, "Hey T, what's up?" They chatted a moment about paint colors and cupboard doors. Disconnecting the call, he asked. "What was up with that look you just gave me?"

"What were you singing?" she asked tentatively.

He sauntered up to her and wrapped his arms around her and kissed her lightly. "Night Ranger."

"Night. Ranger?" she asked.

"You've never heard of Night Ranger? Sister Christian?" he sang the lyrics again.

"Am I?" she asked. "The only one?"

"Yes," he moaned as he kissed her. His mouth was hungry on hers, his hands rubbing her back and lower. When his hands started back up, they went under the jersey and he felt the garments. "Why do you always wear two layers of clothes?" he asked pulling back from her just enough to look at her in focus.

"Those are my garments," she said, not looking directly at him. "They keep me safe, I got them when I went through the temple."

"Interesting," he said, as he gently took her hair out of the ponytail, letting it fall loose around her shoulders. "I'd like to know the statistics on that," He kissed her neck and kept talking, "I'd like to know if Mormons live longer and get hurt less because of the magical underwear," he kissed her neck again and mumbled into her ear, "If it's scientifically provable, my little Lizard, sign me up."

His mouth moved to her mouth. Her mind spun. She was confused. A little defensive because of the comment about her garments, but at the same time, she felt like she was floating feeling his fingers through her hair and his hands on her back, his mouth on her mouth. He walked them both to the bed where he laid her down, they continued to kiss, more urgently. Gaius kissed her mouth, down her neck and to the top of the neckline of her shirt. His hands roamed her stomach and slightly grazed her breasts. Her heart was racing like never before. Elizabeth rubbed her hands over his back and chest, and under his shirt to feel his taut muscles and smooth skin, all while kissing his neck. He took it off in one quick motion and she found herself kissing his shoulders and allowing her mouth to trail down his chest, tasting him. In the bathroom, the blow dryer came on, the noise returning Gaius and Elizabeth back to reality. They pulled away from each other, holding each other in their eyes.

"Wow that was amazing." Gaius said, putting his shirt back on. "I'm going to need a cold shower now," he kissed her lightly on the forehead. "You leave me hot and breathless, Lizard."

"Um, me too," she grinned at him, feeling flush and tingly with feelings of... Love? Lust? She wasn't sure, but she liked it either way.

"Aunt Toni said the Red Iguana is the best restaurant in town and the best Mexican food she's ever had, it's close too," he kissed her again. "Tish? You up for Mexican tonight?" Gaius said loudly.

The bathroom door opened, with a broad smile she answered, "Buddy, if you're buyin', I'm up for about anything."

Chapter Thirty-Nine

The wake-up call was set for 4:20 a.m. Ever the gentleman, he had let the girls take the large bed. Without turning on any lights, he got up and pulled on his jeans and slipped out to find a cup of coffee. When he returned he turned on the light, brushed his teeth in the kitchenette sink with a toothbrush he had gotten from the front desk. He peeked in on the girls. Elizabeth was awake, she had gotten up while he was brushing his teeth and got dressed. She walked past him and he grabbed her around the waist.

"Good morning beautiful girl," he went to kiss her but she pulled away.

"Morning breath, sorry," she said and gave him a sleepy smile on the way to the bathroom. Gaius sat on the chair and opened the curtain to watch the Salt Lake traffic in the predawn light.

Tish rolled over. "Already?" she yawned loudly.

"If you're up for coming." Gaius answered.

"Of course." Tish said, getting up and walking past him in her tee shirt and panties to the bathroom. She tapped lightly on the door and walked in. Gaius heard the two exchange their morning hellos. Elizabeth walked out and went directly to Gaius, straddling his legs, she bent down and kissed him.

"Mmm... Thanks," he said, setting his coffee on the little table next to him. He pulled Elizabeth onto his lap. Gaius rubbed his hands up and down the top of her thighs. Elizabeth ran her fingers through his hair and touched his cheek. They kissed a few more times before Tish reappeared out of the bathroom.

"Get a room," she said walking out of the bathroom, "Oops, I guess you already have one," she grabbed the sweats she had brought and slipped them on, still chuckling to herself. They gathered their few belongings and left the room as quietly as they could.

Gaius noticed it was five to five when they pulled into the parking lot of the Buddhist temple, there were lights on and other vehicles in the lot. The three of them walked to the front doors. They were locked. Looking through the glass in the main doors, they could see people working in the room across the large dark chapel. They went around to the other side and found an open door, fragrant smells lofting out. A nun dressed in a similar robe as the monks, her head just as bald, greeted them with a broad smile. Without actually talking, she led them to a side room and handed them clean aprons and hair nets then led them back to the kitchen. The nun motioned for Tish to come, and set her up peeling carrots. Tish gave Elizabeth and Gaius a look that said 'Oh boy, carrots.' The nun set Elizabeth up washing dishes. The monk from the day before recognized Gaius and came up to him.

"Glad you could make it," he said and held out his hand for Gaius to shake and motioned for Gaius to follow him.

All the volunteers were in the kitchen including Gaius. Bowls of food were lined up along a long table. One of the volunteers stood in front of them, motioning for them to be quiet. Musical chanting began from the dining hall, more and more voices joining in. After several minutes of listening to the chants Elizabeth, Tish and Gaius looked around to see what they were supposed to do. Gaius shrugged at them, the chanting stopped and the distinct crashing sounds of a gong rang out. The volunteer that appeared in charge handed the first volunteer a bowl and he walked into the dining hall, the gong crashed again and the woman in charge handed the second volunteer a bowl and she walked in the dining hall. The gong sounded again, and through another door, the first volunteer appeared and went to the end of the volunteer line. The gong sounded, the second volunteer appeared. This pattern continued. When it was Gaius' turn, he whispered, "What am I supposed to do?"

"You're a smart boy, you'll figure it out." Came the answer.

Gaius took the bowl and walked into the dining room. It had been transformed into a thing of beauty. The lights had been turned off and the only illumination came from dozens of candles plus the soft glow from the eastern windows, the sun was just barely starting to light up the sky. Gaius noticed the volunteer that had been in front of him in line was standing behind a robbed monk, the monks on the left of where the volunteer was standing had bowls in front of them. The ones to the right did not. Gaius walked over and set the bowl in front of the next monk to the right and stood behind as the next gong sounded. The volunteer left from one door as Elizabeth walked into the dining hall from the one he had entered through. She saw Gaius and started walking towards him. When the gong tolled again he whispered to her.

"After I leave, stay here until the next gong, then do what I did."

When the gong sounded, he walked around the long table and out the exit door and Tish walked in. She also figured out what she was supposed to do just by following Elizabeth's lead. There were more nuns and monks than volunteers so each volunteer served at least two people, some served three. Just as the sun crested the majestic mountain range, the monks and nuns began to eat. Back in the kitchen, one of the volunteers explained to Gaius, Elizabeth and Tish that it was an honor to serve the priests and priestesses at dawn, it's the only meal they ate all day and it was one hundred percent vegan.

The volunteer sensed she had a captive audience and continued to explain the people that lived in the monastery lived the Buddhist life to the letter. They eat nothing that they didn't grow themselves. The reason both the men and women had shaved heads and wore identical robes was their philosophy was they were one, and by each of them wearing the same clothes and not having hair, they took away the barrier of sexual discrimination as well as created a uniformity that suggested they were one big unit. The volunteers each got a small bowl of the leftover vegetable curry and rice.

After they ate at a folding table in the kitchen they went into the large chapel and were seated in pews that were lined along the back wall. There was a large golden statue in the center of the room, dozens of incense sticks were lit and set around the statue. Instead of wooden pews, there were more brightly decorated pillows, the volunteers were the only ones sitting on the pews. The monks and nuns walked around the outside of the room, several carrying incense. They sang their chants. There was a large gong at the front of the room and every now and then, a robed monk hit it. While this was going on, people appeared from the street carrying sacks of groceries. They placed the food at the foot of the statue, some lit another stick of incense, and found a cushion to kneel down. Some prayed, some were in the child's pose yoga position, others walked behind the precession of chanting robed figures. The lead volunteer motioned for them to follow her back to the kitchen. She told them they could leave if they wanted to. Speaking softly, she explained around nine o'clock they would gather the morning's offerings and divide it into things they needed here and with what's left, they put together boxes of food for the homeless.

"They do it every day," she explained. "Sometimes we have lots of help, sometimes not so much. I don't come every day, but a couple times a week at least. The younger nuns serve if there are no volunteers, but that doesn't happen very often. I come because it makes me feel good, you know, to help the community and all. Conveniently, it's early in the morning so I just head to work when we're done."

"We can come back at nine." Gaius volunteered.

"Only if you want to." The woman answered. "We have a lot of volunteers today so it's no biggie. We really appreciate your help. Doing the food each morning is such a chore, but it's *all* they eat, you know? So anyway, thanks again."

The three said their goodbyes. Before leaving they decided to walk around the grounds. The sun was barely up and cast long shadows across the grounds. Their gardens were spectacular, every bit as beautiful as the temple grounds. They walked by a large greenhouse and observed robbed figures with chop sticks gently removing the bugs from the tomato and pepper plants and putting them into plastic containers. There were a dozen peacocks wandering around with them, wailing their sorrowful call. To Gaius it sounded like they were saying 'Mom' but stretched out in a long moan. He still missed his mother every day. The pain of her absence still felt fresh when he was reminded of her, or thought of her, or dreamed she was still alive. Being around Elizabeth helped, being around his new grandparents helped, Sassafras helped, but it wasn't the same. It would be nice to share these new relationships with her. They saw a pair of nuns walking side by side towards them. They smiled and nodded as they got closer. The women stopped and motioned for Gaius, Tish and Elizabeth to stop too.

"We are teachers of the Buddhist philosophy and want to welcome you." Said one who appeared slightly older.

"Thank you." Gaius said, "We just wanted to check your place out, you know?"

"The peacocks are really pretty." Tish chirped. "I've never seen so many in one place."

"Yes." The younger looking nun replied. "They seem to know we are peaceful and won't do them harm. They are a terrible nuisance, but it is our way of life to share this world with all creatures. We do not kill or harm. The birds seem to know this and show up to stay."

As they gazed at the three young adults, they smiled, their eyes danced. "If you are interested in learning more about our way of life, we can schedule a time for a lesson." The older nun said, sincerely, still smiling.

"Just like the Mormons." Gaius said softly, beaming at Elizabeth. "Recruiting is recruiting I suppose," he winked at Elizabeth and saw her resigned expression as she agreed with him.

Chapter Forty

Gaius' energy driving home was high. He chattered away recounting his favorite parts of the trip as if he were a little boy. Tish was just the opposite. Her head bobbed as she dozed.

"It's just impressive that there is an organization that doesn't just talk the talk but actually walks the walk," he prattled on. "I was just super impressed. And their food, their one little vegan meal a day, no wonder they were so thin, right?" he took a breath and continued. "Oh, and let's not forget the Catholic nun, wow! She was certainly moved by..." He stopped completely at a loss for words.

"The Holy Ghost." Elizabeth finished the sentence for him.

"Or something." Gaius countered.

"It blows my mind you don't believe in any of this when it's so blatantly in your face, G!" Her tone was sharp and he looked at her apprehensively.

"Did I offend you, Lizard? I'm sorry if I did," his exuberant energy was gone.

"I don't know, Gaius," she sighed. "Sorry I snapped, it's just..." Her voice faded and she leaned her head on his shoulder and took his hand in hers. Suddenly and without warning, she began to cry.

"What's wrong, Elizabeth? Oh my god, I'm sorry," his words were calm and soothing.

She shook her head and didn't say anything, they drove in silence for a few miles. Elizabeth sat up and wiped her face with her free hand, holding tightly to Gaius with the other. "I'm confused, Gaius. It's that simple," she took a deep breath to get a hold of her runaway emotions.

"What are you confused about? Me? Us?"

She laughed and sobbed at the same time. It came out in an unattractive sound through her nose and mouth. "Are we an 'us'? Is that all it takes, a little petting on the bed?"

"Petting?" he replied. "Really?"

"That's what my mom calls it," she shook her head sheepishly and went on. "An 'us' would be lovely, G, but my feelings towards you are not what I'm confused about, my feelings for you are crystal clear." These words caused a fluttering in her stomach. "It's the rest of my life that just got hazy."

"Hazy how?"

"Well, I'm starting to see how things really are, I mean I feel as if someone just took a big cover off life and said 'here, look at it for what it is.' It's not what I expected, this whole adult business. Free will and choices, it was almost easier when my folks just told me what to do and how to do it. I don't know," she struggled to find the right words. "The Baptists impressed me, their exuberance, their music and energy. I mean, I was ready to be saved in Kentucky, my hand almost raised to be re-born. I'm ready to go vegan after only one meal with the monks. Such a simple life they lead. You're right about organizations not walking the walk. They're big *talk*, but..." Tears had sprung in her eyes again, it was *her* church that didn't. "The Catholics impressed me, I'll never forget that confession... And the nun, tied directly to God. I still can't get over that. Those sandwiches were nothing but a miracle, Gaius, a small one, but a miracle none the less. This is freakin' America and there are kids going hungry and living in a shelter? That could have been those kid's only meal for the day, G. That's heartbreaking. Our family throws out more food a day than we gave that little mama?" she let out a long breath and continued. "You and I both know that Montana missionary hunts all the time, and you said it the other night, thou shall not kill is another commandment a lot of Christians don't keep, but the Buddhists do. They pick bugs off their plants for crying out loud. Did you see that?" he nodded, she sighed. "I'm just all messed up. I seriously feel like I just found out Santa Claus isn't real." A tear fell as she looked out the windshield. She put her head back on Gaius' shoulder, her tears flowing silently.

"Sorry sweetie," he said, squeezing her hand. "Reality bites," she nodded and fell asleep on Gaius' shoulder. The girls slept the majority of the way home. They woke when Gaius pulled up to the Anderson house.

"Some company we are." Elizabeth yawned.

"I'm heading home, thanks Gaius." Tish said, opening the passenger side door and sliding out. "Call me later, Liz," she called over her shoulder as she made her way to her car.

Gaius turned and looked at Elizabeth, putting his hands on both sides of her head and looking at her face intensely as if to memorize it. "I'll see you tomorrow?" His sentence a question.

She nodded. They kissed their farewells and she slid across the seat. Standing there for a moment, she looked at him and felt her heart swell. "Thanks for an unbelievable experience, Gaius. I know it wouldn't have happened like that if not for you," she looked down at the ground and back up to meet his eyes. "You're amazing."

"You're amazing yourself, Lizard," he replied. "See you tomorrow."

"For sure."

They smiled at each other as she closed the truck door. Walking into the house, she heard an angry exchange coming from the top of the stairs. *Buzz kill*, she thought. Pausing on the landing she listened for a few seconds, she could hear her dad yelling at someone.

"It's become more than a pattern. You've got to get a hold of this before it ruins your life!"

"Everyone just needs to take one big chill pill!" Elizabeth heard Paul roar back at his dad. "Nothing happened last night! Quit making something out of nothing!"

"If nothing happened, why are we having this conversation?" Alice screeched.

"Because it seems everyone insists on butting their noses in my business!" Paul yelled back.

"Well if you would keep your nose clean we wouldn't have too!" Alice snapped.

That didn't even make sense, Elizabeth thought.

"Son," Daniel began, "When will you look at your accountability with these continued scenarios? It's not difficult to live the way God wants, the covenant of chastity is…"

"Dad, quit trying to control my life!" Screamed Paul. "Nothing happened, for crying out loud!"

Elizabeth headed down the stairs to her room. She didn't want anything to do with this conversation. Jozette and Giselle were on the couch in the family room, watching TV.

"Hey." Elizabeth said. "What's up?"

"Our brother is a freak." Jozette said with distain.

"What happened?" Elizabeth questioned. Jozette just shook her head.

Giselle answered. "No one knows, really. He was at the dance last night, lurking around in the parking lot or something. There's this new kid at school, Shane. He's a senior and transferred for like the last two months of school. He's a year behind, so he's older, something to do with family trouble. I guess he ran away for like a year and then he moved in with his aunt and uncle here in Pleasant. I don't know. The whole thing is weird. So last night, him and Paul were hanging out in the parking lot. Apparently, the school security called the cops. The cops came and told Paul he had to leave," she rolled her eyes. "Of course, he didn't. He told them he had a date and he had every right to be there. That Shane dude just walked back into the dance, he had a high school I.D and stuff. They told Paul he had to leave or they were gonna arrest him. Made all kinds of messed up threats. He told them he would call the news with his one phone call because he hadn't done anything. I don't know, it was a ruckus though. He left, the cops left. Life went back to normal," she sighed and shook her head.

"He's a weirdo." Jozette added.

Aren't we all. Elizabeth thought.

Chapter Forty-One

It was Easter Sunday and Elizabeth woke early to help her mom make monkey bread for the family. It had been years since they dyed eggs or did baskets, but the gooey pastry had remained a tradition. The two of them reminisced about past Easters, the egg hunts and festivities when they were all little. Elizabeth smiled as she thought about the magic her parents created by hiding the eggs and surprising them with baskets with homemade goodies in them. Such an innocent time. One by one Daniel and the kids woke and wandered in the kitchen when the smell of the baking pull-aparts started rousting them.

"Happy first Sunday after the first full moon after the Spring Solstice." Elizabeth said, pulling off some of the warm cinnamon bread.

Daniel gave her a perplexed look. "Excuse me?"

"Oh, I just heard somewhere that Easter was established before the days of Christ, the goddesses' totem animal was the rabbit, that's why the Easter bunny."

"Don't believe everything you read on the internet." Daniel said cautiously. After a moment of silence while they ate their bread, Daniel set his milk down and looked around the table. "I'd like to offer our family a blessing this morning." Like Pavlov's dogs, Alice, Jozette and Giselle immediately put down their food and folded their arms, respectfully. Paul glared at Daniel as he began to pray.

"Our Dear Heavenly Father, thank you for this beautiful day as we gather as a family and remember the sacrifice you made for us. We bow our head in remembrance of your Son, Jesus Christ, we honor you oh Lord, we are grateful for all of the blessings you've bestowed on us, our health and our love. We ask thee to soften the hearts of our family, that they may remember your lessons, that they may read your word and know your truth. That they may honor their bodies as temples and respect the commands you have set for us to live by. We pray unto you for these things. Thank you for the love of our eternal family. Bless us, we ask for these things in the name of the Father, the Son and the Holy Ghost, amen."

"Amen." Elizabeth couldn't help but think of the Holy Ghost as the Heavenly Mother, *her* still small voice. Lately, some ideas made more sense than others. It was as if there were layers of her principles that were being peeled back. Puzzle pieces falling into place. During one of their texted conversations, Gaius had said the reason church was every week was so people didn't have enough time to stray with their beliefs in between meetings. At the time, she thought it was a joke. Now though, that also made sense. She had been skipping Sunday school since she'd been home, and now she found she didn't want to go at all. She was more excited about seeing Gaius afterwards. Her dad was speaking and it brought her attention back to the table.

"While you children are living in our house, whether you are children or young adults, there are some basic things that your mother and I expect from you. The first is Sunday meetings, not just Sacrament either, but Sunday school and Relief Society or Priesthood, Paul," he paused and took a sip of his milk and continued. "You will respect the Gospel while under this roof. This includes the Word of Wisdom, Articles of Faith, the Commandments, weekly scripture reading will be mandatory," his voice was getting louder and more intense as he fell into the groove of preaching to his family. Elizabeth knew none of her siblings would provoke their father in any way. She kept her eye on Paul while her father raged on. "I am still in charge of this household, I am your father." With that last remark, Paul couldn't help but giggle, he looked down at his plate and breathed like Darth Vader, but more subtly. "I mean it!" Daniel roared.

"You got your point across." Alice interjected, placing a comforting hand on her husband's. "It's just your dad and I have been talking and…" She looked at each of her children before continuing. "It's just you all are almost grown and as your parents if we don't instill lifetime values now, we failed and we set you up to fail. It's because we love you so much, like our Heavenly Father loves you," her smile was genuine but Elizabeth sensed a feeling of… of what? It's as if her parents were quoting from a manual on raising young adults. The smile seemed empty with no emotion behind it. What about choices? Free will? Their church lessons were all about choosing and free agency but only if the decisions were the same as their parents'. Was that an actual choice? They were hypocrites.

Where are these feelings coming from? She thought. Is it Gaius? Or the experiences from the weekend in Salt Lake? Crap. This is bad. I shouldn't be questioning this. She remembered once asking a question to the teacher in Primary, the children's class at church. She couldn't remember what the question was but she remembered the reply, 'Don't ask questions. Shut your mouth and listen, you'll learn the answers. Elizabeth listened to her parents without comment. She had definitely been more excited for church before breakfast.

After, they all went their separate ways to get ready for church. Elizabeth had made a light pink skirt, it flared at the bottom. The material had a shimmer to it, her top was borrowed from Giselle, it was light blue with pink floral shaped buttons and puffed sleeves. After braiding her hair straight back, she looked in the mirror. Her hairstyle made the outfit look matronly. Taking out the braid, she shook her hair loose. It fell in her eyes. Carefully, she braided just the hair in the front from one side to the other so it framed her face, leaving the rest loose. She walked upstairs to the sewing room and found some tiny white and pink silk flowers. She placed just a few in her hair, winding them through her braided bangs. Glancing at the clock, she realized it was almost time to go.

Walking back through the kitchen she went over to her dad and put her arms around him. "Love you, Daddy," she said and walked down the stairs.

"See you at church," he called after her.

"Ok." Elizabeth called just as Tish pulled in.

They arrived at the church, Gaius and the Smith's weren't there yet. Tish sat with Elizabeth in the unofficial pew for the Anderson family. The chapel started to fill, the rest of the Anderson's arrived together and slid into the pew. Elizabeth purposely kept herself on the end, she didn't want to take the chance of missing Gaius. The Smith's came in right before the services began. Elizabeth could hear Brother Smith's booming voice as he said his hellos. Elizabeth felt the palms of her hands moisten, she could hear them getting closer. Smiling broadly, she turned and saw Brother and Sister Smith, but no Gaius. Her heart sank as Brother Smith shook her father's hand and greeted her family. As they started to walk towards the front pew, Brother Smith looked at Elizabeth and winked.

Once Sacrament meeting was over, the congregation started filing out. Elizabeth was disappointed Gaius didn't make it. She shuffled out of the chapel with everyone else. Tish followed her talking about Blondie's lunch. When they reached the foyer Elizabeth saw him sitting on the couch, smiling at her.

"Hi," she said a little nervously.

"You're pretty," he said, "Every bit as pretty as Eastre I'm sure." Standing, he took her hand. Tish sauntered up to them.

"Oh my goodness, did you see Shane? He's so super-hot!" Tish was beaming. "We should invite him to our sinners' club."

"Coming?" Gaius asked Elizabeth.

"I can't today." Elizabeth replied. Both Gaius and Tish looked disappointed. "My dad wants us all to go to all three hours of service. I haven't been to Sunday school since I got home from my mission, I'm sorry. He'll be mad. Let's get together after."

"Can't." Tish said, "I've got to go home and help my mom with Easter dinner."

"Well, Tough Stuff," Gaius said looking at Tish, "looks like it's just you and me."

"Okay, I'll meet you there. Happy Easter." Tish hugged Elizabeth and walked out to the parking lot. Elizabeth and Gaius followed but at a much slower pace, their fingers entwined. When they reached the glass door they turned and looked at each other.

"I'm not doing anything later," he said, grinning at her.

"Okay," she blushed and looked at her feet. She felt like her heart was being pulled out the door with him. "I've gotta run." Elizabeth said before she changed her mind, she quickly kissed his cheek. Gaius left through the glass door, blowing a kiss at her. She turned and walked back towards the lobby, slipping into the woman's restroom. While in the stall, she overheard a conversation between a few female ward members.

The first one whined to the others, "It's just not fair for us to have to support it. Bunch of crap if you ask me."

"I know, right?" The second one said. "As parent's we should be able to teach our children the truth. It's just not natural. A sickness really."

"A marriage is one man and one woman." The first one said firmly.

A third voice chimed in. "I agree. It's an abomination. Completely unnatural."

The second woman said, "First it's the lies of science they insist we teach, effing evolution, *please*. We all *know* it's God. And now we have to support freaks? Approve of homosexuality? Not me, sisters, not me."

"Agreed. It's not fair." The first one whined again. "I'll never be for two men getting married, or women for that matter, it's just wrong. What about procreation? What would happen to the world's population if everyone was gay? The whole human race would just die out. And besides, how in the world would I explain it to my kids? Could you imagine? Johnny and Jimmy love each other just like mommy and daddy," she mocked. A combined chorus of horrors filled the small space.

"What's next? Bestiality?" One said laughing as they finished washing their hands.

"The school should teach both evolution and creationism and let the students pray about it, then they can decide for themselves what the truth is." One woman said while dispensing the paper towels to dry her hands. The others agreed wholeheartedly. *Gaius is right, there is no separation of church and state*, Elizabeth thought.

"That's why my kids go to the private school over in Eureka. The parents have so much more say about the curriculum. *No* evolution. None of this global warming crap either, you know? They even have prayer to open the day *and* bless the cafeteria food. Makes me feel so much better about their education. Worth the drive every day, I'm tellin' ya'. Pleasant should have a private school like that."

"No kidding." One answered as they took their conversation out of the bathroom.

Elizabeth shook her head. *How sad*, she thought, *they are wearing blinders and forcing their kids to wear them too*. Looking at herself in the mirror while washing her hands, she realized she had been wearing blinders too. Blinders *her* parent's had put on her. She thought of the other churches they had visited in Salt Lake. Could they all be wrong? Could her church really *not* be the one and only true church? The thought made her stomach turn. Lately it felt like she was walking on uneven and unsteady ground Hurrying back down the hall she walked by a classroom. There was a long window on the right side of a closed door, and the lights were out. Glancing in, she saw Paul sitting on the back row in the darkened room. His head was back and he had a pained look on his face. His eyes were closed tightly.

Elizabeth stopped and peered through the long window. Was he alright? Paul's chest was heaving and he brought both hands to his face as his mouth twisted into a grimace. Elizabeth turned the handle of the door and opened it, leaning her head in slightly.

"You okay, little brother?" her voice broke whatever trance he was in.

Paul's eyes grew wide, his nostrils flared and he hissed at Elizabeth. "Get out, get out, get out," his breath came out ragged and strained. His face turned so red it was almost purple, and his contorted expression turned into pure rage. He leaned over the table, both hands under it and said firmly. "Get...out." Each word came out sharp and clipped.

She backed out confused and darted into the women's bathroom. After a minute she was able to calm her breathing and walked into the hallway. Approaching her was the new guy. It seemed he was coming out of the room Paul had been in, or did he just come from outside?

"Hi. Sorry, I forgot your name," he flashed a handsome smile at her. "We met at the Timpanogos temple on Friday, remember? I was with Laurie and Frida."

"Yes, of course," she said. "It was Shane, right? I'm Elizabeth."

"That's right. Good to see you." Shane said, smiling warmly.

Her thoughts jumped to Laurie putting her arm through his when they were talking to Tish, the pained look on Frida's face, and Gaius' comment about Tish standing a better chance with Frida.

Elizabeth walked towards the room where she had seen Paul. She slowed to look through the window. As she peered in she saw Paul standing with his back to her, he was looking down at his waist and adjusting his belt, he tucked in his shirt. Before he could see her, she quickly walked down the hall to the exit and hustled out into the sunshine. Her dad was going to be mad but church was done for her today.

It was a perfect spring day, the temperature not too hot or cold. After she jogged to the other side of the street, she started walking, the flared hem of her skirt swaying back and forth. As she crested the small hill on 900 East she heard a vehicle coming up behind her. Elizabeth glanced behind her and saw the family truck, she knew Paul would be driving. A tree and small hedge offered her a place to hide while the truck barreled past. Since he hadn't even slowed down, she assumed he didn't see her. Watching the direction of the truck it was obvious he was heading back to their house. Climbing out of her hiding place, she looked back towards the church. Tears stung her eyes. It was a perfect vantage point to see the whole building and surrounding packed parking lot. It was big and sturdy and the sun caught the glistening pillar that ran up from the front entrance. *They all look the same*, she thought, *you can tell a Mormon church from a mile away*. She thought of the Buddhist monks from Salt Lake, the way it was hard to tell them apart when they were serving their breakfast. H ow they worked and lived as a unit. They practiced what they preached, did she? Her family? Her friends?

Was her church just a façade? The members pretentious and haughty? Standing in the shade of the tree she looked at it again, letting her eyes relax like a person does when they want to see hidden pictures in patterns. She thought of the missionary from Montana's conceited smirk as he looked smugly at Gaius. Sister Jolley's wicked smile and the shark look from the bishop in Kentucky popped into her head. She thought of the uncomfortable feeling she had the day she had taken Maximus to church, the Baptist church-goers welcomed her to their church, but her peers shunned Max. Grandpa Bill and her mom's judgmental voices echoed in her mind as well. So what if Gaius' mom wasn't LDS, was that a reason to keep a baby from his daddy? A reason to tear a family apart? She had seen the pained look in Gaius' eyes when he talked about his mother. And what if Paul was gay? Big deal. Big deal! *That's* why he was sent home early, it wasn't a female missionary he was fooling around with, it was another Elder. The thought of her parent's anguish pierced her heart. She saw the angry eyes of her brother. Paul's gay, it made sense in fact, it explained a lot of his behavior over the years.

Their mother would be mortified. For the first time in her life, she felt a twang of empathy for her little brother. She thought of Frida and Laurie and their little secret. It was as if she had been punched in the stomach, her breath shallow. She felt sick. The still small voice in her head told her to walk to the café.

At Blondie's, Tish and Gaius had already sat at the round booth in the corner. They were discussing their Salt Lake trip when their food arrived. Elizabeth walked in, shiny from the heat and walking in her Easter attire. Tish slid around and Elizabeth flopped down on the end of the bench.

"It's hotter than it looks out there," she said.

"You're hot." Gaius smiled.

Elizabeth made a silly face at him, Frida approached. "Hey Liz, biscuits and gravy? Crispy bacon?"

"Hi Frida. Yes, please and a large orange juice, thank you." Frida nodded and walked back to the counter.

"So, what happened? Why are you gracing us with your presence?" Tish asked through a mouthful of breakfast burrito.

"After you guys left, I felt like I was in an episode of the twilight zone," she sighed and slipped her uncomfortable shoes off under the table. Tish and Gaius continued to eat but looked at her with an expression that encouraged her to continue. "So, I was in the bathroom and Sister Cooper, Sister Zimmerman and Sister Hamm were in there talking smack about same sex marriage. It's weird that they are so opinionated about it, how in the world does it affect them?" she sighed, "They also made ridiculous comments about talking to their kids about homosexuality and science and evolution not being legitimate," she took a long drink of Tish's water.

"Science definitely blows the Noah's ark story out of the water." Gaius chuckled, "it's got to be the most ridiculous story in the Bible." Frida appeared with Elizabeth's breakfast.

"You think so?" Tish asked.

"Duh." Gaius said in a condescending tone. "It's physically impossible. Seriously, think about it. Noah would have had to gather *all* the gazelles and deer just to feed the lions, tigers, jaguars, cougars and black panthers. He just saved two so they could reproduce? It doesn't make sense."

"All things are possible with God." Tish answered, finishing her breakfast.

"Well, if that's true, your god isn't very efficient." Said Gaius. Tish knitted her eyebrows together in a look of confusion. "All things are possible with god? You just said that, think about it, just stop and think. Wouldn't it have been easier to just build shelters all around the world for the animals? How did Noah get a polar bear, panda bear and grizzly in his area? None of it, seriously, *none* of it makes sense."

"Noah could have gotten just one bear couple and as they reproduced, they could have moved and found more suitable areas for them, then over generations, they could have changed to adapt to the climate and stuff. You know, the polar bears turned white because of the snow, the grizzlies' brown because of the forest." Tish said in a scholarly tone.

"Oh, you mean, like evolution," he laughed.

"No, I mean they changed because of their environment." Tish explained.

Gaius laughed harder. "Like I said, because of evolution."

"I heard they are making a reproduction of the ark somewhere in the south." Elizabeth commented. "Down by where I served my mission, I think. Kentucky somewhere."

"I've heard that too." Gaius remarked. "It makes me wonder if they'll have animal feces all over the floors and drowning people screaming on the sides, begging for mercy as they drown. God's voice will boom from above, 'Die you sinners, die!'"

"You're twisted." Tish said.

"I'm twisted? It's your story, not mine." Gaius said entertained. "What about the animal life that doesn't even live for forty days and forty nights, I mean some insect's lives are only days or weeks, not a month plus."

Frida stopped by to take some of the empty plates off the table.

"Hey Free." Tish said, "That boy you and Laurie were with the other day, Shane I think was his name. Do you know if he's got a steady girlfriend?"

Frida poured more coffee for Gaius, "No, I'm absolutely positive he doesn't have a steady girlfriend, and..." she hesitated choosing the right words before she continued. "I don't think that's what he's looking for to be honest," her eyes darted to Gaius, there was a look of comprehension between them.

"Hmm, maybe I could change his mind." Tish pondered, her attention returning to her breakfast.

Frida shrugged slightly and walked away.

"No offense, Tough Stuff, but I seriously doubt it." Gaius commented off-handedly.

"Speaking of Shane," Elizabeth said, "the weirdest thing happened today. I saw Paul in one of the empty classrooms at church, and I thought he was praying," she took another sip of Tish's water. "So I didn't knock, but just stuck my head in to see if he was okay, you know? But when I came in, he freaked out. Like *freaked out*! He told me to leave under no uncertain terms, so I ducked into the bathroom across the hall. I washed my hands and walked back into the hall and I saw Shane coming out of the room. I didn't see him in there before."

"Interesting." Tish said.

"Very." Gaius agreed. "What was Paul doing?"

"Well, I thought he was praying, like I said. He had his head thrown back with his eyes closed and a look on his face like he was going to burst into tears."

Gaius choked on his coffee and started laughing.

"What's so funny?" Elizabeth asked.

"You didn't see Shane cuz he was most likely on his knees, but I seriously doubt he was praying," he chuckled again and shook his head.

Elizabeth stared at him not wanting to believe it, but she knew that's what she had witnessed.

"Oh my gosh!" Tish said with a sudden understanding washing over her face. "No, no, no, that beautiful beast of a man can't be..." She looked with confusion at Elizabeth.

"Do you really think?" It was harder for her accept than she thought. This was really *happening,* her brother was gay. It was Shane who was in the parking lot with Paul at the dance. He was sent home from his mission for inappropriate physical contact with another missionary. From what she had gathered, the other missionary had felt guilt over whatever happened between them and had confessed it to the mission president during a routine interview. Most likely his companion was the 'eye-witness.' The whole family had assumed it was a Sister missionary. It was an Elder. No wonder Paul got so defensive when it came up. Elizabeth's mind swam.

"Lucky for the gay men of Pleasant though," Gaius said thoughtfully, "he's a handsome dude."

"The gay men of Pleasant." Elizabeth repeated, her line of thought still muddled. The realization of what had happened in the church classroom washed over her. The color drained from her face. Her mother's worst nightmare, a scandal that would truly rock the family's reputation.

Gaius saw the look on her face. "Lizard, my sweet innocent little Lizard," he smiled at her, "There's no shame in being gay."

"Tell that to my parents." Elizabeth exhaled, her mind spinning. *How is it the church can tell you who you can or can't love?* Various memories of him flooded back. When they were children, he loved her dress-up clothes and when they played she let him wear them. He would pretend her Chapstick was lipstick and would parade around with her proudly. She never thought a thing about it. She remembered her father telling him he couldn't play dress up or wear lipstick, it was sissy and he was a big boy. He shouldn't play with dolls or stuffed animals either. If she remembered right, her dad had bought him a football that day. For the first time in her life, he was exposed to her.

"He could get excommunicated for that if someone found out." Tish commented off-handedly.

Frida stopped by their booth and left their check. The door opened and Laurie walked in and without looking at Frida went to the counter and sat on a barstool while depositing her purse and scriptures on the stool next to her. Frida smiled and walked back to the counter getting a glass and serving Laurie iced lemonade before she even ordered.

Tish reached into her bag and pulled out a ten-dollar bill. "This should cover mine."

"Thanks." Gaius said, taking the bill and adding it to a twenty, he put it in the folder with the handwritten ticket that had Frida's smiley face and 'have a nice day' written neatly at the bottom.

"Sorry, I don't have any money." Elizabeth said. "I shouldn't assume you'll keep paying my way."

"It's cool." Gaius replied. "It's worth it just to have your company."

Tish's phone vibrated. "Crap. I've got to run. My brother needs the car," she announced. "Liz, you comin'?"

Elizabeth looked at Gaius. "Naw, I'll walk, it's a lovely day."

Gaius smiled at her as they all slid out of the booth.

"Should I walk you home?" Gaius asked as they watched Tish pull out of the parking lot.

"I really don't want to go home, but I should change out of these clothes."

"Should we blow this popsicle stand?" he smirked at her and opened the driver's door of the truck.

"Did it ever occur to you there are no Popsicle stands because people like you blow them up?" Elizabeth said as she laughed at him and climbed in. He got in behind her and before starting the truck he leaned in and kissed her, his arms encircling her, pulling her closer. She returned the affection and kissed him back letting her arm reach across him, settling on his waist. Gaius ran his fingers through Elizabeth's hair and studied her face.

"You're so pretty, have I told you that today?" he said and leaned in to nuzzle her neck, giving it light kisses.

Elizabeth saw Laurie come out of the restaurant and unlock her car. Suddenly Frida came running out of the building waving a white sweater over her head. Laurie turned and Elizabeth could tell by her body language it was anticipated. The two girls stood in front of each other, Frida clutching the sweater. Elizabeth nudged Gaius, he saw where she was looking, they watched in silence as the two young women looked at each other, their desire intense. Laurie took a few steps backwards towards the car and Frida followed. Laurie talked animatedly and pulled an envelope out of her bag. She took the letter out and unfolded it and handed it to Frida. She scanned it and handed it back. Laurie's body posture changed, she looked defeated, like she could burst into tears at any moment. Laurie opened the door to the vehicle, Frida handed her the sweater and letter then quickly kissed her cheek. Just as fast, Laurie jumped into the driver's seat. The window was rolled down and Frida placed her hand on the window jam, Laurie ducked her head out and kissed the back of Frida's hand so swift Elizabeth wondered if she had actually seen it happen. The brake lights came on and the car started to back out. Frida stood and watched it pull into traffic and slowly walked back into the diner. As she neared the door, she caught sight of herself and straightened her posture before she walked back in, rubbing her hands over her face as if she had been crying.

"Sad." Elizabeth said.

"That two women as in love as Frida and Laurie can't make out in the cab of a truck in broad daylight like we are doing right now, they can't hold hands, or embrace or kiss in public. That this country claims to be free yet we stifle those that are different from the norm? Stifle is not the right word, ostracize. Ostracize those that don't fit into the mold, into the definition that society deems appropriate," his voice prickled. "Yes. Very, very sad."

After a few seconds of quiet contemplation while they snuggled in the truck Elizabeth made a suggestion. "I don't really want to go home, but I'm not sure I'm dressed for your place," she paused, unsure if she should go on. "Maybe we could go on a little road trip, you know? Back to Salt Lake? Or Provo. The mountains," she added as an afterthought.

He looked at her, a sideways grin on his face, one eyebrow cocked.

"I don't have any money though," she stammered. "And I would have to go to my house to get a change of clothes and my toothbrush, you know."

Gaius touched her face tenderly and leaned in to kiss her. As he drew back, a broad grin broke out across his face and he began chanting. "Camp-ping, camp-ping, camp-ping!"

"Okay. But I do need to go to my house, change clothes and grab a few things."

"Really? Okay, yes, right on!" He bubbled with excitement. "I need to get Sass or make sure Gramps will keep an eye on her. Plus, dig out all the camping gear. We're going to have a blast!" He started the truck and drove to her house. She dashed downstairs to change from the Easter dress. Alice invited Gaius in like an old friend offering him a soda and an invite to stay for dinner. When Elizabeth reappeared in the kitchen, she kissed her mom's cheek and causally asked about the camping tent and cooler.

"Who's going camping?" Alice enquired.

Elizabeth looked at Gaius and back to her mother. "We are," she kept her answer vague.

"You and…" Alice turned, "it was Gaius, right?" he nodded. "You and Gaius? Will there be other kids going too?"

"Yes, of course." Elizabeth answered avoiding her mother's eye. "We were thinking of Provo or American Fork canyon."

"You could drive the Alpine loop." Daniel appeared in the kitchen from down the hallway. "It's a beautiful time of year and you'll probably see a lot of wildlife," he continued, retrieving a grape soda from the fridge and sitting at the table across from Gaius.

"What's the Alpine loop?" Gaius asked. "I've never been in that area."

"If you go up the Provo canyon on the U.S 189 then across on the scenic route, I think its S.R. 92, it winds you up and around and you come out American Fork canyon. It's a beautiful drive. We've taken the boy scouts camping up there to get their Eagle Scout badge."

Gaius glanced at Elizabeth.

"How long are you going to be gone?" Daniel asked Gaius as he took a long drink of his soda.

"I don't know." Gaius said, looking to Elizabeth for help.

Elizabeth was getting the plates and utensils ready for dinner. "Um, I don't know, daddy," she said, avoiding his eyes. "It's a spur of the moment type trip. We were going to leave tonight, but-"

"It's Easter!" Daniel said pointedly, "Certainly you don't want to miss out on Easter dinner," he winked at Gaius and Gaius grinned a little.

"Zeb and Tiffany are coming by as well. You can meet the whole family."

"You're right." Alice beamed at him as she set the dishes on the table. "Besides, it would be dark before you two get to Provo. It's not realistic to leave tonight. Stay and have dinner."

"There's all kind of camping stuff you can help yourself too." Daniel commented. "Besides the cooler and tent, there's also a Coleman stove and first aid kit out in the garage."

"Thank you, sir." Gaius said. "I've got a cooler, but we could certainly use the tent."

"Call me Brother Anderson." Daniel smiled warmly at Gaius. "You two taking Tish? You know, your mother used to bring her best friend on dates with us. I never really understood why, but she did, several times, didn't you, honey?"

"Indeed I did." Alice said proudly. "There is safety in numbers."

"Oh, I'll make sure she stays safe." Gaius commented affectionately.

Zeb and Tiffany showed up and were introduced. Elizabeth thought how wonderful it was to see Zeb. She had missed him. When they were seated around the big table, Elizabeth leaned in and whispered into Gaius' ear.

"Welcome to Sunday dinner, when I was little, this was a weekly ritual."

"Lucky," he said, winking at her and taking her hand under the table.

Daniel blessed the food before they ate. Dinner conversation was light, Zeb updated the family on their landscaping endeavors with their new house, Giselle talked about school and how excited she was about the track meet that was coming up. Jozette didn't comment much but nodded and agreed with her sister, interjecting a 'for sure' or 'totally' every now and then. Alice talked about the Easter egg hunt the relief society had put on for the children of the ward the day before. It had been very successful, over a hundred children had come. Daniel listened and looked interested to each person at the table. Even Paul was in a decent mood and appropriately joined the conversation. He had been avoiding Elizabeth's eye but didn't say anything to her or anyone about the awkward moment at the church. Towards the end of dinner, Giselle commented.

"Have you guys seen that new guy, Shane?" she said, looking at Paul. "He's kinda cute." Jozette nodded in agreement.

"He's probably too old for you." Paul said a bit strained. "He's graduating this year. What are you now, fifteen?" Elizabeth and Gaius' eyes met, neither said a thing.

"Almost sixteen." Giselle announced proudly. Jozette nodded again.

"Too old for you." Paul repeated and scooped a spoonful of potatoes into his mouth. Elizabeth and Gaius exchanged another look.

"Tish thinks he's cute too." Elizabeth added.

"I would think a boy in high school is too young for her." Paul remarked off-handedly without even looking her way.

Gaius and Elizabeth shared another knowing look, one Daniel seemed to pick up on as well. When dinner was over, Gaius was the first person to jump up and start clearing the dishes.

"Leave that to the girls." Daniel boomed. "C'mon Guy, let's go get that camping stove ready for you."

"It's Gaius," he said as he set a stack of plates near the sink.

"That's what I said." Elizabeth caught Gaius' eye and shrugged slightly.

"We've got the kitchen." Alice said, smiling warmly at Gaius, "It was a pleasure to get to know you. I do hope to see you again sometime."

"Most definitely." Gaius nodded towards Alice, "Thank you for the delightful meal. Happy first..." He paused from his usual drawn out title for the holiday and said, "... Easter. Happy first Easter for me, here in Pleasant," he smiled warmly at Alice and Elizabeth.

Gaius followed Daniel and Paul out of the room, Elizabeth put a few items into the fridge and left too, bounding down the back steps to the garage as her sisters loaded the dishwasher.

When she joined her father and Gaius they were talking about the placement of tents to get the most sleep in the morning, or to use the sun as an alarm. There was already a pile set aside with a cooler, lantern, a small shovel and hatchet. Daniel was rummaging through a large wooden box and extracted two sleeping bags and a large denim quilt.

"Your grandma made this so take good care of it," he said as he added it to the other equipment.

"Will do." Elizabeth affirmed as she surveyed the growing pile of camping gear.

After they gathered the necessary items to camp safely and comfortably they loaded them into the back of Gaius' Toyota.

"Wanna just spend the night and we can leave first thing tomorrow morning?" Gaius asked Elizabeth as they finished organizing the back of the truck.

Before she had a chance to answer, Brother Anderson spoke up. "Looks like you've got everything, son. Elizabeth will just see you in the morning," he protectively put his arm around Elizabeth. She forced a smile at Gaius and slightly rolled her eyes.

Gaius held out his hand for Daniel to shake. "Thank you, Brother Anderson. Elizabeth, I'll text you later," he nodded his head once and climbed into the cab of the truck. As he did, Elizabeth realized the nod was a mannerism of Gaius' grandfather's. He must have subconsciously picked up.

Chapter Forty-Two

Glancing in the rearview mirror Gaius saw Brother Anderson steer his daughter back to the front door of their house. Deciding to be proactive about the road trip, Gaius stopped at the C-store to top off his gas tank and grab a couple bags of ice. As he pumped the gas he recognized the little Fiat that pulled on the other side of the pumps. "Hey Frida, fancy meeting you here," she smiled at him and he noticed she seemed to glow. "Well you certainly look glad to be off work."

"Oh, I'm always happy to be away from the cafe," she laughed.

Gaius noticed again how carefree Frida seemed to be. "What are you and-"

"It's our one-year anniversary on Wednesday." Frida cut him off and answered his question before he asked it. "We've got a special dinner date planned."

"Wow, congrats. Tell Laurie hello from me and have fun."

"You too." Frida replied, she held Gaius' gaze for a moment longer, her face smiling but her eyes sad.

"You okay?" Gaius asked.

"Oh, I'm great." Frida answered, "Better than ever," she surprised Gaius by leaning through the opening between the pumps and hugged him. "Glad to have met you, Gaius. You're a special man."

"Thank you." Gaius replied. "You're mighty special yourself."

"Take care," she said and walked into the store to pay for her gas. Gaius headed home.

When he got back to the Smith's, they were just finishing dinner. He noticed an empty plate set at the table. "Sorry I'm late, Gramps. I stayed over at the Anderson's after church. Elizabeth and I are going to go camping this week and I lost track of time while we were gathering things up," he noticed a bowl of cheesy potatoes with cornflakes on them. Since he had been living here, he had learned about 'funeral potatoes' as the locals called them. They were delicious and Grandpa Bill had made them several times. "I'm not too full for a scoop or two of these." Gaius said eagerly and spooned a large helping into his plate.

"Will you be back by Thursday?" Bill asked. "I'd like to volunteer up at the MTC, be on the road by nine to be up there before noon."

"Sure." Gaius said. "Whatever you need Gramps."

"Where are you camping?" Mary enquired.

"I thought we'd explore the Alpine loop. Have you ever heard of that?" he asked, eating the potatoes.

"From canyon to canyon." Mary said smiling. "Are you starting in American Fork or Provo?"

Gaius looked at Bill, their eyes met. It was such a nice thing when Mary was 'all there', it seemed to be happening more and more lately.

"I think we'll start in Provo and end up in American Fork."

"You should do it the other way around." Mary said, finishing the last bite of her dinner. "You could climb to Timpanogos cave and go from there, end up in Provo, you'll be closer to home and you'll love the cave."

Wiping her mouth, she continued. It was as if fifteen years melted off her, "I remember taking Kim and his Boy Scout troop there, years ago. Do you remember that, Bill? Such a great time! We had that old Dodge van, that thing was a trooper, such a reliable vehicle. Anyway, Kim took pictures all day with this cheap little Ninja Turtle camera and when we got them developed, the majority of them were blurry pictures of a chipmunk he chased around the snack bar area. The Davis kid got sick in the van on the drive home, puked orange soda all over the back seat. Ew," she made a face lost in the memory and continued, "It was so sickly sweet smelling. Thank goodness those seats were plastic covered or we wouldn't have gotten the smell out. Fortunately, I had a roll of paper towels and just pulled over on the I-15 and cleaned up the kid and the seat and off we went again."

Bill's eyes scanned back and forth from Gaius to Mary. Whether he wanted to admit it or not, having the young man and the pit-bull here had been good for her. He could see it in her eyes, she remembered more, actively participated in conversations more and was overall more focused. It was interesting the way the brain worked. She could remember a trip to American Fork canyon over twenty years ago but couldn't remember what she had for breakfast even though it was the same thing she had for breakfast every day for the last year plus.

"It's worth the hike." Bill added, standing to clear the table.

"I've got it, Gramps." Gaius said jumping up. "Thanks for the info, we'll check it out for sure."

Gaius cleared the table and did the dishes while Bill and Mary watched the television. Sass was asleep, laying at Mary's feet and Boo-Boo was in his bed on her left. Bill sat in his chair doing a crossword puzzle from the local paper. Watching them, he realized he did have a family that he loved, and he knew they loved him in the way they knew how. Life was weird, circumstantial, but here he was. After putting his cell phone on vibrate, he joined them in the living room, taking the opposite end of the couch. He sent a text to Elizabeth and half-heartedly watched what was on the TV.

> *Hey beautiful! What time should I come get you tomorrow morning?*
> *Anytime. I would have come with you tonight but...*
> *LOL! Your dad!*
> *Right?! Earlier the better for me. I'm ready.*
> *430a? JK, LOL.*
> *LOL! OK. Let's leave before anyone gets up.*
> *Serious?*
> *Yes.*
> *AWESOME! C U then. PS-did I mention I <3 camping?*
> *You're cute. Can't wait. TTYL. XO*
> *It is you that is cute. XO*

Chapter Forty-Three

Elizabeth had packed her backpack with her swimsuit, flip-flops, a couple causal camping outfits and her coat. After thinking twice about it, she grabbed her make-up bag and put it in the zipper part in the front of the bag. She showered and tightly twisted her hair into two French braids. As she got ready for bed, she realized she hadn't packed anything to sleep in and dug through her dresser to find a pair of navy blue sweats and a matching long sleeved print tee shirt. She was so excited she caught herself looking at the clock every three minutes. With nothing more to do she wandered upstairs to say goodnight to her family. Her parents were sitting in the living room and when they saw her Daniel spoke up and motioned for her to come and sit with them. Her stomach tightened. Even if she was an adult in the eyes of the law, her parents could still make her feel like a six-year-old.

"Elizabeth, we were just talking about you. Come, sit with us, let's talk about your adventure this week." Daniel said, motioning for her to join them.

"This is a big step in your life, as you become an adult, we want to remind you of God's plan for you and your covenant to Him."

"Just going camping, dad. No big deal."

"Your father and I would like to talk to you about our Heavenly Father and the commitment you have to Him when it comes to your *body*," her mother said primly, joining them in the formal living room.

"Chasity is a sacred oath. As far as sins go, sex before marriage is right up there with murder." Elizabeth noticed her mother's expression, it was a look of sternness and warning combined with love and concern.

"Your mother is correct." Daniel chimed in. "Alma 39:3-5. I'm sure you're familiar with that scripture, Elizabeth" He pursed his lips together and his brow furrowed. After a long pause, he continued. "Satan has led many people to believe that sexual intimacy outside of marriage is acceptable, but Elizabeth, it is *not*! In God's eyes, this is a very, *very* serious sin. Physical intimacy between husband and wife is beautiful and sacred, it is for the creation of children. But you're a long,

long way from that. Remember, by not honoring this oath you abuse the power God has given you to create life. Not to mention the goal of an eternal partner, one who will be worthy to go through the temple with you."

Both her parents were looking at her with a combination of dread and disapproval.

"We're just going camping." Elizabeth said flatly.

"Sometimes people try to convince themselves that sexual relations are okay because of love or affection, but Elizabeth we are just concerned that perhaps you aren't thinking straight and that's what we are here to do, to guide and direct you into making the right decisions for the long term, not just right now." Alice lectured assuredly.

"Having sexual relationships outside of the vows of marriage often will deteriorate the relationship all together especially if a person begins to feel guilt and shame due to their actions."

Daniel picked up where Alice left off. "We want what's best for you, Elizabeth. That's all parents can hope and pray for. We want eternal life for you in the Celestial Kingdom with a partner that is worthy of you. It's important you don't cross those physical lines in the heat of the moment knowing it could damage your relationship with God for the rest of your life. Knowing that one action could impede you from marrying someone that could have been perfect. Most men don't want to be with a woman that isn't pure, you understand." Daniel reached out and took his daughter's hand.

"We're just going camping." Elizabeth repeated.

"Let's pray about it." Daniel said encouragingly. He took Alice's hand in his other one and Alice took Elizabeth's forming a circle. Elizabeth's stomach tightened. Daniel began to pray.

"Dear Heavenly Father, we come before thee today to pray for our daughter and her choices as she becomes an adult. We thank thee, oh Lord for our opportunity of free-will, we thank thee for giving us your only son so we may have the chance to choose what is right. We pray for Elizabeth's purity of heart and body and mind. We pray for her chastity and that she may know your love is pure and true, that she finds comfort in the oath that she has taken. Dear Lord, we ask that you watch over her as she travels and that she will be protected by you; that they will arrive safely at their destination and return unharmed. We thank thee for the prophets of this church, for the leaders you have sent us to follow and for their guidance they offer in today's challenging world. We say these things, humbly in the name of the Father, the Son and the Holy Ghost. Amen."

"Amen," Alice repeated.

Her parents looked at her, thin smiles on their faces.

"We're just going camping." Elizabeth said for the third time.

"Don't be fresh." Alice scolded. "You act like we weren't young once ourselves. We know the temptations you have. We understand the challenges you face."

"We worry about you, Elizabeth, because we love you." Daniel said soothingly. Elizabeth got up and kissed her dad on his cheek and hugged her mom.

"Thanks. I'm good though, I've got this," she conjured up a reassuring smile for them. Speaking rapidly, she added, "Seriously, don't worry, we're just going camping. He's my friend. Thank you though, it's great to be loved so much. You two are great. I think I'll just head to bed. Good night." *What an awkward conversation*, she thought as she turned and went into the kitchen to retrieve a drink of water before going down the stairs to her room. It was already after ten but she was so excited she knew she wouldn't be able to sleep. It was as if she was a child and it was Christmas eve. After setting an alarm for 4:20 a.m on her cell phone, she lay down to try.

The alarm went off and she grabbed it within a second. As she listened for noises in the house she wondered if she had actually slept because she felt wide awake. She had considered sneaking out the basement window when they had confirmed the early departure time but felt like that would be too juvenile. She was an adult who made her own decisions, like when to leave to go camping, and who to go camping with. If that were true, why was she feeling so guilty about leaving before anyone got up? The backpack lay against the foot of her bed and she grabbed the toothbrush out of it. With the stealth of a criminal, she slipped into the bathroom and brushed her teeth. Her hair looked good considering she had been lying on it for six hours. She adjusted the strands that had come loose and sprayed it with Aqua Net, then snuck up the landing to the front door.

Silently she slipped out and walked across the front lawn and sat cross legged on the sidewalk. She looked back at the slumbering house she had lived in all her life. Truly she was blessed beyond words. Listening to the crickets and sounds of the night, she watched to see if any lights appeared in the windows, they all stayed dark. The stars beckoned to her and she looked up, feeling the enormity of the universe above her. The sky was clear and the air crisp, the stars brilliant. There was a sliver of the silver moon just rising over the eastern horizon. How small she suddenly felt, just a speck of life sitting on a floating mass of rock in the middle of nowhere.

What was God's plan for her? Knowing in her heart that He must have something better than Pleasant, Utah in mind. For some reason, Rebecca and Maximus popped into her head. She thought of Maximus, sleeping peacefully in his sister's house, or was he sleeping peacefully in Rebecca's? A wave of emotion swept over her. She was happy for her friends. Didn't Rebecca suggest they were going to get married? When she thought of Rebecca she got the feeling she was awake and may be looking at the same stars. This time of year, the weather there would be about the same as it was here, the humidity not settling in until later spring. They had brought such a dimension to her mission that no one else had. Had she touched their lives in a similar way? Elizabeth wondered. *Funny how different people come in and out of your life,* she thought. *Each person bringing their own spirit to enhance mine.* She heard Gaius' truck before she saw the headlights. She stood, slung her backpack over one shoulder and waited for him. He stopped and rolled down the passenger window. Sassafras was comfortably lying in the passenger seat.

"You'll have to come around to my side, we don't want to wake the sleeping canine," he whispered. She threw her backpack into the bed of the truck and walked around to the driver's side. He got out and slipped his arms around her waist and kissed her deeply. She leaned in to him and returned the affection, her heart pounding. "I'm so excited I couldn't sleep," he confessed, still whispering.

"Me too," she said and glanced up at the stars. "It's such a pretty night."

"Night?" he nuzzled her neck and inhaled, breathing in her scent. "It's morning, pretty girl, we only have a few hours and the sun will be right in our faces. Ready?"

She looked past the truck at her house, still no lights had appeared. Another twang of guilt flooded over her as the realization of her leaving without saying goodbye to her family hit her.

"Yea, ready," she said as she climbed in and scooted over, careful not to disturb Sass.

Gaius had his iPod plugged into the portable speakers and had selected Moby for their ride. They held hands as they drove east on highway 6. By the time they had reached I-15 Elizabeth had fallen asleep leaning against Gaius. He adjusted his arm so both he and Elizabeth were comfortable and turned north on I-15, pulling into the carpool lane and setting the cruise control. The sun was coming up over the Wasatch front, and the view of Mount Timpanogos was amazing. Golden rays were shooting from both the north and south canyons. Watching the sun create a golden crown of light over it was simply spectacular. He couldn't look away. The show of lights off the mountains and clouds couldn't have been choreographed any better. After an hour, he came to the Alpine exit and pulled off. Elizabeth woke with the shift in speed of the vehicle.

"Oh oops, I must have dozed off."

"Dozed? You were snoring up a storm!" Gaius teased.

She looked uncomfortable. "Really? How freakin' embarrassing. Sorry."

"Just kidding you, Lizard. You weren't snoring, but I bet if you did, you would look beautiful."

"Aw, you're too sweet," she replied, then looked around, "we're in Alpine, already?!"

The sky was slowly turning from gray with gold rays to blue with silver rays. Because they were driving east, directly at the mountain, the world just became lighter, but they stayed in the shadows like the sun was hitting the snooze button.

"Mount Timpanogos. My favorite," she sighed, "see the sleeping Indian princess?"

"The what?"

"A silhouette of a woman lying on her back."

He squinted and smiled, "Yea, okay."

"So, there's this legend of the Timpanogot tribe's princess, Utahna. It's the namesake of the mountain. It's a love story like all the best legends are."

"Indeed, the best legends are love stories," he reached over and took her hand.

"According to at least a dozen documented versions of this story, the princess had a bunch of suitors, but her favorite was a handsome warrior named Red Eagle. He had convinced her he was a god."

"Really? A god?" Gaius glanced at her, "Puts dating nowadays into perspective, huh?" he winked.

"Oh the story gets better," she continued. "The rivals of Red Eagle all got together and plotted to kill him so they would have a better chance with the princess. So they threw him off the cliffs into the river. When the princess discovered what happened, she cried a lake full of tears and died of a broken heart. The End."

"The End?" he chuckled. "What a lovely legend."

"Yea, and inside the Timpanogos cave is her heart."

"What?!"

"Well, it's a stalactite that looks like an anatomically correct heart. Oh, and the waterfalls over in the Provo canyon are named Bridal Veils for the broken hearted Utahna," she pointed towards the south, "That's Mahogany mountain, the G mountain, the Cascade mountain and the Y mountain, we'll come out way over there. I'm excited. You?"

Excited? The way she looked at him made him think there was no other place he wanted to be but next to her no matter where they were. He looked from Elizabeth to the massive mountain range, the immensity of it struck him. "Yeah, way," he replied honestly. When they arrived at the National Park entrance gate, Gaius paid the six dollars for the three-day pass and the park ranger offered them a map. Gaius asked about the cave hike.

"Oh sir, I'm sorry, but it's not open until late May. It's still too cold."

"Well, that gives us an excuse to come back next month," Gaius said cheerfully, taking the receipt and parking pass from the uniformed employee.

The canyon was gorgeous. The early morning light streaming through the curvy branches of the trees formed the illusion of a moving tunnel. A river ran full and fast to their right. The movement of the raging water adding to the beauty surrounding them. Even Sassafras had woken up and was sitting, looking out the window. Gaius rolled it down and turned on the heater, Sass happily stuck her head out and Elizabeth happily snuggled closer to Gaius. The smell of the spring air and the sounds of the river flooded the cab of the truck.

"I'm so happy," Gaius said, looking through the windshield and up at the rock formations. "The scenery is amazing. The company is amazing *and* beautiful. Seriously, how could life get any better than this?"

"You're right. This is perfect. We're so blessed," she leaned her head against his shoulder and squeezed his hand.

Gaius followed the sign that led to the Tibble Fork camping area and pulled into an empty paved parking lot and got out, Sassafras climbed over Elizabeth and followed him.

"Excuse me," she said, laughing.

The dog ran around sniffing, and found a place to pee. Elizabeth climbed out and walked to the back of the truck. Gaius had lowered the tailgate and pulled out a one cup electric coffee pot. He had invested in a converter plug and placed the coffee pot on the floorboards of the passenger side. After pouring the necessary water and adding coffee, he pushed start.

"For you, my lovely," he said. "I brought a choice of green tea, hot cocoa or orange juice. Do you have a preference?"

"Orange juice, please," she answered. He opened the cooler and fished out a small plastic bottle of juice. "I've never tried coffee."

"Mmm... it's wonderful and not as bad for you as people say."

"Really?" she hopped up and sat on the opened tailgate.

"The key is moderation, Lizard, as is the key with most anything. Seriously, think about it, *anything* done in excess is potentially harmful."

"Like what?" she laughed and twisted the top of the orange juice and took a drink.

"Name it. Everything, including the things good for you. Really. Everything, better in moderation. Working out, eating, watching TV, drinking alcohol. Even religion," he winked at her. "Trust me, Liz, living moderately and keeping balance in everything you do is the key to a happy life."

"Not sure I'm buying it about the coffee."

"Yea, for real. It's the crap you put in it that makes it bad for you," he said while getting the cream and sugar out, displaying it as if he was on a gameshow.

"It's delicious though," he poured a splash of cream and a sprinkle of sugar into his cup before getting the pot of coffee. He continued in a radio commercial voice. "Drinking a cup of coffee a day can lower a person's risk of heart disease, diabetes and depression." Then in his own voice, "Seriously, it has antioxidants that can help you live longer," her look was one of skepticism. "I'm not making this shit up, Lizard, it's scientific. I even heard that they may have found a correlation between drinking coffee and reduced risk of getting certain cancers. Wish that were the case with ovarian cancer, but..." His voice trailed off and his mood seemed to darken.

"Is that what type of cancer your mom had?" Elizabeth asked gently.

He nodded, a lump had formed in his throat. *C'mon now*, he thought, *pull it together*. There was no way he wanted to let his loss ruin this beautiful moment in this beautiful place with this beautiful woman. "Yea, and to be honest, she didn't drink her coffee in moderation. She drank a pot a day, not even kidding," he said with a hint of melancholy in his voice. "Wish you could have met her."

"Well, I'll tell you one thing she got right. She did a great job of raising a wonderful man," Elizabeth said and slipped her arms around his waist.

He pulled her close, kissed her, then pulled away and studied her face, "She would have loved you, that's for sure." Tears brimmed in his eyes. "Sorry, when I think about her, I... I just miss her is all."

"Never be sorry for having feelings, Gaius. I'm glad you have good memories and were close with her."

He let her wipe the single tear from his cheek. "Look at this place," he said, suddenly changing the subject and mood. "It's freaking amazing! Listen to me, swearing like a Mormon, *and* we have the place to ourselves, it's like our own private mountain."

He held his arms out wide and circled the empty parking lot taking in the beauty of it and threw his head back and yelled. "I LOVE YOU, *MAMACITA*! I LOVE YOU TO THE MOON AND BACK!" He began to twirl like a child with his arms still outstretched, laughing, crying, she wasn't sure. She reached out and took one of his hands and they spun together like carefree children playing in a schoolyard. He reached for her and grabbed her around the waist, kissing her again.

She whispered in his ear. "She loves you too."

He smiled. "You are amazing, my sweet beautiful little Lizard. Thanks."

"I'm glad we found each other."

"Me too."

With their arms around one another, they walked back to the truck, "Ready to continue this adventure?"

She nodded and they gathered the dog and climbed back into the little truck and continued up the mountain. The sun climbed higher in the sky and the shadows of the trees shortened as the day became warm. Looking at the map, Elizabeth suggested they stop and stay the night in a campground called Timpooneke. It was a beautiful area with a trail that climbed to connect with the summit trail. As they read the informational sign, they both looked at each other with the same excited expression.

"Let's hike to the top." Gaius said.

"Let's do it!" She agreed, her eyes dancing with excitement.

Gaius heard his mother's voice in his head, *Go on foot through the forest*. Wait. Wasn't that a dream he had? There was something else to the message, he struggled to remember, *don't be late*. He took that as a sign that they absolutely had to be back by Thursday morning.

The parking lot was surrounded by an Aspen forest. Gaius got a little day pack from the truck and put waters in it and a couple of sack lunches he had made the night before. He also grabbed his iPod and the small portable speakers. They set off on the trail that meandered along a mountain stream, Sass in front of them, running free and happy. The sun was high in the perfectly blue sky. The scenery was breathtaking. They walked in silence preoccupied by the beauty around them. As they walked they passed a number of small waterfalls, the noise of the water flowing enhancing the amazing setting and spectacular views.

When they reached the little lake, Elizabeth announced it was Emerald lake, the one where Red Eagle had been murdered and the mountain princess died from her broken heart. "It's a bit like Romeo and Juliet," she added. They hiked thirty more minutes and Gaius suggested they stop for lunch. He placed his iPod on a nearby rock and plugged it into the speakers while Elizabeth got the lunches from the knapsack.

"Great music selection. Is that Mozart?"

"Yes," he smiled broadly at her. "My mom used to think it would make me smarter if I listened to it, they say it does. Who knows? I do know I have a greater appreciation for the classics and a passion for a large variety of music genres. My music selection is as eclectic as it comes."

"Do you mind if I bless the food?" she asked.

He shrugged and shook his head.

"Our dear kind and loving Heavenly Father, thank you for this beautiful day and this wonderful world. We ask you to bless this food we are about to eat that it may strengthen and nourish our bodies. That we may find peace in your love and appreciate the beauty around us in which you have given. We say these things in the name of Jesus Christ, amen."

The moment she said 'amen' he took a large bite of the sandwich he had been holding. When she looked at him, he was already chewing a mouthful. They ate enjoying the music, the food and the scenery. Once finished they started up the Summit Trail talking casually about nothing in particular. Gaius bent down and picked up a round little stone.

"Look a fossil of a shell," he handed it to Elizabeth and she studied it. It did indeed look like it was from the ocean, smooth and shell-shaped but a solid rock, even the scallops were perfect along the edge.

"While on my mission, we had a Sunday school class about God creating dinosaur fossils to test our faith. There is some discrepancy as to how old the earth is and..."

Gaius cut her off. "What a dick!"

"What? Who?" Elizabeth was taken aback by the sudden shift in conversation.

"Your god, he's a dick. Seriously, Lizard, think about it. What kind of god would do that? What kind of person would do that? It's like the weird uncle everyone has that says 'got your nose' and puts his thumb between his first two fingers. I mean you know he doesn't really have your nose, he's just annoying. What's the point of that?" They walked a moment, neither speaking. "I'm just saying, Lizard, how is it that you could even trust a god that did something like that? 'Ha-ha, tricked ya'," he shook his head. "That sounds as ridiculous as the magic underwear. Hasn't anyone in your church heard of science? Gawd, Liz, quit being a sheep. *Think* every now and then, use your brain!"

"What?!" Elizabeth felt the hair on the back of her neck stand up. "Eff you, Gaius!"

"What?" he started to giggled. "What did you just say?"

"Eff you!" She stopped walking and started at him. Her tone had settled, but she felt her hands shaking a bit. She had it with his mockery of her beliefs. "For real, eff off!"

"Eff?" Gaius said grinning at her. "Mormon speak for 'fuck'? Did you just say 'fuck you' to me? Fuck off? If you're going to suggest it, Elizabeth, just say it! You do that all the time and it's not necessary, if you want to swear, swear," his words came out a bit shaper than he intended, he really didn't mean to make her mad. They stared at each other. "Just say fuck, Lizard. You can't tell me you're over twenty years old and have never said fuck? Seriously. It's a great word. Try it."

"No, that's not it. I've said it before, it's just I've had it with you making fun of my church, our Heavenly Father is not a..." Her face flushed pink. "Dick. Heavenly Father is not a dick, our garments are sacred, not magic and as for science, well... there are two sides to every story."

"Yes, you meant it. That's what you meant was 'fuck you, Gaius'. 'Fuck off, Gaius.' I know what you meant, your god knew what you meant too, so say it. And as far as science goes, there are *not* two sides! It either is, or it isn't," he stopped walking, it was ridiculous he was getting annoyed. "Say it or I'm turning back and we can go back to Pleasant right now."

"Say what?" she asked, wary of his rising temper.

"Fuck you, Gaius. Say that," his jaw was tight and he didn't smile.

"No," she said, stopping and turning to face him.

"Say it. I know it's what you meant." For some reason, he felt his patience slipping, he felt as if he was getting angry, but for what? It had to be more than this ridiculous conversation. Neither of them spoke for what seemed like some time.

She thought about the morning she lost her temper with Sister Paula, the first time she had said the word in anger, she felt the heat rise in her face, her eyes narrowed. "Fuck you, Gaius."

"There. Was that so hard?" he said firmly, feeling his jaw bone and face muscles relax. "Here's the deal, my dear. I can prove to *you* that science *is* real. There are facts and data and centuries of study on the subject from scientists all over the world. On the other hand, *you* cannot to prove to *me* that your Heavenly Father exists. *You* cannot prove to me that he placed this fossil here just to test your faith. I'm sorry, but the burden of proof is on *you*," he pointed his finger at her to emphasize his point. She had never seen his eyes so cold nor heard his voice so hard. "As for the underwear," he continued. "Were you able to come up with any stats for me on that? Do Mormons live longer because of them? Proof. Where's the proof? I'm that kind of dude, I need proof," she hadn't actually looked to see if there were statistics on it but didn't say anything. He continued as if he was wound up and couldn't stop until he had said it all. "And your god? Please! If he's not a totally one hundred percent dick, he's got a fucked up and very twisted sense of humor. Seriously. Diseases like cancer? Cerebral Palsy? Alzheimer's? Autism? Not to mention an animal food chain that eats other animals while they are still alive, still conscious. And there are horrible human beings that continually destroy the earth with no regard for future generations. People are an entire species that does nothing but harm to this planet, drilling, damming, polluting, draining and then they kill each other in wars over greed and in the name of religion," he sighed and his shoulders sagged.

"Sorry," she said softly, looking at her hiking shoes. "I guess that's why they call it faith."

"I guess so," he said and started walking back up the trail. "I have none."

Elizabeth followed a bit behind, not knowing what to say or how to handle the confrontation. Thinking about him made her heart skip a beat, and she didn't want him angry with her but what she believed, she believed. As they walked in silence, Maximus popped into her head. *Why am I thinking about Max?* She thought to herself. *Especially now that he's with Rebecca.* She remembered the feelings she had at his church that Sunday morning. How she had felt the Holy Ghost and God's presence and almost raised her hand to be 'saved'. *Weird,* she thought. *They all can't be right, or could they? Or maybe Gaius is right and none of them are.* How could she even be questioning her faith? All she had to do was look around her and see God's handiwork. Gaius was not too far in front of her walking at a brisk pace. After a few steps he glanced back and averted his eyes forward again when he realized she was looking at him.

Religious differences. He heard his mother's voice in his head. We weren't together because of religious differences. Remembering when she had said it, he thought she was crazy. He grew up without a dad because of religious differences! This country, this time period? Religious differences? Although no one was telling him he couldn't pursue a relationship with Elizabeth, he could see how religious differences could become a problem. Obviously, Kimball Kay Smith had been just as brainwashed as Elizabeth was. What was it with religion that made perfectly sane people believe in unexplainable and absurd ideas? He glanced over his shoulder. Oops, he thought. She's watching me. Ahead he saw a place to rest and he stopped and sat, watching her approach. "Truce?" he said, looking up at her with the sincerest expression he could muster.

Elizabeth nodded and sat beside him. "I like you," she began. He put his arm around her shoulder and leaned his head against her and nodded once, finding himself at a loss for words. "I don't know what to think of you, though." Shaking her head, she continued. "I am who I am, I was raised how I was raised. There is no apology for it, it's just-" After a pause and a heavy sigh she continued. "It's just you make me think differently. Moving from that comfort zone is, well... uncomfortable. Some of the things you say actually make sense, G. Science makes sense. The idea of the Holy Ghost being the feminine part of the Holy Trinity makes sense. The way the zodiacs came about makes sense. I don't know, Gaius, I just don't know."

"Well, here's what I think," he said softly, "We've only known each other a few weeks, there's no reason to rush into anything. Let's just enjoy this moment. This one, this moment right now. It's all we have. There could be an earthquake tonight and everyone could die, right now is all we've got. Let's not waste the moment," he put his other arm around her, feeling her hip under his hands, he laced his fingers together and felt the slimming of her waist. Neither spoke for a moment. They laid back and curled into each other on the ground.

"This is really nice." Elizabeth said, finally looking at the beauty that surrounded her.

"Agreed," he sat up and looked at her. "I hold you in the highest esteem, Lizard. You're right, you were raised how you were raised and I was raised how I was raised. Let's agree to disagree. We can just respect each other's beliefs, and avoid the subject the best we can. You can bless the food and wear your cute undies and I'll stick with what I know from books I've read and classes I've taken. My mom was a single mother because of 'religious differences'," he made air-quote marks with his fingers. "My parents weren't able to be together because of other people's rules and beliefs, because someone told them they couldn't. We're bigger than that, Liz. If we're meant to be, well... It'll happen."

She nodded and a hint of a smile played at edges of her lips. He leaned in and kissed her, their tongues exploring each other softly, their bodies pressing together.

"I've never felt like this before," she said after the passionate embrace.

"Me neither," he pulled her close again. "I've never met anyone like you, I mean... I don't know how to describe it, but, I've never met a woman that is so completely wrong for me, but makes me feel so amazing."

"Oh, G," she sighed. "I know what you mean."

Chapter Forty-Four

The day grew warmer as they hiked through the meadows and up the ravines. There were waterfalls and lakes, deer, squirrels and birds. Plants and trees were just getting ready to bud and the foliage was early spring green everywhere they looked. Everything seemed to be coming alive from a cold winter. Above one of the lakes there was still a snow glacier and the ice glistened bright in the sun. Elizabeth took dozens of photos with her cell phone, including several selfies of her and Gaius and a dozen or so of Sassafras frolicking in the wilderness.

Finally, they reached the top. It was much colder and the wind snapped at them. There was a small shack. They hurried to it and took shelter. Inside was a large guest book and several pencils. Out of curiosity they thumbed through the pages and noted the dates went back all the way to 1989. There were autographs from hundreds of people, their hometowns and the dates. Gaius took one of the pencils and wrote, 'Gaius K Stewart and Sassafras the Pitbull, Colorado Springs, CO, USA' and drew next to it a small picture of a smiling cartoon squirrel. Above its head he drew a conversation bubble and wrote inside 'Amazing!'

Elizabeth took the pencil and wrote her name in flowing cursive plus Pleasant, Utah. She drew three daisies next to her name. They walked from the shack arm in arm. At the crest they looked down over the valley below. A thick brown cloud hung below them over the cities and towns.

"Oh, that's nasty." Gaius said.

"Agreed. Can't believe we breathe all that crap." Elizabeth added.

"No doubt. This is what I meant about humans destroying the earth, seriously, look at this. Gross! Should we head back down and set up camp?" he asked turning to leave.

Elizabeth nodded and they started back down the trail. As they walked their conversation turned to the brown fog that blanketed the valley. "The thing is, it's not too late, yet. It's still possible to reverse it. If only people could see the damage they are doing by using fossil fuels, eating meat, not recycling..." Elizabeth was saying. "It's ridiculous because of the renewable energy resources we have. Modern technology, we're not using a fraction of our potential when it comes to sustainability."

"You're so right, I love a woman with beauty and brains," he smiled. "Don't even get me started about Global warming!"

"Right?!" Elizabeth exclaimed. "There's tons of people in our ward that don't believe in global warming, but *come on*! Their ignorance drives me crazy! There is proof all around. While I was on my mission, there was a Sunday school lesson that basically said global warming is just another corporate greed scam. I was floored!"

"It's scientifically proven, a fact." Gaius chimed in. "See Lizard, you *do* believe in science. You're even passionate about it, I saw it."

She kept walking, what was there to say? Global warming was real. Those that denied it drove her crazy, couldn't people see what was happening all around them? Thinking about that Sunday school lesson, she remembered how new she had been on her mission. She wanted to say something to the Sister that was teaching the lesson but had conflicting emotions, not wanting to 'rock the boat.'

"I told you I'd respect your belief system, Liz," Gaius was talking, "but just think if you applied that same critical thinking to everything in your life..." He trailed off, not knowing exactly how to finish his sentence. He didn't want to fight. Just by her posture, Gaius could tell she got the point he was trying to make. "It just seems in some ways the folks I've met in Pleasant are picking and choosing their beliefs," he shrugged, "I don't know, but I think it's kinda all or nothing, don't you?"

"I believe it all," she answered firmly.

"Do you?" Gaius paused, "Besides the ridiculous stories like Noah and Moses, where is your stance on abortion? What about Gay and Lesbian rights? The death penalty?"

"Umm...," she paused before answering. "I believe women should have control of their own bodies. If an abortion is the only answer opposed to adoption or something else, anyway, I'm a feminist and I believe women should have the right to choose. Keep in mind though, I also think people should wait until they are married to have sex so..." Their eyes met briefly and she continued. "I think Gay guys and Lesbian girls should be able to get married, for all the legal reasons, you know?

Insurance, taxes, that kind of stuff. And the death penalty, I think that's a case by case situation."

"So, you're a hypocrite too, huh?" he said stopping and turning to look at her.

"What? No." Elizabeth shook her head and stopped, looking at him.

"Yea, you're doing it too" He said, "just pick and choose what to believe. Sorry, sorry, I know, we weren't going to talk about this." Gaius started walking.

"No, I'm not," she declared firmly following him.

"Yes, you are." Gaius' voice was calm and soothing. "Thou Shall Not Kill. Isn't that one of the commandments?" she nodded. "An abortion in some people's eyes is killing. You also said the death penalty is a case by case basis. Both examples are ending a life. You said, case by case bases, so you justify some killing," he sighed. "For the record, you also nailed it on the women's rights. A baby is a twenty plus year commitment. The media is missing a big part of the argument. No one wants more welfare, but no one wants abortion. It's like an Algebra equation, you can't fix one side without fixing the other. You nailed it with the LGBT rights too, the government must and I repeat, *must* give all people the same benefits and not discriminate because of gender, color, etc. But you forgot the most important thing." While walking he started singing. "All you need is love... All you need is love..."

Listening to him sing, she let herself become lost in thought. The point he just made regarding picking and choosing what to live. What other beliefs did she have that weren't in-line with the church? She pondered the question as she joined him, their voices harmonizing together.

They sang and walked back down the mountain. The dog followed in a lazy, around-about-way exploring every cranny, as the shadows started to stretch and day began to cool. As they sang the last line, 'love is all you need', Gaius slipped his arm around her shoulder and she moved her arm around his waist. They stopped, turning into each other and he kissed her. Elizabeth's mouth yielded only a moment before she pressed her body into his and kissed him back.

"Easy there, Lizard," he said pulling back. "I believe you said you wanted to wait until your wedding night and a kiss like that, well... there's only one place a kiss like that leads," his look was smoldering.

Elizabeth blushed scarlet red, she could feel her pulse and her blood swooshing through her veins. Her body tingled, feeling more alive than ever. Breathing slowly, she gained control of herself. "Sorry. You just, I just, this place…" Still short of breath, she found herself at a loss for words.

"Yea, you do that to me too," he said brushing a loose strand of her hair from her face.

"How are we going to sleep tonight? I mean, I could sleep in the truck and you have the tent but I really think we'll both be warmer if we sleep together, I mean, just in the same place, spot, the tent, you know?"

"I could tie you in the sleeping bag like they used to years ago," she smiled mischievously. "I'm not sure it's true, but I heard that way back in the day, dads would tie young men in their sleeping bags and untie them in the morning to save their daughters from unwanted advances."

"That sounds about right." Gaius returned the smile. "I promise I will be a total gentleman," he said as he started to unload the back of the truck. It didn't take long for them to have the tent set up, their bedding rolled out and a fire in the pit. From the cooler, he pulled out two foil wrapped items his grandfather had given him.

"Oh, my gosh!" She exclaimed. "Tin foil dinners!"

He shrugged. "I don't know, Gramps gave these to me, I have no idea what to do with them, I don't even know what's in them."

"I haven't had these in years." Without comment, she took the dinners and strategically placed them for optimal cooking. The vegetables cooked perfectly. The food was excellent. As the sun went down the sky turned brilliant orange before fading to darkness. He went to the truck and retrieved a package of marshmallows, a large chocolate bar with almonds and a box of Nilla Wafers.

"My grandpa told me this was the best part of camping," he said to Liz, putting the items down.

"S'mores!" She squealed like a child. How long had it been since she had s'mores and with Nilla Wafers instead of graham crackers? Excitement bubbled in her as she anticipated the treat.

"We always used graham crackers." Gaius said popping a s'more with a perfectly roasted marshmallow on it in his mouth. "It's good with the cookie though, they are just the right size. Vicki from the C-store suggested it."

"Nilla Wafers are the best that way for sure." Elizabeth said as she took the current marshmallow out of the fire and studied the brownness of it.

After gorging themselves, Gaius called Sassafras to the truck and opened the door. Reclining the seats, he made the dog a bed in the cab, opening the windows enough for air, but not enough for her to jump out. "C'mon old girl. Don't want you to run off chasing a rabbit or get eaten by a bear," he patted the seat and she jumped in, circling twice and plopping down. She yawned at him and made an appreciative noise, and promptly fell asleep. Elizabeth had been moving the coals around so they would die out, it was getting late and she was exhausted. Gaius joined her and nuzzled into her neck. "C'mon beautiful girl, let's go tie me into a sleeping bag."

They went into the tent and got into their individual sleeping bags, Gaius took the denim quilt and spread it over both of them. Propped on his elbows, he kissed her lips then her forehead, her eyes were closed and she moaned softly. He kissed each of her eyelids. "Good night my sweet little Lizard."

"G'night," she muttered. "Had a great day, thanks." Each of them had one hand out of their sleeping bags but under the quilt, they laced their fingers together and almost instantly, they both drifted into a deep sleep.

Elizabeth woke first, just before dawn. She watched Gaius sleep for a minute, his breath deep and steady. Looking at his face, the tiny bit of chin stubble along the strong jawline, the long dark eyelashes and disarrayed hair, *he's so beautiful*, she thought. Her heart fluttered and she silently snuck out of the tent. Sass was sitting straight up in the passenger side of the truck, her goofy grin greeting Elizabeth. She opened the truck door so the dog could get out, Sass stretched and yawned and wandered a bit away from camp to take care of her morning business. Elizabeth wandered to the porta-potty then walked along the path, away from the camp watching the sky come to life, the dog followed.

After a minute she found a large rock that was flat on the top, she climbed up it and snapped a couple shots of the sunrise. She decided to do a few yoga stretches thinking about Sass's perfect down-dog when she jumped from the truck. Elizabeth did a series of warrior poses, keeping an eye on the dog. After fifteen minutes, she jumped down and started walking to camp. She noticed Gaius just a few yards down the trail. He slipped his cell phone in his back pocket and greeted her with a hug and kiss on the cheek. "Got a few great pictures of you with the mountains in the background. You're beautiful!"

She blushed. "Funny, I just thought that about you when I was watching you sleep."

"You were watching me sleep? That's a little creepy."

"You were just taking pictures of me without my knowledge, who's creepin' on who?" she put her arm around his waist and slipped her hand into his back pocket feeling his butt muscles move with each step. They ate a bowl of cold cereal, she had hot chocolate and he had his coffee.

"What's the plan for today?" she asked.

Gaius had been looking at the map. "I thought we'd stay the night over on the Provo side, maybe Squaw Peak? They say there is some great camping over there." They cleaned up and reloaded the truck and continued their journey.

The second day of their adventure was as magical as the first, but different. They spent most of it four-wheel driving, following different trails through the forest, Sass in between them. When they reached Squaw Peak, they found a spot at the top of the campgrounds. It had a spectacular view of the Provo valley, nasty brown pollution cloud and all. They had tried to get the very top camp spot, but there was a two-toned blue Dodge van already in that spot. Elizabeth noticed on the back bumper a 'Families are Forever' sticker and in the back window a stick figure family; Dad, Mom, boy, boy, boy, girl, and a stick figure dog. The opposite window had a yellow diamond shaped signs that said 'Baby on Board'.

"With the exception of the dog, that could have been our van when I was growing up," she motioned towards the vehicle. "They didn't have those silly stickers back then though."

"I swear, Utah is the breeding grounds for blonde hair and blue eyes," Gaius said, "I've never seen so many toe-headed children until I came here."

Her eyes followed where he was looking and saw the young family. The mom was making sandwiches and looked as if she was wearing a maternity smock. *They'll have to add another stick figure*, Elizabeth thought to herself. A toddler of about two years old sat in a squat high chair happily playing with fish shaped crackers. The other children sat at the picnic table plucking green grapes from a bowl, talking and laughing, patiently waiting for their mother to get the picnic sandwiches done. Elizabeth estimated the oldest to be about eight or nine, the youngest around two. The father was putting together a large three room tent. Elizabeth had flashbacks of when she was little and her parent's had taken the whole family camping. Watching the young parents, she realized just what a chore that must have been.

Gaius set up the iPod and speakers and put his music on shuffle. They sat together going through the photos on their phones they had taken during the day. There were several cute selfies and dozens of Sassafras, many of them were blurry and had to be deleted.

"With dogs you've just got to take a lot and be happy with one or two decent ones," Elizabeth said, deleting a series of a jubilant Sassafras running through a field of freshly bloomed wild flowers. Gaius got to the photos he had taken the previous morning of Elizabeth on the rock doing the yoga poses. One was particularly perfect. The way the early morning sunlight lit the mountain scene behind but silhouetted her, the scenery dreamily framing her flawless warrior pose.

"Love this one, I think I'll have it printed and framed. It's art," he twisted his hand so she could see the photo. It did look like something from a motivational poster with the word 'serenity' or 'persistence' printed below it complete with an inspirational quote.

She showed him her favorite selfie of the two of them, both candidly smiling at the camera. "Gonna post this one to Facebook. It's my favorite. You don't mind, do you?"

He shook his head. "Gonna change your relationship status?" he nudged her shoulder with his and avoided her eye.

"To 'It's complicated'?"

"Exactly," he answered. "You can't tag me. I don't have Facebook. In my humble opinion, it's a complete waste of time."

"Probably," she agreed, cropping the photo and enhancing the color and brightness.

The fact he didn't have a Facebook struck her as more old-fashion. After a moment of thought, she was glad he didn't have one. It made her want to delete hers.

"Good for Mark Zuckerberg though, you know?" he was saying looking out over the valley. "I think we live in a cool time, Liz. Technology still an infant and growing at the speed of light. Can you even imagine our life without a cell phone or computer? It's weird, those things weren't everyday items when we were born. Our parents didn't have a cellphone. They wore *watches* to tell time. They used *public* pay phones to make calls with quarters or a long time ago, dimes. There was no computer let alone social media. We're like that lucky generation that gets to see something phenomenal in an industry that didn't really exist before. I'm so glad to have been born in the last century, us nineties kids."

"I totally agree. It's like our phones, aren't even phones anymore even though we call them that. But really, it's like they are computers with phone apps, you know?" she gazed at the iPhone and continued talking, deep in thought. "So you've heard of the scripture in the book of Revelation, chapter thirteen, verses sixteen through eighteen, right?"

"I'm not sure, but if you hum a few bars," Gaius teased in a decent imitation of Groucho Marx.

"It's the scripture about the number of the beast," she said, still looking at the device in her hand.

"666." Gaius said proudly. "A person doesn't even have to be Christian to know the devil's number!"

She smiled and looked at him. "666 is also the number of man." Both her eyebrows raised as she said this to him. "The whole verse has left me scratching my head ever since I got my first cell phone."

"What do you mean? What does your cell phone and the number of the beast have anything to do with anything?" he was deliberately keeping his voice was playful and light. *I do not want a church lecture right now*, he thought to himself.

"Well, the scripture goes something like this," she paused getting the words right before she began speaking as if she had rehearsed. "Also, it causes all, both small and great, both rich and poor, both free and slave, to be marked on the right hand or the forehead so that no one can buy or sell unless he has the mark, that is, the name of the beast or the number of its name. This calls for wisdom: let the one who has understanding calculate the number of the beast, for it is the number of a man, and his number is 666."

"I don't get it."

"Everyone is marked on their right hand," she held her phone up with her right hand and wiggled it towards him slightly, "or the forehead." Exaggeratedly, she moved the phone to her ear next to her forehead. "No one can buy or sell unless he has the mark? Do you not need a cell phone to do practically anything nowadays? Who has cell phones? Oh, I don't know, everybody? The small, the great the poor the rich, the free, the slave? I mean couldn't the beast be the corporation that has control of the man because of the number? Politically speaking, the corporations are going to be the downfall of this country. Anyway. It's one of those scriptures that has left me wondering."

"My phone has a menacing look all of a sudden." Gaius remarked.

"Right?!"

After a pause he asked. "So what's your favorite science?"

Elizabeth stopped playing with her phone and looked at him. "Astronomy," she said without hesitation.

"So glad you didn't say Astrology, Lizard. Too many people think they are one in the same, seriously."

"Astrology?" she asked incredulously. "Is that even a real science?"

He laughed. "To some people, I suppose."

"Yea? I love to think about the stars, the other planets, the moon cycles. How consistent and unfailing they are, you know? I can't tell my family or friends this because I'll have to admit I believe the earth is billions of years old, not thousands like they believe. You struck a nerve with me yesterday, G," she sighed and looked out over the dirty valley. "You're right. I don't know what else to say but you're right."

"I am?" His eyes lit up. "About what?"

"The all or nothing thing. You're right. I've never thought about it, because it's blasphemy where I come from. Science isn't something you believe in, it's something that is a fact. The proof lies on me and if I had to prove to someone God exists the only thing I have is what is in my heart. There is no proof but that," tears stung her eyes.

Gaius put his arm around her and she leaned her head into him as he softly said, "I'm sorry. I certainly didn't mean to burst your bubble."

Elizabeth sighed and spoke, "I feel like I just slid headfirst into adulthood, a nasty reality. Not a happily-ever-after reality, but real reality, like a veil has been removed from *my* reality. All of a sudden, my beliefs feel more like a security blanket, thoughts to comfort me, but not solid. Does that even make sense?"

He looked at her with a hint of sadness in his eyes, "I don't want to be the bad guy."

Placing her hands on the sides of his face, she leaned in and kissed him. "I've never been that bold with a boy," she said. "I don't know what you do to me, but it's definitely me, not you. You'll never be the bad guy. When I'm with you, I just feel like my mind is opening. Stretching. For the first time really."

"You've heard the old saying about a mind being like a parachute? Once opened it can never go back to the way it was, or maybe the mind is like panty hose, once stretched out they can't ever go back in that little egg looking thingy."

She laughed. "I don't know. I haven't lost faith. I still have my testimony. I still love my Heavenly Father. Maybe I do pick and choose. Maybe there is a science devil on one of my shoulders and an angel on the other, but I don't feel like it makes me a hypocrite, it's more…" her voice trailed off, after a moment she said, "It's just I need to find the balance, like you suggested." Elizabeth's mind wandered to her beliefs, the world she had known her entire life. She thought about the second coming of Christ. How disappointed would Jesus be if he came back tomorrow and saw how the people he had given his life for had used and abused the earth? How would He feel if he saw firsthand the suffering of so many of His children? What would He say? In her mind, she pictured the CNN special report.

"This is so-n-so from CNN, live in the land of Zion. Jesus has returned and it is rumored he has said he is sorely disappointed in the way the planet has been treated. To be sure, we've gotten an exclusive interview with the Son of God, Himself."

In her mind the news panned to a handsome, well-groomed, bearded Jesus being interviewed by the station's anchor.

"Welcome back, Jesus, er, Mr. Christ. We're all so glad to see you. Have you had a chance to look around? There's been some changes since you were crucified. A lot of changes. Have you had a chance to review these changes?"

The camera then zooming in for a close up of Jesus's face, his forehead knitted, his mouth in a slight frown. "I have indeed seen the changes and quite frankly, this is ridiculous. What were you all thinking?"

Her thoughts were distracted by a little boy's voice.

"Hi, I'm Todd," he said. A smaller boy held his hand. "This is my brother, Travis."

"I Twavis," the smaller one said, his smile starting from his eyes and encompassing his entire round face. Travis had the distinctive features of a child with Down Syndrome.

"Where's your children?" Todd enquired.

Elizabeth laughed. "We don't have any children, sweetie."

"Where's your mommy and daddy?" Todd asked suspiciously.

Gaius laughed and Elizabeth looked at him with a smirk on her face. "They had to work today," she explained as their mother called them.

"Todd, Trav, c'mon over here and don't bother those nice people. C'mon now," she motioned with her arm for them to come back to their campground. "Sorry." The young mother hollered to Gaius and Elizabeth.

"Not a problem." Elizabeth called back as the boys began to wander to their parents.

"You pwetty." Travis said to Elizabeth as they turned to return to camp.

"You're a smart boy." Gaius said to Travis, "A very observant and incredibly smart boy. Don't you forget that now, you hear?"

"Tank you," Travis said over his shoulder, the smile still radiating from him, "Twavis is smart boy."

"See you later!" Todd squealed, looking back over his shoulder as he led his brother away.

The sunset was exceedingly dazzling, the oranges and reds enhanced by the cloud of dirty air. As it got darker they watched a campground below them start to fill with cars. Gaius noticed one of the trucks had a pony keg in the back, it was tapped and the red Solo cups were passed around. Dozens of young adults began to party, their music filling the canyon. Gaius got his binoculars out and looked down at the campsite.

"Let's walk down there and have a beer, Liz," he said, jumping up and getting Sass's leash from the cab of the truck.

"Well, you don't have to have a beer, but I haven't had one since I moved from the motel and it sounds great, c'mon."

Elizabeth got up and hurried to catch up with them, slipping her arm into the crook of his, the dog leading the way. They walked up to the party as if they had been invited. Gaius smiling and greeting people as he made it to the truck.

"Five bucks a cup." The young man at the tap said. Gaius fished in the front of his jeans pocket and took out a ten, the guy offered him change.

"No, two cups please," he said and motioned towards Elizabeth.

Two foamy cups of beer were handed to Gaius. "Thanks, man," he said taking the cups and handing one to Elizabeth.

"I don't want this," she said into his ear not loud enough for anyone else to hear.

"Just carry it around, it makes you look like you're supposed to be here. I'll drink it, we can switch every now and then, and it will look like you're drinking too. You're over twenty-one, don't sweat it."

Elizabeth shrugged her shoulders and lifted the drink to her nose and inhaled. It didn't smell too bad but not too good either. She didn't really see the point of her carrying it around. Gaius had downed half of his already and switched glasses with her.

"See, now it looks like you are part of the party," he said, smiling. They found a place to sit on the outskirts of the gathering. The young adults were drawn to Sassafras and several people had come over to pet her and meet them. Gaius introduced himself to numerous party-goers and explained to them they were camping in another spot. Watching him Elizabeth pictured a chameleon knowing he had gone from care-giver of his sick mom to surrogate son of an elderly LDS couple to the life of a random party in Provo canyon. She vaguely smelled the same sickly sweet smoke from Hattie's house and knew someone was smoking marijuana close by.

Fall Out Boy came on over the speakers, *My song's know what you did in the dark*. She felt the heat rise to her face thinking about the sexy, topless dance she had done in the privacy of her own room. She brought the beer to her lips and took a large drink. The bitter, foaming liquid caught her off guard. Her eyes grew wide and she swallowed hard, not wanting anyone to notice her spit it out. *I should have brought a bottled water*, she thought.

"Elizabeth Anderson?" she heard her name and looked around to see who was talking to her.

"Pru?" It was Tish's youngest sister, Prudence.

"What are you doing here?" Elizabeth asked.

"Party!" Prudence answered, throwing her head back and thrusting her red cup in the air.

"Did you bring Jozette and Giselle?" Prudence started looking over Elizabeth's shoulder. "How about Molly?" she sang the word Molly and noticed Elizabeth's confused look.

"Who?"

"Ecstasy?"

Elizabeth looked even more confused. "Ecstasy? Are you asking me if I brought ecstasy? Are you suggesting Jozette and Giselle are bringing ecstasy," her question came out more a statement as her mind flashed to the small baggie of pills taped discreetly to Jozette's hanger.

"I sure hope so!" Pru sang and glanced down at Elizabeth's beer.

"Wow, I didn't realize you were so cool, Elizabeth. Your sisters always painted you out to be such a square. Cheers." Prudence held up her glass so Elizabeth could tap them together. She did and sipped another drink while Pru chugged hers.

"Gonna go for a re-fill, want me to fill yours too?" she asked.

"No, thanks though. Are my sisters coming tonight?"

"Maybe. I don't know, they were invited. Who are you here with?" she looked around and spotted Gaius. The younger woman gave Elizabeth an approving look accompanied by a thumbs-up motion. Pru sauntered away towards the keg.

Elizabeth's mind was spinning. Her sisters doing drugs? Was that why they still shared a room, because they were doing ecstasy together? Was that why Jozette was so anti-social? Is that why their parents wanted to keep them right across the hall? What else did they do behind that closed door?

Gaius strolled up and handed her an empty glass and took hers, downing it in one gulp. "Having fun?" he asked and bent down and kissed her, "You taste like you are," Gaius commented.

She rolled her eyes a little. "My sisters are supposed to be here tonight. They are supposed to bring Molly from what I understand," she explained making quote marks in the air when she used the nickname for the drug.

"Wow, cool, I've never tried ecstasy, have you?"

Her face contorted. "No. No. Not cool. And of course I've never tried ecstasy. Crap Gaius, this just came out of left field."

"I love baseball talk," he said sitting next to her, beaming ear to ear.

"Baseball talk?" she looked at him in astonishment. "I just found out my sisters provide illicit drugs to the locals and you're talking about baseball?"

"No, you did. You just said it came out of left field," he took another drink of the beer.

She sighed, took the beer cup from him and swallowed another large drink then handed it back. He finished it. "Going for re-fills," he kissed the top of her head. "So glad we're here."

Elizabeth smiled up at him and watched him walk back towards the truck with the keg, passing Prudence and her friends. She looked around at the other guests and saw a few familiar faces, but for the most part, they were all strangers. It was odd to think of her little sisters here. She would have never suspected them to hang-out with this crowd. Who was she kidding? She had no idea Tish's little sister was 'that crowd.' Gaius returned with two more filled cups of beer. He handed her one and they clinked the plastic cups together.

"To your health," he said, and downed half of his cup full. She took a little sip and they switched glasses again. "You okay?" he asked, looking at her with concern.

She nodded. "You could say this is my first party."

"And it's a kick-ass kegger! Cheers," he tipped his cup back towards hers.

"Hey dude," a male voice said swaggering up to the couple. The young man was holding a red Solo cup and smoking on a joint. "Here," the stranger passed the joint to Gaius who took a long draw from it and handed it back. The young man took it, drew on it and went to hand it to Elizabeth. Shaking her head, she looked at it and then to Gaius.

"Go for it. Seriously, what do you have to lose, I'll make sure you stay safe, Lizard. You've come this far," Gaius toasted his red glass in her direction.

Tentatively she took the pot and held it to her lips, sucking softly. She blew out and tried again, the tip of the joint glowing a little brighter as she inhaled. As she exhaled, she started to cough.

"Gotta cough to get off," the young man said, laughing. "Hey, I think I know you, aren't you Jojo's sister? Is she here?" he looked around the crowd. She raised her eyes and looked at him as she tried to pass the joint back. He shook his head, "It's going the other way, to your boyfriend," he nodded towards Gaius, Elizabeth turned and held the joint towards him.

"Puff, puff, pass," he said happily, taking the joint and inhaling deeply, "Cheers to your boyfriend," Gaius added and winked at Elizabeth. She sighed and smiled.

"Jojo?" Elizabeth returned her attention to the young man as Pru ambled towards them.

"Well glad good ole Mary Jane could make it even if Molly couldn't," Prudence said taking the joint from Gaius.

"Hey Pru, isn't this Jojo and Elle's big sister?" The young man said, motioning to Elizabeth.

"Sure as heck is!" Prudence said putting her arm around Elizabeth.

"Jojo? Elle?"

"Nicknames, honey." Pru said, "Jozette and Giselle of course!" she laughed loudly and smiled big as Gaius took a picture of them with his phone.

"Now don't go and post that on the FB, I'm still a minor, you know?" Pru laughed again, "Where's my sis? Did you ditch her for your cute man over there?"

Prudence's words slurred slightly. Elizabeth shook her head. "No. Yes. I don't know," she took a long swallow of the beer, the taste seemed to be growing on her. This whole night was turning into something from a television show. Prudence was laughing. Gaius was smiling at her, and the unidentified young man was bobbing his head to the music. Lady Gaga's song Pokerface had begun to play. Suddenly they were all dancing and singing, the whole party getting caught up in it. Elizabeth was swept up in the hubbub. It felt magical, her head was light and she felt disconnected from her feet. Pru grabbed one of Elizabeth's hands and started to spin with her, singing wildly.

"*Oh, oh, oh, oh, ohhhh, oh-oh-e-oh-oh-oh... I'll get him hot, show him what I've got...*"

Prudence started to shake her backside and motioned for Elizabeth to do the same. At first she felt awkward, but between the little bit of beer and pot, her inhibitions were lost and she began to move more fluently, sexy. She looked around to be sure she wasn't making a spectacle of herself, but no one was watching her. Everyone was shaking something and singing and laughing. Her heart swelled and she smiled with her whole face, moving her body to the rhythm and wondered if this is what it felt like to be happy. Truly happy.

"Oh, oh, oh, oh, ohhhh, oh-oh-e-oh-oh-oh... I'll get him hot, show him what I've got!"

Elizabeth sipped another beer, Gaius had a couple more and they bade their farewells and started back up the hill to their tent. When she had said goodnight to Prudence, the younger woman had held out her pinky finger. "Pinky promise me you won't tell Tish," she said as they entwined their smallest fingers together and embraced in a bear hug.

"Promise," Elizabeth assured her. When they got back to the tent, Gaius let Sassafras run around for a few minutes and put her in the cab of the truck. Elizabeth had slipped in the tent and changed into the pink panties from Kentucky and nothing else. The beer had left her feeling bold and sexy. She sat and waited for Gaius to come in. When he did, he turned away with embarrassment.

"Sorry, Liz. Didn't know you were changing," he averted his eyes and ducked his head back out of the tent.

"I'm cool," she said feeling a flush from her head to her toes. "You can come in."

"Are you decent?" he asked coming back in. She grabbed the back of his neck and kissed him hard, pressing her breasts into him. "Whoa, whoa, whoa!" He said pulling away from her. "How many of those beers did you drink, girl?" Gaius couldn't help but look at her near naked body. "You look amazing, good enough to eat, seriously, but..."

"But I don't turn you on?" she asked disappointed.

"Oh, no, you definitely turn me on. Yes, the answer to that is affirmative," he said feeling the blood rush to his face and elsewhere. "It's just I'd be a royal asshole if I took advantage of you tonight after your first beer 'n bud. That's not my style, little Lizard. Besides, you told me you wanted to wait until your wedding night, remember? And I don't remember jumping any brooms this evening or anything like that," he took the oversized night shirt she had left on her sleeping bag and helped her into it and assisted her into the sleeping bag.

"Should I tie you in or can I trust you not to molest me in the night?" he asked, a sparkle in his eye.

"I'll probably have to pee, so don't tie me in," Elizabeth answered, suddenly feeling very sleepy. "I try not to molest you in the night..," she slurred as she slipped into sleep. Gaius lightly kissed her forehead and grabbed his sleeping bag pulling it from the tent. He found a place near the fire and made himself comfortable enjoying the view of the stars and the noises of the wilderness as the last of the sliver of moon set.

Chapter Forty-Five

Elizabeth woke to the sounds and smells of the brewing coffee. Rolling on her side, she noticed Gaius' sleeping bag was gone. Peering out the front of the tent, she saw him sitting on a folding chair rubbing Sass' head, his sleeping bag on the ground by the fire pit. She pulled on her sweats and climbed out of the tent. "Good morning."

He smiled at her setting his coffee on the cooler. "Good morning, beautiful!" He slipped his arms around her and nuzzled her neck. "How are you feeling?"

"I'm just waiting for the hangover to hit," his expression was quizzical. "My hangover, when does it come? I've never had one before." Elizabeth explained matter-of-factly.

Gaius giggled. "You're so cute," he let her go and picked up his cup of coffee. "Seems you've never had a hangover and still don't. When you have one, you know the second you open your eyes, that is *if* you can open your eyes."

"Weird. I feel great."

"Not weird. You didn't drink *that* much and I only saw you have one hit from the doobie."

"Doobie?"

"The joint," he arched one eyebrow up and looked at her. "Do you even remember smoking? Did you inhale or were you like President Clinton?"

"Doobie is a cool word. I like the way it sounds, doobie, doobie. Doooo-beee. And as for if I inhaled or not, I don't really know. It felt amazing, I do know that! When we were singing and dancing, I felt like I was floating, so happy!" She said opening the cooler and retrieving a bottled water. She took a long drink and continued. "I remember seeing Tish's sister, Prudence, and they were looking for *my* sisters. *That* was weird. But for real, I felt great last night, I feel great this morning," she looked down the hill to the campground and noticed only two vehicles, the truck with the keg and one car.

"Where'd everyone go?" she asked.

"They left hours ago, I'm sure they all had to sneak back in their houses before their folks realized they were gone. My guess is most those kids were under age."

Elizabeth felt a laugh bubble from her. "Ya' think?" she said sarcastically and shook her head, "I think Pru is only fifteen, I can't remember if she is Jozette or Giselle's age, or should I say Jojo and Elle. Good grief, so much I don't know about the people that are supposed to be the closest to me. I'm ninety-nine percent sure my little brother is gay and a hundred percent sure my little sisters are freaking party animals," she sighed and downed half the water in one drink.

"I'm one hundred percent sure your brother is gay and ninety-nine percent sure your sisters are party animals," he said, putting water on the stove to boil. "I've got instant oatmeal on the menu for this morning. Do you want apple cinnamon or maple brown sugar?"

"Maple brown sugar," she answered going back into the tent. The memory of her being topless and throwing herself at Gaius came rushing back. She could feel her face turn red all the way to her ears and she zipped herself into the tent. *How humiliating*, she thought, *thank goodness he was the gentleman he professed to be*. Digging through her bag, she found her garments and stripped down putting them on first, then pulled the clean tee shirt over the top and slid into her jeans from the first day. After donning her shoes and socks, she began to roll up her sleeping bag and heard Gaius tell her the oatmeal was done. Bowing her head, she prayed silently to herself. The guilt she was feeling was the only hangover she had. What was she thinking? She stuffed the rest of her belongings into the backpack, grabbed the rolled bag and exited the tent.

Once they packed up the campground they explored the Provo side of the canyon, enjoying lunch at the Sundance's Foundry Grill and doing a light hike at Bridal Veil Falls. They walked holding hands under the mist, the roar of the water making it difficult to talk, the sheer cliff hiding the sun. The great water falls were incredible and Elizabeth took dozens of photos. About dinner time they loaded up Sass and headed down the canyon. As they drove down the scenic road, the traffic began to slow and completely stopped.

"Wonder what's up." Gaius said. "It's too late in the day for construction."

"Probably an accident."

"Probably." After a couple of minutes, Gaius turned off the engine and looked in his rearview mirror, the traffic was stacking up behind him. After twenty minutes, people were starting to get out of their cars and talk amongst themselves. Another half hour went by, fortunately the weather wasn't too hot nor too cold. Sassafras had curled up with her head in Elizabeth's lap. Elizabeth was going through the pictures on her phone, editing the best ones and deleting the bad ones. She got a text.

"Wow, look at that, I have service."

"Cool. I think we're almost to the bottom of the canyon. Is it your mom? Your folks gonna kill me when we get back?" Gaius' voice was supposed to sound light and humorous, but it didn't come out that way, "I'm going to grab a granola bar. Want anything?" he asked opening the door and climbing out.

"Bottled water, please," she answered, "And a granola bar."

"You got it, pretty girl," he said. They heard the rotors of a helicopter approaching. Gaius looked up and saw a red life-flight helicopter coming down just around the bend in front of them. He also saw two news channel helicopters flying a bit higher. "Must be a bad accident."

The text was from Giselle.

> *Hey Sis, U OK?*
> *Yes. What's up?*
> *Saw on the news there was a fatal accident in Provo canyon. Pru said she saw you last night. Just wanted to make sure it wasn't you.*

At first, Elizabeth couldn't believe Prudence had told Giselle. In retrospect, the pinky promise was not to tell Tish. She should have added her own stipulations.

> *We're stuck in the traffic. What'd the news say?*
> *Head on collision. Family coming home from camping with their kids, some drunk driver swerved and nailed them. News said the dad was driving and he's the only one that made it, but it doesn't look good for him either. Sucky deal.*

Elizabeth's stomach rolled as she thought of dead children only a dozen cars in front of them. Gaius was getting back in the driver's seat. "Might as well get comfortable, doesn't look like we're going anywhere soon," he commented, handing her a water and snack.

"Nope. Giselle said it's on the news, a head on crash. People died." For a moment, she imagined it was her family in the accident, the morbid theme seemed to be stuck. She sent a text back to her sister.

>*Sucks for sure. Thanks for checking on me. LOVE YOU! Tell mom we're fine.*
>
>*Will do. She was mad you didn't say bye before you left, but I think she's over it now. The news said the canyon will be closed another hour. Good luck. Be safe.*

Gaius' head was leaned back and his eyes were closed. Sass was asleep. Again images of her family, dead in the crash, invaded her mind. Thoughts of losing her siblings tumbled from her head to her heart. Sadness washed over her, she asked Heavenly father to comfort the family that was going to receive the worst phone call of their lives. The prayer offered no comfort.

Approximately two hours after they had stopped, the red helicopter took off and a car in front of them roared to life waking Gaius. "Are we moving? Sorry, did I fall asleep?"

"Yea, and you were snoring up a storm," she said, a hint of a smile playing at her lips. The train of cars started to snake down the canyon. As they approached the accident Elizabeth let out a cry of horror. "Oh no, oh *no!*" She covered her mouth with her hands and began to cry.

Gaius saw it too. The two-toned blue van with the stick figure family and 'Families are Forever' bumper sticker was completely crushed. The metal was bent like a giant had stepped on one side. The jaws of life had ripped open the driver's side. A large GMC pick-up was on the back bed of a tow truck, also heavily smashed, the windshield broken out. Besides the tow truck, there were two ambulances and six police cars. As they rolled by, they noticed a gurney behind one of the ambulances, there was a person on it, covered in a white sheet. Elizabeth got a glance of an ankle when the breeze blew the sheet back slightly. *Was that the mom?* She wondered, still crying, the tears flowing silently down her cheeks.

"Here's a million-dollar question for you. Which is worse, Lizard?" he asked, forcing himself to keep his eyes forward on the car in front of him instead of looking at the mangled mess of the accident. "Dying or waking up in the hospital to learn you are the sole survivor?"

She couldn't answer and shook her head trying to block out the sweet faces of Todd and Travis, blocking out the young mother's voice calling to them, the memory of the baby in the high chair, happily playing with the fish crackers. She noticed the 'baby on board' sign had fallen.

"I think I would want to just die," he said. "I'm glad their family has their faith to hold on to. This is a situation Liz I really wish I could just believe that mama is making those kids their sandwiches just on the other side of the pearly gates. That there was a kind and merciful god. Seriously, Liz, I do." A lump clotted in his throat and tears stung his eyes. Elizabeth was speechless and shook her head and cried softly. They stopped at a restaurant on Center Street in Orem called Joe's café. Elizabeth ordered the biscuits and gravy. She wanted comfort food and there was nothing more comforting than a large helping of biscuits and sausage gravy. It was difficult to block out the vision of smashed vehicles, the exposed ankle of the corpse near the ambulance, the smiling faces of the blonde haired, blue eyed brothers. By the time they left Orem it was already getting late.

"Wanna just stay at my house tonight?" Gaius suggested, "By the time we get back I'm going to want to just hit the hay. If you stay at my place, we can get up early. I've got to be back home by nine so that way we can get your things out of the back when it's light."

She nodded. Since seeing the mangled blue van, she hadn't felt much like talking. Trying to be considerate, she sent a text to her sister to inform their mother she would be home in the morning.

"Damn." Gaius said. "Life is so fucking precious."

"And so fucking fragile," she added, the third time she had ever said that word. It seemed fitting for this occasion. No other word could have summed up how she was feeling at that moment. He looked at her and reached over the dog to take her hand. When they pulled into Pleasant and drove towards 700 North, they saw the distinctive strobing lights of two police cars down one of the side streets. Elizabeth tried to remember who lived down that dead ended cul-de-sac, but her mind was tired and she couldn't think.

Once they got to the Smith's house, Gaius had Elizabeth open the gate and he backed in while Elizabeth closed it behind him. As soon as Gaius opened the door to his little apartment over the garage, Sassafras ran up the stairs and immediately jumped up on her chair, turning twice before flopping down and sighing. Gaius and Elizabeth didn't say much to each other as they stretched out on Gaius' bed, curled up together and fell into a deep sleep.

Chapter Forty-Six

Gaius woke early. It was a little weird having another person in his bed, especially a beautiful blonde he had feelings for. Remembering she had told him she watched him sleep, he watched her in turn. She looked like a child, her blonde hair spilling over the pillow and framing her angelic face. A warm feeling crept through him, she was unlike anyone he had ever dated.

They held each other throughout the night, their arms and legs entwined. When he woke, they were back to back. Not wanting to disturb her, he got up slowly. Sassafras' keen ears heard him and got off the chair, shook her floppy ears and yawned. "Shhhh…" He whispered. Sass followed him down the stairs and out the door. He started to unload the back of the truck. Grabbing the cooler first and retrieving the little bit of leftover food, he tipped it on end so the melted ice would drain on the lawn. The back sliding glass door opened and closed. Boo-Boo tentatively walked down the steps. Standing in the bed of the truck, Gaius shuffled around what was Elizabeth's and extracted what was his and his grandpa's gear. Behind him, he heard the sliding glass door open and close again. He looked up and saw his grandfather walking towards him.

"G'morning, son." Bill said, striding up to the truck. "Glad to see you're home. Me and Mar saw on the news last night there was an accident in the canyon, since we hadn't heard from you, well…"

Gaius looked at him and saw the relief in his face. "Sorry Gramps. I should have called. With me, you can bet, no news is good news." Gaius saw the worry dissipate from the old man's face and turn into a sincere smile. Elizabeth appeared in the doorway.

"Hi," she said. Gaius and Bill looked at her. She had taken out the braids and brushed her long blonde hair; it had taken on a wave and laid exquisitely over her shoulders. She was wearing the sweats and a tee shirt she had gone to bed in.

"Good. Morning." Gaius said brightly, hoping down from the back of the truck.

"Hi," she repeated, looking at Gaius with love in her eyes. He grabbed her and kissed her. Bill made a noise clearing his throat and Elizabeth pulled away. "Good morning, Brother Smith," she said cheerfully. "Thank you for letting me crash here last night. Gaius and I got in awfully late and it was just more convenient for me to..," she trailed off as her and Grandpa Bill's eyes met.

"You two aren't, um..." Bill stumbled on his words, "aren't, um..."

"No, Gramps we are not sleeping together in the sexual sense, we really just slept," Gaius reassured his grandpa. Bill nodded once and grabbed the cooler from the lawn giving it a good shake and closed the lid. Sassafras had come to greet Elizabeth and she dutifully rubbed the dog's head. "Gotta run Liz home, then I'll be back so you can leave, okay Grandpa?" The older man nodded once and eyed the two young people with suspicion. He returned to the house as Gaius got into the cab of the little truck and Elizabeth walked towards the gate. Sassafras stopped running and sat at the edge of the drive, panting and smiling and watching them leave. "You in a huge hurry?" Gaius asked. Elizabeth shook her head. "Cool. I'm going to stop at the C-store and grab some coffee and gas."

She nodded and looked out the window as they drove down the empty streets. They drove to the convenience store in silence. After pulling up to a pump, Gaius took out his wallet and handed his debit card to Elizabeth.

"Tell Vicki I'm going to fill up on pump seven," he handed her the card. "If you don't mind, grab me a coffee too. Twenty-four ounces, two creams, one sugar." Their eyes met and he leaned over, taking her hand and kissed her gently. "There's a proper good morning kiss, my fair lady."

"Thanks," she muttered.

"You okay?" he asked.

"I just want to hug my family," she replied. He could almost see the reflected canyon accident in her tear-filled eyes as she got out of the truck. "Be right back."

"Good morning Elizabeth Anderson!" Vicki announced loudly as she walked through the front doors.

"Good morning, Vicki. Fill 'er up on seven, please," she said as she slid the card across the counter and walked towards the coffee. Once she had fixed the beverage to his liking, she returned to the counter and placed the steaming cup on the counter.

"He's almost done." Vicki said smiling at her.

Elizabeth looked down and saw the morning paper. The headlines read 'Family of six dies in Provo canyon'. She picked up the paper and began to read the front-page article. It said the dad had died during the night, only the driver of the other vehicle had survived. As she skimmed the article she discovered the instigator of the accident was not only drunk but a first counselor at a local Provo ward. "We were in that traffic." Elizabeth said without looking up.

"Glad you all are okay," Vicki said, and added, "poor Sister Walker, you know? My heart just breaks for her."

Elizabeth looked up at Vicki with a confused expression. "What do you mean?"

Vicki motioned to the paper, "You haven't heard? It's at the bottom, front page, I feel so bad for all their parents. Such a shame. Such a horrible tragedy."

Elizabeth flipped the still folded newspaper. There was Frida and Laurie's senior pictures smiling up at her. The headlines read 'Suicide pact shakes small town'. *What?!?* Her mind reeled as she scanned the article.

> *A couple from Pleasant, Utah came home from their temple volunteer work late Wednesday night to find their twenty-two-year-old daughter and what appeared to be her lesbian lover dead in the garage. The two women had apparently been celebrating an anniversary and had prepared a dinner for themselves. After eating, they sealed the roll up garage door with a large padded moving quilt and started a 1997 Fiat. They laid together in a small cot until the carbon monoxide fumes took both their lives.*

"Did you know they were gay?" Vicki asked.

Elizabeth shrugged and nodded slightly. "Lesbians. Yea, I knew," she took the debit card, coffee and newspaper and exited the store. When she climbed into Gaius' truck, she handed him the coffee and dropped the newspaper with the suicide headline facing up. Tears silently streaked down her face as she handed over the debit card.

"Lizard, what's wrong?" he asked and glanced from her face down to the paper. "No, no, no, no, no, no, no, no." The single syllable became a chant. Gaius pictured Frida's face on Sunday when he had seen her getting off work. She had been so happy. He thought of the hug, how could he have known that ending her life was on her mind. *Take care*, was her last words to him. A wave of nausea passed over him as he read the paper.

> *Frida Walker and Laurie Rasmussen had been friends since high school, their families were surprised to learn their friendship was something more. Both women were said to be wearing lingerie and a makeshift dining table was set with candles and china dinnerware. Flowers decorated the table and cards to each other were found at the scene as well as a letter from Miss Rasmussen's local bishop requesting a meeting with her for the following Sunday. The other Rasmussen children had come home from school and had not known the girls were in the garage. The paper had reported their afternoon was normal, like any other. Mr. and Mrs. Rasmussen discovered the young women when they returned from their volunteer services and opened the garage to park for the night. Both sets of parents have declined further interview. More information regarding the funeral services will be published as soon as they are available.*

The next page went into the epidemic of therapy and suicides that had been plaguing the schools and young people in Utah. Apparently, Utah had a higher suicide rate than the national average. Gaius felt like he was going to be sick.

"The cop cars we saw last night when we were coming home." Elizabeth heaved a heavy sigh. "They were down fourth, Rasmussen's live on fourth, I remember now. That letter from the bishop... They were going to excommunicate Laurie for loving Frida!" The cries came. She leaned forward and put her hands over her face, her body racked with sobs. Gaius put his arms around her and laid his face on her back, crying with her, his tears leaving wet dots on the back of her tee shirt. It was 7:47a.m. "If we hurry to my house, I can hug my little sisters," she sniffled.

He nodded and sat back straight in the driver's seat and started the truck. They pulled into her driveway only minutes later. Elizabeth had opened the door and taken off her seatbelt before the truck had stopped. Racing up the stairs, she flung her arms around her mother and started sobbing again.

"What's wrong?" Alice said, folding her arms around Elizabeth and glancing at her other two daughters with puzzlement.

Gaius appeared in the doorway of the kitchen with the newspaper in his hand. He looked as if he had been crying too. Elizabeth released Alice and turned to Giselle and Jozette, hugging them in turn and back to her mother's embrace. Her tears were starting to subside. Gaius walked over to the breakfast table and sat heavily on a chair, almost as an afterthought, he put the folded newspaper on the table. Giselle and Jozette's eyes fell onto the headlines.

"Holy crap!" Giselle exclaimed, "That's Michaela and Michael Rasmussen's sister," she slid the paper so it lay between them. Jozette looked at the pictures of the two girls as Giselle started to read the article. Alice steered Elizabeth to a chair and was standing behind the younger girls looking at the periodical.

"It was like they were lesbian lovers ending it like Romeo and Juliette, but in this case, more like Juliette and Julia. What a bummer," Giselle commented as she continued to read, opening the paper to read the second page. "I wonder what the bishop would have said to her if she went to the interview. Wow that sucks so bad!"

"For sure," Jozette commented.

"Oh, their poor mothers," Alice exclaimed. "Horrible to think what they are going through, how embarrassing. Let this be a lesson to all of you about homosexuality. Nothing good can come out of it, it is an abomination, a sin against God. This tragedy is proof." Gaius watched as Alice shook her head and made tsk-tsk noises.

The younger girls announced it was time for them to go. Jozette walked behind Elizabeth and bent to kiss the top of her sister's head, her lips barely brushing against her hair. Giselle stopped and put her arms around her big sister and pressed her cheek to Elizabeth's as she spoke. "Sorry about your friends. So glad you are alright," she squeezed Elizabeth's shoulders and kissed the side of her face. "I love you, Sis." Giselle announced.

"Love you, too," Elizabeth mumbled and nodded her head.

"Can I make you something to eat?" Alice asked.

Gaius shook his head, "No ma'am, thank you. I've got to be getting back. It's my turn to watch my grandma."

"I want to go with you," Elizabeth sudden exclaimed. "Wait for me, I'll be right back," she jumped up and ran down the stairs.

Alice slid the paper across the table so it was upright for her to read. "So sad," she commented. "I can't even imagine what I'd do if one of my kids were gay, I think it would be better if they were retarded or something."

Gaius stared blankly at her. No wonder Paul was still in the closet. He thought Elizabeth had been exaggerating when she said her parents would freak out but it was obvious she was not. "So, let me get this straight." Gaius said cautiously. "You would rather have a child with a mental handicap than to have them love someone of the same sex?"

"Well, it's kind of the same thing, wouldn't you say?" she turned the paper over and saw the story of the family that had been killed in the canyon and started to read it.

"No, actually I would say it was not the same at all." Gaius sighed heavily. "In all due respect, Sister Anderson, you would rather have your child be alone than to know love, that is if the love is coming from someone of the same sex? Do I understand you correctly?"

Alice sighed, "Yes. It would be too much to have a child so deranged, I would absolutely rather they be alone than to be an abomination, you know, there is therapy for that. I heard all about it, most psychologists treat homosexuality as a disease, you know? Medications and therapy, it's something that someone can change about themselves if they want to. Give it to God, trust He knows best. It's a sickness, nothing more." Alice nodded her head and continued to read the paper. Gaius looked at her and shook his head in disgust.

Chapter Forty-Seven

Elizabeth had sent a quick text to Tish instructing her to call when she was up. She dumped her bag onto her bed and grabbed a clean change of clothes and her make-up, stuffing them back into the pack, then bounded up the stairs and back into the kitchen. She looked at Gaius and noticed his jaw was tight, his lips pressed together. Glancing at her mom, she noticed Alice was oblivious to Gaius' icy stares.

"We gotta run, Ma." Elizabeth said, scooping up the paper.

Her mom looked up at her. "When should we expect you home?"

"I don't know," she said as Gaius got to his feet. "Before church on Sunday."

"What?!" Alice's brow furrowed and her eyes narrowed at Elizabeth. "Your father and I will not…"

Elizabeth interrupted her mother. "I'll see you before church on Sunday. That could be later today, later tonight, tomorrow, the next day or Sunday morning. I don't know, Ma, I don't know. C'mon G," she headed down the stairs, Gaius on her heels. Elizabeth heard her mother call her name, the tone turning high pitched as if fury was about to bubble out of her mouth. They returned to the Smith's and as they entered through the sliding glass door, Bill was just putting the muffins in the oven.

"Oh good, you're back," he said as he turned, surprised to see Elizabeth.

"Hey Gramps, I'm going to grab a quick shower. I know you need to leave, so Liz will sit with Grandma for a minute," he headed down the hall towards the spare bathroom, the one he had taken over the last month. Elizabeth set her bag on the table and sat on one of the chairs then heard the water of the shower come on. Bill walked over and sat across from Elizabeth, he glanced in the living room to be sure Mary was still watching the television.

"I'm beginning to worry about you, Sister Anderson." Bill began. "It would be a shame to have history repeat itself."

Elizabeth cocked her head to one side and stared at him, not knowing exactly what to say to head off the lecture that would surely ensue.

"It's a shame what happened to Kimball and Gaius' mother. It's an example of what can happen when two people try to get together when they are clearly not meant to be together in God's eyes," he shook his head and continued. "Your friends, Sister Walker and Sister Rasmussen are another prime example of God's law, two women or two men, that isn't the way God's plan is set up, Elizabeth. This should be as clear to you as the nose on my face. You come from a good family with good morals, if anyone should be able to understand God's plan for us, it should be you, young lady." Elizabeth just stared at Bill, she heard the T.V go to commercial. The shower water was still running. "I'd like to offer a prayer for us this morning, if you could bow your head with me," he said a bit louder. "Mary, I'm going to offer a prayer, could you put the television on mute for a moment?" Obediently, Elizabeth crossed her arms over her chest and closed her eyes, the television sound disappeared and Grandpa Bill began to pray.

"Our dear kind Heavenly Father, thank you for this glorious day you have bestowed upon us. Thank you for the friendship that has blossomed between Gaius and Elizabeth. We pray Lord that they may see your eternal plan and strive to stay pure and true to your word. That they may understand how important chastity is for young people in today's world. We pray that they will be delivered from temptation and will embrace your will. We thank you for our health and are grateful every day for all the blessings you have provided to us. I ask thee humbly to watch over Gaius, Elizabeth and Mary today that they may feel your presence, that they may feel the prodding of the Holy Ghost and act accordingly. Please watch over me, your humble servant, as I travel to and from Provo to do your work this afternoon, that I may return unharmed and that I may bring the young men and women faith and courage as they train to embark on their missions to serve in your name. Again, thank you. Thank you, Heavenly Father for the sacrifices you have made so we have the free will to make our own choices. I say this, humbly in the name of the Jesus Christ of Latter Day Saints, amen."

"Amen," came from the living room and the volume of the television returned. Still a commercial. The water from the shower turned off. Elizabeth just stared at Bill, his smile looked painted on. There was no humor or goodwill in his grey eyes. Her own eyes dulled as if the very light of her belief system was extinguished by the comment Bill had made about Frida and Laurie. She thought of her brother and the new boy, Shane. Her jaw tightened, the whole ugly picture was pushing her to the very edge. Gaius returned to the kitchen in clean clothes, his hair still wet.

"My turn," Elizabeth stood up and matched Bill's fake smile. "See you this afternoon Brother Smith," she turned to Gaius, "Did you leave me any hot water?"

Gaius smiled at her and bent in to kiss her cheek lightly, he whispered in her ear. "Of course, I did. I'm perpetually taking cold showers when you are around," his tone seemed lighter, even though the normal playfulness was missing.

She grabbed her bag and headed down the hallway. There was no rush, processing the morning's events while the hot water splashed down upon her was therapeutic. It seemed like it had been a week since they returned from the mountains and it had barely been twelve hours. Frida's face appeared in her head, pouring Gaius' coffee, serving them their Sunday meals, the way she looked at Laurie during the temple tour. Tears began to stream down her face, mixing with the shower spray. When Elizabeth went to get dressed, she thought of the family that perished in the car accident. Certainly, the parents were wearing their garments, even the driver that had been drinking was LDS. *The drunk driver was the only survivor*, she thought. Pain hit her stomach as she pictured what he must be going through. She was sure sometime today he would wish he were dead too. How in the world would he ever look at his own wife and children the same again? And would the church turn their backs on him because he had alcohol in his blood?

She slipped on the garments anyway, even though she realized for the first time in her life the underwear only represented a concept. Gaius was right, there was no special protection when wearing them. Right now, it was comforting and that's what she needed. Maybe today they would offer her some peace, or not. It was going to be a long day, as long as she was with Gaius she could get through it.

Her mind wandered to Brother and Sister Walker. Frida had been their only child. How would they cope? They were parents for over twenty years and woke up on a random Thursday to find they no longer had a daughter. And what about the Rasmussen's? She wasn't sure how many kids they had, but losing one would create a hole in their hearts and in their family.

Suicide.

She had never known anyone who took their own life. Her stomach lurched. She turned on the water in the sink. Falling to her knees, she covered her face with her towel and screamed. A torrent of tears streaked down her face as she tried to breathe deeply. The bile in her stomach pitched up and she lunged towards the toilet a moment too late as the contents of her stomach went down the front of her garments and into the towel she held in her hands. Another heave took control of her and made it into the bowl. Her body was shaking. She tried to control her sobs and her stomach by looking up and breathing. Through the nose, out the mouth, through the nose, out the mouth. Sitting there on her knees looking up, she couldn't help but think of her Heavenly Father and wanted to pray but the words that came to her were harsh.

How could you? she thought, looking up to the ceiling. *How could you make defective people? Laurie and Frida's love was real. How can you reject that? Why is their love not good enough for You? Why? Why? Why?* Her tears were hot on her cheeks, Because He doesn't exist, the thought overwhelmed her. It came as a quiet still small voice from within her heart. Gaius was right, there was no kind and merciful god. Another sob bubbled out of her open mouth and her body folded into itself as she bawled, she didn't think about the noises she could be making. There was a light tap on the door and it opened slightly.

"Lizard? You okay?" Gaius saw her crumpled on the floor and immediately kneeled down and took her in his arms. "It's okay, baby. It's okay," he cooed to her as if she was a child.

"No," she cried, "it's not! Frida and Laurie are dead, Todd and Travis, dead and I'm covered in vomit. Don't. You're clean, stop."

Her shoulders shook under his hands and the tears continued to flow. He could smell the sour stench of vomit. Tears sprung into his eyes as well, it pained him to see Elizabeth like this. He sat on the edge of the tub and rubbed her back with one hand while she cried into the soiled towel. After a minute he spoke. "I'm going to go check on Grandma."

She nodded and wiped her face. "I'm sorry. I'm okay, I'm good." Taking the towel, she wiped the toilet seat and stood up. "I'll get dressed, I'll be right out. Gaius, I'm so sorry."

"Oh sweetie, don't be sorry. What did you tell me? Don't be sorry for having feelings? You're cool. You're tough. This is a horrible tragedy. You have every right to cry," he picked a piece of her wet hair that had stuck to her cheek and gently moved it behind her shoulder, then let his fingers run lightly down her cheek. "You're beautiful, even when you're upset. And you have every right to be upset. As hard as it is, be upset, cry, let it out," he kissed her forehead. "Muffins will be done momentarily. Did you want some tea?"

She shook her head. He walked out of the bathroom. Looking in the mirror she saw the throw-up on her garments and carefully pulled them over her head. She peeled the bottoms off and got back in the shower, rinsing herself thoroughly. When she was done, she couldn't put the stained underwear back on so she carefully wrapped them in the soiled towel and put her clothes on without anything underneath. Elizabeth brushed her hair and put two little braids in the front to keep it from hanging in her face. With the wadded soiled laundry in her hand, she walked into the kitchen inhaling the smell of the fresh muffins.

Gaius smiled at her. "Lemon poppy seed," he said.

"Okay, I'm going to run these clothes out to the washer." The washer and dryer were in the detached garage below Gaius' room. As she neared the door she veered right and walked up to the large garbage can on the side of the house. She stood in front of it for a long moment then opened the lid and deposited the towel and garments in the container. As she walked back to the sliding glass door she looked back over her shoulder wondering if she should go back and pull them from the rubbish but decided against it. "What day does your trash go out?" she enquired when she returned.

"Oh my, gosh, Thursday, today," he bounded past her, through the sliding door and grabbed the city trash can and hauled it to the curb. "The neighbor's trash hasn't been picked up yet so we made it," he declared victoriously when he returned.

"I owe you a towel," she said as she sat on one of the kitchen chairs and plucked a muffin from the plate. He looked confused so she explained. "I didn't wash the towel and my garments, I just tossed them."

"You didn't," his eyes grew wide as he looked at her. "Like I said before my little Lizard, don't lose faith because of me."

She shook her head. "I'm not, it's not *because* of you," heaving a heavy sigh, she peeled the paper from the poppy seed muffin and placed it on the little plate Gaius had placed in front of her. "It's just…" She stammered a little lost for words. How could she explain it to him? How could she explain losing faith to someone that never had faith to begin with? "It's just God doesn't make junk. And homosexuals aren't junk, their love is real. I witnessed it, we witnessed it. Homosexuality isn't a disease that can be fixed, it's a way of life that should be embraced. You're right Gaius, you've been right all along. This life is precious and fragile and…" A sob escaped her lips. "And the only one we get. You are so right, if one believes this is it, it does make the few years we have here more precious, more extraordinary. Life should be embraced and lived, I mean really lived! Experienced. Lived without regrets, lived with no remorse." Tears threatened to fall. She sighed and took a bite of the still warm muffin.

"I love you," he said softly.

Her head snapped up and she looked at him, terrified.

"Oh no, did I say that out loud?" she watched as his face turned many shades of red and he stumbled on his words. "Crap, I so thought I just thought that, I'm sorry, Liz. It just came out. I didn't mean it, well I did mean it, I just didn't mean to…"

She interrupted him. "Shhh…," she looked down at the muffin and back up to him. The look on his face was almost comical, she could see in his eyes he didn't know how to handle this slip of the tongue. "I love you, too," she spoke softly, "Well, I think I do, I'm not sure because I've never been in love before."

He reached across the table and took her hand. "Does holding my hand make your stomach somersault?" she nodded. "Do I make you laugh?" she nodded, a flash of a grin across her face. "When you wonder 'who do I want to hang out with today?' Am I the first person that pops into your head?" she nodded. "Do you think about me when I'm not with you?" she nodded. "Does the idea of never seeing me again make you sad?" she nodded, a bit more aggressively as tears sprung into her eyes. "Can you see us growing old together like your folks or Bill and Mary?" she shrugged and nodded, keeping her eyes adverted to her muffin. A single tear dropped onto her sky blue skirt leaving a dark dot. "Well I would say six out of six yes answers would lead me to believe, indeed, you love me too," he squeezed her hand and she looked up at him.

There wasn't anything to say, she had answered the questions correctly. It was entirely possible she was in love. The world seemed to grow brighter and scarier at the same time. Brighter because Gaius was in it. Scarier because Gaius was in it. The idea of leaving Pleasant, leaving Utah excited her with a queasy feeling. She didn't want to have her heart broken but at the same time, how could she not fall head over heels in love with this guy, Gaius.

"I'm scared," she admitted to him.

"Well, it's not called 'falling in love' because it's a controlled graceful act, it's called 'falling' because you're not in control, have you ever fallen and been in control of that shit? No, it doesn't happen, maybe a little twist here or a roll there, but really, not much control in falling and not being in control is scary, Lizard. Seriously scary."

Gaius leaned as far as he could across the table and Elizabeth pushed herself forward to meet him, taking his other hand they kissed, softly at first but then with more passion, leaning across the kitchen table. He took one hand and put it on the back of her neck, she grabbed the front of his shirt. There kissing became more passionate, a low moan emitted from Gaius' throat.

"I do love you, I do. I'm just so scared," she said pulling away from him, looking deep into his eyes, searching for confirmation of his feelings.

"We'll go slow, I promise, Liz," he kissed her forehead when they both realized Grandma Mary was sitting on the chair on the opposite end of the table. They slowly sat back down and turned towards her, Elizabeth could feel her face flush with embarrassment.

"The show is better in here." Mary said. "Muffin, please."

Chapter Forty-Eight

There was a heaviness to Sacrament meeting on Sunday. The church was packed for some reason. Elizabeth thought that tragedy must bring out a need to want to be a part of something bigger than just yourself. Or the busybodies that usually skipped Sacrament showed up to listen to the local gossip. Dead lesbians were as big as news got in Pleasant. They were all sitting in the same spots as they had the weeks before, the Smiths on the front row, the Andersons in the pews on the right, two rows back. She looked at the back of Gaius' head and thought about the week before. It seemed like months, but was only seven days since Easter. Their camping trip, hiking to the top of Timpanogos, the innocent conversation with Todd and Travis, being stuck in traffic because of the accident, Frida and Laurie's suicide. She had stayed with Gaius and Mary throughout the day on Thursday and spent the night with Gaius on Thursday and Friday.

Both nights they had made-out passionately. Tearing off each other's clothes, their kisses more like a hunger. She thought about feeling their naked bodies against each other, his hardness pressed against her stomach. They hadn't had sex but it was close, further than she had been with anyone, Saturday night being hotter than Friday. Never in her life had she been so turned on. She had wrapped her hands around his hard penis, examined it, felt it jump with excitement from her touch and heard his moans of pleasure. It was empowering. She felt sexy and desired. He had kissed her breasts and eventually had gone down on her, his tongue softly exploring her most private places. He left her quivering and begging for more. As for having intercourse, he told her they could wait until she was ready and he wasn't convinced she was ready.

"We've taken this far enough", he had told her, breathless. "I don't need your dad and brothers hunting me down with torches and pitchforks."

Elizabeth respected him for that, but still, she wanted him. After the two nights of passion that left her dizzy and craving, she was absolutely sure. Not at the Smith's house or not at hers. She had some romantic idea about them being somewhere beautiful and perfect, maybe married, maybe not.

Her fantasy vacillated between the ideas. She only had one 'v-card' and wanted it to be as perfect as it could be. A thought crossed her mind, the only nights all week she had stayed at her house was last Sunday and last night. They had been together the rest of the week. Besides the Sister missionaries, there was no one she had spent that much time with, not even Tish. Not a whole week all at once anyway. She was completely lost in thought and was brought back to reality with the congregation saying 'amen' in unison. Opening prayer. The bishop had taken his place at the podium.

"Good morning," he began. "Our first order of business is to offer our condolences to the Walker and Rasmussen families. We may never know what our Heavenly Father was thinking to call these two young women back to him so soon, but it is not our place to question but to accept His divine plan." Gaius looked over his shoulder at Elizabeth, his brow was furrowed. She shrugged slightly and he returned his attention back to the bishop. "Services for Frida Walker will be held here on Tuesday at two o'clock p.m., interment to follow immediately after. An open casket viewing will be held Monday night, also here at seven p.m. Services for Laurie Lynn Rasmussen will be held Friday at three thirty, here, interment immediately after with the viewing Thursday night at seven p.m. The Relief Society ladies are looking for volunteers to help with food preparation for both Tuesday and Friday," he took a breath and looked down at his notes.

"Excuse me, bishop," Gaius' voice rang out as he stood.

"Sit back down, boy," Grandpa Bill quietly hissed.

The bishop's eyes turned towards Gaius before he could say anything Gaius asked,

"Why wouldn't you have them together, the same day? Frida and Laurie's services. They died the same day, the same people will be mourning, seriously, I highly doubt they would mind, in fact, they would probably prefer it that way."

"Young man, if you could see me after Sacrament meeting is over, I'd be happy to discuss it with you. This is neither the time nor place."

"Just give me an answer, sir. I mean no disrespect, but Frida was my friend and I think she would approve of her and Laurie's services being combined," Gaius continued as a murmuring spread throughout the chapel.

"It was a family request." The bishop said without emotion. "Now if you would please sit down."

"A family request, is that so? Sister Walker are you in here? Sister Rasmussen?" Without warning, Paul jumped up and strode two steps to Gaius, taking his arm.

"That's enough. Let's go." Paul said sharply.

Gaius jerked his arm from Paul. "I'll go. Don't get your panties in a knot." As he walked up the aisle, he caught Elizabeth staring at him, her eyes round, her mouth slightly gaped. Paul continued to follow Gaius out into the foyer. As Gaius walked out the front doors, Paul followed him and suddenly, without warning, pushed him in the back with both hands open. Gaius staggered and turned to Paul, straightening up his posture. Even at his full height, he was several inches shorter than Paul. "What the fuck?" Gaius shrieked.

"Get out of here you freak!" Paul shouted. "We don't need your kind coming around here!"

"My kind? My kind!" Gaius repeated almost laughing. "My kind? You mean the kind of people who are comfortable without made up stories and myths about zombies and ghosts? Someone like me that doesn't have a need to worship a deity? My kind that is comfortable in my own skin? That kind is what you can do without?"

Suddenly Gaius' butt hit the ground, his head flew back and hit the sidewalk. There was no way to know what just happened, like he had been in a car accident but he wasn't in a car. Confused. Everyone was moving in slow motion and he couldn't hear what they were saying. Paul's face was contorted in a hideous snarl. Elizabeth pushed her way through the door. Gaius was grateful his backside had taken the brunt of the fall and somewhat spared his skull. He lifted his hand to the back of his head, no blood. The pain flashed in his jaw as the realization that Paul had just punched him settled in his brain. His eyes were slightly out of focus as he watched Paul's snarling mouth scream, his hand out pointing a finger in Gaius' direction. Elizabeth grabbed Paul's arm and turned him towards her, they were still moving in slow motion. He couldn't make out what they were saying. Gaius was snapped into reality as Paul pushed Elizabeth backwards. She staggered but didn't go down. Her hand flew up and slapped her brother across the cheek, she hurried towards Gaius. He had already gotten to his feet, but was a little wobbly. She put her arm around his waist and talked to him.

"Let's go, G. Let's just get out of here," Elizabeth pleaded.

A small crowd had gathered in the foyer and was watching them through the glass doors. Elizabeth noticed Shane was standing in the doorway, holding the door open, a look of concern on his handsome face. Elizabeth and Gaius slowly walked to his truck as Paul went back in to the church, pushing past Shane. Elizabeth put the car in gear and drove to Blondie's. "Are you okay?"

"I think so," he pulled the visor down and looked at his reflection, checking the pupils of his eyes and the bruise that was starting to show on his jaw.

Elizabeth pulled the Toyota into Blondie's. They both noticed a memorial that had been constructed near the entrance of the diner for Frida, her senior picture smiling from a standing plastic frame. Flowers, candles and cards had been placed there with a light brown teddy bear dressed like a waitress. They got out and walked over to it, reading some of the notes when Gaius noticed another memorial on the opposite side of the diner. He walked over to it and exclaimed loudly. "Oh hell no!"

Elizabeth looked up from reading a sympathy card. Gaius was holding a large plastic frame with a picture of Laurie in it. There were just as many flowers, candles and cards as well as a bright pink teddy bear dressed in a ballet tutu.

"They were separated in life, there should be no reason to separate them in death," Gaius said, scooping up the flowers and cards. "Help me, Liz," she rushed to his side and they collected all the items that had been placed near Laurie's picture. They brought them over to the side where Frida's tokens were gathered. Together they placed the pictures side by side and the candles on either side of the frames, they took the flowers and arranged them so they created a large heart around the pictures and candles. Elizabeth took the ribbons from the bouquets and braided them into a long rainbow link and laced it in between the flowers. They placed the teddy bears side by side behind the picture frames and arranged them so they looked as if they were holding hands. "Much better," he said, she nodded in agreement. Gaius sighed and took Elizabeth's hand as they walked into the restaurant.

They took their normal round booth, sitting side by side they could peer out the window and see the memorial they had put together. The hostess and waitress were both people they had never met before. The hostess gave them menus and told them their waitress would be right with them. It seemed as if it was business as usual. The waitress came up and brought them waters with lemon wedges placed on the side and asked them if they were ready to order. Gaius said he had never tried the biscuits and gravy and glanced at Elizabeth. She smiled at him and said she'd have the same with a side of bacon, extra crisp. At that moment, Tish came in.

"Hey you guys! Breakfast burrito for me, please," she hollered sliding into the booth. The waitress walked away, Tish continued. "Nice memorial outside, did you guys check it out?"

Gaius and Elizabeth nodded and smiled sadly. Tish retold the story of Gaius getting sucker punched from her perspective and that the bishop calmed everyone down and went on with his sermon on Families Being Forever and the blessings of being sealed in the temple.

"Glad I didn't stay for that one," Gaius commented. Their food came and they ate with minimal conversation.

"I heard they looked like they were sleeping all cuddled up, but their lips were blue," Tish said solemnly.

"I can't think about it," Elizabeth answered, tears springing in her eyes. "I just can't."

They tried to talk to the waitress about what she knew, but she said she didn't know anything about anything, she was just asked by a family member to step in for a few days, or maybe a week. She was from a neighboring town and was just there to help out. "Is there anything else I can get you guys?" The waitress's smile was all teeth.

The three of them shook their heads. Elizabeth recognized the fake friendliness. "I've got to get out of this town," Elizabeth said to no one in particular.

"Me too," Tish agreed.

"Me three," Gaius chimed in.

He and Elizabeth passed a sad look between them. The waitress came and cleared their dishes and refilled their beverages. Gaius looked out the window and noticed his grandparents pulling into the parking lot. He watched as they parked and Bill got out and walked around to help Mary out of the car. It was so endearing the way he treated her. As they walked towards the entrance, Gaius noticed Bill's eyes cut across to the makeshift memorial. Gaius jumped up and went to get the door for them but they walked through when he was still about ten feet away.

"Hey Gramps, Grandma Mary," he waved and continued walking towards them.

"We just stopped by to see if you are okay," Bill said.

The hostess appeared and offered them any table, Gaius explained they were all together and started to steer his grandparents to the booth. "Want a menu, Gramps?"

"We just stopped by to see if you are okay," Bill repeated.

"I'll have some tea," Mary said and added, "Do they have muffins?"

The imitation waitress said they did have bran muffins available and they came with a cup of fruit. Gaius said that would be perfect and they all slid around making room for Bill and Mary. The waitress brought a small tray with an assortment of teas, Mary picked an orange blossom tea and Bill poured the hot water into the cup.

"Glad you're alright, you got sucker punched good," Bill said looking closely at Gaius' face.

"That I did," Gaius said, "But I'm okay, Gramps. Don't worry about me."

The waitress brought the muffin and bowl of fruit, "Hope you don't mind, but I doubled up on the fruit since there are so many of you," she said and refilled everyone's water glass.

Grandma Mary reached over and picked all the strawberries from the plate and set them on the saucer with her muffin, "I just love fresh strawberries," she commented, popping one into her mouth.

After an awkward moment of silence, Elizabeth noticed another car pull into the parking lot. It was odd, each Sunday they had the café to themselves, but today other patrons. Another car pulled in after the first, and then another and another. From the first car, a woman got out as soon as the car had come to a complete stop and rushed to the memorial. Gaius caught Elizabeth's eye and indicated out the window with his own, he didn't want to bring the event everyone else's attention. She glanced out and back then leaned into Gaius.

"Free's mom," she said quietly but not quietly enough, Tish and Bill both turned their heads to look out the window behind them.

Sister Walker had fallen into a heap in front of the memorial, a man rushed from the car once it was parked and came to her side kneeling and putting his arm around her. Frida's mother heaved in sobs as she rocked back and forth in agony. Several of the other occupants of the additional cars had joined them. One woman sat next to Sister Walker and took her hand and held it with both of hers. The others just stood behind, not knowing what to say or do.

More cars started filling the parking lot, one after the other. By this time, all five of the booth's occupants had a front row view of the memorial and the people that were beginning to crowd in. Laurie's mother, Sister Rasmussen marched from her SUV through the gathering crowd. It was obvious she was furious. Her brow was knitted and her mouth and jaw was set firm. Once she reached the memorial, she reached down and snatched the framed picture of Laurie. She started to scream at the crumpled woman on the ground but no one could hear what was being said from inside.

"Oh shit," Gaius said tumbling from the booth. He moved as quick as he could with Elizabeth following through the doors to the commotion in front of the restaurant.

Brother Walker was on his feet, his wife still a heap on the ground. "Leave her alone," he wailed, "you can take the picture, I don't care, but just leave her alone!"

"What's going on?" Gaius asked calmly.

Sister Walker looked up at him and howled, it sounded like a wounded animal. Instinctively, Gaius lowered himself to the ground and held the weeping woman in his arms as Mr. Walker started to explain that Sister Rasmussen didn't want Laurie's picture here with Frida's that she seemed to think there was some type of mistake. Before he could finish Sister Rasmussen screamed louder than Sister Walker's wailing, *They were not a couple!*"

"Sure they were," Gaius said as calmly as when he first spoke. He was still holding Sister Walker, her crying starting to subside, "How on earth could you say they weren't?" Gaius continued, "I've only known them a month and I saw the love they had for each other. You're Laurie's mother?" Elizabeth watched as he looked around. The majority of the ward had gathered.

"Was!" She screamed, "I *was* Laurie's mother." Suddenly Sister Rasmussen started to cry loudly which seemed to calm

Sister Walker. Gaius stood and helped Sister Walker to her feet as she wiped her face with the back of her hand. Mary reached into her sweater pocket and took out a handkerchief. She walked over and put her arms around Sister Walker, offering her the cloth. When she pulled back, she continued to hold Sister Walker's hand. Brother Walker had joined them and had his arm around his wife's waist. Brother Rasmussen was sobbing as well. He was attempting to put an arm around Sister Rasmussen but she was too distraught and kept waving her hands for him to stay back. She was still holding the portrait of Laurie. Elizabeth noticed the bishop and other high counsel members of the ward had also joined them. The entire parking lot was filled with the locals of their ward. Gaius cleared his throat.

"Excuse me, please. Could I have everyone's attention?" Elizabeth felt a surge of panic bolt through her body. "Excuse me, please!" He said louder and his eyes locked onto the bishop's. "I would like to offer a few words from an outsider's point of view, if everyone could please hear me out," he paused and waited for everyone to quiet down. Both Sister Rasmussen and Sister Walker had slowed to an occasional sniffle. Still looking at the bishop he said in a loud voice. "You all are a bunch of freaking hypocrites!" Gasps and comments could be heard rippling through the crowd as Gaius made a motion with both his hands for everyone to quiet down. Elizabeth kept her eye on Paul. She wanted to make sure Gaius wasn't going to get a surprise attack again. Shane was standing just a foot or two behind him. Shane caught Elizabeth's eye as if to say, *he's safe*. The crowd's comments died down.

Holding the bishop's stare, Elizabeth stepped to Gaius' side and spoke. "Enough Mormon speak. I'm going to speak plain, simple English…" She paused and looked at the faces of her peers. "We are all a bunch of *fucking* hypocrites," she exhaled and continued. "I think what Gaius was trying to say is, was your, um, my, um, *our* narrow-mindedness was what killed these girls. This ward is all one big family! You've all known me, them, since we were kids. We all know each other's kids and kid's kids. You know Frida and Laurie loved the church just as much as I do, as much as any of us do, but yet we were going to just toss them out because they loved each other. Their love wasn't within our guiding principles? Throw them out like something that wasn't of value?" she took a deep breath. Her hands had become sweaty. "Bishop, I know that's what you wanted to talk to Laurie about. I know she got a letter from you about her relationship, I know Frida and Laurie had discussed it, I know they had concerns about it..." Her words trailed off as her eyes sliced to Paul and Shane standing closely behind.

Elizabeth's heart felt as if it would burst as Gaius began again, "Frida and Laurie's love wasn't a threat to you people, it wasn't hurting you or your life or the way you raise your kids. It didn't affect you. Bottom line is, their love wasn't to your standards, wasn't what you deemed right or normal. Their love wasn't written in some book thousands of years ago. Sad. Sad. Sad. This entire town's messed up beliefs killed these girls, these wonderful, beautiful and perfect young women." Gaius' voice cracked with emotion. From the front row, Mary shuffled over to her grandson and placed her hand softly on his arm. "I'm sorry, Grandma." There were tears suddenly rolling down his cheeks. Mary took his hands and held them, her own eyes filling. She turned to Sister Rasmussen and spontaneously hugged her, holding on to one hand. She turned to Sister Walker and took her hand, the three of them linked. Elizabeth fought the emotion welling in her chest as she watched Gaius' grandmother. After a long moment, Mary spoke.

"No one here knows the anguish these two women are going through now. No one here knows the heart break of losing a child except those of us that have been unfortunate enough to have lost a child," she paused, the tears streaming down her wrinkled face. The bishop had made his way to the front and approached Mary and the two women.

"Are you ladies okay?" he asked.

"No!" Mary screamed at him. "If I could be so bold and speak for Sisters Walker and Rasmussen, we will never be alright!" Laurie's mom began to cry again and turned to her husband. Frida's father approached and put his arms protectively around Sister Walker. Mary moved so she was out of the bishop's reach and pressed into Bill, Gaius on the other side of her. It surprised Elizabeth how coherent Mary was as she continued. "This is all very wrong," Mary stated. "Love is love. My grandson and his girlfriend are right," she nodded once and turned to her husband. "Let's go Bill."

Bill looked at the people who stood their gawking and nodded once as his wife had done. He started to steer Mary through the crowd towards their car. Gaius followed close behind. Elizabeth walked over to Sister Rasmussen and hugged her tight. When she pulled back, she gently tugged at the photo frame. Resigned, Sister Rasmussen let it go and Elizabeth placed it back in the circle of flowers next to Frida's. She turned and hurried through the crowd trying to catch up with Gaius and his grandparents. Cars started to leave meandering out as they had come in. Elizabeth noticed Paul was in the passenger seat of Shane's silver Honda Civic. She sighed knowing the conversation that would need to take place in her home, and sooner than later.

By the time, she reached the Anderson's car, Gaius had already buckled Mary into the passenger seat. Bill had climbed into the driver's seat and started the car. Some of the people that had gathered had gone inside to eat while others had left or were in the process of leaving.

"See you at home, Gramps." Gaius said through the open window. Bill put the car in gear and pulled out into the light traffic. As soon as they were gone, Gaius threw his arms around Elizabeth and began to cry. "I can't do two funerals this week, Lizard. Two is two too many."

She felt his chest heave with sorrow. A lump formed in her throat, tears stung her eyes. Putting her arms around him, she pulled him closer to her. "We'll get through this together," she said softly.

He nodded and pulled away from her, wiping his face with his hands. "Did you hear my grandma?" he asked, one eyebrow cocked up.

She smiled. "Yea, according to her, I'm your girlfriend. How could I have missed that?"

He leaned down to kiss her. As he did she suddenly became aware of the people still gathered in the parking lot. It didn't matter, she was his girlfriend, who cares who was watching. She kissed him again.

Chapter Forty-Nine

Gaius had talked to Toni on Sunday night. He had told her about Frida and Laurie and more as an afterthought, filled her in about his and Elizabeth's trip to the mountains. Toni filled him in on the progress of the house. "It's basically done, G. You come on home anytime you're ready."

He heard the familiar inhale of smoke and longed to be back there, to have a beer and pizza with Toni. It would be emotionally challenging to live in the house he and his mother had called home, but he had to get away from Pleasant. The thought had crossed his mind more than once to invite Elizabeth to come back to Colorado with him. He wasn't ready to make a marriage proposal, but he didn't want to leave Pleasant without her and he didn't think she would come if he didn't. *You'll never know if you don't try.* He heard his mother's voice in his head clearly.

"You're going to love what we did with the place. Kept it simple but elegant," Toni was saying. "It doesn't even look the same, the contractors blew out the entrance to the kitchen and made it one of those open space floor plans. Your mom's room is a hundred percent different, you're going to love it and if you decide not to sell that should definitely be your room. We stuck with the original hard wood floors. Once we tore out the carpets. It wasn't too hard to make them look nice. Saved a grip of dough too, plus the bathroom is amazing! We retiled it with super nice travertine. Looks so fancy shmancy." Gaius heard a male voice in the background and Toni added, "Oh yea, we added French doors to the bedroom too. We widened the entrance and it added some great natural lighting."

"We? Who are you talking to?" Gaius asked.

"You silly," there was a pause and Toni exclaimed, "oh my gawd, I totally forgot to tell you, G. I met a man!" Toni's voice took on a lightness and lilt he had never heard, "I can't believe I forgot to tell you! The company that bid the work on the house, the site supervisor, his name is Alan, well..." She heard Toni cover the mouth piece and a quick exchange took place between Toni and someone, he assumed Alan "Well, I don't know what to say, but I'm crazy about him. And he, likes me too." Gaius could hear the happiness in her voice. "The best part is we saved a shit ton of money because Alan and I did a lot of it ourselves. He did the hard stuff, so I was the cook, clean-up crew and general gopher, it looks so good!"

"The best part is you're happy, T. That is the very, *very* best part. Congrats! I hope it works out with you 'n him, that's awesome!" Gaius said. "I'll be home soon. I've got to get these funerals out of the way and figure something out with Bill and Mary, but yea... It's time."

"What about Lizard?" Toni asked, concern in her voice. "She's still in your life, right?"

"I don't know what to do about her." Gaius answered honestly. "I'm going to ask her to come, but she's super close to her family and I think she'll want to get married and although it's entirely possible I love her, I'm not ready for that whole ball and chain thing."

"Oh, come on now, Gaius, it's not that bad."

"Really? I have no idea. My mom never gave me much of an example on how to have relationships."

Toni sighed. "This is true. She always put you first, kiddo. You were her main man, so to speak. You were her everything." Gaius felt the tears sting his eyes. Toni continued. "It's all trial and error, buddy. Ask her to come. There's that old saying about if you love something let it go... if it comes back to you it's yours, you know the rest. If you two are meant to be, she'll come. Maybe not next week, but eventually."

He nodded his head and realized she couldn't see him. "Yeah, you're right. We have a funeral date on Tuesday, I'll talk to her then."

"That sounds dreadful," Toni answered. "The funeral date, not the talk."

"If she's set on staying here, both may be dreadful."

Tuesday late morning Gaius picked up Elizabeth. She was wearing the black skirt she had made when they first met and a dark grey silky blouse with a loose woven black sweater over the top, no garments underneath. Her hair was combed back and straight, there was a black head band at her crown holding it all in place. He wore his church pants and a white shirt with a simple black tie. They decided to eat at Blondie's before the services. After they were seated and ordered Elizabeth told him about the viewing the night before. "She looked good. The way the mortician did her face made it look like she had a little smirk, she would have loved that."

"Yea," Gaius agreed. After a moment of silence, he blurted out, "I'm going back to Colorado."

"What? When?" she asked, alarm spreading across her face.

"Next weekend, after Laurie's services. I can't stay here anymore, Liz. This place isn't right for me. The only thing that feels even remotely right is you. Come with me," his eyes were pleading.

"I can't."

"Why? You don't like being here either. I don't understand."

She shook her head, "Where would I live? What would I do? Gaius, my family is here, everything I know is here."

"You'd live at my mom's with me, duh," he explained, exasperated. "As for what you'd do, that would be your choice, you could do anything you wanted. You could work, you could go back to school, you could stay home and weave baskets for all I care. I just want to be with you, Elizabeth."

"I don't know," was the only answer she could muster.

"I'm not asking you to make a decision now. I'm leaving at the end of the week, maybe as late as Sunday. You're welcome to come with me. Your life. Your call."

The waitress brought their food and they ate in silence.

Gaius had never been to a Mormon funeral. It reminded him of the Sunday church services with the one exception, there was a casket adorned with white flowers at the front of the chapel. The prayers and talks sounded the same. Many people, including the bishop, stood and said wonderful things about Frida, the casket was taken out the side door and loaded into the hearse. The precession of cars followed to the cemetery where there was an additional prayer offered, a few more words from the bishop and Frida's body was lowered into the ground. The crowd gathered back at the church where the Relief Society women had prepared a lunch buffet. Two lines formed as the congregation took their paper plates and loaded them with ham, funeral potatoes and Jell-O salads.

"Hard to believe we're going to do this all again on Friday," Gaius remarked as he glanced around. There were a lot of people here he didn't recognize, relatives from out of town he supposed.

Laurie's would have the entire town gathered. There were nine children in that family. Everyone knew at least one

Rasmussen kid, the Walker's only had Frida. Not that it made it any easier. Losing a kid was losing a kid. It was something so horrible he couldn't even think about it. The smashed van in the canyon had come to his mind a few times and he thought about the family. It was all too sad. How could this month have gone from total happiness to horrible in just a week?

He looked at Elizabeth and knew it was going to get worse when she told him she couldn't go to Colorado with him. What was he thinking? Since he had never been in love before, he couldn't tell if what he was feeling was normal. He wondered if she felt the same way. It hurt to look at her. It hurt to think about his life without her in it. It hurt to be here at church in the middle of the week mourning a precious and beautiful life. It hurt to think of not having Frida in his life too, and he barely knew her. Precious life. Tears welled in his eyes and blurred his vision. He reached for Elizabeth's hand under the table. He squeezed and leaned a little into her.

"Let's get out of here," he whispered. They gathered their still full plates and cups and made a hasty exit.

Chapter Fifty

As they suspected, the services on Friday were extremely crowded. The church parking lot overflowing up the street both east and west. Gaius had worn the same clothes. He explained he thought the services should have been together, so he was going to wear the same thing and pretend it was just the same service but part two. She wore the same skirt, but with a dark green blouse and the same black sweater. Gaius suggested parking the furthest away so when they left it would be easier to get out. They walked two blocks to the church where the line to get in was through the doors, down the steps and all the way around on the sidewalk to the back of the church.

"Holy shit, this is ridiculous," Gaius said quietly.

Elizabeth nodded. She wasn't sure if she had ever seen this many people at her church, she had seen crowded weddings and funerals, but this was definitely the biggest gathering she could remember. The Baptist church in Kentucky popped into her mind, that church could have accommodated all these people. As they drew nearer to the church, Gaius leaned into Elizabeth and put his hand around her waist.

"I don't think I can do this again," he said with sickness in his voice, "And besides, look at how many people there are, it's going to be standing room only."

Elizabeth sighed. She agreed. There was a huge crowd and even with the accordion doors that slid open between the chapel and gymnasium to accommodate such numbers, the church would still be packed.

"We hardly knew Laurie. It was Frida who was our friend. I'm not trying to justify not going but-wanna get out of here?"

"Yes, no, I don't know. I'm not ready to go home, that I do know," she sighed, "you're right about the number of people here and the fact we paid our respects to both Frida and Laurie on Tuesday. We could take off and stop by the cemetery on our way home to say our final goodbyes."

"Let's go for a drive, my pretty little Lizard."

They walked the two blocks back to Gaius' truck and climbed in. She reached out and put her hand on his leg while he maneuvered the truck into a three-point U-turn and headed out of town. They drove west to the foot hills and parked.

"I know you're not really dressed for it, but do you want to go for a little walk?"

"Sure," she said, getting out and taking off her sweater.

It was a beautiful day, the sky radiant blue and not a cloud to be seen in any direction. They started to walk up the trail. Approximately a quarter mile up, there was an old cemetery.

"Wow, check it out." Gaius said, suddenly excited. "I love old cemeteries. There's history here no one reads about in books," he was already walking down the rows reading the inscriptions. "Here's one from 1889! That's crazy to think about, seriously."

"Oh how sad," Elizabeth said, "here's a baby from 1919. It says Bartholomew, Beloved Son, one year, two months and five days. Weird how they put it down to the day."

"Because every day is a precious day. They should still do that."

"This is probably his mom," she said, pointing at the headstone next to it.

It also said Bartholomew, 1919. The second one said Beloved Wife and Mother, twenty-one years, five months, nineteen days.

"She was younger than I am now," Elizabeth pondered. "I wonder if she died during child birth. How awful."

"Yup, awful like fucked up cancer and dying when you're only forty-two, after an awful car accident killed both your parents. Awful like going to war and not coming home before you're old enough to buy yourself a beer. Awful like a head-on crash in the canyon that wipes out a whole family. Awful like coming home and finding your kid dead in the garage. Death. It's awful, it's final, it's... part of life, I suppose," his voice faded and he shook his head as he took her hand. They continued up the hill to the farthest side of the cemetery where a large tree stood. They found a comfortable spot and sat in the shade looking down at the town below. From where they sat, she could see the church and Blondie's, the cemetery and the high school. "I talked to Toni Sunday night. The house is done. I'm pulling out of here Sunday morning. I'm sure my job is still waiting for me, I haven't been gone *that* long. Donovan has always been so good to me," he paused. "I still want you to come with me, Liz. I don't know if it's possible to fall in love with someone in a month, but... I think, I love you."

"You think?" she smiled mischievously at him.

"Yea, I don't know. Seriously, I've never been in love before, I've never had sex before. The other night getting naked with you was the first time I've even done that with a hot chick like yourself. I mean sure, we've all made out in high school, but not like that! For real! You. You're. I don't know what you do to me, but I don't want to live without you and I don't want to settle in Pleasant. A classic catch twenty-two as my mom would say."

"Wait. You're a virgin?"

"Um, yea. Why do you think it was so easy for me to not ravish your body? I'm as inexperienced as you are."

"Well, I doubt that," she said modestly. "But that's pretty freaking cool, you're still a virgin."

"Is it?!" He said laughing, "You're probably the only person in the world that would say that. In most people's opinion, it doesn't make me freaking cool, it makes me a loser with a capital L."

"Not where I come from," she said, joining in with laughter.

"True dat," he said, then grabbed her and kissed her passionately, her arms instantly wrapping around his waist, her mouth eager for his.

I think I love you too. She thought to herself, breathless.

He leaned back in the fresh spring earth and pulled her on top of him, her skirt gathered and bunched around her, she leaned down and kissed him again feeling him get hard underneath her.

"I want you so bad," he moaned.

"Me too," she agreed, kissing his neck, breathing in his scent.

"Here? Now?"

"Probably not," she giggled while sitting astride him and looking down at his face. It was flush with excitement, his eyes dancing, looking at her with desire. She felt her own heat and wanted him, loved him, yes, this feeling had to be nothing short of love. "I can't think of a more romantic place to give up my V-card than under an oak tree above an old cemetery overlooking the town I was born and raised in, however; we don't even have a blanket to lie on and I have nothing as far as birth control, you know?"

"I have a condom I've carried around for years in my wallet."

She climbed off him and saw the bulge in his pants, she was just as turned on. He pulled out his wallet and extracted the foil package. "March, 2009. Yea, I suppose I *have* been carrying it around for years. Do we trust it?"

"I don't know," she answered honestly.

"Well then, let's wait," he said pulling her close.

When and where was it right to have sex? Her upbringing rang in her head. The line she had been fed since she could remember, no sex until you've gone through the temple and sealed for all time and eternity. Sex before marriage was a sin, such a sin it rated right up there with murder. How could something that felt so right be so wrong?

He heaved a heavy sigh and sat up, "I see the wheels turning behind those beautiful blues you've got there, Liz. What's on your mind?"

"You. Duh!"

He laughed, "What about me? Duh."

"What am I going to do with you?" her smile was warm but sad.

"What do you mean? Do you need a commitment from me? Aside from me joining your ridiculous church, what do you want from me?" his tone had changed. It was pleading and exasperated at the same time.

"It's not ridiculous," she said, the words sounding flat even as they came out of her mouth. Maybe it was, she looked down at the cemetery. Even from here she could see the fresh dirt of Frida's grave, facing east like all of them did. It was tradition for the Mormons to bury their dead facing east so when the Savior came, the second coming of God, and all worthy souls rose to greet him, they would all be facing the same way. She tried to picture it, the cemetery coming to life. The bodies lined up like a military formation. She thought of the hundreds of cemeteries up and down the Wasatch front, and the cemeteries throughout the country. Would only the Mormons rise? Only the ones facing east? She glanced at the little cemetery below them. Only the ones that had gone through the temple and became worthy would rise? Right?

What about Frida and Laurie, would they rise and still be lesbians? Would that even be fair? Her stomach reeled as she thought about the primary lessons she had when she was a child. The primary teacher explaining to the children that everyone would be perfect when the second coming happened. No one would be old, sick or deformed. Everyone would rise and have perfect bodies. Diseases like Down syndrome and Cerebral palsy wouldn't plague those humans that had been cursed with them in this life, they would be resurrected flawlessly whole. Were those children not perfect in this life? Little Travis's face appeared in her mind, his beautiful and innocent smile, his sparkling eyes. He seemed perfect to her, as she was sure he seemed perfect to his mother, as perfect as Todd or the other children, as perfect as any child of God. Were these children as defective as the world viewed Frida and Laurie?

She could feel her faith begin to crack, anger rising at the thought of what Frida and Laurie had done. As sad as it was, it was sadder they couldn't just love each other the way other couples do, the simple reason that pushed them over the edge. For the first time in her life, she realized when it came to her religion, too much relied on faith.

"Ok, perhaps there are a few things within my religious beliefs that are ridiculous," she commented after several minutes of silence between them.

"A few?" His eyebrow arched up the way it always did.

She smiled thinking to herself how handsome he was and how happy she was, right now, in this moment.

They heard men's voices and leaned in to each other not wanting to be discovered. Looking towards the noise, Elizabeth realized it was Shane talking and laughing. There were several trailheads going further up the mountain. Shane and someone else were coming down one just a few yards from where they sat. Paul came into view and grabbed Shane from behind, spinning him and planting a kiss on him. Shane leaned into the embrace and wrapped his arms around Paul.

"You're amazing!" Shane said loudly, "You're beautiful and amazing and all mine!"

Shane grabbed the sides of Paul's face and kissed it hard again. They walked, their fingers slightly entwined. Elizabeth watched her brother knowing he hadn't seen her, knowing he didn't know he was being observed. She had never seen him happy like this. It was as if she was looking at a different version of Paul, one without the bitterness and scowl he so often wore. They continued down the trail head without looking towards the tree where Gaius and Elizabeth sat. Once they were out of earshot, Elizabeth said.

"I'm sorry my brother punched you in the face, I'm not sure I ever said that."

"No worries," he said. "What are your parents going to do when they find out about Shane?"

"I don't know," she sighed, "not sure I want to be there when they do though."

After a few minutes, Elizabeth saw their family truck pull down the dirt road. She got up and brushed off her backside.

"Ready?" he asked, jumping up and doing the same.

"Sure."

They walked hand in hand back down the dirt road towards Gaius' truck. When they rounded the bend before the parking lot they saw Shane was leaned against his little Volkswagen texting on his cell phone.

"Hi Shane." Elizabeth greeted warmly. "Did Paul leave?"

"Paul?" Shane's face contorted into confusion.

Elizabeth remembered her mom saying she always knew a lie was coming when she answered a question with a question. Perhaps it was just human nature. She saved him from lying. "We just saw you two, I mean, it's no biggie you guys are together. I was just wondering if he was still here."

Shane's face drained of color, "You saw us? Where?"

"Oh, um..." she thought of the day at church when Shane was under the table, "we didn't see anything other than you two walking down the trail, that's all. We were above the little cemetery, under the oak tree."

"That place gives me the creeps," Shane stated, then to Gaius he added, "You okay? Paul popped you a good one on Sunday."

"Yea, I'm fine. Thanks for asking."

There was an awkward silence between them, Shane's phone chimed with an incoming text. "Saved by the bell," he said smiling. "Gotta run. Great seeing you two."

"Thanks for making my brother so happy," Elizabeth blurted.

Shane turned to her, his eyes sad and sharp, "Don't be so quick to say that, Elizabeth. I would love to be able to make your brother the happiest man on the planet. That being said, he needs to figure out a way to come out. I can't be his big dark secret forever. If he can't come to grips with who he is, well... I'm just going to break his heart. It's that simple."

"He's scared," Elizabeth volunteered.

"Of course he is. It isn't easy being gay in this red neck part of the woods. He's a great guy and all but I'm moving back to Salt Lake as soon as I can graduate. I only came here to finish high school. My parent's refuse to claim me since I came out to them. They disowned me. I lived on the streets for about a year until my sister took me in. I can't get a job without a diploma, can't make any money without a job, so here I am for one more month. Sad deal about Frida and Laurie, they took the easy way out. What else can be said? You know? It's one of those things, we're damned if we do and damned if we don't," he heaved a heavy sigh and climbed in the VW and started the engine. "See you around," he held his hand out the window for Elizabeth to touch as he rolled away.

They walked to Gaius' truck and climbed in.

"Let's not be like Shane and Paul, damned if we do and damned if we don't. Lizard, please. Come to Colorado with me. I love you. I don't think I do, I do, seriously."

She looked at him. "You can't be my big dark secret forever?" he shook his head. "Colorado. Maybe."

"Maybe is better than no. In my eyes, its progress," he started the truck.

That night during dinner at the Anderson's, there was a tension between Elizabeth and Paul. She assumed Shane had told him she and Gaius had seen them. Towards the end of the meal Paul announced he was moving to Salt Lake to go to University of Utah.

"Well, son, how are you going to pay for that?" Daniel asked.

"I don't know, Dad. I'll probably have to get a job and just pay as I go," Paul said as evenly as he could, "there will be more job opportunities in the city." Both parents agreed as everyone finished their food. "So, yeah, I'll probably move out in about a month or so," Paul continued as Giselle and Jozette started clearing the table.

"That soon, huh?" Daniel said, looking at his son.

"Yeah," Paul nodded. "If I get a job now, I can start saving my money for college."

"Where are you going to live?"

"With friends, you know that new guy, Shane?" Paul's eyes darted to Elizabeth, "I think him and I are going to look for an apartment, split the costs, you know?"

Daniel's eyes narrowed and his jaw firmed up. There was just Elizabeth, Paul and him at the table. "So, son. Will you be looking for a one or two-bedroom apartment?" The insinuation was out there, hanging between them like a fog. Elizabeth's eyes cut from her dad to her brother, a look of dread leaking into her face.

"Two-bedroom, of course," Paul said with a nervous laugh, he got up and started to help his mother and sisters clean the kitchen.

Daniel looked at Elizabeth. She nodded her head as slightly as she could and reached over to hold her dad's hand. He looked resigned, tears had welled in his eyes. Still holding Elizabeth's hand, he took his free hand and covered his face as the tears silently rolled down his face. Paul shot Elizabeth a look that could have killed, she shrugged and squeezed her father's hand. The girls, oblivious to the silent conversation, finished their chores and headed to their bedroom. Paul headed towards the stairs.

"Paul, we need to talk." Daniel said, his voice shaky.

Alice turned to him. "Honey, are you alright?" she rushed over and put her arm around her husband and glanced at Elizabeth and then up to Paul, a look of confusion across her face. Paul's back was still turned towards them.

"What'cha wanna talk about, Dad?" Paul's voice was as shaky as his father's.

"Come, sit. Join us."

"Do you want me to leave?" Elizabeth asked.

"Yes," from Paul.

"No," from their father.

She didn't move. Daniel addressed his son as Paul turned and joined them at the table, his shoulders sagging and his eyes downcast. "Could you, please explain to me a little more about you and ... err ... Shane's ... um ... friendship?" Elizabeth heard an intake of breath from her mother as she lowered herself into a chair. Paul began to shake his head and with his elbows on the table, he covered his face with his hands.

No one said anything for what seemed like a very long time. Paul began to speak. "I'm going to move in with Shane in

Salt Lake when he graduates," he sighed and brought his eyes up to meet his father's.

"That doesn't tell me anything about..." Daniel began but Paul interrupted him.

"I'm gay, Dad."

The sharp yelp that came from Alice was the only sound in the room. Elizabeth reached over to take her brother's hand.

"Don't you touch me!" he yelled at her. "You probably told them, didn't you?! How could you do that? Traitor!"

"I didn't say anything," Elizabeth said, "I swear I didn't."

"You knew?" Daniel looked at his daughter in astonishment, "How? When?"

Alice began to cry loudly, "This isn't happening!" she sobbed. "What are people going to say? The Relief Society ladies, what will I tell them? Ashamed. My children have..."

"Mom!" Elizabeth shouted, "Paul is your son! He should be more important to you than a bunch of biddies from the ward. You wouldn't turn your back on Paul if you found out he was suicidal like Frida, would you? Is that how you would rather his life be, a big fat lie, a sordid secret that pushes him to end his own life? I saw firsthand the torture that Frida and Laurie went through. They were in love, mom! They could have had a happy life together! What about Paul? What about *his* happiness? Do you not ever want him to feel what it feels like to be in *love*? If you could for one freaking minute put your own feelings aside and think about your child and what's important here!" She hadn't realized she was yelling at her parents. Her eyes cut to Paul's, his expression was of utter disbelief. "There are a lot of worse things for Paul to be than gay. He could be a hypocrite. And a liar and a fraud." Elizabeth said much calmer, turning to her sibling. "Sorry bro, I swear I didn't say a thing to them, you gotta know, I've got your back. Say what you've got to say."

There was a moment of intense silence.

"I'm moving to Salt Lake with Shane after graduation, you can tell whoever you want whatever you want, I don't care," Paul said flatly to his parents. "Mom, Dad, I'm sorry. I am who I am. I'm not going to change. Believe me, I've prayed about it. I've begged God for an answer or direction. He brought me Shane. I've tried to like women, I've wondered why I'm like I am, but bottom line is, plain and simple, this is who I am. I'm attracted to men. I'm in love. I'm in love with Shane."

Elizabeth reached out for Paul's hand and this time he let her take it. Before she could think, Elizabeth said. "I'm also in love, but obviously, with Gaius. I'm going to move in with him. In Colorado Springs. The day after tomorrow." The statement surprised her as much as it did her parents and brother, but it was the truth. It's what she truly wanted. She couldn't stay here anymore, she had outgrown this town. It was time to go. Spread her wings, figure out how to be an adult. Paul gave her hand a reassuring squeeze, she could see the hint of a grin at the corners of his mouth. Their mother looked the opposite, ashen and horrified. Elizabeth continued, "Free agency, it's what's been crammed down my throat my whole life, but you know what?! Free agency means *making choices*, choices aren't just doing what you're told. *Choose* the Right?!" She looked at her hand and pulled the CTR ring off, tossing it on the table. "I choose to be happy, I'm moving to Colorado with Gaius. And we *will* be sharing a room."

"What?! No. What are people going to say?" Alice said shaking her head furiously. She got up and moved down the hallway to her bedroom stifling her sobs.

Daniel's posture had slumped forward, his face in his hands.

"I'm sorry, Dad. Really I am." Paul sighed heavily. "It's pretty obvious why I haven't said anything up to this point, I knew this would be your and mom's response."

Elizabeth sighed. "I'm sorry too, Dad. It's called falling in love because a person has no control, it's *falling*. I want to be with Gaius though. It's what I want, it feels *right*. I'm not sure if we're going to get married or go through the temple or have kids, but right now, I just want to be with him. And he wants to go back to Colorado, so... I'm going to Colorado too." Elizabeth looked at her brother. "You okay?"

"Better than I've ever been in my whole life," he responded. "You?"

"Yea. I feel as if a huge weight was just lifted off my shoulders."

"You have no idea," Paul said, getting up and heading downstairs to his room.

Elizabeth stood and kissed the top of her dad's head. "Love you, Daddy," she followed her brother down the stairs. Daniel began to quietly pray, tears silently running down his cheeks.

Chapter Fifty-One – Five years later

Elizabeth pulled in the driveway and gathered the groceries. She and Gaius celebrated the holiday season on the Winter's solstice each year by hosting a dinner get-together. Toni and her husband, Alan, were coming, as well as Rebecca, Maximus and their adorable two-year old daughter. After depositing the groceries on the kitchen counter, she went back out to plug in the lights for the Pagan tree they had decorated in the front yard and grab the mail. Walking back in, she glanced at the photos on the foyer wall and thought about how much her life had changed and how much more it was going to change.

Rebecca and Max had gotten married in Aspen the year after Gaius and Elizabeth had left Pleasant. Elizabeth and Gaius stood as the Maid of Honor and Best Man and then vacationed with the newlyweds. They looked so young in the photo. Rebecca and Max had fallen in love with the area and moved just outside of Denver within the year. Gaius and Max had become partners in a joint business venture that had done so well, Elizabeth and Rebecca didn't have to work but instead spent their free time together volunteering in the community. Or traveling. The foursome loved to travel together. She looked at framed snapshots of the four of them in Hawaii, Canada, London, Costa Rica and Moab. Her eyes continued to scan the wall, family portraits, her sisters' graduation photos and Giselle's bridal picture taken in front of the Draper temple. Her favorite photo was the wedding selfie of Paul and Shane taken on the steps of Utah's State capital on the Winter's Solstice, 2013. The back was signed in Paul's all block print, 'We're making history.'

She glanced at the mail. There was a postcard from Tish, *Merry Everything and greetings from the Congo*. Elizabeth smiled, happy her friend was seeing the world. Tish had been traveling with the Peace Corps for more than three years. She opened the next envelope. *Merry Christmas, see you soon*. It was from her mother. The second part of their yearly December traditions was to drive to Pleasant on the twenty second and home on the twenty fifth. It was the only time they caught up with her parents, Gaius grandparents and Sassafras.

They had made the decision to leave the old pitbull there when they moved as Gaius was convinced that was what the dog wanted based on her facial features and body language. Boo-boo passed away only months after and everyone was grateful for the companionship Sass offered Bill and Mary.

Elizabeth began preparing dinner. The Beatles played on her iPod, All You Need is Love. It made her smile. She heard Gaius' Chevy before it turned into their driveway. Gaius loved that truck. Bill had given it to him when they moved from Pleasant and he had restored it making it a collector's dream. Elizabeth moved towards the garage door. Doobie came bouncing in. She still was rambunctious even at five years old. She still remembered picking the pup from the litter at the grocery store the day they left Utah. She named her Doobie, partly because she liked the sound of the word, and partly because they called her Debbie when they were in Utah and the dog still answered. Doobie sniffed her hellos and plopped down on her doggie bed in the family room.

"Hey beautiful," Gaius said, kissing Elizabeth's lips. She could feel the cold from outside on his face and coat. "The weather outside is frightful…" he murmured, pulling her closer to him and nuzzling his face into her shoulder.

"Inside is so delightful," she returned.

"Yes it is," he agreed running his hand down over her rear end.

She pulled away, "Not now lover boy, gotta a ton of things to do," she walked back into the kitchen.

He followed and took off his coat and hung it on a hook in the hallway. "What can I help with?"

"You can set the table," she said and indicated the dinnerware sitting on the counter.

"Sure," he took them and set them around the big table. She walked in and leaned against the door frame and watched him work. He glanced at her, "You know, Lizard, never in my wildest dreams could I have imagined being this happy," his attention went back to his task. "I mean, you, Max, the farm, all of it. Having Toni in my life, my dad's parents too, you know?" she smiled and nodded keeping her eyes on his every move. "What's up with you?" he asked. "Cat got your tongue? Ever wonder why people say that? Such a weird saying," his eyes met hers and she dropped her gaze to a small package on the table. It was wrapped in silver paper with a green ribbon tied around it. He followed her gaze. "Tell me this is a center-piece and not a holiday gift, Liz," she shrugged and remained silent. "You're freaking me out, Elizabeth Ord Anderson. We don't get each other gifts, remember?" he shook the box. "For me?"

She nodded and said with love in her eyes, "You're my gift," she looked back at the little package in his hands, "Open it."

"You know I don't have anything for you."

"It's not that kind of gift," her smile couldn't be restrained any longer and she began to giggle, "Open it!" He beamed at her. With the excitement of a three-year-old, he ripped the paper off the little box containing a test strip with two visible blue lines.

BIO

D.W. Plato has wanted to write books for as long as she can remember. As a child, when asked what she wanted to be when she grew up, she always answered "an author." After raising her daughter and spending 20 years in corporate America's rat race, her dream has finally come true. Utilizing a lifetime of experiences, she has created stories for her readers to get wrapped up in, and characters to fall in love with. Living in New Mexico has given her the motivation and inspiration to create fun fictional sagas.

www.ingramcontent.com/pod-product-compliance
Lightning Source LLC
Chambersburg PA
CBHW061312170626
46817CB00001B/156